reading too. Ali lives in Cambridgeshire with her family and two Labradors. When she isn't writing, she likes to travel, read and people-watch, more often than not accompanied by a good cup of coffee. Her dogs and a love of exercise keep her sane!

To find out more about Ali visit her website at
www.alimcnamara.co.uk
or follow her on Twitter: @AliMcNamara

Further praise for *From Notting Hill With Love . . . Actually*:

'Perfectly plotted, gorgeously romantic, has some great gags and leaves you with that lovely gooey feeling you get at the end of a good Hollywood rom com'
Lucy-Anne Holmes, author of *The (Im)Perfect Girlfriend*

*Also by Ali McNamara*

From Notting Hill with Love . . . Actually

Breakfast at Darcy's

From Notting Hill to New York . . . Actually

Step Back in Time

From Notting Hill with Four Weddings . . . Actually

# The Little Flower Shop by the Sea

Ali McNamara

sphere

SPHERE

First published in Great Britain in 2015 by Sphere

3 5 7 9 10 8 6 4 2



*All characters and events in this publication, other than those clearly in the public domain, are fictitious and resemblance to real persons, living or dead, is purely coincidental.*



A CIP catalogue record for this book is available from the British Library.

ISBN 978-0-7515-5861-6

Typeset in Caslon by M Rules

Printed and bound in Great Britain by
Clays Ltd, St Ives plc

Papers used by Sphere are from well-managed forests and other responsible sources.

*For Jake, my Basil.*

# Acknowledgements

This book has been one of the hardest to write, but in a strange way one of the most satisfying now it's fully in bloom!

Watching this book grow has been a long process, but during that time I had much support and necessary watering from my wonderful family – Jim, Rosie and Tom, and the constant calming breeze of my fantastic agent, Hannah Ferguson.

I would like to thank everyone at my publisher, Little, Brown, who helps me grow my books, especially my editors: Rebecca Saunders who planted the initial seed of this one, and Maddie West who helped harvest the final buds!

And finally, my fabulous dogs Jake and Oscar, who never fail to make me smile when life doesn't, and who cast the essential sunshine into my life to allow me to grow my stories for you, my lovely readers, to enjoy.

# Prologue

## 1993

My brother and I run through the town, weaving our way through the holidaymakers as they bustle along Harbour Street. It's a Saturday, and the town is packed with people; some eating ice creams and pasties, some choosing souvenirs from the many busy little shops, and some simply enjoying the fantastic sunny weather.

But Will and I don't stop to browse in the shops or eat ice cream, though I do look longingly at a lady carrying a large, white, whippy ice cream with a chocolate flake. It's a really hot day and I'd love an ice cream, even though we've just had our lunch. My grandmother says my tummy is an empty pit that she can never fill up, but I can't help it, I'm always hungry, especially when we're here at the seaside.

Today we don't have time to stop for ice creams, however tasty they look. Because Will and I are on our way to see one of our favourite people.

As we run along together Will clutches a paper bag and I'm holding a posy of flowers my grandmother pressed into my hand moments before we left her flower shop and headed for the bakery.

'Say hello to Stan for me,' she'd said in the same way she always did. 'Send him my love, won't you.'

'We will!' we'd called before rushing out of the shop and up the street.

At last we escape the hustle and bustle of Harbour Street and run to the harbour, where people are crammed on benches soaking up the sun, trying to prevent the hovering seagulls from snatching their fish and chips, or their delicious cakes bought from the lovely bakers a few doors up from my grandmother's shop.

Mmm, I think again as I see the cakes, I could just go a custard tart.

Finally we leave the holidaymakers and their tempting food smells behind, and begin climbing the narrow path up Pengarthen Hill.

'Here you are, my lovely young friends,' our old mate Stan says as we find him sitting high up on the hill, looking out over a glorious view of the town and harbour. 'And you come bearing gifts – what might they be, I wonder?'

'A pasty, of course!' Will says happily, handing him the bag.

'And flowers from my grandma,' I say, handing him the posy.

'Ah, they always brighten up my little home so well,' Stan says, smelling the flowers. 'So what would you like to do today? A story, perhaps? Or straight up to the castle?'

'Story!' I cry, at the same time as Will says, 'Castle.'

Stan smiles. 'How about we do both? I'll tell you a story as we walk up the hill to Trecarlan.'

Will and I grin with anticipation as we walk side by side with Stan, and he begins to tell us one of his strange and glamorous tales about his wonderful home.

It was so exciting back then. We had a friend who lived in a castle! I thought I was a fairy princess.

As I recall us all walking happily up the hill together, I wish I'd known then that those precious summers we spent in St Felix would be the happiest time of my life.

# One

## Daffodil – New Beginnings

This can't be it, surely?

I stand in front of my grandmother's old flower shop and gaze up at the sign. *The Daisy Chain* it states in curly yellow writing. But the paint is beginning to peel away from the edges, so in reality the sign reads *he Daisy Chai*, which makes it sound more like an oriental tearoom.

I look around me at the cobbled street where as a child I'd run up and down to fetch delicious cakes and pasties from the bakery, my grandmother's daily paper from the newsagent, and where at the start of our holidays we'd spend ages choosing a shiny new bucket and spade from the beach supply shop at the end of the road.

Yes, this is definitely it; I can see the bakery a few doors up, but now it's called The Blue Canary, not Mr Bumbles like it used to be back then. The newsagent is further up the hill that this street winds its way up, and there's still a shop that looks like it might sell buckets and spades in the summer, but today, a wet Monday afternoon at the beginning of April, its doors are closed, and the lights are turned off.

I can't blame them for shutting up shop early; it isn't the best of days to be by the coast. A dank sea mist hovers over the town, making everything feel damp and lacklustre, and in the short time since I arrived in St Felix I haven't seen many holidaymakers. Or come to think of it, many people, full stop.

It's a strange phenomenon – the seaside wet weather effect. A resort can be packed with people out enjoying themselves in the sunshine one moment, then the next, as a changing tide brings dark showery clouds in with it, they will all suddenly disappear, back to whatever hotel, holiday cottage or caravan they are calling home that week.

When I used to stay here with my grandmother in the peak holiday seasons, I would sometimes pray for rain, just so I could wander the beaches and clifftops in total peace, away from any holidaymakers.

My eyes follow the cobbles up the winding street. Beyond the bakery, newsagent and beach shop, I can see a small supermarket, a charity shop, a chemist, and what looks like an art gallery – it's right at the top of the street so it's difficult to make out from here. But that's it: a few small businesses in amongst an awful lot of empty shops with white paint covering their windows. Where have all the gift shops gone? They were always so popular when I used to come here. St Felix prided itself on the quality and variety of its souvenirs; none of that tacky seaside stuff like Kiss-Me-Quick hats, or T-shirts with rude slogans. St Felix had always been a haven for local artists and their work. What has happened?

My grandmother's shop stands at the bottom of Harbour Street, at the point where the cobbles lead out on to the harbour. My first thought was that it looked a bit ramshackle, but having seen all the other derelict shops, I'm just glad it's still here. Down in the harbour I can make out a few fishing boats, and a patch of pale yellow sand – the tide must be on its way out. Maybe it will take this miserable weather with it.

It's been a long day already, with a tiring drive from my flat in north London to St Felix, the little town on the north Cornish coast where my grandmother's shop was. My mother had hired a car for me, a brand-new black Range Rover, thinking it would help cushion the journey. But for all the car's comfort and luxury, it hadn't made the journey to somewhere I really didn't want to go any easier.

My stomach grumbles as I stand looking forlornly at my slightly bedraggled reflection in the shop's window. No wonder that guy at the service station I'd stopped at had given me a look when I'd pulled up in the Range Rover; with my long black hair dangling around my pale face, I look much younger than my thirty years. He probably thought I should be sitting in the back rather than the driver's seat.

An elderly couple holding hands with two cute toddlers – twins, by the look of their matching outfits – pass by. The lady stops briefly to help one of the twins fasten her coat, and as she pulls the hood over the child's face to shield her from the strong wind gusting today, she gives her a kiss on the cheek.

I feel my heart tug.

*My grandmother used to do that to me when I was small . . .*

I turn away from them and stare up at the shop again, feeling guilty – not for the first time today. Guilty about moaning so much about returning to St Felix, and guilty I hadn't done so sooner.

You see my grandmother has just died.

Not passed on, moved to a better place, or any other term that people use to make the obvious sound easier to accept.

She'd simply died and left us – like everyone does eventually.

Afterwards everyone had cried. Not me, though. I never cry now.

Worn black – that part was easy, I liked that.

Went to her funeral and talked about how wonderful she was; eaten all the food they could stuff inside them at her wake – again, neither of these proved difficult for me.

Her family had been summoned to a will-reading with a solicitor who had travelled up from Cornwall to meet us at a posh London hotel.

We being myself, my mother and father, Aunt Petal, and my two annoying cousins, Violet and Marigold. Actually, after the awfulness that was the funeral, the will-reading was quite amusing to begin with. The look on Violet and Marigold's faces when my name was read out as the sole beneficiary of my grandmother's estate was hilarious – for a few seconds. But then as everyone recovered from their shock, and my mother with tears in her eyes hugged me and proclaimed that this would be the making of me, the reality of what my grandmother had done began to envelop me in a way that made me feel so claustrophobic it was all I could do to breathe.

'I'm afraid you won't get any flowers in there today, miss,' a voice behind me says, making me return to the present with a start.

I turn to see a very tall young policeman with a mop of black curly hair protruding from underneath his hat, standing with his hands behind his back. He nods at the window of the shop. 'There's no one in there on a Monday – not any more.'

'And there is the rest of the time?' I ask, surprised to hear this. As far as I'm aware no one has been in the shop since my grandmother became too ill to look after herself just over a year ago, and was admitted to a specialist private hospital in London which her daughters had insisted paying for.

He shrugs, and I note, from the lack of rank insignia on his shoulders, that he's a police constable.

It's not something I'm particularly proud of, knowing how to spot the rank of the police officer you're dealing with, but when you've had as many encounters with the police as I have . . . let's just say it becomes second nature.

'Yes, there's someone in there five days a week. Well, sort of . . .'

I wait for him to continue.

'You see, the florist that was there before sadly passed on. Lovely lady she was, apparently.'

'Apparently?'

'Yes, I never knew her. I'm new to this patch, only been here a few months.'

'So who runs the shop now then?'

'The local women's group.' He looks about him, then lowers his voice. 'Fierce bunch, they are. Not really suited to the gentle ways of a delicate flower, if you know what I mean. They quite scare me.'

I nod sympathetically.

'However,' he continues, 'I don't like to say a bad word

about anyone. The ladies run the shop voluntarily out of the goodness of their hearts – which is never a bad thing in my book.'

'Yes, of course.' I smile politely at him.

'But they close on a Monday, see. So if you're looking for flowers, then I'm afraid you're out of luck.'

'Oh, never mind then,' I say, hoping he'll leave me alone. 'Maybe another time.'

'Staying in St Felix long, are you?' he asks, obviously wanting to continue our conversation. He looks up at the sky. 'Not the best day to see the town at its finest.'

'I'm not sure. Hopefully not too long.'

He looks surprised at this.

'I mean, maybe a few days.' I look up at the sky like he had. 'Depends on the weather . . .'

'Ah, I see. Good plan. Good plan.' He smiles. 'Sorry about the shop, but – and I don't mean any offence to the ladies when I say this, you understand – their ways with flowers are a bit old fashioned. If you're in need of something more modern you could always pop up the hill to Jake. He'll see you right.'

'Jake being . . . ?' I enquire, wondering if I'll regret asking.

'He owns the local nursery up on Primrose Hill. They deliver flowers all round the area. Just between us –' he leans in towards me and lowers his voice once more – 'I always go there when I need flowers for the *special* lady in my life.'

'And would that be . . . your mum?' I can't resist teasing him. This constable is completely unlike the officers of the Metropolitan Police I've encountered in London. Although, thinking about it, most of those encounters hadn't exactly been amicable, I was usually being arrested. Nothing serious – my misdemeanours ranged from disturbing the peace, to drunk and disorderly, to my favourite: trying to climb on top of one of the lions in Trafalgar Square. I'd been a bit of a rebel in my younger days, that's all. I wasn't exactly a criminal.

'Yes. Yes, that's right,' he mumbles, his cheeks reddening. 'Flowers for my mum. Well, I must be off – things to do, you know. This town doesn't run itself.'

I feel bad for teasing him, he seems a nice enough fella.

He gives me a quick salute. 'Nice meeting you, miss.'

'Yes, and you, PC . . . '

'Woods,' he says proudly. 'But everyone around here calls me Woody. I try and stop them, but it's kinda stuck now. I dread to think what my superiors would say if they knew – it hardly conjures up an air of authority.'

I grin. 'I think it suits you. Well, thanks for the tip about the flowers, Wood—, I mean PC Woods. I'm sure it will come in handy.'

He nods. 'Just doing my job, miss.' Then he turns smartly on his shiny black shoes and sets off briskly up the cobbled street, arms swinging by his sides.

I turn and look at the shop again.

'Right, let's see what you've left me, Grandma Rose,' I say, reaching into my pocket for the key my mother had pressed into my hand this morning, just before I dropped her and my father at Heathrow ready to fly back to the States. 'Or should I say, let's see what you've left me to sell . . . '

*

As I warily open the shop door for the first time in fifteen years I feel my throat begin to tighten as yet again I'm cast back to the day of the funeral.

'Why on earth has Grandma Rose left me her flower shop?' I'd protested in the quiet of the hotel lounge. 'I hate flowers, and she knew that. Did she really hate me that much?'

'Poppy!' my mother had admonished. 'Don't say that about your grandmother, she loved you very much, as you well know. That shop is the original link in The Daisy Chain empire, she wouldn't have left it to you unless she thought . . . ' There was a pause, and I knew what she was thinking: her mother must have been losing her mind to leave her precious shop to me.

You see I've heard it all before, too many times – how flowers have been in my family for ever . . . passed down through every generation. How at least one person in every branch of the Carmichael family owns, runs, or works for a florist. It was like a broken record that never came off the turntable. But it didn't stop there. The Daisy Chain was now international: my mother had opened a flower shop in New York, a distant cousin had a florist business in Amsterdam, and another would be opening a shop in Paris later this year. Every Carmichael loved flowers – every one except me. I may have been burdened with my family's tradition of calling all children flower-inspired names, but that's where the floral affinity stopped. There were no flowers in my life, and I didn't intend for that to change any time soon.

'Go on . . . ' I'd prompted. I wanted to hear my mother say it. I knew I was the black sheep of the Carmichael family; I knew I was the one they talked about in hushed tones at family parties. Maybe my grandmother had seen past that, maybe she thought by leaving me her shop it might help me. How could she be so wrong?

My mother took a deep breath. 'She wouldn't have left you her shop unless she thought you could do some good with it.'

'Perhaps.' I'd shrugged.

'Poppy,' my mother said, rubbing her hands comfortingly over my upper arms, 'I know this is difficult for you, really I do. But your grandmother has given you an opportunity here. An opportunity to do something good with your life. Please, at least give it a chance.'

My father had stepped forward then. 'Couldn't you at least go and *look* at the shop, Poppy? For your mother, if not for yourself? You know what your grandmother's shop means to her – and the whole Carmichael family.'

It's begun spitting with rain, so I stop dithering on the doorstep of the shop, and dart inside, swiftly closing the door behind me. The last thing I want is for any of the other shop owners in the street to see I'm in here and come banging on the window for a chat. I'm not intending to stay long.

I resist the urge to turn on the light, so I have to try and make out the interior of the shop as best I can from what little daylight there is coming through the window.

It's bigger than I remember. Perhaps that's because I only ever saw it filled to the brim with flowers. When my grandmother was in here you couldn't move without bumping into a tin pot filled with brightly coloured blooms waiting to be arranged into a bouquet and sent out into the world to brighten someone's day.

The shop is still filled with the same long tin pots, but today they stand eerily empty, as if waiting for someone to come along and fill them with the latest buds.

I sigh. Even though I don't like flowers or want anything to do with them, I loved my grandmother, and I can remember spending many a happy, sunshine-filled holiday here in St Felix with her. It was here that my brother and I graduated from building sandcastles on the beach, to learning to surf when we were that bit older and stronger. When the evening tide was high in St Felix, huge waves would crash down on to the Cornish sand, wiping out the day's carefully built, but now abandoned sandcastles. My grandmother would cheer us on from her red-and-white striped deckchair, a steaming hot flask of drinking chocolate ready to warm our wet and aching bodies when we could battle the waves no longer . . .

I shake my head.

That's all in the past now. I have to remain focused on what I'm here to do. So I begin to step carefully about in the dim light, trying to gauge the fixtures and fittings. I might have to sell those on separately if I put the shop up for sale and the buyer doesn't want them. But to be honest, they don't look like they're worth much. Everything I can see is made of heavy dark oak. Huge dressers and cabinets all stand empty, pushed up against grimy cream walls. Who's going to want to buy those? Shops these days opt for modern, light-coloured fixtures – to make the 'shopping experience' as pleasurable as possible for the consumer.

I once spent a ghastly few months working on the tills in a large supermarket during the run-up to Christmas. I nearly went insane passing people's huge festive shops over the bar-code scanner hour after hour. It got so bad I began having nightmares about '3 for 2' and 'BOGOF' offers, until it reached the point where I leapt on to the checkout conveyor belt in the middle of one of my shifts and used it like a treadmill, shouting to anyone that would listen that greed would kill us, and we should all – staff and customers alike – be ashamed of ourselves.

If that incident had only been a dream like so many others about the shop, it wouldn't have been so bad ... But I was dragged down from the checkout by two security guards who thought I was marvellous for giving them something to do other than look at security screens all day, then escorted to the manager's office where I was fired on the spot and banned from every branch of this particular chain within a fifty-mile radius.

It was one more item on the ever-growing list entitled: *Unsuccessful jobs Poppy has had.*

Would this shop – my grandmother's pride and joy – turn out to be yet another?

'The rest of us would have jumped at the chance of taking on Grandma's shop,' Marigold had piped up at the will-reading. 'It would be an honour. Goodness knows why she left it to you, Poppy.'

'I *know* ...' Violet joined in whining. 'You of all people. I mean, can you cope with that sort of thing these days?' She'd tipped her head to one side and regarded me with fake pity. 'I heard you were still taking *medication*.'

'The only medication I'm taking is a pill to help me deal with annoying and ignorant cousins,' I'd told her as she'd glowered at me. 'I've been fine for some time, Violet, as you well know. Perhaps Mum's right, perhaps Grandma Rose knew that and she wanted to give me a chance. Unlike *some* people.'

Violet had then stuck her tongue out at me like a petulant child.

'I'm really not sure about this, Flora,' said Aunt Petal, turning to my mother with a look of concern. 'The Daisy Chain is such an important part of our heritage. Should we allow Poppy to be put in charge of it with her ... *history*.' She'd whispered the last word as if it was poison.

'I am here, you know,' I'd reminded her.

'Poppy,' my mother had put her hand up to quieten me, 'let me deal with this.' She'd turned back to Petal. 'Poppy may have had her *issues* in the past, we all know that. Just as we all know,' she'd added pointedly, 'what caused them.'

The others had all looked slightly ashamed, and I'd closed my eyes; I couldn't bear people pitying me.

'But she's a changed person now, aren't you, Poppy. How long were you at your last job?' my mother asked, nodding with encouragement.

'Six months,' I'd mumbled.

'See!' Marigold shrieked. 'She can't stick at anything.'

'It wasn't my fault this time. I thought the guy was coming on to me in the hotel room, what was I supposed to do?'

In my last job I'd been quite content working as a maid in a 5-star hotel in Mayfair. It was hard work, but not taxing, and I hadn't minded it anywhere near as much as I thought I would. In fact I'd stuck it longer than any job I'd had before. That was until one evening a guest had got a little too frisky for my liking when I knocked to turn his bed down one night – a pointless part of the job, if you ask me. I mean, who can't pull their own sheets back? However, it was part of my job description, and every evening at around six o'clock I'd begin knocking on doors. On this particular occasion I was told I'd *over-reacted* by tipping a jug of water over the guest's head after he'd suggested from his bed that I might like to help him 'test his equipment to see if it was working'. How was I to know that five minutes earlier he'd called down to reception to ask if someone could come and sort out his room's surround-sound system, which didn't appear to be working?

So I'd been *asked* to leave yet another job . . .

Ignoring the interruption, my mother had fixed her smile and continued:

'Well, however long it was, it's an improvement, and that's all we want to see.' She'd nodded at the others, hoping to gain their approval. 'I think we need to give Poppy a chance to prove herself to us, and to herself. I know you can do this, Poppy,' she'd said, turning to me. 'And Grandma Rose knew it too.'

I peer through the gloom towards the back of the shop to see if the old wooden counter that I remember my grandmother serving behind still remains. To my surprise it does, so I make my way carefully across the shop towards it. As I do, I knock into one of the empty tin buckets standing on the floor and it crashes to the ground. I quickly stand it upright again and continue on my way.

I approach my grandmother's desk slowly; my brother and I had spent many fun-filled hours hiding under here when customers came into the shop; for a laugh, sometimes we would leap out from our hiding place to make them jump. Well, I did;

Will was always too polite and well mannered to go through with it and scare someone.

I run my hand gently along the soft, warm, now heavily worn wooden surface, and recollections of the three of us fill the room as I do. It's as if I've rubbed a magic lantern and released a genie made up of memories.

*I wonder?*

I crouch down behind the desk and pull out my phone, activating the torch on the back. The underside of the desk is suddenly filled with light, and I direct the beam into a corner.

*It's still there.*

In the upper left-hand corner of the desk is an inscription. It had been carved roughly with a pair of my grandmother's floral shears in a moment of madness; it might well have been a dare – from me.

W & P WAS 'ERE JULY 1995

That's what Will had written. I smile at his correct use of an apostrophe to represent the missing *h*. Even graffiti had to be grammatically correct with Will.

Rebels together forever . . .

That's what I had scribbled underneath.

Except we weren't really rebels; we were good children, if sometimes a bit mischievous. I was ten when we wrote that, Will was twelve.

*I never thought I'd still be rebellious twenty years later.*

*

'I . . . I don't know,' I'd stuttered to my expectant family as they had awaited my decision. 'I hate flowers – you all know that, and I don't like responsibility either, it's just not my thing. Maybe I should sell the shop?'

There had been gasps from all round the room.

My mother had sighed heavily. 'Give me a minute,' she'd told the others before they could all jump on me. She grabbed my hand and pulled me into the hotel foyer.

'Poppy, Poppy, Poppy,' she'd said sadly, shaking her head, 'what am I going to do with you?'

'Well, I'm a bit too old to be spanked,' I'd joked, my usual defence mechanism when faced with a serious situation. 'You don't see many thirty-year-olds being spanked with a hair-brush – well, not in the foyer of fancy hotels like this. Perhaps in the rooms . . . ?'

My mother looked at me reprovingly. 'This –' she'd placed her finger gently on my mouth – 'will get you into very big trouble one day. You're feisty, Poppy, feisty with a sharp wit and a quick temper. It's a dangerous combination.'

I'd smiled ruefully. 'Already has, on a number of occasions.'

My mother had stepped back to look at me. 'You probably get it from her, you know,' she'd said reflectively, 'your temperament. I remember your grandmother keeping my father in check with her sharp tongue. She never meant anything by it though, it was always in jest – same as with you.' Then she'd reached out to stroke my hair. 'When she was younger, your grandmother had a mane of raven hair just like yours. I remember spending ages combing it for her in front of her dressing-table mirror. In those days, she didn't have the joy of straighteners to keep it tamed the way yours is – I guess that's why I remember her wearing it up most of the time.' She'd sighed as her pleasant memories made way for present concerns, which as usual involved me. 'I don't know what my mother was thinking of, leaving her precious shop to you, Poppy, really I don't. She was under no illusions about what you're like. But knowing Mum she had her reasons ... and although I would never admit it when I was younger, she tended to be right about most things.'

She'd looked at me then; her dark eyes imploring me to change my mind.

'OK, OK – I'll go,' I mumbled quietly, looking down at my Doc Marten-clad feet. There was an unusual gleam to them today because I'd polished them up especially for the funeral.

'Really?' Her face had lit up, like I'd just told her she'd won the lottery. 'That's wonderful news.'

'But here's the deal. I'll go to St Felix and check the shop out, but if it's not for me or I have any ... *problems* while I'm there, then I'm selling it. OK? No guilt trip.'

My mother had flinched slightly, then nodded. 'Sure, Poppy, you have a deal. I just hope St Felix can work its magic on you like it used to when you were small.' Then she did something she hadn't done in a long time: pulled me into her arms and held on to me tightly. 'Maybe it can bring back my old Poppy. I do miss her.'

As I'd returned my mother's embrace, I knew that, unless St Felix could turn back time, there was no way I'd ever be *that* Poppy again.

# Two

## Camellia – My Destiny in Your Hands

'Is anyone there?'

As I sit under the desk, comfortably wrapped in my memories, a voice breaking into my thoughts makes me jump up, banging my head.

'F—iddle.' I manage to say, as a male face looks questioningly at me over the top of the desk.

'What are you doing down there?' the concerned face, which is attached to a tall, broad body, asks.

'Looking for something.' I stand up, rubbing my head. 'Why, what concern is it of yours?'

'Should you be in here?' he asks, his dark chocolate eyes looking me up and down suspiciously.

'You think I'm a criminal? If I was, I wouldn't be a very smart one: there's nothing here to take.'

'You'd also be a noisy one.'

I stare at him blankly.

'I was walking down the street and heard the crash from outside,' he explains. 'That's why I came in to investigate.'

I glance at where I'd knocked over the pot earlier. '*Oh* . . . I see.'

'So what *are* you doing then?' He stands with his legs apart and his arms folded. *The classic male defensive position*. One of my early therapists was a body-language expert – she taught me a lot.

I sigh, and jingle a set of keys at him. 'New owner, aren't I?'

He looks surprised at this. 'I thought Rose's granddaughter was taking over the shop.'

'How do you know that?' I demand.

'Her mother phoned and told me to expect her. I'm Jake Asher, I own the local flower nursery.'

'Oh, *you're* Jake!'

'Yes . . . ' Jake says, looking puzzled. 'And you are . . . ?' But he quickly holds up his hand before I can speak. 'No, wait, *you* must be Rose's granddaughter.' He nods confidently. 'Yes, that would explain it.'

'Explain what?'

'Nothing, just something your mum said on the phone about your temperament . . . '

He tails off as I narrow my eyes at him.

'Perhaps we'd better start again, hmm?' he says, holding out his hand. 'Welcome to St Felix.'

I eye him suspiciously before taking his hand, which is surprisingly large. His fingers wrap themselves around my hand and shake it.

'Thanks.'

Suddenly there's a rustling from the top of one of the

wooden cabinets, and in the shadows I can just make out something climbing down the shelves.

'What the hell is that?' I cry out, about to duck back down behind the desk.

'It's OK,' Jake says, holding out his arm. 'It's just Miley.'

Something jumps from the shelves and lands on Jake's shoulder.

'Is that a monkey?' I ask in astonishment, still not quite able to see properly in the unlit shop.

'She is indeed.' Jake moves towards the door and flicks on the shop lights. 'A capuchin monkey, to be precise.'

'But why?' I ask, still staring at the tiny, furry creature.

She eyes me warily, while licking her left paw.

'Why is she a capuchin? Because Mummy monkey and Daddy monkey got together and—'

'Funny. No, I mean why have you got a monkey? Isn't it cruel to keep them as pets?'

'Normally I'd agree with you.' Jake rubs the monkey under her chin, and she nuzzles into his hand. 'But Miley is different. She was trained to be a helper monkey over in the States for people with disabilities, but she didn't quite make the grade. She was a bit too rebellious for the charity's liking. But she couldn't be put back into the wild, or into a wildlife park, because she's too humanised. So when friends of mine who live over in the US told me her story, I agreed to take her.' Miley strokes Jake's sandy-coloured hair, then to my horror she begins to preen him.

I pull a face.

'It's OK, she won't find anything in my mop to eat!' Jake jokes, pulling a nut from his pocket. He passes it to Miley and she greedily leaps up on to an empty dresser to begin removing the shell. 'She's just doing what comes naturally.'

I watch Miley suspiciously from behind the desk.

'So you agreed to look after a monkey, just like that?' I ask doubtfully. Monkeys were something you saw in a zoo or on television. I wasn't used to someone keeping one as a pet.

'Yep,' Jake says tersely, to my surprise. 'Just like that. Why, do you have a problem?'

'Noo ...' I hold up my hands. 'What you do with your monkey is no business of mine!'

Jake's expression changes and his lips twitch.

Realising what I've said, my cheeks redden. I look at the monkey; she's now finished her nut, and is eyeing me warily again.

'Does she eat fruit?' I ask hurriedly. 'I have an apple in my bag.'

Jake nods. 'Yep, Miley loves apples.'

I scrabble about in my leather rucksack and produce a slightly battered green apple. I hold it out.

'Er ... ' Jake begins to say.

'Oh, doesn't she like Golden Delicious?'

Jake smiles. 'She's picky about food, but not that picky. It's a little too big for her to handle.'

'Oh! Oh right, of course.' I hurriedly look around me for something to cut the apple with. 'Wait right there,' I say, heading out to the back room where my grandmother used to arrange her flowers into the exquisite and often exotic bouquets that would bring a huge smile to the lucky recipient's face.

It's as if I've stepped back in time: the room has hardly changed. If anything, it's tidier – probably thanks to the local Women's Guild or whoever's been looking after the shop.

On a shelf I find a pot with an assortment of florist's tools, and the very thing I'm looking for – a knife. My grandmother kept it for slicing the ends of flowers off at a sharp angle, so they could take up their water faster. It's funny what you remember, I think, picking up the knife and a wooden board and heading back into the shop.

'You don't need to go to all this trouble,' Jake says. 'She's had a nut, she'll be happy for a while.'

'It's fine, really. I've offered her the apple now, so it wouldn't be fair to go back on a promise. I never do that.'

Jake watches me while I chop the apple into small pieces. 'There, what should I do now?'

'Just hold it out to her. If she wants it, she'll come to you. But I warn you, Miley doesn't usually like strange— oh . . . '

Miley is already sitting on the desk in front of me taking a slice of apple in her tiny paws.

' . . . but she obviously likes *you*,' Jake finishes.

We watch in silence for a few moments as Miley nibbles delicately on her apple.

'Why did my mother call you?' I blurt out at the same time Jake asks, 'So what are you going to do with the shop?'

'Ladies first,' Jake says. 'She called me because I supply the shop with flowers, and she wanted to let me know you'd be in charge from now on. I don't know if you realised, but some ladies from the town have been looking after the place since your grandmother went into hospital. They do their best, but their ideas on flowers aren't quite what St Felix is used to.'

*A flower is a flower, isn't it?* I think of Woody. *Why did the people here seem to think otherwise?*

'It's good of them to do it though.'

'Yes, of course,' Jake agrees. 'Your grandmother was well loved around here. A few people went up to London for her funeral.'

'Yes, I know.'

'So you need to answer my question now,' he prompts. 'By the way, don't let Miley have all that apple, will you. She gets terrible gas and bloating if she eats too much.'

I stifle a giggle. 'The answer is I don't know what I'm going to do with the place.' I look around the shop again. 'Flowers and me . . . well,' I gesture down at my clothes – today a pair of skinny black jeans, my favourite burgundy Doc Marten boots, and a baggy long black sweater – 'we don't really go together all that well.'

'I didn't think so,' Jake says matter-of-factly. 'I could tell when I first saw you that you weren't the floral type.'

I should feel pleased at hearing that. But for some reason I'm insulted by his assumption.

'You'd probably be best selling the shop then,' he continues. 'Take the cash and jet off to a hot climate to sun yourself. You look like you could do with a bit.'

'Cash or sun?' I demand, folding my arms.

Jake pulls a wry face. 'Ah . . . I'm in trouble there, whatever I say . . . I meant sun: you look a bit pale.'

'This is my natural colour!' I protest. 'Just because I don't plaster myself in fake tan like some Barbie doll!'

Miley flinches at my raised voice.

'Sorry, fella,' I say in a gentle voice. 'I mean girl . . . lady . . . oh, how do you address a female monkey?' I ask Jake.

'Just use her name, that usually works.'

'Sorry, Miley,' I say quietly. 'I didn't mean to scare you.'

Like two plump raisins buried in a furry head, her tiny eyes look up knowingly at me, as if she's reading my mind. Then solemnly she holds out her paw.

'She wants to make friends,' Jake instructs. 'Hold out your hand.'

So I do.

But instead of Miley shaking my hand as I expect her to, she carefully places the pips of the apple into my palm. Then she darts off back to Jake's shoulder.

'Sorry,' Jake says, 'she can be a tad erratic sometimes, to put it mildly.'

'It's OK,' I say, looking at the pips. 'It wouldn't be the first time I've carried someone else's trash, and I doubt it'll be the last. It's usually all people trust me with.'

Jake looks quizzically at me, but I don't enlighten him.

'Drink?' he asks. 'There's a pub down the road. You look like you could do with one – sorry,' he hurriedly apologises. 'I'm making assumptions again.'

I study him for a moment. He looks harmless enough, and it seems unlikely that a guy who goes around with a monkey on his shoulder will turn out to be a serial killer.

I nod. '*That*, Jake Asher, is the first sensible thing you've said since you walked into this shop.'

# Three

## Snapdragon – Presumption

The Merry Mermaid must have been carved from the same piece of rock St Felix originally grew from. This pub hotel has stood on the harbour front for as long as I can recall, and even though I haven't been back to St Felix for over fifteen years it's still exactly as I remember.

The décor and the owners may have changed over time, but the ambience inside remains the same – warm and welcoming to friends old and new, visitors and tourists alike.

'What can I get you?' Jake asks as we wait by the bar.

I think for a moment. I haven't got to drive; I'm supposed to be staying in my grandmother's old cottage while I'm here.

'A pint, please.'

Jake looks surprised.

'Never seen a girl drink a pint before?' I ask, raising my eyebrows.

'Yes of course I have,' he says brusquely. 'I assume you mean a pint of beer though . . . not spirits?' Jake's eyebrows rise to match mine – but beneath them his eyes twinkle.

I have to smile. 'Yes . . . a pint of *beer* will be fine, thank you.'

'Two pints of my usual, please, Rita.' Jake turns towards the lady behind the bar, who is wearing the most fabulous fifties-style floral dress. Her bright red hair, which is piled up into a beehive, adds to the retro effect.

'Of course, lovey,' Rita says. 'Anything for Miley?' She waves at Jake's monkey.

'She's good at the moment, thanks, Rita.'

Miley is currently sitting on the bar, playing with the beer mats.

'Righty-ho!' Rita looks at me with interest as she reaches for two pint glasses. 'Have we met before?' she asks. 'I feel I might know you.'

'This is Poppy,' Jake explains before I can answer. 'She's Rose's granddaughter.'

Rita's face lights up. 'Oh my love, I knew I recognised you – you are the spit of your grandmother!' Then her face falls and she takes on a more sombre expression. 'I'm so sorry for your loss,' she says. 'Rose was well loved around here. How are you bearing up?'

I open my mouth to reply.

'Silly question!' Rita says, shaking her head. 'Of course, you're still in mourning, aren't you? I should have known by your clothes. Richie!' she shrieks, making me jump, as a man appears at the other end of the bar. 'Come see who it is.'

Richie finishes serving his customer and ambles along

behind the bar. He's wearing blue jeans and a brightly patterned floral shirt. He nods at me.

'It's only Rose's granddaughter,' Rita gushes.

'Yes, I can see that.' Richie holds out his hand. 'Very pleased to meet you. Poppy, isn't it?'

'Yes, but how do you know?'

'Your mother called yesterday, said to expect you.'

Is there anyone in St Felix my mother hasn't called?

'I see you've already met Jake,' he says. 'And Miley.'

Miley has given up her game of trying to balance the beer mats into a tower and is now busy shredding them into as many pieces as she can.

'I have, yes. Jake popped into the shop earlier.'

'Oh, are you going to take over the florist's?' Rita asks excitedly. 'How wonderful!' She looks with relief at Richie. He nods.

'Poppy is probably going to sell the shop,' Jake tells them before I can speak.

I glare at him, but he carries on calmly sipping at his beer.

I smile awkwardly at Rita and Richie. 'The truth is, I haven't decided yet.'

Jake's statement seems to have temporarily silenced them both. But it's Richie who speaks first: 'I see. Well, it would be a real shame if you did, young lady. But it's your decision, and if that's what you want, I can only wish you a speedy and profitable sale.'

Rita has turned a shade of red that is on its way to matching her hair.

'You can't sell the shop!' she suddenly explodes. 'Sorry, Richie, I know the customer is always right and everything, but she can't sell that shop – Rose loved it. It's special is that place. *You* know it is.' She gives him a meaningful look.

A few people in the bar turn around to see what Rita is venting about.

'Rita!' Richie warns. 'We've talked about keeping your opinions in check behind the bar. Sorry, Poppy,' he apologises.

'It's fine,' I say, surprised by Rita's passion for the shop. 'I like people who say what they think, and Rita is entitled to her opinion. Like I said before –' it's my turn to give Jake a meaningful look – 'I haven't decided what I'm doing with the shop yet. I'll know in a few days, I guess.'

'You have to try and persuade her otherwise,' Rita says grabbing Jake's hand. 'Tell her how important that shop is to this town.'

Jake squeezes Rita's hand then puts it gently down on the bar.

'Poppy will make up her own mind, Rita,' he says. 'She's a grown woman, with her own opinions.'

Rita huffs.

'I won't do anything rash, I promise,' I say, trying to appease her.

Rita gives me a terse nod. 'Good. Well, that's something, I suppose.'

'We'll leave you with your drinks,' Richie says. 'Let us know if you'd like food. I've a cracker of a spag bol on the menu tonight, and –' he looks around him at the near empty pub – 'unless it picks up a bit later, me and Rita'll be eating it for the rest of the week. No, the drinks are on us,' he says when Jake holds out a note to pay for our beer. 'In memory of Rose.'

Richie leads Rita away in search of thirsty customers.

I take a sip of my beer.

'Is that why you brought me in here?' I ask Jake. 'Because you knew they'd react like that and try and persuade me not to sell.'

Jake shrugs. 'Not at all. I brought you in here because it's the only pub in St Felix and I wanted a beer.'

I eye him over my pint glass.

'Honestly. It makes no difference to me whether you sell the shop or not.'

'Yes it does,' I say, following him as he gestures for us to sit at a table that's become free by the window. 'If I sell the shop to someone who doesn't intend to run it as a flower shop, then you'll be out of business.'

Jake laughs.

'What? What's so funny?'

'As lovely as your grandmother was, her shop's not my only source of income. I supply flowers to shops all over Cornwall.'

'Oh, I didn't know that.'

'Do you know anything about flowers at all?' Jake asks, putting his pint down on the table. 'I thought it was the family business.'

'No, not a lot,' I admit. 'I've always steered away from getting involved.'

'Why?'

I shrug. 'Dunno, flowers just aren't my thing.'

'What is *your thing* then?'

I think about this. 'I don't think I've found it yet, to be honest.'

Jake watches me as he drinks from his pint glass.

'What?' I demand. 'What are you thinking?'

'Nothing, guv, honest!' he says holding up his free hand. 'Tetchy, aren't you?'

'No, I'm not. Just because I haven't gone into my family business, it doesn't mean I have a problem!'

'I never said you did.' Jake shakes his head. 'I think I'll just sit here in silence and drink my pint. It'll be easier.'

We both pick up our glasses and drink, looking anywhere apart from at each other. I watch Miley playing over the other side of the bar; Rita has given her some monkey nuts – appropriately. She's carefully breaking open each nut one by one, then neatly brushing the shells under a beer towel before she greedily eats the inside.

'Sorry,' I say after a bit, looking back at Jake. 'For snapping at you before. It's a bad habit of mine.'

'Not a problem,' Jake says, shrugging amiably.

'It's only I've heard it all a hundred times before,' I continue, wanting to explain. 'How I should go into the family business with everyone else. How I'm odd because I can't settle into anything in life.'

'I never said you were odd,' Jake says, looking at me differently. 'Do you think you are then?'

'Now you sound like one of my therapists,' I reply, rolling my eyes. 'Turning my words around on me like that.'

'You've had counselling?' Jake asks, sounding very interested. He sits forward in his chair.

'Yeah, so what? Loads of people have.'

'I didn't say there was anything wrong with it. Gosh, you're hard work.'

I look at Jake. I've been giving him a tough time and it isn't fair, he's only trying to be nice. 'I know. I've heard that before too. Some people call it "high maintenance".'

'What do you call it?' Jake asks, his dark eyes twinkling again in a very attractive manner.

'I'm just an awkward bitch really,' I reply, lifting my glass and taking a drink while I wait for his reaction.

To my delight, Jake laughs. We smile at each other across the table, and any previous tension between us melts away.

'Shall we order some food?' Jake asks, looking at his watch. 'I know it's only five o'clock, but I'm starving.'

'Yeah,' I reply keenly, never one to turn down food. 'So am I.'

'I'll get us some menus,' he says, standing up. 'Then I have to make a quick phone call.'

'Sure,' I say, watching him as he wanders over to the bar. He collects Miley and couple of bar menus, walks back and hands me one. 'I'll just be a sec,' he says, holding up his phone.

I pretend to take a look at the menu while Jake goes outside to make his call, but really my mind is racing. Is this wise, Poppy? I ask myself. You've only been here a couple of hours and you're about to have dinner with a complete stranger – a fairly hot stranger, yes, but that shouldn't make any difference.

Jake isn't my usual type at all. He's a bit more mature than the type of guy I'd usually go for – I'm guessing he might be in his late thirties to early forties. His broad shoulders and well-developed arms suggest he works out regularly too, but that could be because he does a lot of manual labour at his nursery. He seems like a nice guy, but I don't want to get involved with anyone right now, especially anyone who lives here in St Felix, or I might never get away.

No, I need to remain calm and focused on what I came here to do, even if Jake does have one of the cutest smiles I've seen in a long time . . .

Jake returns, sitting down opposite me again with Miley on his shoulder, and I pretend I've been busy with my menu.

'Sorry about that,' he says, as I look over my menu at him. 'Had to tell the family I'd be late getting home.'

'No problem,' I reply casually, as my mind races again.

*Family?*

I covertly glance at his left hand while pretending to examine my menu, and notice a gold wedding band for the first time.

Damn, I knew it was too good to be true. He's married.

'Is your wife OK about you having dinner out?' I feel very uneasy about this. Having a meal with a man you've just met is one thing, but a married man . . .

'It wasn't my wife I was calling,' he says. 'It was my children.'

Oh God, he has children too! I begin to run through ideas for getting out of this pub as quickly as I can. This is why I try to steer clear of the male of the species. I've only been here five minutes and already I've been duped by a nice smile and a tight butt. 'Ah, I see,' I reply carefully, my menu swiftly becoming very interesting again.

'They're teenagers, so they're quite capable of getting their own dinner,' Jake continues, apparently unaware of my unease. 'But I like to let them know where I am if I'm going to be late.'

'Sure.'

'What's wrong?' Jake asks, looking at me questioningly over the table. 'You've gone all quiet on me. And you may be many things, Poppy, but you're certainly not that.'

Never one to mince my words, I tell him straight: 'I don't see married men.'

Jake looks around him. 'Where don't you see them?'

'No, I mean I don't date married men. It's one of my rules.' I sit back smugly in my chair and fold my arms. Actually I'm lying, I don't have rules for dating, but it makes me sound good.

Jake's tanned forehead furrows at first, puzzled by what I'm saying, and then his expression changes to one of mirth. 'You think this –' he waves his finger backwards and forwards between us – 'this is a date?'

Miley, sitting on his shoulder, mimics him by shrieking and holding her tummy as if she's belly-laughing.

My cheeks annoyingly redden once more. 'Well, what is it then? You ask me out for dinner, then you tell me you're married. I'm sorry, but the two *never* mix in my world.'

Jake nods. 'Ah, now I see.'

'What? What do you see?' I demand.

Jake takes a long drink, draining the last of his pint, then he places the glass firmly back down on the table.

'Well, thanks for making me feel like the local letch – which I can assure you I'm not. I was merely being friendly, that's all. Rose was a lovely lady and a good mate of mine, and I thought it would be the right thing to do to look after her granddaughter. Obviously I was wrong.' He stands up. 'Enjoy your evening, Poppy. Maybe I'll see you around before you leave St Felix.'

Then to my horror, without a backward glance he turns and walks with Miley in his arms through the doors of the pub.

Sitting still in my seat, my cheeks flaming as hot as the plates of steaming fajitas Richie is serving to a couple at a nearby table, I lift my glass of beer and sip quickly, glancing around me to see if anyone else has witnessed what's just happened. But the pub is fairly empty and the few people who are in here are too involved in their own business to be watching me. So I quietly stand up and slip out of the door unnoticed.

Which is exactly the way I like it.

# Four

## Snowdrop – Hope

Snowdrop Cottage, my grandmother's old home, is a tiny two-up two-down terraced house in the middle of another narrow street, bizarrely called Down-Along, which leads up from the opposite end of the harbour to The Daisy Chain.

It's not that far from the shop, but I need to pull up in front of the narrow whitewashed cottage to unload my stuff from the Range Rover, and in doing so I manage to block the entire road for a few minutes.

Eventually, after apologising to the queue of drivers I've held up, I park the car back at the nearby Pay and Display car park then return to the house to unpack.

It doesn't take long, I haven't brought that much stuff with me, so as soon as I've hung a couple of bits up in the bedroom I used to sleep in as a child with my brother, found some bedding and made up one of the twin beds, I take a quick look around the house.

The downstairs is much as I remember; the quiet, pretty bedroom I've chosen to sleep in is at the back of the house next to a tiny bathroom. At the front, looking out on to the street, is a cosy kitchen with pale blue wooden units, a black Aga range cooker, and a kitchen table with four chairs. Upstairs, my grandmother's old bedroom at the front of the house is exactly as I remember it; there's a huge wooden bed with a feathery patchwork eiderdown, standing in the middle of whitewashed wooden furniture that belongs in a much bigger room. At the back of the upstairs of the house there's a light, bright sitting room, with a plump scarlet sofa covered in further patchwork cushions, a rocking chair, a small TV, and a large bookshelf packed with books, magazines and papers. The reason my grandmother had chosen to have her main living room upstairs is easy to see when you enter the room. Through an ornate pair of French windows that lead out on to a small balcony, the back of the house commands a glorious view of St Felix Bay that I remember vividly.

I take a quick peek through the windows. Sadly much of the view is blanketed in a dense sea mist and it's tipping down with rain. But what I do notice standing out on the balcony, drinking up the raindrops pelting down on them, are bunches of drooping yellow daffodils and colourful tulips in a series of wooden planters.

My stomach growls as I stand there, and I realise I've not eaten since I stopped at the service station earlier. So I head downstairs and pull on a big navy mac with a hood that's hanging on a peg outside the kitchen. I toy with the sou'wester that's hanging next to it, but decide I look daft enough already in this get-up without adding to my humiliation.

Then I grab my bag, lock the door and head down into the town to find food.

It's not long before the smell of fish and chips comes wafting towards my nostrils, so I head into Harbour Fish & Chips – shaking myself like a dog before I go through the door to remove as much water as possible from my person.

There are a couple of people already queuing in front of me so I stand back and wait.

'Just the one portion tonight, is it?' I hear the round, jolly-looking counter assistant ask. 'That's not like you, Jake. With your lot it's usually a bulk order!'

*Oh no, it isn't, is it?*

But it is.

'Change of dinner plans, Mick,' a familiar voice says. 'The kids have already eaten. It's just me tonight.'

I shrink back against the wall and pretend to be examining their noticeboard in great detail – a meeting of the Town Council; a bring-and-buy sale; a missing cat . . .

'Ah, I see, that makes sense.'

'But they won't be best pleased if I waltz in with take-away when they're not involved. I'll probably eat this in my van.'

'Good plan,' the counter assistant says. And I hear paper being expertly wrapped around chips. 'Nah, this one's on me, mate. The wife loved them flowers you got for her. I owe you one.'

'Cheers, Mickey!' I hear Jake call. 'See ya later, Lou,' he says to the woman ahead of me in the queue, and as he leaves, the bell rings above the shop door.

*Phew, he didn't see me!*

The lady called Lou orders, but has to wait for her chicken to be cooked; so then it's my turn.

'Yes, my love,' Mickey says, grinning at me with a set of perfect teeth, which look even whiter against Mickey's dark skin.

'Cod and chips, please.'

'Certainly, my love. Large cod?'

'Oh yes, please, and large chips too.'

Mickey smiles over the counter. 'Got an appetite, have we, tonight?' he asks jovially.

'A bit.' I smile.

'Cod'll be ready in two minutes,' he says. 'Be good and fresh though. That OK?'

'Of course.'

I stand back and smile at the other customer. Lou is an older lady wrapped up in a similar fashion to me to protect herself from the rain.

'It's a rare old night out there,' she says, nodding at my mac. 'Forecast is clear for tomorrow though.'

'That's good.'

'It's been a quiet day today in the town, I barely saw any customers.'

'Which shop are you in?' I ask, wondering if she's one of The Daisy Chain's neighbours.

'I run the post office and newsagent,' she says. 'April can be a funny month; you see your regulars, obviously – they're always about, whatever the month – but your tourists, they can vary so much at this time of the year, depending on the weather. We sell ice creams, drinks, sweets, all that kind of thing. Trade will rocket in a sunny week and dive in a wet one.'

I nod, wondering why she's telling me all this in so much detail.

'I notice a lot of the shops are empty these days.'

'Yes, it's very sad to see. It's only really happened over the last year or so. Place used to be a bustling little town. It's a real shame.'

'Lou, yours is ready,' Mickey calls from the counter. He hands her a large bag of wrapped food. 'Blimey, where are all these appetites coming from tonight?' he asks, grinning at us.

'Oh, this isn't all mine,' Lou says. 'My brother is down from Birmingham for a few days. He likes his food.'

Mickey nods. 'Bon appetit to both of you then!'

Lou thanks him and heads out of the door. 'See you around, Poppy,' she calls, smiling at me.

I lift my hand and sort of half wave goodbye before it hits me: *Hang on a minute, how did she know my name?*

I try to watch her through the misty window as she stops to untie a large basset-hound whose lead is tied to the shop door opposite so he's in the dry; then they head off down the road together.

'Right,' Mickey says, not allowing me time to think about it further. 'Large cod and chips it is!'

He proceeds to pull a huge piece of cod from the fryer and lay it on some paper, then he fills a paper bag with chips. 'I hope you won't be eating this in your van alone?' he asks.

I look blankly at him.

'Oh, you mean like Jake?' I say, then wish I hadn't.

'Yeah, poor fella. He's never quite got over it, has he?'

Mickey has assumed because I know Jake's name, I also know Jake.

I shake my head. 'No . . . ' I say cautiously. 'Do you think he ever will?' I try, hoping this will prompt an appropriate answer.

Mickey finishes filling my parcel with chips, then deftly wraps white paper around the outside.

'I don't know. Losing your wife like that, it's gonna hit any man hard, ain't it. He's done well though – I reckon the kids kept him going.'

'Yes . . . ' I nod hurriedly, hoping Mickey will continue.

Does this mean Jake is a widower? Or did his wife leave him?

'That gravestone at the church is one of the best kept you'll ever see,' Mickey says, totting up my bill on his cash register. 'That'll be £7 please, love. Fresh flowers every week without fail.'

So he's a widower . . . Now I feel really bad.

'Yes, that's lovely,' I say, paying him. I pick up my parcel. 'Thanks for these.'

'No worries, my love.' He looks at me quizzically. 'Have I seen you before around here? You look very familiar.'

'Not for a while,' I say truthfully. 'I'm just back in town on some business.'

Mickey seems pleased with this explanation. 'Never forget a face, me,' he says, winking.

'Bye for now!' I call as I leave the shop. 'I'm sure I'll be back again while I'm here.'

I close the door behind me, pull up my hood, and I'm about to run back to the cottage with my food when I see a white van parked down by the harbour.

Painted in red on the side it says *Jake Asher – Flowers*.

I pause for a moment to think, then before I can chicken out, I purposefully change direction and head down towards the harbour and the van . . .

# Five

## Hazel – Reconciliation

Knocking on the driver's side window I see that Jake is hungrily tucking into his fish and chips, lying in their paper on his lap.

He looks up and sees me staring through the window at him, the rain pelting down on my industrial-strength mackintosh. His eyes narrow as he tries to see who it is under the huge hood, disturbing his dinner.

When he realises it's me, he winds down the window.

'Yes?'

I hadn't expected this. I'd thought he'd immediately invite me into the dry and warmth of his van.

'I . . . I wanted to talk to you,' I stutter.

'About what?' Jake asks, looking up at me, expressionless.

'About earlier . . . in the pub. I'm sorry.'

'That's OK,' he says. 'Apology accepted.' And he begins to wind the window back up.

'No, wait!' I call.

Jake stops the window halfway up and looks expectantly at me.

I think fast. 'I wanted to talk to you ... about flowers ... for the shop.'

Jake considers this. 'OK then, I guess you'd better come in.'

He moves some papers off the passenger seat as I rush around to the other side of the van.

I climb in and try to remove my sodden mac, but I get caught up in the confined space while trying to balance my dinner on my lap. So Jake has to help free my arms from the coat.

I notice as he leans near to me the very pleasant aroma of a good quality aftershave mixed with something much sweeter, which I realise a few seconds later is the scent of freshly cut flowers.

'Better?' he asks, when I'm finally free of the coat.

'Yes, thanks. It's not mine,' I hurriedly tell him. 'It was in my grandmother's cottage.'

Jake smiles. 'I didn't think it was quite your style.'

I'm about to demand, 'What's that supposed to mean?' but I take a deep breath instead, and seeing the half-eaten fish supper on his lap say, 'Please, carry on eating – don't stop on my behalf.'

Jake looks oddly at me. 'All right – on two conditions.'

'Which are?' I ask warily.

'One, you eat your dinner too, before it gets cold. And two, you tell me why you're being nice and polite all of a sudden. It's not like you.'

*

We eat our fish suppers companionably in Jake's van.

'So, you wanted to ask me about flowers?' Jake says, when we've exhausted the polite topics of the weather, St Felix, and Mickey's fish and chips. And when I say exhausted, I mean it; polite conversation has never been one of my strong points.

'You've changed your mind and decided to stay on and run the shop?' Jake asks, looking quizzically at me when I don't answer.

'Er . . . yes . . . well, I'm considering it.'

'Great, what's changed your mind?'

'OK, OK, I can't do it!' I cry, running my hand through my damp hair – probably not one of my best ideas when I've just been eating fish and chips with them.

Jake looks puzzled. 'You can't do what?'

'I can't sit here and have idle chitchat, then tell you a pack of lies about me wanting to keep the shop. It's not me.'

'So why did you force yourself into my van then?' Jake asks, the tiniest hint of amusement on his face. 'If not for my flower knowledge – extensive and fascinating though that is.'

'I didn't force myself into your van, you invited me in!' I say, my voice rising, as my usual defence mechanism kicks in.

'I could hardly leave you standing in the rain, could I?' Jake grins. 'What sort of man do you think I am?'

Every time I start to get wound up, Jake manages to defuse my rage – how does he do that so easily?

'I told you, I wanted to apologise,' I say in a calmer voice.

'But you did that outside. So what changed? You were adamant I was some sort of adulterous perv earlier.'

'I never said that.' I notice his hand resting on the steering wheel. 'It was your ring. I assumed you were married.'

'Ah, my ring,' Jake says, looking at it thoughtfully. 'Yes, I suppose that is a pretty obvious sign.'

He looks at me, his earlier amusement now gone as his voice takes on a more sombre note. 'The truth is, I was married, for quite some time. But my wife, she . . . ' he swallows, and immediately I feel his pain. 'She died.'

'I'm really sorry to hear that.'

He half smiles, in that way people do when it's the last thing they feel like doing. 'It's one of those things, isn't it? Happens every day to hundreds – no, make that thousands of people. The thing is, you never think it's going to happen to you.'

I want to reach out and take his hand, tell him I know exactly how he feels. But I don't. I sit very still in my seat and wait for him to continue.

Jake faces forward and stares at the rain falling on the windscreen.

'You don't have to talk about it if you don't want to,' I tell him.

He shrugs. 'You may as well know. Someone will fill you in at some point if you're thinking of spending any time here in St Felix; I'd rather you heard it from me.' He pauses for a moment. 'Felicity – that was my wife – she had a rare heart condition. We never knew anything was wrong with her. One day she was here, and the next . . . she was gone.' He looks at me again, his face now full of pain and anguish. 'She was out jogging when it happened. Jogging – it's supposed to be good for you. That's what they tell you, don't they?'

He seems to require an answer, so I nod.

'They say it could have happened at any time – the fact she was running was probably not a factor. But you know, whenever I see someone jogging, I want to rush up and tell them: "Don't do it. You could be on borrowed time."' He smiles wryly again. 'Do you think I'm mad?'

I shake my head.

'That's something, I guess. A lot of people did for a while after. But it's just the way I dealt with it. That's how come I ended up with Miley.'

Suddenly I remember.

'Oh, where is she?' I ask, looking around, expecting her to pop up in the back of the van.

'Do you really want to know?' Jake asks, a genuine smile returning to his lips.

I nod.

'Put your seat belt on then, and I'll show you.'

I hesitate.

'Sorry, I forgot about the perv thing.' He pulls a silly face and crosses his eyes.

'OK, stop with that now; I said I'm sorry, didn't I?' But I'm pleased to see him return to his normal self. I'm not very good at dealing with other people's emotions.

Jake grins. 'Yes, you did. Sorry, couldn't resist.'

'So . . . where is Miley?'

'Seat belt first!' Jake instructs. 'And then we'll be on our way . . .'

We drive out of the main town, up a hill and pull up outside a secondary school.

Jake gets out, so I follow him.

'Where are we going?' I ask, scuttling along to keep up with his long confident strides.

'You'll see,' he says as we enter through the main school doors. 'It's just down here.'

We walk down the main corridor and through into an art block. There are examples of the students' work framed and hung carefully on the walls we pass, some of which are really very good. We stop by a glass cabinet before we enter one of the classrooms. 'That's my daughter's work,' Jake says proudly, indicating a piece of pottery in the case. 'She did that last year.'

'Wow, that's amazing,' I say, looking at the intricate turquoise papier mâché pot. 'It's like something from a gallery.'

'I know,' Jake says. 'She's very talented. She was only fourteen when she did that. She paints, too.'

'Really? Does she get her artistic abilities from you?'

Jake shakes his head. 'No, her mother was the arty one. I'm more hands-on practical, you know?'

I nod.

Jake pushes open the door of the classroom, and we find ourselves standing on the edge of an art class in full flow. There are about a dozen full-length easels dotted about the room with adults standing and sitting at them, painting and sketching. Some are using pastels, some charcoal, some pencils, but what all the pictures have in common is the subject.

A monkey.

There are pictures of a single Miley, multiple Mileys in different positions, abstract Mileys that look nothing like a monkey but more like a treble clef, and, sitting in amongst all this, high up on a shelf nibbling on a slice of banana – but by the look of some of the paintings it would appear she's been in many places tonight – is the real thing.

She sees Jake at the door, squeals with delight, then makes

her way over towards him, first by climbing the shelves, then by scuttling along the floor into his arms.

'Perfect timing!' calls a slender young woman with long blonde hair, who I guess is the tutor. 'I think you'll all agree it's been a challenging, but very rewarding class tonight. I should like to thank Miley for allowing us to capture her – she's been an absolute star.'

The class applauds, and Miley, now sitting on Jake's shoulder, gives a tiny bow.

The students begin packing their kit up and the tutor wanders over towards us.

She smiles at me, then speaks to Jake.

'Thank you so much as always, Jake,' she says touching his arm. 'Miley was wonderful to work with, so animated and interesting to sketch.'

'I'd have thought you would have preferred something more static,' Jake replies. 'Be a lot easier to draw.'

'But that's the challenge!' she exclaims, leaning in towards him, laughing.

'Oh, let me introduce you two. Poppy, this is Belle, our resident artist here in St Felix. Belle, meet Poppy, she's . . .' he hesitates. 'She's new to St Felix.'

'Hi,' Belle says, looking me up and down, clearly deciding very quickly I pose no threat to her quite obvious interest in Jake. An interest Jake appears completely unaware of. 'And what brings you to St Felix, Poppy?'

'I've inherited the florist's on Harbour Street,' I tell her, deciding it's not worth trying to keep it quiet any longer, considering so many people know.

'Really? How fabulous,' Belle says, sounding like she means

it. 'You're not far away from me. I have the studio a few doors down from you.'

'Oh, yes, I saw it earlier today.'

'So, what are we all up to now?' Belle asks, already losing interest in this thread of conversation. 'Can I take you for a quick pint down the Mermaid to thank you for lending us Miley, Jake? You too of course, Poppy,' she adds as an afterthought.

Jake hesitates. 'Actually, I was in there earlier, Belle.'

'Really?' She seems surprised. 'That's early for you. Feel like popping back in again?' She leans in towards both of us and whispers: 'Just between the three of us, I can *always* do with a quick drink after teaching this class! Yes, goodnight, Bob!' She waves at a man carrying an easel and box of paints. 'See you next week.'

'Poppy?' Jake asks. 'Would you like to attempt another drink at the Mermaid?'

'Goodnight, June!' Belle turns away from us for a moment to speak to a woman making her way past us. 'Great work tonight, those charcoal sketches you did were amazing.'

'Promise it won't be a date this time,' Jake whispers in my ear. 'Belle can be our chaperone.'

'Well, if you put it like that . . . ' I whisper back. 'I guess a drink with you would be perfectly acceptable.'

But as we wait for the rest of Belle's class to file past us carrying easels, brushes, and pictures of Miley, a tiny part of me wishes it *was* just going to be the two of us again.

# Six

## Lavender – Mistrust

When we arrive back down at the harbour, the Merry Mermaid is busier than it was earlier, but far from packed out, so we easily manage to find ourselves a space at the end of the bar.

'What are you girls having?' Jake asks, while Miley takes up her spot from earlier with a fresh pile of beer mats.

'Dry white wine, please, Jake,' Belle says. 'Gosh, it's busy in here for a Monday evening.'

*This is busy?*

'Women's Guild,' Jake says, leaning over the bar to see where Rita and Richie are. 'A lot of them come in here after their monthly meetings.' He lifts an imaginary glass and pretends to empty it a few times into his mouth.

Belle laughs a bit too loudly for the strength of Jake's joke.

'Poppy?' Jake asks. 'Same as before?'

'Oh, *both* of you were in here earlier?' A flicker of annoyance crosses Belle's pretty face.

'Only for a quick drink,' I tell her. 'Yes, same as earlier, please, Jake.'

I wonder whether I should have chosen a slightly more elegant drink, but beer's what I like. I'm not going to change just to keep up with Belle.

And even if I did, a different-shaped glass wouldn't change much about me. Belle is pretty, delicate and graceful. With her long, flowing, blonde locks and her petite frame she's like a perfect china doll. I glance down at my heavy boots and black baggy clothes. At five foot nine I suddenly feel very tall and cumbersome. I might as well be Darth Vader standing next to Princess Leia.

'Back again?' Richie enquires of Jake as he finally arrives at our end of the bar. 'And this time you've got *two* lovely ladies with you. I don't know how you do it, Jakey-boy!'

Jake grimaces and puts his order in while I look around to see who Richie means. Then it dawns on me that I'm supposed to be the second of the two lovely ladies.

I don't get referred to as *lovely* very often. In fact it never happens at all.

'Did you get settled into your grandmother's cottage all right?' Richie asks me while he carefully pulls two pints of beer from the pump. 'She has a stunning view of the bay from there, I believe.'

'Yes, thank you, and yes, she does. It was a bit too misty today to see anything, but on a clear day it's beautiful.'

'Sorry about Rita earlier,' he says as he places the first pint down on the bar, and lifts a glass to begin pouring the second. 'She gets a bit carried away sometimes.'

'It's fine, really. I'd rather someone said something to my face than behind my back any day.'

'Hear, hear to that sentiment, young lady!' Richie's blue eyes flicker briefly from the pint glass towards me, then back down again as if he's considering something. 'That flower shop is very special to the two of us, you know?'

'I got that feeling earlier. Rita seemed very keen for me to keep it going.'

Richie nods, he places the second pint down next to the first, and reaches for a bottle of white wine.

'Usually I'm not one to believe in anything magical, you see,' he continues, focusing on pouring the wine into a glass. 'But your grandmother and her flowers were kind of instrumental in us getting this place.'

'Really?'

He nods and places the white wine down with the other drinks. 'Yes, I don't know what she did, Poppy, or how she did it, but we have a lot to thank that lady for. That'll be £9.80, please.'

'But how did she help you?' I begin to ask, as Jake automatically reaches into his pocket and hands Richie a ten-pound note.

'You bought the round earlier,' I protest, reaching for my purse. 'Let me pay for this one.'

'No, I didn't, it was free, remember?' Jake says. 'Plus I can't have ladies buying me drinks.'

I look to Belle for support, but she doesn't say anything, she simply picks up her wine glass and takes a sip, so I'm torn between pressing Richie for more information about my grandmother, and pursuing this misdemeanour on Jake's part.

'Don't be so old fashioned,' I tell Jake, letting Richie escape along the bar to new customers, after Jake refuses his offer of change. 'Women can buy men drinks.'

'Hmm ... yeah, I know,' Jake says, absent-mindedly sipping on his own pint and looking around to see if there's a table for us. 'Belle, is that a table over there? Are those folk leaving?'

Belle moves along the bar to take a look.

'But you don't like it though, do you?' I persist, the feminist in me bubbling to the surface.

'What?' he asks, turning back to me.

'The thought of me buying you a drink?'

'I can't say I've given the thought of you buying me a drink any consideration, since we only met for the first time this afternoon. Oh look, Belle's waving, she's got that table.'

Jake summons Miley and starts to make his way across to the other side of the pub, so I have no choice but to follow him. Oh my God he can be so irritating. How did he always seem to get the better of me, whatever I said? And more to the point, why did I care so much about someone who, as he had quite rightly pointed out a few seconds ago, I'd only just met?

'So what are you going to do with the flower shop?' Belle asks after we've been sat down a while.

I'd misjudged Belle when I'd first met her. Aside from her perfection, and her obvious interest in Jake, she is very nice. Belle seems to be one of those very irritating, naturally pretty people that you want to hate, but can't find any reason to.

'I'm not sure right now,' I reply truthfully in answer to her question. 'The shop stirs up a lot of memories for me – some good, some bad. Part of me would be relieved to see the back of it, but then another part . . . '

'Doesn't want to let it go?' Belle answers knowingly.

I nod. 'Yes. However, what I do know is I'm not really cut out for selling flowers, it's definitely not my thing.'

'What makes you say that?' she asks, sounding genuinely interested.

'I just know,' I tell her, without explaining further. 'Whatever happens with the shop, me and flowers – it's never going to happen.'

Jake smiles into his beer.

'What's so amusing?' I ask.

'Nothing,' he says, swilling his pint around, still grinning. But then he changes his mind and looks up at me. 'Well . . . you actually.'

'Go on,' I tell him, as my arms automatically fold across my body protectively. I lean back in my chair and I raise one eyebrow.

Teresa, my current therapist, would have a fit if she could see me now. This was exactly the type of pose she'd spent months easing me out of adopting every time I felt threatened. That was the next stage after coming up with strategies to prevent me from verbally attacking anyone who I felt criticised me in any way.

'For someone so young, you're very set in your ways,' Jake says, regarding me thoughtfully.

I'm unsure which part of his statement to tackle first, so I take both at the same time. 'Firstly, I'm not sure what you mean by young? I'm thirty, so I'm hardly a teenager.' Both Belle and Jake look astonished by this. Which does not surprise me; most people think I'm younger than I am. I guess I should be flattered. 'And as for "set in my ways",' I continue, before Jake can speak, 'what about you, back there at the bar?' I gesture towards Rita, who's pulling a pint. '"I can't have ladies buying me drinks,"' I say in a deep, dull-sounding voice, supposedly mimicking Jake, when really he sounds nothing like this at all. His voice *is* deep, but it's also gentle and soft at the same time. 'However,' I eye Jake across the table, 'I guess you can't help being stuck in your ways when you reach your age, can you?'

Belle sits with her empty wine glass held up to her lips, her mouth open in astonishment as she witnesses my acerbic response.

Jake watches me, his impassive face not telling me anything at all.

'I'm forty this year, since we're sharing birthdays,' he says steadily. 'Don't worry about a card though, and I know you won't be sending flowers. It's not *your thing*, is it?'

Damn, he's got me again!

I'm about to reply when I feel a tap on my shoulder.

I turn to find a small, slim woman with auburn hair pulled up into a tight chignon standing behind me. She's wearing a navy cardigan, a white blouse, a string of tiny pearls around her neck, and tan three-quarter-length trousers with flat black pumps.

'Caroline Harrington-Smythe,' she says, thrusting a cold hand into mine.

'Hi . . . ' I reply, cautiously shaking her hand.

'You know who I am, obviously, so I won't go through the formal introductions. Jake, Belle,' she says, nodding curtly at them both.

'Actually, I don't,' I say, feeling like I should put my hand up before I ask her a question.

She looks extremely put out by my admission, as though anyone entering St Felix should have been given a leaflet explaining who Caroline Harrington-Smythe is, with her opening times, fire exit locations and parking arrangements included.

'Oh . . . oh, I see.' She glares at a smirking Jake. He hastily picks up his near-empty pint glass and tries to find a few last dregs at the bottom. 'Let me start again then,' she says in her clipped, cultured voice. 'I'm Caroline Harrington-Smythe, president of the St Felix Women's Guild, and chairwoman of the Parish Council.'

She waits for my response.

I stare blankly back at her. Am I supposed to congratulate her on her achievements?

She sighs impatiently when I don't respond. 'Rita behind the bar informs me you are the new owner of the flower shop on Harbour Street?'

'Yes, that's correct.'

'Only the Women's Guild have been running the flower shop for some time now—'

'Yes, thank you, it was very kind—'

'—and I'm not sure how the ladies are going to react to this news. The Daisy Chain has become very dear to them. Have you purchased the shop?'

'No, I'm Rose's granddaughter. She left it to me in her will.'

'*You*, are her granddaughter?' she asks, her eyes wide, as though this information has come as something of a shock to her.

'Yes, does that cause you a problem?'

I don't know whether Caroline has this effect on everyone, but judging by Jake's reaction to her arrival at our table tonight I suspect she probably does. All I know is she's beginning to wind me right up.

'That depends on what you intend to do with the shop.' Caroline straightens her cardigan in a business-like manner. 'We can't have just anything on Harbour Street. If you're thinking of selling up, then the Parish Council need to be informed.'

'Like I keep telling *everyone*,' I glance around the table at the other two, 'I'm not sure what I'm going to do with the shop yet. I haven't decided.'

Caroline's steely grey eyes look me up and down. 'I have to say, you don't look the florist type,' she announces with disdain. 'Perhaps it is time for a change?'

My usual reaction to this sort of provocation would be to bite immediately, but we're in a public place and people are beginning to look. I don't want to cause a scene on my first day here. So I bite my lip instead.

'Your grandmother was never much of a businesswoman,' Caroline continues. 'The shop wasn't exactly raking in money when she had it. I should know, I saw the books when I was in charge. I think bringing in fresh blood to St Felix could be just what the town needs, and you must admit the shop is starting to look rather shabby.'

*Enough.*

I push my chair back and stand up to face her, and I'm surprised to find that I tower over her tiny frame. Her forceful manner had given the illusion she was much bigger.

'Maybe my grandmother's shop wasn't the newest, or the most sleek,' I tell her, surprised to hear a clear, calm voice coming from between my bright-red cheeks. 'But it had something else *you* may have failed to notice, Caroline, though many others did . . . it had *heart*.'

I feel my legs shaking as I stand there facing her. Public displays of emotion are definitely not my thing either. But something had ignited inside me when I'd heard Caroline dissing my grandmother and her shop, and I had to respond.

Caroline looks as surprised as I feel by my outburst. She glares at me, then glances around the room to see if anyone else is hearing this. As people sense an argument brewing, the pub is already beginning to quieten.

'I'm surprised I didn't recognise you to be Rose's granddaughter before,' she says, obviously deciding she needs to save face by taking this battle on. 'The family likeness is definitely there.' Then, as if she can't quite stop herself from saying something to goad me, she adds, 'She was a troublemaker too.'

'Oooh,' I hear Jake say, as he watches Caroline and me begin to battle it out. 'Fifteen–thirty. Poppy to serve.'

'My grandmother – a troublemaker?' I question, desperately trying to remain calm. 'I doubt that. She was a good, kind woman. She lived in this town nearly all her life, she loved it here, and she loved her shop. How long have you been in St Felix, Caroline? Long enough to make you an expert on the place, apparently.'

'Thirty all,' Jake whispers, loud enough for us to hear him.

Caroline raises a knowing eyebrow at me. 'In all the time I've lived here I've never seen you visiting her shop, Poppy. What sort of granddaughter does that make you?'

Sharp intake of breath from Jake, and a murmur of, 'Thirty–forty.'

Calm, Poppy, I tell myself. You must remain calm.

'And you know everyone that passes through this town, do you?' I ask, my face reddening still further as I feel my fists clench by my sides. 'Oh, that's right, I bet you're the local busybody, nosing into everybody else's business, so of course you'd know.'

Caroline is the one with the red face now as I hear a few sniggers around the pub.

'Deuce!' Jake calls, and we both glare at him.

Caroline opens her mouth to defend, but I gain the advantage.

'I should like to thank the ladies of the St Felix Women's Guild very much for helping to keep my grandmother's shop up and running, it was most kind of you.' I smile in the direction of the table some of the ladies are still sitting at, although most have gone home now as Richie has already called last orders. Then I score the winning point: 'But *I'm* here now, Caroline. The Daisy Chain is now *my* concern, and no one else's. I may not be the perfect granddaughter, or the perfect person to run a flower shop, but I'm prepared to give it a damn good try, and I'm going to do it in a way that would have made my grandmother proud!'

I stop as I realise what I've just said. Oh no! Me and my big mouth – my mother was right.

Have I just stood and publicly agreed to run a flower shop?

I turn towards Jake and see he's grinning. 'Game, set and match!' he mouths at me.

It seems I have.

Then I hear applause break out from behind the bar as Rita begins cheering.

'Yay for Poppy and our magical flower shop.'

*Magical? There's that word again.*

As people offer to buy me drinks and congratulate me on my new venture, I notice Caroline has melted away with the rest of her cronies. But I have a feeling it won't be the last I see of her. I've met the Carolines of this world before; they don't take defeat well.

'So,' Jake says, when my temporary fan club has dispersed. 'It looks like you might be needing that chat about flowers after all . . .'

# Seven

## Gerbera Daisy – Cheerfulness

The next morning I awake early to sunshine streaming through the curtains in the bedroom downstairs.

Yuck, I'm used to sleeping with blackout blinds in London. I immediately roll over, pull the eiderdown over my head and try to get off to sleep again. But I can't, my mind begins churning over the events of yesterday, particularly last night, so I roll on to my back and stare up at the uneven ceiling above me.

After my accidental admission about the shop, Jake had walked me back to my cottage, and then taken himself off home, sensibly leaving his van at the harbour because he'd been drinking. He didn't mention anything more about the shop, obviously sensing by my silence I had much to think about, and for that I was grateful.

What on earth had possessed me to announce that to Caroline and the rest of the pub? I was no more certain I wanted to stay on in St Felix and run the shop than I was of the coastal weather forecast.

But as I'd said to Jake only yesterday, if I say I'm going to do something, I do it. I don't back down.

However, by sticking to my guns this time, it would mean I'd have to give this flower shop thing a go. *Flowers and me.* I screw up my face. Not exactly a match made in heaven.

It's getting quite warm in the little bedroom now, and I wonder if perhaps today will be a nice sunny day in St Felix, and I'll get to see the town in a better light. I kick the eiderdown off, and begin thinking again:

Would staying for a while in this quiet little seaside town really be so bad?

What had I got to look forward to if I went back on my word and sold the shop and cottage and returned to London? I'd just been fired from the hotel job, I didn't really have any friends, and I lived in a tiny flat above an off-licence in Barnet, having insisted on paying my own way when my mother wanted me to take a job in Violet and Petal's shop in Liverpool. Also I'd have an excuse not to visit Teresa for a while; her receptionist had been chasing me to reschedule the appointment I'd cancelled four times already. Much to my annoyance, my mother had insisted on continuing to pay for my therapy, even when I had taken to paying for everything else. As hard as I tried, I couldn't get away from it.

But *selling flowers* . . . Just the thought of it is making me feel very uneasy indeed.

Maybe I could get someone in to help me? Then I might

not have to have too much contact with the flowers. I could concentrate on the day-to-day running of the shop, and let my assistant do the rest!

Brilliant! Yes, I could try that for a while, and if it didn't work out I could leave before the rough winter weather set in. It might be nice to spend the summer here in St Felix …

I lie there in bed, happy that I have a plan, and not a bad one by my standards. One that will not only keep my mother happy, it will appease the people of St Felix for a while.

Suddenly I hear banging on the front door.

'Who on earth is that at … ?' I glance at the bedside clock and realise it's nearly 8 a.m. I must have been lying here thinking longer than I thought.

I get up off the bed and head through the hall and across the kitchen in my PJs. Then I open the wooden front door and peek through the gap.

I don't know who or what I expect to find standing outside my door at 8 a.m. on a Tuesday morning, but it's not the riot of colour, wild hair, and general exuberance that greets me.

'Oh boy, are you Poppy?' she asks, trying to poke her head through the gap.

I open the door a bit wider.

'Yes … ' I say hesitantly. 'Who are you?'

'Amber – your mom sent me,' she says, as though I should know exactly what she means.

'She did?'

'Yeah, to help you with the shop. She did tell you, right?'

'Nope.'

'That's odd. She said she was gonna call you … ' Amber appears to be thinking. She runs a bejewelled hand over her wild red hair while she screws up her freckled nose. 'It is Wednesday, right?' she suddenly asks.

'No, it's Tuesday.'

'Ah!' She throws her hands up in the air. 'That's why. She's supposed to call you today. I must have lost a day somewhere over the Atlantic.' She looks at me and smiles. 'Can I come in?'

I shake my head to try and wake myself up. An enthusiastic American hippy was not what I was used to before I'd even had coffee in the morning.

'If Mum sent you, then I guess you'd better,' I sigh, moving aside to let her into the cottage.

Amber and her luggage are now scattered across the sitting room while I make tea – herbal for Amber, which she has produced from one of her many bags, and black for me, after I realise I don't have any milk in yet.

All I've discovered so far is that Amber flew in to Bristol Airport early this morning from New York via Dublin. Then she got a train, and finally a taxi to St Felix. She says she hasn't slept in twenty-four hours, which is why she's acting 'pretty wired' and has got her days mixed up.

I carry our two mugs of tea upstairs to the living area.

Amber is already out on the balcony, her face absorbing the sun's morning rays. 'Your view is to die for,' Amber says, turning towards me as I join her.

'Yes, it is pretty special.' I pass Amber her tea while I take a look at the view myself. It looks a lot prettier than it had out here yesterday. Today I can see right across the bay to the harbour. The sea is a crystal clear azure blue, and where the sun's rays burn into it, it's almost translucent in places. What a difference a new day and some sunshine makes.

'Your mom promised me St Felix would be special,' Amber says, 'but I had no idea just how beautiful it would be.'

'So why are you here? I know you said Mum sent you, but why?'

Amber takes a sip of her tea. 'Mmm, camomile ... so relaxing. I'm your new florist,' she announces. 'I usually work with your mom at her store in Brooklyn. She knew you'd be needing someone and, well, I don't like to sing my own praises too highly, but I am one of *the* best florists in New York State.'

'Fantastic.' I nod. 'I'm sure you're really talented, Amber. But why did you want to leave New York to come here to St Felix? It's a bit different.'

'Change is good,' is all Amber says, before sipping her tea once more.

'But Mum was taking an awful chance, sending you all the way over here on the off chance I'd be keeping the shop, wasn't she? What if I'd decided to sell?'

'Oh, she knew you'd be keeping it,' Amber says knowingly.

'How could she, when I didn't even know it myself until this morning? In fact I only decided thirty seconds before you knocked on my door!'

'I read her petals,' Amber says, wandering back into the lounge. She sits down on the rocking chair. 'Oh, how very quaint!' she exclaims as she begins rocking to and fro.

'What do you mean – read her petals?' I ask, following her.

'Her flower petals; I gave her a flower reading. It's like a cross between reading tea leaves and tarot cards.'

I blink hard. Could she be for real?

'I may regret asking this,' I say, sitting on the sofa opposite her, 'but tell me: just how do you read someone's flower petals?'

Amber smiles dreamily. 'It's a gift. I'll read yours while I'm here, if you like?'

'Er, no, that won't be necessary, thank you.'

'Why, what are you afraid of?' Amber looks above my head with a glazed expression. 'You know your aura is very muddy. I could cleanse that for you, if you like?'

Before I can politely reject her offer, Amber continues, 'I see a lot of darkness around you, Poppy.' She flinches slightly. 'A lot of darkness and a lot of pain.'

'What's my mother been telling you?' I shout, jumping up. 'It's no one's business but my own!'

'Whoa, easy, sister. Your mom said nothing. I'm just telling you what I see, that's all.'

'Well don't.' I walk back towards the open French windows and stare out at the wispy white specks of cloud in the bright blue sky. 'I don't mean to seem rude, Amber, because I'm happy you're here to help me with the shop, really I am. I know nothing about running a florist.'

Actually I can't believe my luck. This means I won't have to look for someone. One item crossed off what I expect will turn out to be a very long list of things that need to be done before I can get the shop up and running again.

'But I'd appreciate it if your flower knowledge is all you share. I have my reasons, but all this spiritual stuff – which I'm sure works for you – it's not my scene at all.' A giant gull lands right in front of me on the balcony. He flaps his wings a couple of times and stares at me as if to enquire why I'm on *his* landing area, then decides to fly off again in search of food. 'I'm sure your floristry skills will be a wonderful asset to The Daisy Chain,' I say, watching the gulls dive into the water looking for fish. 'I haven't thought too much about what sort of shop it's going to be when we re-open; you caught me unawares with your sudden arrival this morning. So if you've got any ideas that you want to share, I'd really appreciate hearing them . . .'

I turn to hear Amber's response; but the chair has stopped rocking and she's fast asleep.

*Great!*

There's a blanket lying across the arm of the sofa, so I pick it up and gently cover her. She doesn't stir, so I hurry back down to my bedroom to get dressed.

Leaving Amber still snoozing in the rocking chair I head out in search of breakfast. All I'd had time to do last night was buy fish and chips, so I head down to the supermarket and stock up on a few basic provisions – like milk, butter, jam and bread. I decide I'll have to pop back later and stock up properly when I've had a chance to make a list.

On the way back I pause outside The Blue Canary bakery. The cakes in the window look delicious – just like they had when I was a child. The only difference was now I could see through the window with ease instead of having to stand on tiptoe.

A man wearing a pair of mustard-yellow trousers and a tight, white short-sleeved T-shirt with a blue canary on the front comes out of the shop carrying a sign. He places it down on the pavement, then smiles at me.

'Howdy,' he says jovially. 'Can we tempt you into something naughty but nice?'

'Yes, I think you might be able to.' I grin back. 'It all looks so good.'

'What tickles your fancy – in the cake sense, that is!'

'Erm . . . ' And then I remember. 'I don't suppose you do a custard tart, do you? I used to buy a lovely one here when I was small.'

'My darling, of course we do! It's one of our specialities! Come, come!' He encourages me into the shop. 'Declan!' he calls, as we go into the shop together. 'Are the tarts ready yet?'

'Coming right up, Anthony!' I hear a voice from the back respond merrily, and then another, slightly thinner man, this time wearing bright-red trousers and the same white T-shirt, with the addition of a blue apron, appears carrying a tray of freshly baked custard tarts.

'How many would you like?' Anthony asks, now behind the counter.

'I'll take two, please,' I say, thinking of Amber back at the cottage.

'Coming right up.' Anthony begins to bag up the cakes. 'So how long ago was it you used to buy the tarts?' he asks.

'Oh, many years ago. I used to holiday here in St Felix as a child.'

'How lovely. You would have known Declan's uncle then. Declan inherited the shop from him.'

'And all his recipes!' Declan calls, bringing through yet another tray of delicious-looking cakes – Chelsea buns this time – which he sets down on the counter. 'Those tarts are made to his exact recipe.'

'Then I know they'll be delicious!' I smile, offering Anthony a £10 note. 'They were always my favourite.'

'Are you holidaying here again now?' Declan asks, coming over to the shop counter. 'We don't see too many holiday-makers at this time of year.'

'At any time of year,' Anthony mutters, tapping the buttons on the till.

Declan glances at him.

I take a deep breath; I've made my decision, now I must stick with it. 'No, as a matter of fact I'm taking over the florist shop along the street. I'm Poppy – Rose's granddaughter.'

Anthony and Declan look shocked at my announcement one moment, then overjoyed the next.

They both speak at once: 'Oh my darling, why didn't you say so! That's fabulous news. We adored Rose. We were devastated when she passed.'

Anthony opens the till again, puts back the change he was just about to give me, and retrieves my £10 note. Then he presses it into my hand.

'Those are on the house,' he says. 'I should have known. Custard tarts were always Rose's favourite too.'

'Really?' How had I forgotten?

He nods. Then he reaches into his pocket and pulls out a hankie. He dabs it at his eyes.

'I'm sorry,' he says, turning away. 'Seeing you here, and knowing you're going to take over Rose's wonderful shop. It's just too much!'

Declan smiles at me.

'Ant is always a bit overemotional,' he explains. 'I'm used to it.'

'Oh!' I exclaim, suddenly realising. 'Your names! You're Ant and Dec!'

Ant spins around, his sorrow now turned to joy. 'I know, isn't it cool? We used to hate it when we were first together and they were PJ and Duncan, but now they're international celebrities it's rather fabulous!'

'They're hardly international celebrities, sweetie,' Declan says. 'But it's a good hook for the business.' He looks up at the back of the shop, and I see an elaborately painted sign:

**Welcome to**
**The Blue Canary Bakery**
**Where your hosts**
**Ant & Dec**
**will be pleased to serve you today.**

'The customers love it,' Declan continues. 'And they never seem disappointed when it's just me and Ant serving them.'

'As well they shouldn't,' I say. 'I'm sure the two of you are just as entertaining, if not more so.'

'When do you think you'll have the shop open again?' Anthony asks. 'The ladies of the Women's Guild have been running it since your grandmother went into hospital, but their ways . . . ' He pulls a face. 'Let's just say they're not quite up to your grandmother's standards.'

'Let's be honest, no one could replicate Rose's touch with a bloom,' Declan says wistfully. 'That was something extremely special to behold.'

They both exchange a knowing look.

*What on earth did my grandmother do with flowers that was so wonderful? I remember people often leaving her shop incredibly happy, even crying on occasion, which had seemed odd to me at the time. But what was she doing with flowers to make them so special?*

'I'm not too sure when we'll be open again,' I tell them. 'But luckily I do have someone to help me with the shop – a new florist, all the way from New York!'

'Oh, how decadent!' Anthony says. 'I can't wait to see what they do. Let's just hope she . . . or is it a he?'

'She.'

'*She* can sprinkle some Manhattan magic into your grandmother's shop. It's sure been lacking it of late.'

They exchange another glance.

'I'm sure we'll both give it a good go,' I assure them, wondering again what all these looks were about.

'It'll need more than that, sweetie,' Declan says. 'The way things have been here lately, it'll need a miracle.'

# Eight

## Monkswood – Chivalry

Amber and I stand and look up at the outside of the shop.

It's 9.30 a.m. and we've breakfasted on custard tarts and more tea, and even though I'd suggested Amber stay and try and get some more sleep, she insisted on coming with me to visit the shop this morning, so she could see just what she was letting herself in for.

'It needs work,' Amber says. 'A lot of work.'

'Yes, I know that,' I say, taking a step back to get a better view. 'But in what way? I mean, we can't just give it a lick of paint, can we? I've a feeling it needs more than that.'

'I could tell you about your mom's shop, if you like?' Amber suggests.

'I know what it's like; I've seen it when I've been over there.'

'I don't remember you visiting,' says Amber. 'Was I there?'

'No, I don't think so. It was some time ago.'

The truth was I'd visited years ago when Mum first opened the shop. It had seemed super exciting, Mum opening a florist in New York, and I'd jumped at the chance of a free trip over to the Big Apple. I'd had such a great time seeing the sights and living it up in the city that never sleeps, that I hadn't taken much interest in Mum's flower shop at all. I feel guilty now as I stand looking up at my grandmother's old store, as though a piece of my history has died along with a member of my family.

'Anyway,' I try to sound bright, 'I don't want to emulate one of my family's many flower shops from around the globe. If I'm going to do this – and believe me, Amber, this isn't coming easy to me – I'm going to do it my way.'

'Would you two youngsters move aside please, we've flowers to get into the shop.'

We both turn to find three ladies of varying ages and builds unloading flowers from a small white van.

'I'm sorry,' I say to the one fast approaching the shop door carrying a large pot of carnations. 'The shop isn't open today, and it won't be for a while until it's refitted.'

'What?' a middle-aged woman, who's wearing a Barbour jacket and a paisley headscarf tied jauntily around her neck, demands. 'Don't talk nonsense. We only close on Sundays and Mondays. Stand aside at once.'

'No.' I step in front of her. 'You can't come in today, I'm afraid. As I just said, the shop *won't* be opening.'

Amber barricades herself across the doorway, her arms outstretched in a dramatic fashion, so the sleeves of her brightly coloured blouse billow like sails across the frame.

The woman regards Amber and then me as if we're minor irritations she could do without.

She sighs. 'Beryl, Willow!' she calls to the women offloading the van. 'Do you know anything about this?'

Beryl and Willow poke their heads around the side of the van.

'These *girls*,' she says with disdain, 'won't let us into the shop.'

Beryl, a well-built older lady with grey curly hair, and Willow, a tall, slim girl of about twenty, put down the boxes of flowers they're holding and stand side by side in front of the van, folding their arms across their chests.

The woman in the Barbour turns her head back to me. 'I don't know what you think you're doing,' she says in a low voice, 'but I suggest you both move. Beryl, Willow and I have work to do. We don't take kindly to being held up.'

I defiantly fold my own arms now, and stare hard into her face. Is this woman really spoiling for a fight here in the middle of St Felix? Goodness, things have changed!

Beryl and Willow begin to walk silently towards us.

As I steel myself against the women's approach, I've never been so glad to hear the dulcet tones of the local constabulary asking: 'Good morning, ladies. Can I be of any assistance here?'

Woody! Thank goodness.

'Police Constable Woods, just the person,' the Barbour-jacket woman says, smiling sweetly. 'These girls won't allow us access to the flower shop.'

As Woody looks at us, he jumps in surprise, firstly at seeing me again, and then at Amber barricading the door.

'Is this true, ladies?' he asks.

'It sure is!' Amber cries. 'We will not, we will not be moved!' she sings.

'What my friend means, Woody,' I say sweetly, 'if you don't mind me calling you that?'

He nods.

'What Amber means is, I own this flower shop now and the shop will be closed until further notice.'

Woody looks back at Barbour-jacket woman. 'Well, Harriet?'

'What proof does she have?' Harriet demands. 'Aren't you going to ask her that, PC Woods?'

Woody turns back to me. 'She has a point.'

'I have a key,' I say, reaching into my pocket. 'I think that's proof enough.'

'Well, I have a key right here too,' Harriet says, holding up a key on a piece of rope.

Woody begins to look a bit panicky.

'This was my grandmother's shop. I'm Poppy, her granddaughter, and I've inherited it. You can ask Amber here, or Ant and Dec up the road, or Rita and Richie in the Merry Mermaid or—'

'Or me.'

Jake.

Woody turns to see Jake and Miley standing on the opposite pavement watching the proceedings.

'I can vouch for Poppy; her mother phoned me to say she'd be coming down to take over the shop a few days ago.' He walks over towards us. 'And as for you, Harriet, I'm surprised Caroline didn't phone and tell you that you wouldn't be needed today. She knew all about Poppy taking over the shop last night.'

I notice when Jake speaks to Harriet how coy she is with him to begin with, but then when he imparts the news about Caroline, she immediately begins to bristle.

'Caroline knew?' she demands. 'Then why didn't she say?'

'Why do you think?' Jake says with a shrug of his shoulders. 'To cause trouble, as always. She likes to do that when she doesn't get her own way.'

Harriet quickly evaluates the situation, working out how she can extricate herself without losing face.

'If what you say is correct, and you, Poppy, are indeed the new owner of The Daisy Chain, then I must apologise to you.' She holds out her hand to me, and I shake it. She nods firmly. 'As you have heard, it is our president, Caroline, who is apparently to blame for this mix-up. Although I'm sure this is a complete oversight on Caroline's part – she was very much involved with the shop to begin with, but lately she hasn't had quite so much time ...'

Jake coughs loudly.

'... it is unforgivable,' Harriet continues, after giving Jake a steely glare, 'that the St Felix Women's Guild should welcome you here to our town in this way. I do hope you can find it in your heart to forgive us.'

I nod, a little taken aback by her speech. 'Yes, of course. Apology accepted.'

Woody, standing next to us watching all this, bursts into spontaneous applause, then hurriedly hides his hands behind his back and adopts the typical policeman's stance while his cheeks flush bright red.

'Can I just thank you all for looking after my grandmother's shop while she was in hospital. It was very good of you.' I turn and smile at Willow and Beryl. Willow beams back; Beryl sort of snarls something that might be a smile.

'Not at all,' Harriet replies for them. 'Rose was thought of very highly here in St Felix, it was the least we could do. Any member of Rose's family will always be welcome at our guild meetings. I do hope you might consider joining us, Poppy. We could do with some younger blood.'

Willow nods eagerly. From behind me I hear Jake chuckle.

'I'll think about it,' I say politely.

'Can I join too?' Amber asks, stepping away from the door of the shop. 'I've never been a member of a Women's Guild. I don't think we have them in the States – what is it? It sounds fun!'

While Amber discusses the benefits of the St Felix Women's Guild with Willow and Harriet, I go over and talk to Jake and Woody.

'Thank you,' I say.

'Not a problem, miss,' Woody replies. 'All in a day's work.'

'I meant Jake actually, for vouching for me like that.'

Jake grins smugly.

'But if you hadn't arrived when you did, Woody,' I quickly add when he looks upset, 'I don't know what might have happened. It was starting to get a bit aggressive.'

Jake snorts now.

'It was!' I tell him. 'You weren't here. That Beryl woman looks quite vicious.'

'Ah, Beryl's harmless enough,' Jake says. 'She's the verger at the local church, has been for years. Clarence would be lost without her.'

'Clarence?'

'Father Claybourne,' Woody explains. 'He's our vicar. Lovely man; he was most helpful to me when I first came to St Felix. Poppy, you know I would have vouched for you if I'd known. You didn't tell me who you were when we met yesterday.'

'I know, I'm so sorry, Woody.' I gently touch his arm and Woody's face flushes again. I don't know what it is about Woody. Unlike most women, I don't go for men in uniform at all. But Woody was just so cute. Cute like a puppy: you wouldn't want to make him sad or upset.

'So, I'm gathering from all this hoo-ha this morning you really *have* decided to keep the shop,' Jake says quickly, changing the subject. He looks up at The Daisy Chain. 'I wondered last night if you might change your mind.'

'No, of course I wouldn't change my mind,' I lie. 'Why would I do that?'

Jake shrugs. 'Just thought you might have rushed into your decision a bit, and then had second thoughts in the cold light of day.'

I shake my head. 'Nope.'

'Good, I'm pleased. So the question is, now you've decided to keep the old girl, what are you going to do with her?'

I liked how Jake referred to the shop like it was a person. 'Run it as a flower shop, you'll be pleased to know,' I tell him. 'I think I'd be lynched around here if I did anything else. Plus my mother has sent me Amber over from New York.' We both look over at Amber. She's got her eyes closed and is waving her hands rhythmically around Willow's head, while Harriet and Beryl look on sceptically.

They've obviously moved on from discussing the Women's Guild.

'She's supposed to be some hotshot florist over there.'

Amber suddenly clicks her fingers, snaps her eyes open, and pronounces Willow's aura clean.

'Time will tell, though,' I add.

Miley climbs on to Woody's shoulder and begins fiddling with his uniform buttons. Woody looks apprehensive.

'She won't hurt you, Woody,' Jake insists. 'I've told you a hundred times.'

'I know, I know, I'm just concerned about my uniform – this is police property, you know?'

'Oh, a monkey!' Amber cries, leaving her new Women's Guild friends and coming over. 'Is he yours?' she asks Woody. 'A monkey cop, how cute!'

'Definitely not,' Woody says, trying to shrug Miley off his shoulder.

Miley takes the hint, and climbs on to Amber. She delights in examining the colourful braiding in Amber's hair, and then moves on to the many beads and chains around her neck.

'Miley!' Jake warns. 'Behave.'

'No, she's fine,' Amber says. 'The guy across the street from the florist's shop back in New York has a monkey. I love animals.'

'As much as I hate to break up the impromptu street party that's building here,' Harriet says, 'we need to sort out what to do with all these flowers we've got for the shop. We can't just put them into storage until you open again, Poppy, and we can't just throw them away.'

'Ah, yes, that ... erm?' I look to the others for help, but they all stare blankly back at me.

'I know,' Amber says calmly, with Miley now sitting cross-legged on top of her head looking like some sort of weird Buddha statue amongst all Amber's hippiness. 'You won't make much money out of it, but it will be fun ... '

# Nine

## Lady's Slipper – Capricious Beauty

'Are you sure?' I ask Amber for about the tenth time as we sit on the floor of the shop amongst rolls of ribbon, wire, and the heads of hundreds of flowers.

'Yeah, they're gonna love it, and they'll love you for doing it too.'

Amber's idea, so we wouldn't waste all the flowers the ladies had in their van, was to make floral hair garlands, then give them away to the ladies of the town. She said it would be a nice friendly welcoming gesture.

I think Amber had visions of us standing in the street giving out flowers to passers-by like peace-loving hippies from the seventies, while Bob Dylan played in the background.

But I, with my more sensible head on, had suggested we should look on it as an early marketing campaign for the new shop, and we should ask for a minimal donation to cover our costs, then donate any leftover money to a local charity.

'That's what you call a loss leader,' Jake had helpfully told us, before he and Miley had rapidly disappeared when the Guild ladies started to produce tools, wire and ribbons by the bucketload from the back of the shop. 'Nope,' he'd said, shaking his head. 'I grow flowers – I definitely don't arrange them! But,' he'd suggested before he'd departed, 'I'll have a word with my daughter Bronte. This sounds just the sort of thing she and her friends would like. I'll see if they can come down from the school in their lunch break and take a few off your hands.'

'He's a nice guy, that Jake,' Amber says now, as I pass her another carnation head and she winds it expertly on some wire. 'Hot, too.'

I don't say anything, but I casually glance at the rest of the ladies to see if they react to her statement.

'Jake has had a very unfortunate past,' Harriet says as she begins to form another circle of wire – just as Amber had shown her.

'Oh, why?' Amber asks. 'I thought I was picking up some sadness from him but I couldn't place it.'

Harriet looks at Willow and Beryl.

They both give a sombre nod of approval.

'His wife, Felicity, was taken from us very suddenly a number of years ago. Felicity was such a bright light all over St Felix – from the school PTA to our own Women's Guild, our lovely Felicity would always be there, raising funds and helping out with a cheerful smile and a kind word for everyone.'

'She sounds wonderful,' Amber says.

'Oh, she was,' Harriet continues. 'Everyone in St Felix loved Felicity.'

'We were all heartbroken when she died,' Willow says, cutting a long length of ribbon. 'Felicity was wonderful to be around; always a kind word, always time for you, whatever you were doing. So gentle, so delicate, so—'

'Willow, you make Felicity sound like a saint,' Harriet says. 'Yes, of course she was a lovely lady, and I wouldn't hear a word said against her. But she had her faults like the rest of us. Nobody is perfect.'

'Ain't that the truth,' the usually silent Beryl mutters.

'But Jake has kids – yes?'

I'm thankful to Amber; she's asking all the questions I want to, but without appearing nosy.

'Yes, and what a wonderful job he's done in bringing them up since their mother passed away,' Harriet says with approval. 'Bronte is fifteen now – she's in the same class at school as my son. And Charlie, he's seventeen.'

'Wow, he doesn't look old enough to have kids that age,' I hear Amber say, while I'm still absorbing this information. 'He must have had them young.'

'Felicity and Jake were childhood sweethearts,' Willow says wistfully. 'It was very romantic. Met at sixteen, engaged at eighteen, married at nineteen, first baby when they were in their early twenties.'

'Then separated by death over a decade later,' Beryl finishes for her. 'Very Romeo and Juliet, if you wish to romanticise the pain of death, Willow.'

I'm beginning to like Beryl more every minute. She may be

quiet, but when she does speak there's no beating about the bush – an admirable trait, in my book.

Willow pulls a sulky face and goes back to her job: tying the ribbons on the ends of the garlands.

'Are you OK, Poppy?' Amber asks me. 'You look a little pale.'

'I'm fine,' I reply quietly. 'Let's just get on with these garlands.' But I can't help looking towards my grandmother's old desk while I cut the heads off more flowers, and remember . . .

As Amber predicted, the flower garlands are a huge success.

After we've finished making them up, the ladies of the St Felix Women's Guild leave the two of us standing outside the shop. Willow and Beryl, both wearing flower garlands in their hair, walk down the high street together arm in arm.

We manage to give away a few garlands to the odd passer-by in return for a donation, and then Ant and Dec arrive and delight in parading a couple back up to their bakery, where I know for a fact they wear them for the rest of the afternoon, because when I pop by to get a couple more custard tarts later (Amber had enjoyed hers as much as I had) they still have them on.

It's when lunchtime arrives and the girls from the high school come marching down the hill led by Jake's daughter, Bronte, that our trade really takes off. In fact in the space of forty-five minutes we shift nearly all of our garlands.

'This is so cool,' Bronte says, spinning around with flowers in her hair. There can be no mistaking whose daughter she is. She has Jake's sandy brown hair and deep brown eyes. 'We never get anything like this here; it's like having our own festival. Will you be doing cool stuff like this all the time when you open up for real?'

'Yes,' I assure her. 'The Daisy Chain will definitely be very cool.'

She smiles. 'I thought it might. With you two running it, it would have to be.'

I smile at her and am about to say thanks when she continues.

'I mean, an ageing Goth and an American hippy coming together in one store, what sort of mega mash-up is that going to be! The two of you will be wicked together. I can't wait.'

With that Bronte and her friends merge into one big pack of short school skirts, bottle-green jumpers, shrieks and giggles, and disappear back up the hill.

I look at Amber, still holding the near-empty box of garlands.

She smiles awkwardly. 'I'd say I was more New Age than hippy.'

'I'd say *you* got off lightly. I'm not a Goth! Let alone an ageing one!'

She looks me up and down. 'How old are you then?'

'I'm thirty!'

'Really?' Amber looks surprised. 'I thought you were much younger. You look it. Maybe it's your clothes, like Bronte said. You are a *little* . . . how can I put it politely?'

'Just say it, Amber.'

'Dark.'

'What do you mean *dark*? Just because I don't wear all the colours of the rainbow like you, doesn't make me a Goth!'

'No, but look at what you're wearing now,' she gestures at my clothes. 'They're all black.'

'Today, perhaps. Yesterday I had on burgundy DMs.'

'With . . . ?'

I sigh. 'OK, with black leggings, but that doesn't mean—'

'I'm just saying what I see, which is exactly what Bronte did. Plus your personality is also a little . . .'

I roll my eyes. 'Go on, you might as well get it over with.'

'Harsh.'

'I'm harsh?' I snap.

'See.'

'OK, but not all the time, surely?'

'No, not all the time.' Amber smiles and plucks a stray flower that has fallen from one of the garlands from the bottom of the box. 'I think you have a softer side hidden somewhere in there, my new friend. But the question I can't answer yet is . . .'

'Go on.'

She places the flower behind my ear and I shudder internally.

'Why do you keep it hidden from us?'

# Ten

## Flax – I Feel Your Kindness

It's funny how once you really set your mind on doing something it suddenly starts to come together very quickly.

The day after Amber and I had stood outside selling flower garlands in the street, everything began to fall into placc regarding the new shop.

When I realised Amber had nowhere to stay in St Felix and had planned on staying at the Merry Mermaid until she found somewhere, I'd asked her to stay with me at the cottage.

This went against all my natural instincts, as I hated living with anyone. I was always better on my own. But I couldn't let Amber live at the pub when I had a spare room, especially when she was being so helpful to me and the shop. Besides, for all her 'alternative' ways, Amber was fun. She made me smile – which was a tricky thing for anyone to do.

So I moved my stuff into my grandmother's old room

upstairs, which was very odd to begin with, but turned out to feel a lot less odd than sleeping in Will's and my old room, which I'd found very unsettling for the one night I spent there. Then we turned our attention to planning our new shop.

Both Amber and I agreed from the beginning that whatever sort of shop my grandmother had run in the past, or the ladies of the St Felix Women's Guild had been running for the last year, this new generation Daisy Chain should be something with our own unique stamp on it.

Even though I was officially the new owner, in my eyes Amber was as much a part of the shop as I was. She was the florist; I was just someone who had been thrown in at the deep end.

We quickly decided between us that, along with fresh flowers, we should stock flower-based trinkets too – cool pieces of jewellery and pottery. We wanted Daisy Chain to be somewhere that the ladies of the St Felix Women's Guild would want to come to buy their fresh flowers from, but at the same time somewhere Bronte and her girlfriends would want to hang out in. If you loved flowers in any form, then you'd love Daisy Chain.

And that was my big problem in all this.

I didn't.

Love flowers, that is.

Amber knew everything there was to know about them: their names, their scents, their colours, how long they lived for, what temperature of water they liked, and what temperature you should store them in. Her knowledge and enthusiasm for flowers was endless.

We spent lots of time together at the cottage dreaming up ideas for our new shop – some helpful, like my idea to sell flower-related items, and some not so much, like Amber's idea of laying a trail of fresh petals outside the door every morning to entice people inside. We agreed on a slight name change: Daisy Chain instead of The Daisy Chain – we both thought it sounded funkier. We also agreed that an overhaul of the dark interior of the shop would be needed, yet we both wanted to retain the essence of what had made my grandmother's shop so special.

We surfed the Net on Amber's iPad, doing image searches and looking on Pinterest for photos of modern flower shops and florists, trying to get a feel for what everyone else was doing these days. After much discussion, we decided on a seaside theme to complement the shop's surroundings.

Bright blue walls would be our backdrop, with whitewashed wooden units displaying all our flower knick-knacks. Scrubbed wooden tables would hold the cast-iron buckets of fresh flowers that we'd sell and Amber would arrange into bouquets on request. We were also going to keep the original desk my grandmother had served behind. Amber said it felt lucky, and she could feel the spirit of all the former owners who'd stood behind it. Besides, I didn't want to see it go – that desk held too many memories for me. So the desk had been worked into the new design.

We also discovered some vintage floral china hidden in the drawers of the wooden dressers, and we were going to display these pretty pieces on the newly painted units, as a tribute to the shop's long history.

We hoped the overall look would be eclectic, yet chic.

Hopefully it would not only be the perfect tribute to my grandmother, but the perfect setting for a new and successful business.

Today is Sunday, and it's almost two weeks since I made my momentous decision about keeping the shop. Well, it's momentous for me, I've never embraced responsibility in my whole life! And this morning we're about to attempt our first stab at decorating the shop. We've decided to do it ourselves, as the quote I got from a local painter and decorator would have eaten into far too much of the money my mother had sent to help me get the shop up and running.

Even though my mother had lent me the money without any strings attached in an attempt to entice me into staying at the shop, I'd insisted I would pay her back as soon as the place was up and running and hopefully making a profit.

If I'm going to do this, I'm going to do it my way.

So here we are, wearing our white painting overalls from the DIY shop in the next town. Amber has brightened hers up by tying back her unruly red hair with a brightly coloured head-scarf, but I remain in my usual monochrome, the only difference being that my predominant colour on this occasion is white instead of black. There are unopened paint pots at our feet and we hold clean brushes and paint rollers in our hands.

We both sigh as we look at the empty walls, dressers and tables.

'Where do we begin?' I ask, looking up at the bare wall.

'I have no idea,' Amber says. 'Have you ever decorated before?'

I shake my head.

'Me neither,' she says. 'We always had someone in when I lived at home. The house and the rooms were too big to do it ourselves. Not that my mom would have sullied her hands decorating. It might have chipped her nails!'

I look across at Amber. The way she dresses and acts, I'd assumed she didn't come from a wealthy background. I'm cross with myself; I of all people should know not to judge someone by their appearance. I only had to look in the mirror.

'So, where do you think we start?' I ask, looking down at an unopened tin of paint. 'With that?'

'Putting the kettle on is usually a good place to start when you've got the workmen in!' a voice calls at the door, and we see Jake and a posse of people, including Woody, Belle, and some of the Women's Guild ladies, wearing an assortment of mismatched outfits, and carrying brushes, rollers, sandpaper and a whole host of tools I hadn't even considered we might need.

'Come in, my friends!' Amber calls, as everyone pours through the door. 'If you don't mind an American making you tea, I'll put that kettle on at once!'

'What are you doing here?' I ask Jake, still astonished by the many folk pouring through the door.

'We thought you could do with a hand,' Jake says, propping a long-handled roller against the wall after Miley has left his shoulder and scampered after Amber. 'You told Rita at the Mermaid you and Amber were going to be starting to decorate today, didn't you?'

'Yes . . . '

'So she put the word out, and here we all are!'

I couldn't believe how many people had come up to me in

the days following my decision to keep the flower shop, all wanting to congratulate me, thank me, and tell me I'd done the right thing.

The Daisy Chain obviously held a very special place in many people's hearts here in St Felix, and I was determined to find out why.

'This is brilliant,' I say, still finding it hard to believe everyone has turned out like this. I'm not used to people helping me. 'I . . . I can't pay you all though.'

Jake looks at me oddly. 'Why would we want paying – we just want to help you.'

'But why?'

'Because that's what friends and neighbours do – help each other.'

'Sure. Yes. Of course.' I smile awkwardly. 'Well, thank you, this is . . . brilliant – I said that already, didn't I?'

Jake smiles. 'Yes, you did. But don't thank me, thank Rita; she and Rich will be along later when they've done the breakfasts at the Mermaid.' He looks around. 'Right, so what should we do first?'

Luckily there are a few people in the decorating posse that know what they're doing. So between them they organise us into teams, so we can get going in some sort of orderly fashion. Apparently there's much rubbing down to be done first to remove flaking paintwork, and then cracks that must be filled. These things hadn't occurred to me at all.

I thought you just painted over cracks: in decorating, and in life.

A while later I'm helping Charlie, Jake's son, sand down one of the big wooden tables. Charlie is a lovely boy, tall like Jake, but whereas Bronte takes after Jake in colouring, I assume Charlie must take after his mother. He has bright blue eyes and pale blond hair, and his manner, although polite when spoken to, is quiet and unassuming.

'Sorry you've got dragged in here on a Sunday morning,' I say, trying to make conversation.

'That's OK,' he says, rubbing the table leg with his piece of sandpaper. 'Not much else to do. The weather forecast isn't that great.'

'What would you be doing if it was?'

He looks at me as if he's wondering why I care.

'I dunno, go down to the beach maybe, watch the surfers if the waves were good.'

'Don't you surf yourself then?'

'No.'

'Why?'

'Do I look like a surfer?'

The only thing that looks surfer-like about Charlie is his blond hair. His frame, although tall, is lanky and slight. He looks as though the slightest gust of wind would knock him off a stationary surfboard, let alone one careering through eight-foot-high waves.

'Not all surfers are the same,' I suggest, remembering my brother Will and my own attempts at surfing. 'Sometimes it's just about taking part and having fun.'

'Not in St Felix it isn't. It's taken very seriously here. If you're not in the "gang", you're not in the surf.'

I'm about to protest further when a lady wearing a red head-scarf and denim dungarees comes over. 'Can you go and help your father lift that dresser, Charlie?' she asks. 'They need another pair of strong hands.'

Charlie looks at her as though she's joking. Then he sighs. 'Sure, Aunt Lou.' He gets up and hands her the sandpaper, then heads over to where Jake and another man are trying to move a dresser away from a wall.

'I'm Lou,' the woman says, holding out her hand. 'I believe we met in Mickey's chip shop the other day?'

'Oh yes, that's right, I remember you. Thanks for coming along to help out today. As I said to Jake earlier, it's most kind of everyone.'

'People are like that here in St Felix, and Rose was very well thought of.' Lou sits on the floor next to me and begins sanding the leg that Charlie was midway through smoothing down. 'I do miss seeing her cheery face every day.'

I smile at Lou; underneath her red headscarf I can see tufts of grey hair poking out, belying her youthful complexion. 'Did you know my grandmother well?'

'Oh yes, we were very good friends. I came to her funeral up in London.'

I thought her face had looked familiar the other night at the chip shop. 'I'm so sorry I didn't remember you the other evening,' I apologise. 'If it's any consolation, you did look familiar.'

'My dear, don't worry at all. You had a lot to contend with at the funeral without remembering every face that turned up to pay their last respects to Rose. And there were an awful lot of people wanting to do so.'

'Yes, there were. Oh, that's how you knew my name at the chip shop – from the funeral.'

Lou smiles. 'It was partly that.'

I wait for her to enlighten me.

She stops sanding, lowers her voice and leans in towards me. 'Rose told me you'd come one day.'

'What?'

'She said one day her granddaughter Poppy would come back to St Felix to take over her flower shop. She often talked about you.'

'When did she tell you this?'

'Years ago.'

'Before she became ill?'

'Oh yes, well before that. She was always adamant you'd be the one to take over The Daisy Chain.'

I stop midway through sanding, my hand poised on the leg of the table.

'But why would she have been so confident? It's a big enough mystery to me that she left me the shop in the first place. But to be so certain I'd choose to run the place ... ' I lift the sandpaper away from the wood and twiddle it around in my hands while I think. 'When she was ill in hospital I'd go and visit her, but she never mentioned any of this. I assumed that if anything happened, the shop would go to my mother or one of my aunts – someone who was actually interested in flowers.'

'She was right, though, wasn't she?' Lou says gently. 'Because here you are, about to open the shop up as your own. And here we are, all helping you out, as she knew we would.'

'She was always right,' I laugh. 'It was very annoying.'

'Wasn't she just!' Lou smiles. 'Try having a best friend who's right all the time. It's very wearing.' Her expression changes to sadness as she remembers her friend is no longer here.

Never comfortable when it comes to dealing with emotions, I fall back on my usual strategy and change the subject. 'So you're Charlie and Bronte's aunt?' I ask, wondering if Lou was Jake or Felicity's sister. She looked a bit old to be either.

'Great-aunt, actually. I'm Jake's aunt – his mother's sister.'

'Oh . . . that makes more sense,' I blurt out.

'Because I'm an old biddy?' She grins. 'I'll have you know, I'm the reigning over-sixties surfing champion for North Cornwall.'

'Really?'

'Yep,' she says proudly. 'There may only have been three of us entered, but I still stayed on my board longer than those other pension-drawing wusses!'

I hold out my hand to her to high five, and she responds appropriately by slapping my palm.

'You should take Charlie for a spin on the waves,' I say, looking over to where Charlie is now helping Amber sand some already filled cracks flat before they can be painted. 'I think he'd like it.'

'Tried,' Lou says. 'He won't have it. He's a bit too worried what he'll look like. It's an awkward age for a boy – seventeen.'

I nod.

'It's a shame,' she continues. 'They miss out on so much when they're young because they're worried what they'll look like, and then when it's too late and they can't—' she stops hurriedly. 'Oh my dear, I'm so sorry, I didn't mean . . . I meant . . . ' She reaches out her hand and places it gently on my arm, and in one touch does everything I couldn't do for her a few minutes ago.

'I know,' I reply, suddenly needing to examine the knots in the wood very closely. 'It's fine, really.'

'No, it's not. I know it won't be easy for you, being here in St Felix again. Rose told me everything.'

I look at Lou. 'Everything?'

She nods.

'What are you two up to, hiding under there?' Jake says, sticking his head under the table. 'Poppy, I see you've met my aunt Lou.'

'I think Poppy could do with a break,' Lou says. 'Is that kettle on at the moment?'

'Er, I'm not sure, I'll go and find out,' Jake says, craning his neck to look in the direction of the back room.

'Maybe a little walk might be better?' Lou suggests. 'Mickey said he'd lay on some lunch for us – perhaps you could go and find out about that?' She raises her eyebrows at Jake.

'Sure,' Jake says. 'You want to come, Poppy?'

'I don't know – it doesn't seem right to abandon everyone.' I look at the current team of helpers busying themselves in the shop.

'They'll be fine,' Lou says. 'A good lunch will be much more important to them in a few minutes than your presence right now.'

'OK, if you're sure.'

Jake holds out his hand, I take it, and he pulls me up.

'Right,' he says, giving my hand a squeeze. 'Off in search of chips we go!'

# Eleven

## Lilac – First Emotions of Love

Jake and I walk along the harbour towards Mickey's chip shop, with Miley back on Jake's shoulder. Even though Charlie had said the forecast was dismal, the clouds are now lifting, and it's turning into a beautiful day in St Felix.

'Do you want to sit a bit and wait, or walk on?' Jake asks after we've found no sign of life at Mickey's. Even though it's Sunday, Mickey had offered to come in early to fry up some chips for the decorating volunteers – another act of kindness which completely took me by surprise.

'Sit, I think,' I reply, shielding my eyes from the bright sun. 'I could do with a rest after this morning.'

We find a bench and sit down by the harbour wall, both of us looking out at the sea and the boats swaying rhythmically up and down on the waves now the tide is in.

'Your children are very good, coming out to help us today,' I say to Jake after we've been sitting for a minute or so admiring the view.

'Yes, they're good kids, they always have been. Especially Charlie. Bronte can be a bit of a tearaway at times.'

I smile.

'What?' Jake asks.

'She called me an ageing Goth when Amber and I were giving away the flower garlands outside the shop the other week.'

Miley, appearing to understand what I say, chooses this moment to screech with laughter, while Jake pulls a face. 'God, I'm so sorry.'

'It's OK,' I say, eyeing Miley until I realise she's screeching along with a seagull sitting on the harbour wall. 'Bronte's young; she sees everyone as old, I guess. Although usually it's the other way around for me.'

'People think you're younger than you are?' Jake asks. 'I certainly did when I met you.'

I nod. 'Yeah, I've kinda got used to it over the years. Never felt the need to grow up gracefully.'

'Why?' Jake enquires. 'Are you the Peter Pan of floristry?'

'Hardly. I dunno, I just feel more comfortable not taking life too seriously.' I look down at my boots. 'If wearing Docs makes me seem younger, then so be it. Amber tells me I wear too much black though,' I concede.

'Really?' Jake teases. 'I would never have guessed.'

'I'm not today though, am I?' I protest, gesturing at my painting overalls.

'Yes, I have to give you that – a pair of white dungarees is quite the rainbow of colour,' Jake says, grinning. 'So how does it feel to liberate yourself from your cloths of mourning?'

I wince at his joke. 'I'm not that bad, am I?' I reply, shaking it off. Jake has no idea how close to the truth he is.

'You've been here in St Felix how long – a couple of weeks?'

'About that.'

'And the only colour I've ever seen you wear, apart from black, is your burgundy boots.'

He noticed?

'I like black, so what? Is it a crime to wear black clothing in this town?'

I expect Jake to come back with one of his usual witty retorts. I've been enjoying our banter, sitting out here in the dazzling Cornish sunshine. The town looks like a vibrant, colourful oil painting today – vivid shades and bold brush-strokes masking any dullness that a plain white canvas underneath might betray.

'No, of course not,' he says awkwardly, fiddling with his sleeve and attempting to roll it up his arm. 'It's just . . . well, you don't drown out the perfection of a pale, delicate lily by surrounding it with something heavy, you let its beauty shine through for everyone to see.'

I'm pretty sure my skin isn't pale and delicate right this moment; it's most likely red and ruddy, as I feel my cheeks flush hot at Jake's words. What does he mean? He can't be referring to me, can he, with his flower analogy? No, surely not. It must be the way these flower types talk – using flowers instead of normal words.

Except none of my family ever talk like this – so why does Jake?

Jake's cheeks, I notice, are doing something very similar to mine. They're pink and he looks flushed as he proceeds to roll the same sleeve back down his tanned arm.

'I appreciate the advice,' I tell him awkwardly, uncertain how to deal with this side of Jake. 'But I think I'll just stick with black for now. I've kind of got used to it over the years. It suits me.'

'Fair enough,' Jake says, shrugging amiably. He crosses one long leg over the other, so his large tan Timberland boot rests on his knee, and he visibly relaxes as he leans back against the bench and looks out to sea. 'If you want to look like an ageing Goth,' he says, the merest hint of a smile spreading over his lips, 'then that's up to you.'

Phew, I breathe a sigh of relief. Jake's back to normal. I can handle his banter, but compliments, they're a different matter.

'I think you'll find I'm *not* a Goth, ageing or otherwise,' I reply, able to look at him properly again. 'Being a Goth is about more than wearing dark clothes. I don't wear heavy make-up, or listen to that sort of music. I don't do colour, that's all. It's just not my thing.' I lean back against the bench and fold my arms, happy that we've returned to behaving naturally with each other.

'What about your attitude, though?' Jake asks sombrely, still looking ahead, apparently intrigued by the exploits of a very large seagull ripping up the remains of an unsuspecting tourist's ice-cream cone.

Miley also watches, probably wondering if she can get in on the action.

'What do you mean, my attitude?' I snap, a little too fast.

Jake holds out his hand in a 'there you go' gesture. 'We had a similar conversation in the Mermaid the first evening I met you, if I remember rightly. You called yourself an awkward bitch.'

'I *may* have said that,' I reply, remembering. 'I'm just not a people person, that's all.'

Jake turns and looks at me in part amusement, part confusion. 'How can you even say that with a straight face?'

I look at him, not understanding.

'Do I really have to explain?' Jake asks.

I nod.

'Right, examples ... OK, here's one: Since you've been here, you've welcomed our American friend Amber into your home. And from what I can tell, she seems to love living with you.'

I smile at the mention of Amber; she's been like a breath of fresh air in my life since she arrived at the cottage. I'm almost jealous of her sunny disposition and unfailingly positive nature.

'She didn't have that much choice who she lived with,' I try, but Jake is having none of it.

He shakes his head. 'Uh-uh. Don't even go there with that self-deprecating attitude of yours. I have seen you actually talk to people since you've been here. And not only that, you seem to have a knack for it. You were even chatting to my son earlier, and it takes some effort to get more than two words out of him these days.'

'Charlie's a nice lad,' I tell him. 'He reminds me of someone I used to know.'

Jake waits for me to explain, but I don't.

'Well, maybe there's a few exceptions,' I admit. 'But believe me, Jake, I'm better left on my own most of the time. People, *in general*,' I add when he opens his mouth, 'annoy me. I rarely annoy myself.'

'Rarely?' Jake enquires, and I notice a slight twitch at the corner of his lips.

'Only when I try and wear colour!' I announce, and to my relief this time he smiles.

Then I notice the chip shop.

'Oh, there's a light on in Mickey's,' I say with delight. 'Look's like it's lunchtime for everyone!'

We carry as many portions of fish and chips back to the shop as we can manage, and I'm relieved and happy to feel relaxed in Jake's company once more.

However much I protested, I knew he was right: I had interacted with people more in the two weeks I'd been here than I would in two months in London. And more significantly, I'd enjoyed it.

Back at Daisy Chain our paper parcels of lunch are well received, and after everyone has eaten their chips sitting on the floor, in the doorway, or propped up outside in the sunshine against the wall of the shop, we resume work.

'Poppy!' Late in the afternoon, Woody, who looks very different wearing casual clothes, calls me over. 'We found these earlier when we were changing those rotten floorboards out back. They must have been your grandmother's.'

He hands me a cardboard box containing some old journals and notebooks.

'Thanks,' I say, taking a quick look inside. 'I'll take them back to the cottage and keep them safe. They're probably the shop's old accounts books.'

Odd that they were hidden under the floor though.

'How do you think it's coming along?' Woody asks. 'As you'd hoped?'

Jake and Charlie have just finished applying a coat of the bright blue colour to a second wall, and Amber and Bronte are admiring their handiwork, having stained the first of the dressers. It looks like new with its translucent white coating.

'Yes,' I say, looking proudly around me at the transformation taking place. 'I think it's going to look even better than I'd hoped.'

'Great,' Woody says. 'I think I might have to get this same team in when the station wants a new lick of paint.'

There are shouts of derision at Woody's suggestion, and a chorus of voices telling him this is strictly a one-off, a special case.

And as I look around me at the St Felix massive, as Bronte had named them earlier, all pitching in and helping me get my grandmother Rose's shop back in business, that's exactly how I feel: special.

I really shouldn't tar all people with the same brush, I think, wincing at my awful pun as I lift the brush that's in my hand so I can continue painting the window frame in front of me. The people of St Felix have been nothing but lovely and helpful since I arrived.

Being back in St Felix would never feel the way it had when I used to come here with Will, I knew that.

But with the help of my new friends, it was already beginning to feel just that bit special again.

# Twelve

## Acacia – Secret Love

'I'm just going to hop in the bath, Poppy!' Amber calls up the stairs. 'Even without salt crystals, a bubble bath is gonna ease my aching muscles.'

Amber had tried everywhere in St Felix to get some sea salt crystals to add to her bath tonight, telling us all that the salt would draw out our impurities and aches a treat. She refused to believe she couldn't buy sea salt in a town so close to the sea; she'd even tried Mickey's chip shop. But the type of salt Mickey used to fill the cellars that stood on his shop counter wasn't conducive to the sort of spiritual healing that Amber had in mind. So instead she's having to make do with Radox and some lavender bath salts that I found in my grandmother's bathroom cupboard.

I'd stepped into a lovely hot shower as soon as we came in from our long day of decorating – which amazingly was nearly finished. I couldn't believe how much we'd managed to achieve in one day. I guess the saying many hands make light work really is true.

I flop down on the sofa in my PJs with a mug of hot chocolate and one of the doughnuts left over from the huge box that Ant and Dec had popped round to the shop in the afternoon when spirits and energy had been beginning to lag.

What a day it's been. Not only the progress in the shop itself, but getting to know the St Felix townsfolk who came along to help with the renovations. Especially Jake's family. His kids are a real credit to him; Bronte, like he'd said, seems a bit of a tearaway, but nothing compared to what I'd been like as a teenager. Charlie's a quiet, unassuming, lovely young boy. But what they, and their aunt Lou, quite obviously have in common is their love for Jake.

I think about Jake as I finish off my doughnut and sip on my hot chocolate.

He's a strange one. One minute he'll say or do something that seems to imply he sees me as more than just a friend, and the next he'll make it quite clear that that's not on his agenda at all. Jake wouldn't be the first male to confuse me; most relationships with the opposite sex end up leaving me bewildered, but usually I'm the one making things complicated.

Maybe I have been imagining signs because I hoped they were there. I mean, why would Jake be interested in me? He's a nice guy; he probably wants to help me because he knew my grandmother. Perhaps there really are good guys out there who don't want anything from you, only your friendship.

I've not had that many male friends in the past that were *just* friends, but then I've never had that many friends full stop.

It wasn't always that way. At primary school I had loads of friends; there'd been parties, and play dates, and I was never the last to be picked for anything. Even when I went to secondary school all was fine to begin with. I was on the hockey team, and the netball team, and the school council too. I played the flute in the school orchestra, and appeared in countless school productions. I was quite the swat too – the teachers reckoned I'd get A or A* in every one of my GCSEs. I was the archetype of the perfect pupil.

But then one summer everything had changed . . .

I go to the French windows and pull back the doors. As I step out on to the balcony a gust of sea air is strong enough to billow my long, freshly showered hair up and around my face. It licks my cheeks, and I have to push it back to restrain it. But I don't go indoors, I stand there willing the salty air to blow away my memories and remove them from my mind like Amber's salt bath was going to purge the aches from her body.

'I won't go back there,' I shout into the wind. It immediately whips the words from my mouth and tosses them high into the sky where no one can hear them. 'I won't think about how my life changed the day I lost you.'

Angrily, I storm back inside the room, slamming shut the French windows.

'Everything OK up there?' I hear Amber call from the bathroom downstairs.

'Yes, everything's fine. Just enjoy your bath!' I call back.

Lovely as Amber is, I need some space right now. A breather for a few minutes.

The cardboard box that Woody gave me earlier is sitting on the table next to the sofa. In an effort to steer my mind away from the painful memories that have suddenly resurfaced, I decide to investigate its contents.

As I had thought, the box is full of old financial records, individual customers' accounts, and lists of flowers supplied for various events. I set the latter to one side in case they might be of use to Amber, and I'm about to give up on the box and get another doughnut, when I spot something lying right at the bottom. It's a bundle of worn-looking books of varying sizes, bound together by a frayed and faded piece of white ribbon. I fish the bundle out, untie the ribbon, and take a look inside the first book.

It's an antique hardback called *The Language and Meaning of Flowers*; its dust jacket is so delicate and worn at the edges that I can barely open the cover without the jacket crumbling between my fingers.

It seems to be a glossary of flowers. There's a very detailed drawing of each flower, plus a description and the growing habits. At the top of each page the name of the flower is given in both English and Latin, along with its symbolic meaning. Daisy, for example, symbolises innocence; Marigold – grief, Iris – message. I laugh at the meaning of Poppy: Fantastic Extravagance. *As if!*

I flick gently through the pages, reading each flower's meaning and the occasions when it should be given, and then I notice a handwritten inscription at the beginning of the book:

*To my darling Daisy,*

*One day I hope to make your dream come true, and these and many more flowers you shall sell in your own Little Flower Shop . . .*

*All my love and deepest admiration today and forever more,*

*Your William*

*February 1887*

'What's wrong?' Amber asks appearing in the doorway still towelling her hair dry. 'I was sensing negative vibes coming from up here a few minutes ago, so I got out of my bath.' She looks at me, still staring at the book in shock. 'What's that? What do you have?'

'This book belonged to my great-great-great-grandmother,' I tell her holding the book up. 'Look, here at the front, it's inscribed "To my darling Daisy from your William". Those are the names of my great-great-great-grandparents. That Daisy is *the* Daisy, the Daisy who owned the original Daisy Chain shop.'

'You mean the lady that started your family's empire?'

*I wouldn't exactly call it an empire . . .*

'Yes, that one,' I agree, for the sake of argument. 'Do you know the story then?'

'Some,' Amber says, grabbing a doughnut from the box and settling down next to me on the sofa, her damp hair cascading over her shoulders. 'Tell me again though, I love a good story.'

I'd had this story told to me so many times over the years, I'd long since stopped listening when it was being recounted. But this is the first time *I've* ever been asked to tell it to anyone. I look at Amber's expectant face, and suddenly it feels very important I get this right.

'Daisy was a flower seller on Covent Garden Market in the late nineteenth century,' I tell her, closing the book up and placing my hand on the front cover. 'She came from a big family, and a very poor background, so she was delighted when she managed to get a job selling flowers.'

Amber smiles, already enjoying the story.

'Apparently her sisters had all gone into service, and that was what was expected of Daisy. But she decided differently, and took the job on the market. It didn't pay that well, but she loved it.'

Amber nods approvingly.

'In 1886, she met my great-great-great-grandfather William. William's family owned a large company that grew and distributed flowers all over England. They met when he was delivering flowers to the market one day – the romanticised version of this story tells it as love at first sight, but I don't buy that.'

Amber pulls a disapproving face, and waits for me to continue.

'Anyway, at *some stage* they decided they wanted to get married, but William's family didn't approve of Daisy's background and thought he was marrying beneath him. Again, there's talk here of planned elopements and the like, but it depends who you talk to in my family and how romantic they want it to sound. I don't think the guy would have given up all his inheritance for love, not back then . . . All right, all right,' I say, as Amber folds her arms across her chest. 'I'll stick to telling the story. OK, so in a weird twist of fate, William's father died unexpectedly and, as the only son, William inherited the family business. The first thing he did was to ask for Daisy's hand in marriage, and she immediately accepted. They moved to Cornwall, opened Daisy's longed-for flower shop, and the rest, as my family always say at this point, is history.'

'That's a great story,' Amber says. 'I never tire of hearing it.'

'So you did know it! Why did you make me tell it if you knew Daisy's story?'

'So *you* could hear it again,' she says, raising her auburn eyebrows.

'What? Why?'

'Because she's like you, isn't she – Daisy?'

'How on earth is a genteel Victorian girl who goes from selling flowers on Covent Garden Market to owning a shop here in Cornwall *anything* like me?'

'How do you know she was genteel? She could have been feisty and ballsy, just like you.'

I look at Amber as though she's lost it.

'Just because she was Victorian doesn't mean she didn't hide a passion for life underneath all her corsets and long skirts,' Amber says, brushing doughnut sugar from the tiny towel she has wrapped around her body. 'She must have had some guts to stand up to her family and not go into service like all her sisters did. Hmm?'

Oh, now I see where Amber is going with this . . .

'*You* didn't do what your family wanted you to, did you? You stayed away from the family business for years, and—'

'Amber,' I hold up my hand. 'Let me stop you there. I appreciate the sentiment, and what you're trying to do. But you're forgetting one thing. Where have we been all day?'

Amber thinks.

'Ah.'

'Yes: Ah. I'm not like Daisy at all. I've folded. Given in to it all. I'm joining the family business by reopening Daisy's original flower shop. I'm not a leader like she was. I'm a follower like the rest of them.'

I sigh heavily, the weight of it all enveloping me like a strait-jacket.

'No,' Amber says, not standing for my self-pity. 'You're wrong. You, Poppy, are here for a reason. Just like your great-great-great-grandmother was, and all the other generations that have had that little flower shop since.' She stops to think, twiddling her long hair around her fingers while she does. 'I didn't know your grandmother Rose, but I've met enough people since I've been in St Felix that did know her, and it's obvious she made a huge difference to people's lives.' Amber unwinds her hair from around her finger and swivels on the sofa to face me, an eager look on her face. 'You've been sent here to change people's lives too, Poppy, I know you have. And do you know how I know?'

'You read my petals?' I ask darkly.

Luckily, Amber smiles. 'No. The reason I know is because I think I've been sent here to help you.'

# Thirteen

## St John's Wort – Superstition

'So what's in the rest of your pile?' Amber asks calmly, while I'm still staring at her.

Is she for real? All that stuff about me making a difference to people's lives and being here in St Felix for a reason?

The only reason I'm here is because I had nothing better to do.

OK, that's a bit harsh. St Felix is a nice enough town, the people have been nothing but kind to me since I arrived, and I have to admit it's been nowhere near as bad as I thought it would be, coming back here after all these years. And I'm quite looking forward to opening up the shop with Amber – except for the flower part, but I'd deal with that when it happened.

'Er . . . ' I shake my head and look down at my lap. I'd only got as far as the hardback flower book. 'I'm not sure.' I hand Amber one of the little brown notebooks, and I open one of the others.

Inside mine each double page is carefully ruled into four columns. In the first column, written in beautiful ornate handwriting that's faded in places and has the occasional ink blot where the author's fountain pen has leaked, is a list of names; the second column lists ailments and conditions; the third flowers; and the fourth comments. The entries all date from the late 1800s.

It's the strangest list I've ever come across; from small turns in people's financial fortunes, to their love lives changing for the better, even their health improving. It would appear that it was all down to a single visit to The Daisy Chain, and the flowers they were given.

'What's in yours?' I ask, wondering if Amber's book contains anything similar.

'This picture fell out,' she says, passing me a tiny embroidered picture of a purple rose. 'It looks quite old. There's also a quarter handwritten on the back, which is odd.'

I examine the embroidered card; the stitches on the rose are tiny, but perfectly sewn; it's very sweet, and as I turn it over, handwritten on the back is indeed a number one over a number four.

'Are those letters woven into the petals too?' Amber asks, looking over my shoulder at the picture. 'Look there.'

I look at where she's pointing, and it does appear there's a V and an R stitched into the flower.

'Maybe it was the initials of the person that sewed it,' I suggest. 'That was the kind of thing they did back then, wasn't it? So what about the book?' I ask, more interested in the book than a picture of a rose. 'Anything interesting there?'

'It's the cutest thing,' Amber says, holding up the book. 'It's like a dictionary of flowers, but it lists things that can be cured with their petals. I've never seen anything like this before and I know *a lot* about alternative healing.' She looks at me. 'What do you have? Do you wanna swap?'

We exchange books, and silently examine the pages.

'This is utter madness,' I say, at the same time as Amber says, 'This is so cool!'

'How can it be cool?' I ask. 'It's all nonsense! As if people's lives could be changed just by coming into a flower shop. Even you can't believe that, surely?'

Amber thinks about this.

'See, there's three schools of thought when it comes to alternative healing,' she says, pulling her feet up on to the sofa and resting her chin on top of her knees. I notice she's wearing pretty silver rings on some of her toes. 'First, you've got the people who believe everything, whether it's Reiki, homeopathic medicines, acupuncture – you name it. If the doc says it doesn't work, they will argue to the death that it does.'

'Go on.'

'Second, you've got the type who pooh-pooh everything, and won't give any of it a chance.' She puts on a Deep South accent: 'If ah cain't see it or touch it, honey, then how *can* it be doing me good, let alone, heaven-to-Betsy, actually working!'

I'm pretty sure I fall into that category.

'So what's the third?' I ask quickly before Amber has time to make that judgement.

'And the third . . . see, they're the most interesting.' She drops her knees and leans back against the multicoloured sofa cushions. 'These folk don't diss alternative healing. No, they're way too sensible for that. They know it works, but the question is how?'

'What do you mean?'

'The placebo effect,' she says, pointing her index finger at me. 'They don't want to believe in all this weird stuff they can't understand, but they can't deny the evidence, especially when they find some of it actually works on them. That's when they bring in the old *placebo* excuse.'

'The placebo effect isn't an excuse,' I tell her. 'It's a well-documented scientific reaction.'

'So you're taught to believe by those that can't explain how the human body can supposedly heal itself,' Amber says knowingly. 'There's all sorts of energies going on in and around us that are brought into play by our own bodies when necessary for healing and pain relief, and that effect can be intensified by specialist practitioners when our bodies need some assistance.'

I don't want to get into an argument with Amber about the placebo effect. Especially as I think I might be able to see where she's going with this.

It was actually quite worrying to me how easily I was able to understand Amber and her wacky thought processes.

'Correct me if I'm wrong, Amber, but are you saying that the Daisy Chain is a placebo?'

Amber grins with delight that I've got it.

'I am! Kind of . . . '

'Kind of?' Here we go.

'Placebo, in that when people that come to the shop needing help – they believe the Daisy Chain is there to provide that help. Placebo, in that when the people leave they take something away with them that makes them feel like they're going to get better – specific flowers.'

I nod. I've got it so far.

'Placebo, in that it seems by the look of these notebooks –' she holds the bundle up '– and I'm pretty sure wherever they came from there will be more like them – these people do get better as a result of visiting the shop and their lives improve and change for the good.'

'I guess . . .'

'They do, Poppy,' she insists. 'Look at the evidence.' Amber taps the covers of the notebooks. 'But not a placebo, if you're suggesting that the change is only in their minds, and that the shop and what happens to them there is of no consequence.'

'So what *are* you suggesting then?' I ask, knowing what she's going to say before I even open my mouth.

Amber's bright green eyes light up.

'I'm suggesting that with the knowledge these books contain, my legendary skills with flowers, and one magical little flower shop by the sea, we have got ourselves a wonderful opportunity, not only to help anyone that needs us, but also to put your grandmother's shop back where it belongs: in the hearts of the visitors and people of St Felix.'

# Fourteen

## Passionflower – Faith

The big day has arrived at last – the grand opening of Daisy Chain.

It's taken us just under a month to get the shop ready to open. After everyone had turned out to help us decorate – which I thought would have been the hardest part of getting the shop ready to trade again – it turned out to be an uphill struggle, on a gradient steeper than any of the hills you could climb around St Felix, to persuade suppliers to provide us with the flower knick-knacks and trinkets we wanted to sell as part of the Daisy Chain experience.

In the end I'd gone to see Belle in her studio at the end of Harbour Street to see if she could suggest anyone.

'Keep it local,' Belle advises me as she sits at her desk painting a piece of pottery in the colours of the sea. 'The few tourists we get here want to buy things made by local people. They don't want something that's been made in some awful sweatshop in India.'

I'm about to protest, indignant at the suggestion I'd sell goods that had been made in that way, when I realise she's only trying to help. Belle's colourful studio-cum-shop is filled with her own creations; she of all people knows what sells.

So I bite my lip. 'Yes, of course, that's what I was hoping to do. But it's so difficult to find people that want to supply you. Most of them want money up front, and we've used most of our budget on doing the shop up.'

'When do you open?' Belle asks, putting down her paint-brush and wiping her hands on a cloth.

'Saturday first of May.'

'That's just over a week away!' she exclaims.

I pull a face. 'Yes, I know, but I have been trying. Amber is doing all the real flower stuff, she's been really good liaising with Jake about supplying us the way he used to my grand-mother.' I notice her eyelashes flicker when I mention Jake's name.

'Jake's involved in your shop?' she asks innocently.

'He's supplying us with flowers – yes.'

Belle nods. 'I see ...' She stands up and wanders over to the shop window. She's so willowy and graceful as she stands there silhouetted against the sunlight streaming in through the glass. In her tight white vest, long blue skirt and bejewelled sandals, she makes me feel very dark and heavy standing in a corner of her shop in my usual attire of black on black. I have mixed it up a little today, I'm wearing dungarees – black, obviously –

with bottle-green DM boots and a black-and-grey-striped long-sleeved top.

'I think I might be able to help you,' she offers, like a queen offering her subject a pardon.

'Really?'

'Yes. How about I ask my students at evening class if they can produce some flower-related items for you to sell in the shop? Before you say no,' she adds, seeing me about to say just that, 'I'm only talking about my top class. They're very good, and it would be such an honour for them to have work for sale in a real shop.'

'It's very kind of you to offer, Belle,' I begin. I'm not sure a local evening class is quite what we're looking for. 'But—'

'And I'll do you some pieces myself,' she continues, looking around her. 'I usually work with the sea as inspiration, but flowers . . . hmm. Yes, I could go with that. It would be a challenge, especially with the timescale involved. That's sorted then. Problem solved!'

I have no choice but to smile politely, thank her, and promise to pop along in a few days to see how she's getting along.

I walk back to the flower shop and Amber feeling as if I've just been ambushed. I'd thought these artistic, spiritual types were supposed to be relaxed, easygoing people, but both Belle and Amber have turned out to have more drive, tenacity and determination than I have black leggings.

As Amber and I put a few last-minute finishing touches to the shop ahead of our grand opening at 10 a.m., I'm surprised at how nervous I feel.

I'm not sure if it's the thought of the shop opening to real people that's freaking me out, or the fact that the whitewashed cabinets lining the sea-blue walls are now filled to the brim with brightly coloured fresh flowers and the assortment of flower-inspired knick-knacks – some of which are stunning, but some of which are somewhat ... *unconventional*, to put it politely – provided by Belle and her students.

'What's wrong?' Amber asks as she expertly winds floristry wire around some delicate pinks and gypsophila, turning them into the little posies we're to give away to our first customers. 'You're very jumpy this morning. Are you nervous about the shop? Let me give you my amethyst pendant to wear, that will help calm you.' She puts the flowers down and begins to reach around her neck.

'No, really!' I protest, waving my hand at her. 'I'm fine, honestly.' I manage a nervous smile. 'But thanks for the offer, Amber.'

While Amber rests the amethyst back on her chest, my eyes dart anxiously towards the flowers for about the hundredth time. Did we have to get so many types of roses in for today? There were pink ones, yellow, deep blood-red ...

I swallow hard.

Amber notices.

'What is it with you and flowers?' she asks as she pops yet another posy into a small trough of water to join the others. 'You've been on edge since Jake brought them in this morning.'

'Nothing. There's just a lot of them, that's all. I didn't realise there'd be quite so many.'

Amber laughs. 'This is a florist's, Poppy, what did you expect?'

I shake my head. 'It's fine. I'll be fine. Don't worry about it.'

'No,' Amber says, leaving the desk to come over to me. 'I'm sorry, I shouldn't have laughed. What's wrong, tell me.'

'Morning, ladies!' Harriet cheerily bangs on the shop window. 'How are we feeling? All ready for the off?'

Amber goes to the door and unlocks it, and Harriet, wearing a floral dress and green wellingtons, is suddenly upon us. 'Well, it's all looking marvellous,' she says, surveying the premises. 'You've done a splendid job. I'm sure today will go swimmingly for you. I can't stop – far too much to do, as always. We've a huge cub and scout jamboree at the church hall later today. Will you be able to pop along for a few minutes in between customers to support us? We've lots of stalls along with all the fun!'

'We'll have to see how it goes, Harriet,' I reply cautiously. 'If we're busy, there'll need to be more than one of us serving in the shop.'

'Of course, of course. I understand!' She salutes. 'Right, that's me off. Toodle pip and good luck!'

As Harriet leaves, Woody arrives. They exchange pleasantries outside, and then Woody appears in the doorway.

'Good morning, ladies,' he says, removing his hat and tucking it under his arm. 'How are we today?'

'Good thanks, Woody,' I reply, as Amber returns to her flowers. 'How are you, busy as always?'

Woody is rarely busy. St Felix isn't exactly a hotbed of crime. The most he's had to handle since I arrived was a mix-up over two neighbours' recycling bins.

'I'm very well, thank you, Poppy,' he says, puffing his chest out. 'A policeman's work is never done. You never know when there might be a need for authority.'

Amber and I glance at each other, but decide to humour him.

'Of course,' Amber says, wandering over to Woody with a tiny white flower in her hand. 'I'm sure your presence would make any criminal think twice.' She smiles at him and deftly tucks the flower into his lapel. Woody flushes red, all the way from his neck up to his curly hair.

'Yes . . . well,' he stutters. 'Luckily I'm not often needed to exert my authority, but—'

'If you were, we'd feel safe knowing you're there to protect us,' I finish for him. 'Wouldn't we, Amber?'

'Oh yes.' She nods. 'If I *was* to be arrested here in St Felix, I'd definitely want it to be by you, Woody.'

I grin at Amber – assuming she's winding Woody up. But instead she virtually flutters her eyelashes as she looks coyly up at him.

'Right, well – let's hope I won't be required to do that,' says Woody, trying for brusque, but it comes out as a squeak. He clears his throat and continues, his voice softer now: 'However, if I was to arrest you, Amber –' he takes the flower from his lapel and offers it back to her – 'I'd be very gentle about it.'

'I have no doubt you would be, Woody,' Amber says in the same tone, taking the flower gently from his hand.

'Ahem!' I say, grinning at the two of them. This, I hadn't seen coming.

'Yes, well, I must be off,' Woody says, straightening up. 'Ladies.' He nods at us and puts his hat back on. 'I'll be back later, for your grand opening – crowd control, you know.'

I very much doubt we'd be in need of that. We'll be

lucky to get any sort of a crowd, let alone an unruly one, but I play along with him. 'Yes, of course, Woody,' I say. 'See you later.'

Woody leaves and I look at Amber as she bolts the door behind him.

'What?' she asks, trying to look innocent.

'Are you serious, Amber?'

'About . . . ?'

'About Woody.'

'He's nice – I like him,' she says coyly, pretending to rearrange some irises in a long vase as she passes.

'I *like* him,' I say, 'but not like that.'

'Well, we all have different tastes in men, and Woody isn't like anyone I've ever met before. He's kind and gentle – I'm not used to that.'

I watch Amber return to the desk and furiously begin rewinding pink ribbon on to one of the many multicoloured rolls we have stashed under the desk. I wait for her to continue, but she doesn't.

I'm about to come right out and ask what she means when Ant and Dec appear outside with the tray of cupcakes I've ordered to give away to our customers this morning along with the posies.

So we open the door for a third time.

'Well, doesn't she scrub up well!' Ant says, looking around him as Dec carries the cakes through to the back with Amber. 'You two have done a fabulous job. It's so bright and breezy! Not at all like the old place. Oh, no offence,' he says, slapping a hand over his mouth.

'None taken,' I say, smiling. 'It was a bit dull in here before, you're right. But my grandmother was getting on a bit; I guess the décor of the shop wasn't her main priority.'

'And neither should it have been,' Dec says, emerging from the back of the shop. 'She was a wonderful woman, Poppy, and she had a magical touch with flowers; everyone who came in here knew that. They weren't bothered about what colour the walls were.'

'Did you two ever buy flowers from here?' I ask.

They look at each other. 'Of course, all the time,' Dec says.

'Any particular occasions you'd like to share with us?'

They both look shiftily about the shop.

'Wow, look at that!' Ant says, exclaiming with delight over an abstract ceramic coaster in the shape of a tulip head. 'That's ... *interesting.*'

'It's by one of the students from Belle's art class,' Amber explains. 'Some of their work is really diverse and unusual.'

'Mmm, that's one way to describe it,' Dec says, peeping over Ant's shoulder. '*Unusual.*'

'So, about this time you bought flowers,' I prompt. 'What happened?'

'I don't know what you mean, Poppy,' Ant says. 'Like I said, we bought flowers here all the time.'

'You know my grandmother kept records of all her *special* transactions,' I tell them. 'Amber and I have found notebooks dating back years and years ... '

Since the first box had turned up, we'd discovered more boxes in my grandmother's cottage with records going back over a hundred years. The magical goings-on at the Daisy Chain had started long before my grandmother took over the shop. It seemed to have been providing help to anyone who needed it for well over a century.

Dec looks at Ant. 'Go on,' Ant says. 'We have nothing to hide. You may as well tell her.'

'I think you'd better put the kettle on, Poppy,' Dec says, 'this is a long story.'

We're all perched on wooden stools in the back room of the shop clutching large white mugs, each with a different flower on – one of Amber's ideas for the shop. I have a Poppy of course, Amber has a sunflower, Ant has a daisy, and Dec a pansy.

'Right then,' Dec begins, 'I'll try and keep this as brief as I can.' He glances at Ant, who nods his encouragement. 'When I first inherited my uncle's bakery here in St Felix, I was a bit of a lost soul. I'd been blissfully living the gay scene down in Brighton to its absolute extreme. And when I say living it to the extreme, I don't think I need to explain what that means, do I?'

We all shake our heads.

'I had money, far too much money, from a lottery win – and boy did I know how to spend it. I'm not proud of how I behaved back then. But I was young and living the high life for the first time, and enjoying every debauched, decadent minute of it.'

He takes a moment, to gather himself, and Ant lays a reassuring hand on his shoulder.

'I thought I had friends,' Dec continues, 'but of course they weren't real friends, they were only interested in my money and what it could buy them. In the end all it bought *me* was danger. I had a couple of very nasty experiences that . . . well, let's just say they knocked the wind out of my sails.'

Again he looks to Ant, who comfortingly squeezes his shoulder.

I glance at Amber, but she just takes a long drink of her coffee.

'So I gambled all my money away, and as a consequence lost all my so-called friends. I was literally on the brink of suicide – and that's no exaggeration,' he assures us, 'when my uncle died.' He smiles. 'You would think *that* on top of everything else would have pushed me over the edge, but it didn't. When I found out he'd left me – his favourite nephew, apparently – his business, it gave me new hope. Something to look forward to.'

He looks at us all sipping our drinks, listening intently to him.

'I know I'm sounding like some godawful candidate for Jeremy Kyle here with my tales of woe and redemption. But this is a true story, I promise you.'

'Nothing truer than real life,' Amber says sympathetically. 'You'd be a lot more shocked if I told you some of my stories.' We all look at her with interest, but she just winks at Dec. 'Go on, what happened when you got here to St Felix?'

'When I arrived at the bakery and found all my uncle's secret recipes, some of which had been handed down through the generations, something changed, I began baking and people began buying and telling me they liked what I baked. It was odd, but I just felt special. Like I belonged.'

'Tell them about the flowers, Declan,' Ant encourages.

'Ah yes. So I'd had the bakery open a while, and I was doing

OK. I was enjoying living here by the sea. Brighton had been by the sea, of course, but it wasn't like this. St Felix is . . . ' He thinks about this. 'St Felix is different. I hate to use the same word again, but it's special. You don't know it is until you've lived here a while, but it really is. People say the sea air is healing; well, St Felix's sea air is super healing, whatever is wrong with you. Anyway,' he says, when only Ant acknowledges this, 'even though I was happy, I still felt a bit lonely. I wasn't really into flowers, but occasionally when the bakery was quiet I'd wander down and talk to your grandmother. She'd always have a kind word to say, or some friendly advice to give. But she never made you feel like she was preaching.'

I nod. I remembered that about her.

'One day I came down to the shop for a chat – it was a Monday afternoon in late April, never the busiest of times for either of us. Your grandmother sensed something was wrong, even though I didn't really let on what it was, and before I left she presented me with some flowers to take back to my shop.'

'Ooh, which ones?' Amber asks excitedly.

'A single peony, a long stem of verbascum, and a spray of freesia, all bound together with a white ribbon. That became her trademark – the ribbon, didn't it, Ant?'

Ant nods. 'If ever you saw someone leaving Rose's shop with flowers bound together with a white ribbon, you just knew.'

'Knew what?' I ask impatiently.

'Knew something special was about to happen to them, like it did to me. To us,' Dec says, taking hold of Ant's hand.

'Come on, guys!' pleads Amber. 'I wanna know what happens next.'

Dec smiles. 'Patience, my American friend, all is about to be revealed. So, I took the spray of flowers back to my shop and put them in a vase of water. I didn't give them another thought until about three days later when Ant appeared at my door asking if we sold – of all the things you could have asked for,' he says, waggling his finger at Ant, 'cream horns. It was one of the few recipes of my uncle's I hadn't tried out yet.'

'I was holidaying in Cornwall with my then boyfriend,' Ant explains. 'We hadn't meant to stop in St Felix, but our hire car had broken down because I hadn't remembered to put petrol in it that morning, and boy was he *mad* at me! He loved cream horns – the cake, you understand!' Ant reassures us with a wink. 'And I thought if I got him one it might pacify him until the garage filled us up and got us on our way.'

'And did it?' I ask, not really understanding where this story is going.

'*No*, that's the point, isn't it? Dec didn't have any.'

'So . . .?'

'I found myself explaining to Dec why I was so stressed over a cream horn, why I needed one so badly. And do you know what he said?'

I shake my head. This story, far from telling me anything about my grandmother and her old shop, is fast veering into the realms of something you see advertised on the front of *Take-a-Break* magazine.

'I know! I know!' Amber shouts, her hands in the air like she's answering a question in class. 'I bet Dec said, "If it's that important to you, I'll bake some cream horns for you right now!"'

Ant looks at Dec reprovingly. 'Amber's right. That's exactly what you *should* have said, Declan!'

Dec tuts. 'I couldn't, could I? I was on my own in the shop back then, I couldn't go out back and start baking a load of *puff* pastry for an angry *poof*!'

The two of them smile good-naturedly at each other.

'So what *did* Dec say?' I ask. 'You still haven't said.'

'Go on, you tell them,' Ant says, flashing his blue eyes at Dec.

Dec blushes. 'I said he shouldn't worry about filling the guy's car up. If he was going to get mad over something as silly as that, then he wasn't worth it.'

Amber nods approvingly.

'Go on . . . ' Ant says, nudging him. 'Tell them the rest.'

I get the feeling that it's not just in looks that Ant is larger than Dec. His personality is much bigger and more boisterous than Dec's too. Dec, I think, likes to keep something in reserve.

'And I also said,' Dec swallows hard, 'that if he ever felt like popping back to sample my cream horn, then he'd be most welcome.'

'Nooo!' Amber and I cry at once. 'You didn't?'

Dec is bright red now.

'He did indeed,' Ant says proudly. 'And I'm pleased to inform you that I most definitely did come back, and I sampled many of Dec's splendid cream horns. And –' he pats his tummy – 'a few too many other fine cakes in the process.'

'That's wonderful. I'm pleased for the two of you,' I say, genuinely meaning it; they seem like a lovely couple. 'But you haven't told us the significance of the flowers in all this.'

'Ah yes, the flowers,' Dec says, smiling. 'I wondered myself afterwards what they meant, so I looked them up. Peony means anger. Verbascum – take courage. And freesia – lasting friendship.'

'I still don't see—'

'It was a message from your grandmother. Ant turned up on my doorstep because Dominic, his partner, was angry with him – the peony. I had to take courage – the verbascum – in inviting Ant back to taste my wares. And as a result?' He takes hold of Ant's hand. 'We now have a lasting friendship – the beautiful delicate freesia – that's been getting stronger every year for the last ten years.'

# Fifteen

## Columbine – Desertion

After Ant and Dec's revelation about the flowers, and the story of how they met, we all suddenly realise what the time is.

Ant and Dec rush back to the bakery to see if Neil their Saturday boy has coped in their absence, while Amber and I get ready to open the doors to our first customer.

'What are you doing?' I ask as Amber begins tying some white floristry ribbon across the shop doorway.

'It's for you to do the official opening,' she says, tying one end with a fancy bow.

'What official opening? I thought we were just opening the door at ten?'

'Poppy, you can't let a significant occasion such as this go by without at least a bit of fuss.'

'Can't we?'

'No.' She finishes tying the other end. 'I was going to use a red ribbon, but after what Ant and Dec said I thought white would be more appropriate.'

'You don't believe all this flower nonsense, do you?' I ask. 'That thing about Ant turning up after Dec got the flowers – that was just a coincidence.'

'Albert Einstein once said: "Coincidence is God's way of remaining anonymous."'

'Einstein said that? I thought he was all into science and stuff, not airy-fairy quotes.'

Amber pauses before she unbolts the door. 'Einstein was a very clever man, Poppy. Do you know why?'

I shake my head.

'He didn't let his incredibly smart brain cloud his thinking on any subject. Instead, he allowed his super-intelligent mind to be opened up to a whole world of new possibilities,' she says, sliding the bolt back. 'Gosh, I hope you're good at speeches!'

'What do you mean?' I ask as Amber flings open the door and I see a small crowd has formed on the cobbles outside the shop. 'Oh fu or goodness sake,' I recover just in time, and put on my best welcoming voice. 'I didn't expect to see so many of you. Hello, welcome, how good of you all to come.'

The crowd look up expectantly as I dither in the doorway.

'The ribbon, Poppy!' I hear Jake shout from amongst them. 'You need to cut the ribbon before we can come in.'

A pair of silver scissors miraculously appears over my left shoulder, courtesy of Amber.

'Speech!' Amber calls from behind me, trying to disguise her accent.

Cheers, Amber, I'll get you for that later . . .

'Right . . . well . . . ' I grin manically at the people in front of me. 'Like I just said, thank you all for coming, I'm sure my grandmother would be very touched to see you all here.' I hear someone mumble, 'Probably turning in her grave, more like.'

I run my eyes over the sea of eager faces in front of me, but I can't spot anyone who would have said that, so I carry on:

'The shop wouldn't be opening today without the help of many of you standing here right now. Jake Asher –' I gesture towards him and Miley – 'the ladies of the St Felix Women's Guild –' I wave quickly at Harriet, Willow and Beryl along with a few others. Then I notice that Caroline has joined them today, although she had been notably absent when we'd been setting up the shop. Then there's Bronte and Charlie, Woody, Lou, Mickey, Belle, Rita and Richie from the Merry Mermaid, Ant and Dec and a few other shop owners from Harbour Street – even Father Claybourne the village priest is here. 'Wow!' I exclaim, taken aback at seeing them all standing here. 'Actually, so many of you have been absolute stars at helping us out, Amber and I really couldn't have done it without you all, honestly we couldn't. So from the bottom of our hearts, thank you.'

I stare out into the crowd, and they look awkwardly back at me, and then at each other, wondering if I've finished or not, and whether they should applaud.

'Ribbon, Poppy!' Jake prompts helpfully. 'Cut the ribbon!'

I jump. 'Yes! The ribbon, of course!' I place the blades of the scissors either side of the white ribbon. 'So, without further ado, I would like to declare the all-new Daisy Chain flower shop well and truly open!'

I cut through the ribbon, and as the two pieces fall to either side there's a polite round of applause. Then I stand back and accept their congratulations as one by one the people of St Felix – for that's who all these early visitors are – enter the shop, exclaiming with joy how pretty it is, how much it's changed, and how proud Rose would be to see it up and running once more.

'Well done, Poppy!' Lou says as she munches on a cupcake decorated with a daisy. 'Rose would be delighted to see this, and very proud of you for making it happen.'

'It wasn't just me,' I insist, waving my hand in front of my face to get some air. Is it really that hot in here? No one else seems to think so. 'I couldn't have done it without everyone's help – especially Amber and Jake.' I look towards the shop door, wondering if we should prop it open, but I find it's already open as people continue to pour in.

'Did I hear my name?' Jake calls, weaving his way through the crowd towards us. 'I was just looking for Miley, but she's happy over there handing out posies for Amber.'

I look over to the desk and see Miley passing Amber's mini posies out to everyone, whether they want one or not. I turn and smile at Jake. 'I was saying how I couldn't have opened the shop up like this without your and Amber's help.'

Jake smiles at me, and then for some bizarre reason I feel the need to reach up and kiss him on the cheek. 'Thank you,' I whisper.

He stares at me for a moment. 'Not a problem,' he says quietly, still looking at me. Then he clears his throat. 'So, that was quite a speech you gave out there – you seem to have lost your fear of speaking to people.'

'What do you mean? I'm not afraid of speaking to people. I just—'

'Yeah, yeah, you just prefer being on your own. I remember.'

He winks and I want to glare at him, but I can't. Instead I find myself smiling wryly as I gaze up into his kind, thoughtful eyes.

We get jostled and separated as the shop continues to fill with people, and I wonder as I watch Jake take up polite conversation with Harriet if the townsfolk's interest has been piqued by the thought of a new florist on Harbour Street, or more likely by the smell of a free cupcake.

I'm aware as I stand here, continuing to greet people like a bride on her wedding day, with a polite word of thanks and a smile, that I'm getting hotter by the minute. I'm aware that it's happening again, and if I don't do something to rectify the situation very soon I'm going to be in big trouble.

I look around the shop as yet another person squeezes inside; Amber seems to be in her element, showing off our new shop. She looks gorgeous in her outfit, a long, flowing green velvet dress, with graceful bell-shaped sleeves edged with gold. With her long auburn tresses cascading down over her shoulders, she's almost fairy-like as she flits around the shop amongst all the flowers.

The flowers.

There are just too many of them in here today. When Jake began unloading them early this morning, I'd almost fainted there and then at the sight and intense sweet smell that greeted me when he opened the back doors of his van.

Over the years, I'd learned to deal with seeing a few flowers provided it was just a few at a time. I could handle seeing the odd bunch outside a petrol station, in a vase in someone's home – that kind of minor floral exposure didn't faze me at all, as long as there weren't too many roses. And while they weren't my favourite places, I'd coped with visiting the odd florist's shop when I had to – with my family, I didn't have a lot of choice.

It hadn't been easy, but I'd managed to deal with my issues with flowers in my own way, and as a result I'd thought, perhaps naïvely, I was going to be able to deal with this.

That was one of the reasons I'd wanted the shop to sell floral merchandise as well as real flowers; I thought the less fresh flowers we had in here at one time, the easier it might be for me. When Jake had unloaded his van this morning we'd been standing outside, so I was able to take a deep breath of the sea breeze wafting up Harbour Street. Perhaps a few gulps of salty air would quash the nausea that was beginning to overwhelm me now.

Slowly I edge towards the door. As I do, the room begins to spin, and all the chattering voices seem to blend into one. The scent of the flowers is overpowering with this many people squeezed in here, and I can pick out the scent of the roses so easily they might as well be the only flower in here . . .

Panic sets in as I realise I'm stuck in an enclosed space full of flowers and people, my two worst nightmares . . . My throat feels tight, my head's spinning, and I can't breathe. So I throw myself through the door, out on to the cobbles outside.

As I begin to gulp in long, deep, healing breaths of sea air, I still feel a little dizzy, as if I might faint, so I hold on to the doorframe for support.

'Don't you like crowds?'

The voice makes me jump. It's Charlie, Jake's son. He's leaning against the shop window, watching everything that's going on inside with a disinterested look on his face.

'No, not any more,' I reply, turning to face him. 'Do you?'

He shrugs. 'Nah, never have. Bronte's always trying to get me to take her to these concerts, up in Bristol – mosh-pit jobs. Dad won't let her go on her own. But I can't see the fascination myself. Who wants to be squashed into a tiny space with a load of drunks for hours on end with nowhere to pee and everyone smelling of BO? Not my idea of fun.'

'You sound like my brother,' I tell him, as another familiar, unpleasant feeling begins to build inside me. 'He never liked those sort of gigs either.'

'Sensible fella,' Charlie says, putting his hands into his pockets and turning so his back is against the window.

'Yes,' I say, thinking about Will. 'He was.'

Charlie briefly turns his head to look at me, but doesn't ask any further questions. And I like him all the more for that.

'You gonna go back in?' he asks, with a nod in the direction of the shop.

I shake my head. 'Not right now.'

'Probably best, looking at the state of you,' Charlie says. 'You're mighty white. You wanna go for a walk – get some air?'

'I would love to.' I smile gratefully. 'But it's my shop, I can't just leave everyone.'

'Ah . . . ' Charlie says knowingly. 'And there was me thinking you were a bit of a rebel with your black clothes and your Docs 'n' all.'

I stare at him. 'Say that again.'

He looks puzzled. 'Which part? About your Docs?'

I shake my head.

'Oh ... about you being a rebel?' He grins. 'So you are one then?'

I glance into the shop, and amongst all the people I can just make out my grandmother's wooden desk, and for a brief moment I'm transported back in time ...

'Charlie Asher, you're about to find out.'

# Sixteen

## Periwinkle – Tender Recollections

Charlie and I run off together like a couple of school kids – well, technically Charlie *is* a school kid, but I don't want to think about that now – along the harbour, back out through the town and up Pengarthen Hill towards the cliffs that tower above St Felix Bay.

I know I shouldn't have run off like that, not on our opening day, but if I'd stayed inside the shop in amongst the flowers and the crowds I would have passed out. It's happened before, and I don't want people making a fuss. It's bad enough I have these issues, without everyone knowing about it. I've been dealing with it pretty much on my own for fifteen years, and aside from the odd therapist I'd spent time with, I had no intention of sharing my reasons why I felt like this with anyone.

The wind high up on the cliffs is strong and gusty, and it blows my hair around my face so much I have to keep pushing it away so I can see where we're going. But I don't care; up here all those feelings of nausea and dizziness have gone. In fact they disappeared practically the moment we ran from the shop.

'Where are we going?' I ask Charlie, as eventually we stop climbing the footpath that leads up and away from St Felix, and he begins to cut across the grass towards the sea.

'You'll see,' he says. 'Be careful though, the ground is a bit unstable underfoot.'

I stop for a moment to look around. We've reached a sort of junction in the footpath; one way leads up to Trecarlan Castle, and the other further along the cliffs.

I hesitate, debating which route to take – the castle holds such special memories for me, I must take time to go up and visit while I'm here. It's not far away from this spot at all.

But Charlie has stepped off the path and is rapidly descending the grassy slope of the cliff, so I begin to follow him, watching my footing as I go. But when I next look up, Charlie has disappeared.

'Charlie?' I call out. Where has he gone?

I'm beginning to have visions of him lying in a crumpled heap at the bottom of the cliffs when I hear his voice.

'Down here, Poppy!'

I can just see the top of his blond head poking up from below me.

'How did you get down there?' I ask, sitting down on a grassy mound on the side of the cliff so I can edge forward enough to see where he is.

'Look to the left of you,' he calls. 'There's some rough steps carved into the side of the cliff. If you take those – carefully, mind – it'll bring you down here.'

I look where he suggests and find there are indeed some worn stone steps half-hidden by the long grass and wild flowers that have grown up around them.

I clutch the tufts of grass on the side of the cliff as I descend gingerly down the narrow steps, making sure I have a secure foothold before I attempt the next. We are perilously close to the cliff edge here and the jagged rocks that poke up menacingly from the waves that crash below me. So it's not until I get to the very bottom step, and on to firm ground again, that I dare to look up properly.

'Wow,' I exclaim as I find myself standing next to Charlie in a tiny hollow of smooth stone that cuts into the side of the cliff. 'This is amazing!'

But it's not only our little viewing platform that's astounding me – remarkable though it is, hidden away down here – but our view.

From our hidey-hole tucked into the side of the cliff, we can see nothing but deep blue sea and pale blue sky extending for miles and miles into the distance.

'What an incredible view,' I tell him as I stare out at the never-ending seascape. 'How on earth did you find this? By accident?'

'Yeah.' Charlie sits down cross-legged on some dry bracken that's obviously been left here on purpose for people to sit comfortably for long periods and gaze out at the view, so I sit down next to him. 'When my mum died I needed somewhere to come to get away from everything, and one day I found this place while I was out wandering, not knowing what to do with myself.'

'That was lucky,' I say, and immediately feel stupid. Why could I never say the right thing in these situations? 'I mean, we all need somewhere to go when we lose someone close to us.'

Charlie looks across at me.

'Have *you* then?'

'What?'

'Lost someone close to you?'

I hesitate for a moment. 'Yes, my grandmother,' I say swiftly. 'That's why I'm here in St Felix, isn't it?'

'Ah yes, of course.' Charlie nods. 'Your grandma. I forgot. Sorry.'

We sit and watch the gulls for a few minutes as they circle over the sea, waiting for the chance to dive down and snatch a fish from the waters below.

'So why don't you like crowds then?' Charlie asks. 'You were obviously having problems in the shop earlier.'

'I had an incident involving a big crowd when I was younger. I've had a bit of a phobia ever since.'

'Oh.' Charlie pauses to think. 'Is that why it was so easy for me to persuade you to leave?'

'Maybe. That and some other stuff.'

'Do you want to talk about it?' Charlie asks, sounding as awkward as I'd felt earlier when he mentioned his mum. 'That's what people always ask, isn't it? I'm not sure they always want to listen, though, when they say that.'

I smile at him. 'No, not really. I've done too much talking over the years, to be honest. Not sure it ever helped that much.'

'Me too,' Charlie says. 'After Mum, we all had counselling – lots of counselling.' He pulls a face. 'I think it helped Bronte, but she was younger. Not too sure about Dad, he kept everything hidden. But then he's like that about most things. I reckon Miley helped him more than any counsellor ever did.'

'Really?' I think about Jake and Miley, and how they seem to dote on each other.

'Yeah, thank God for Aunt Kate and Uncle Bob in the US, that's all I can say. Dad was in a real bad way before they asked him to take Miley. Once she became a part of our family, life seemed to start getting better – not just for him, but for all of us. It was a real turning point in our recovery as a family. We have a lot to thank that monkey for.'

'She's a lovely little thing.'

'Miley?' Charlie pulls a face. 'You want to try living with her! Stroppier than Bronte ever knows how to be is that one.'

I grin. 'Your sister isn't so bad. You should have known me when I was young.'

'Bit of a rebel, were you?' Charlie asks, winking at me. 'You seemed to like it when I called you that before.'

'Definitely. I was much worse than your sister.'

'I can't believe that!' Charlie looks sceptical.

I hesitate. 'Well, apart from messing up all my GCSEs, and getting into a *lot* of trouble at school, I got in trouble with the law too.'

Charlie looks surprised. 'How bad?'

'Bad enough to get me arrested a few times. Let's just say a night in a police cell soon cures you of a rebellious streak.'

'I bet. Was the rebellion anything to do with your brother? You mentioned before he was quite sensible.'

'Gosh, look at those dark clouds over there,' I say, suddenly pointing to some clouds that are probably a good hour away from us yet. 'Perhaps we should be getting back.' I glance at Charlie, and hope he doesn't realise what I'm doing. We've been getting on well until this moment, but I can't talk about Will with anyone.

'Sure,' Charlie says, standing up. 'I understand. But you know where this place is now, so if you ever find things are getting a bit too much, it's always here for you like it's been here for me.'

I'm about to thank him when he continues.

'You know, I lied before,' he says, looking me right in the eye. 'About finding this place. I made it sound as though I stumbled across it by accident.'

'And didn't you?'

'I did stumble across it,' he says, turning and looking out to sea. 'But it was because I was thinking about jumping.'

'What do you mean?'

'Jumping,' Charlie says, 'into the sea. It was just after Mum died, and things were at their absolute worst at home. So when I say I stumbled across it, my stumble luckily took me down these very steps, and landed me where we are now. If it hadn't . . . well, I probably wouldn't be talking to you today. This place saved me, in more ways than one.'

I can't believe he's told me this. I've been in some dark places over the years, but I've never attempted to take my own life. But as usual, faced with someone else's emotions, I have no idea how to respond.

'Thank you, Charlie . . . ' I hesitate. I feel like I should hug him, but I don't want to make either of us uncomfortable. 'I know how hard it is to share that kind of stuff. Really I do.'

'I know you do,' Charlie says. 'I could tell the minute I met you. I may not be the rebel you or my sister are, but let's just say it takes one to know one, eh?'

I nod, and before I can change my mind I reach my arms out to hug him.

And I'm relieved to find Charlie hugging me back.

Charlie and I walk back to town together, and I'm thankful to find us talking about normal stuff once more, our emotional revelations left behind us up on the cliffs. As we get closer to St Felix the signal on my phone picks up and texts start pouring in.

Beep beep.

Amber: *Where are you? Manic in here. Hurry back x*

Beep beep.

Amber: *Poppy, what's going on? Getting worried. A x*

Beep beep.

Jake: *Are you all right? Amber says you've disappeared. Let us know you're OK. Jake*

'Have you been missed?' Charlie asks as his own phone beeps too. He pulls it from his pocket and looks at the screen. 'It's my dad,' he says. 'I'd better give him a quick ring.'

I'm about to text Amber when Charlie speaks to Jake.

'Hey, Dad ... yeah, I'm fine ... Yes, I have – she's with me ... OK, sure. Yeah, will do. See you in a bit.'

Charlie ends the call.

'Dad's at your shop. Apparently Amber is getting a bit worried about you.'

I pull a face. 'Oh dear, best head over there, I guess, and face the music.'

*

The Daisy Chain we return to is a lot quieter than the one we'd left a couple of hours ago. As I cautiously head through the open door I find Amber standing behind the big wooden desk I'd seen my grandmother behind so many times, arranging the few remaining cupcakes on one plate, and Jake sweeping up a mixture of crumbs, leaves and petals from the floor with a long-handled broom.

'So, the wanderer returns,' Jake says, looking up. 'Both of you, it would seem,' he adds, glancing questioningly at Charlie.

'Where have you been?' Amber demands. 'It was manic in here, people everywhere. They were asking for you, wanting to talk to Rose's granddaughter, I turned around to find you, and you were nowhere to be seen.'

'I'm really sorry,' I say, feeling even more guilty about leaving Amber to cope on her own. 'I just had to get away for a bit.'

'On your opening day!'

'I know . . . I know, I panicked.'

'Poppy has a problem with crowds,' Charlie explains helpfully. 'Don't you, Poppy? She needed some air, so we went for a walk to clear her head.'

I nod. 'I'm sorry, it's no excuse. I know I should have been here to help you.'

'Crowds?' Amber exclaims in relief. 'That's it? Thank the Lord. As you can see, the crowd situation didn't last too long once everyone had been in to have their five-minute gawp, and I can't imagine it will ever get like that again. After the way you were behaving earlier, I thought for one teeny-weeny moment you might have a problem with flowers. But then I thought, who would be silly enough to open a florist shop if they had a flower phobia?'

'Haha,' I laugh, a little too forcefully. 'Flower phobia, how silly would that be?'

'Not as silly as you might think,' Amber says knowingly. 'We did this wedding in New York for a woman who hated fresh flowers – something happened to her in her childhood, I think. Anyway, we had to do the whole thing in silk flowers! It was quite the challenge, but your mom coped brilliantly. The venue looked amazing!'

'Really . . . ?' I reply uncomfortably. 'That's great. Well, no worries about that here.' I gesture around the shop. 'Everything in Daisy Chain is good and fresh!' My glance rests on Jake as I turn around, and I notice how his brow crinkles between his eyebrows as he stares thoughtfully at me. So I quickly look away.

'Right then,' Jake says. 'As long as you're back safe and sound, I guess I can go now. Miley,' he calls to the monkey, currently decorating herself in a roll of floristry ribbon. 'Time to go.'

'Thanks, Jake,' Amber says, 'for staying back and helping. It was good of you.'

'No worries,' Jake says, smiling as Miley bounds up on to his shoulder, still with the ribbon. 'Any time.' He looks at Miley and rolls his eyes. 'We're bringing that home, are we?' he asks her, as she twirls the ribbon above her head like a rhythmic gymnast.

'Keep it,' Amber says. 'I'm not keen on orange anyway.'

'Right, you,' he attempts to ruffle the top of Charlie's head, which is almost level with his, but Charlie ducks out of the way. 'Let's go. See you guys later.'

Jake, Miley and Charlie head off, and I turn to face Amber.

'Right,' Amber says. 'It's your turn to man the shop for a while.'

'Where are you going?' I ask as she heads for the door.

'To get some milk so we can have a cuppa, of course,' she says, grinning at her use of the English slang. 'Then you can tell me all about where you went with Charlie.'

# Seventeen

## Thistle – Misanthropy

The shop is quiet through what little is left of the morning and through lunchtime. In the early afternoon we see a few tourists, but most people pass us by on their way down to the harbour carrying pasties, ice creams and cakes for impromptu picnics in the spring sunshine.

'Don't worry,' Amber says as she begins to cash up the till at the end of our first day. 'We're new here, people aren't used to buying fresh flowers on their high street yet, and remember there's that – what did Harriet call it, a "jamboree"? – at the church today. That might be taking a few people away. It'll pick up.'

'Possibly,' I say from my position by the door where I've been on and off for much of the day, gulping down fresh air as the waves of nausea return whenever I get a waft of the sweet scent of roses.

'It will,' Amber says positively. 'I just know it. And I'm never wrong!'

I smile at her. Amber is the complete antithesis to me. She's always so upbeat and optimistic. Whereas I tend to expect the worst in people, Amber invariably sees the best. She's good for me to be around, and I feel lighter as a result of spending so much time with her.

'What's so interesting outside?' Amber asks. 'You've been standing by that door all afternoon.'

'I was looking up at Trecarlan,' I tell her. This wasn't a lie; I had spent some of my time doing this.

'That old castle on the hill?' Amber asks. 'I've seen that. Who lives there, do you know?'

'I'm not sure about now, but when I was a child the castle was owned by Stan, an elderly eccentric who everyone thought was a bit mad.'

'Really? How fabulous. I love eccentric old people. Who was this Stan? Was he like a duke or something grand like that?'

'No.' I smile, remembering. 'Stan was the least grand person you could meet. He lived at Trecarlan on his own with no family. But there was a rumour he'd once eaten a dozen giant Cornish pasties in one sitting, and so he'd earned himself the nickname Mad Stan the Pasty Man.'

'Wow, I love it!' Amber claps her hands together enthusiastically. 'Tell me more. I adore this Stan already.'

'Everyone thought Stan was a bit doolally,' I recall, as I'm taken back to a period in my life when I seem to have been happy all the time. 'But I had many a lovely conversation with him, and we often played up at Trecarlan Castle in the summer months. Stan loved talking about Trecarlan's history, and if you took him a pasty, he'd happily tell you tales about the castle – which isn't really a castle,' I explain, 'it's more like a big country house that looks a bit castle-esque from outside.'

'How fantastic. I would love to have played in a castle when I was young. Did you pretend you were a princess?' Amber asks, her eyes gleaming with excitement.

'Yes,' I grin, 'I did sometimes.'

And Will would usually play the prince, or more often a knight brandishing a pretend sword he'd fashion from a twig.

Will and I had loved Stan, and spent many happy hours with him. Mad or not, we found him to be a lovely, kind man with a good heart.

'Anyway,' I say, shaking myself from my reverie, 'that's in the past. We need to get this shop shut up for the night. What can I do to help?'

I close the shop door and pull the bolt across. Then I move towards the desk.

'You're good. I've got this,' Amber says as she counts out some notes from the till. 'Why don't you begin carrying the buckets of flowers back to the cold store?'

I'd have rather cashed up the till. But I still feel bad about abandoning Amber earlier, so I do as she asks, trying to hold the first bucket at arm's length from my face without being too obvious about it.

'So what do you think of the people in St Felix now we've been here a while?' Amber calls as I'm just returning to the shop for my fourth bucket. I'm leaving the roses till last in the hope Amber might finish cashing up and help me.

'Er . . .' I'm surprised by her question. 'They seem very

nice. I'm not keen on that Caroline, though. She's definitely got it in for me. Gives me the evils every time I see her – which thankfully isn't too often. I've no idea why though. I've done nothing to her – except for the night in the pub, but that was ages ago.'

'She's like that with everyone,' Amber says dismissively, busily writing figures in a book. 'You should see her at the Women's Guild meetings. She rules them with a rod of iron.'

Encouraged by Willow and Beryl, Amber had joined the Women's Guild and had very much enjoyed the first meeting she'd attended.

'I can imagine that,' I say, thinking about Caroline as I carry a bucket of carnations out to the back and place them in the cold store with the others. 'What does she actually do in St Felix though?' I ask as I return. 'I mean, apart from be a busybody. Does she have a job?'

Amber shrugs and begins sweeping the piles of coins into tiny plastic bags. 'I don't think so. I don't know what she does. She lives in that nice house as you drive out of town, the big red one.'

'Caroline lives there? It's massive! She and her husband must be loaded.'

'I've only met Johnny the once. I think someone told me he was a banker. Seems like a cool guy though. Talking of which,' Amber says glancing at me, 'Jake is a really nice guy too. Don't you think?'

'Yeah,' I try to sound noncommittal as I lift the last bucket not to contain roses. 'He seems it.'

'Hot, too.'

'Perhaps.'

'Come on, Poppy, even you must be able to see that.'

'What do you mean "even me"?' I ask, putting the bucket down.

'Well, you hardly try with anyone, do you – let alone men.'

'I do try,' I protest. 'I'm just not a people person.'

'What are you then – an animal person?' Amber enquires, grinning. 'I hardly see you jumping to play with Miley when she's around.'

'I'm better on my own, that's all. People end up hurting you when you let them get close.'

I expect Amber to say something to the contrary, but instead she nods. 'That is sadly often the case. But you can't let that stop you from trying to find people who *won't* let you down.'

'Are you suggesting Jake might be that person?' I ask, opening my eyes wide.

'He might be, he might not. But why don't you let him in? He obviously likes you.'

'What? When has he ever suggested that?' I'm trying to act shocked, but inside I'm intrigued by Amber's suggestion.

'Like I said before: I know these things.' Her eyes dart to the window behind me. 'Ooh how about you pop down to the shop and get some milk while I finish up here?'

'Didn't you buy milk earlier?' I say, frowning at her. 'How much tea have we drunk?'

'But we don't have any in the refrigerator back at the cottage, and you know how partial I am to your English cuppas. Go to the shop for me, Poppy, will you, *please*?'

'OK,' I sigh, thinking about the bucket of roses still waiting ominously for me. 'Your wish is my command!' I wink at her.

'I'll grab my bag then meet you at the cottage – you're sure you're OK locking up?'

'Yes, of course. Now go, go!' Amber flaps her hand at me.

I shake my head. 'Anyone would think you wanted me out of here.'

Amber grins. 'Nope, I just want you to go to the shop. And if you see anything else you fancy while you're there, why don't you pick that up too?'

At Amber's request I walk across the street to the little supermarket, and head for their dairy section. I pick up a litre of semi-skimmed milk, and as I head past the biscuit aisle I stop to pick up a packet of chocolate HobNobs and a packet of Tunnock's Teacakes, both of which Amber has become addicted to since she's been here.

'Moment on the lips, lifetime on the hips!' I hear behind me, and I turn to see Jake carrying his own basket of food.

'They're for Amber,' I tell him quickly.

'I thought Oreos would be more her thing,' Jake says, grinning as he lifts a packet from the shelf.

'Nope, apparently our English cookies are the best. She's completely hooked on tea and biscuits these days.'

'And so she should be,' he says, putting the packet down. 'You can't beat a good cuppa.'

I stare at him. That's it, that's why Amber was so desperate for me to come in here. She'd seen Jake passing by with a cotton shopping bag, apparently heading for the supermarket.

At the same time as I'm growling internally, I notice that the shop, which was almost empty when I entered, is suddenly filling with a bottle-green sea of children all clambering to buy sweets and fizzy drinks.

'Cub and scout jamboree,' Jake informs me as we watch them swarm all over the shop. 'Clarence said he was expecting quite a few in the grounds of the church today. It must have just finished.'

I nod, and look desperately towards the exit. I need to get out of here and fast; the kids are everywhere, and already I can feel my temperature starting to rise.

But there's no way I'm going anywhere: the aisles are crammed with green shirts and hats, and would remain that way until all sugar cravings had been extinguished.

I grab a packet of Kit-Kats from the shelf and begin fanning my face.

'Are you OK, Poppy?' Jake asks. 'Is this crowd of kids too much for you?'

'I'm fine,' I insist in a tight voice. 'Just fine.' But I can feel my head beginning to swim, and a familiar feeling of nausea making an unwelcome return.

'Right, let's get you out of here,' I hear Jake say, just as I feel my knees buckle.

'Out of the way, kids!' Jake instructs in a firm voice as he puts my arm around his strong shoulders and half guides, half lifts me out of the shop. 'That's it, move aside.'

Like a diver rising to the surface of a deep, dark sea, I register daylight, that had seemed so far away a few moments ago, rapidly getting closer as we weave our way through the children to the exit, then outside into the fresh air.

'Here, take a seat,' Jake instructs, sitting me down on the bench outside the shop. Amber and I have taken to calling it the 'gossip' bench, as it usually houses two or more of St Felix's elderly residents discussing the events of the day in great detail. 'Now, take some deep breaths.'

I do as he says, and as always, now that I'm safely removed from one of my 'trigger factors', I begin to feel better almost at once.

'Sorry,' I tell him, as Jake watches me with great concern. 'I'm fine – really.'

'I thought you were going to pass out on me back there,' he says, nodding at the shop.

'I probably would have if you hadn't got me out. Sorry.'

'Nothing to apologise for. We all have our demons.'

I wonder what he means.

'I'll be fine, really,' I say, attempting to stand up, but I wobble slightly.

Jake catches hold of my arm. 'Steady! Let me walk you back to Daisy Chain.'

'No!' I almost cry, thinking of the sweet flower scent that would only make things worse. 'I mean, no, I'd rather take a walk – get some sea air, you know?'

'Sure,' Jake says, and with his arm linked firmly around mine we begin to walk down towards the harbour.

'You know when you nearly fainted earlier,' Jake asks after we've walked all the way along to the end of the harbour and the small lighthouse that proudly stands ready to guide the fishing boats into St Felix, 'that was your problem with crowds again – yes?'

I nod.

Now that I've recovered, I'm mortified at my little episode, and how Jake had to rescue me from a bunch of school children.

In one day I'd come up against both my *phobias* – I hated calling them that – and Jake had witnessed it. Having a problem with crowds meant I invariably became centre of attention when I had one of my panic attacks and I found it excruciatingly embarrassing. My issues with fresh flowers I always kept well hidden. People had a certain amount of sympathy for you if they understood your phobia. The more common varieties, like agoraphobia and claustrophobia, were well known and people *got* why someone might be terrified. Fear of spiders, birds or certain animals – yes, that was understood too. But someone who has an irrational fear of flowers? That was just weird.

One of my therapists had informed me that the correct term for my anxiety was anthophobia – fear of flowers. But knowing it has an official name doesn't make me feel any better or able to share my concerns with anyone. I know why I don't like flowers, and no amount of therapy or counselling is going to change that.

We lean against the railings at the end of the harbour and look out at the sea. It's high tide, and the waves are crashing against the harbour wall, sending spray up and over the rails. It feels fresh and revitalising against my skin. The glorious sunshine has given way to grey clouds that are being blown across the sky by a gusty wind.

'Are you claustrophobic as well?' Jake asks. 'Did being in that small shop bother you when it got busy?'

'No, it wasn't that. Look, do you mind if we don't talk about this, please? I'm feeling much better.'

'Sure, if that's what you want.' Jake turns so we're both facing out to sea, both leaning up against the green railings, both getting splashed with the salty spray.

'It's just you said you'd had therapy before and I wondered—'

'Did I not just say I didn't want to talk about this?' I snap, and immediately feel bad. Jake has been very kind, he doesn't deserve this. 'I'm sorry, I didn't mean to snap at you,' I tell him. 'I don't like talking about my problems, that's all.'

'Sure, I understand.' Jake nods, but doesn't look at me.

A silence falls between us, broken only by the sounds of the sea, brazenly continuing to batter the wall below.

'There's no shame in having had therapy,' Jake says, obviously deciding to ignore my request. 'I had therapy when Felicity . . . left.'

I notice he says *left* and not *died*.

Knowing how therapy works, I wonder if this deliberate choice of words is the result of one of those sessions.

'I know, Charlie told me earlier.' I immediately regret saying that. What if Charlie didn't want his dad to find out he'd shared that information.

Jake looks surprised. 'Did he?'

'Yes. He said you all had. But he thought Miley had probably done you more good than any therapy session. Where is she, by the way?'

'With Bronte. Miley and supermarkets don't go well together.' Jake thinks for a moment. 'Charlie is probably right though, about Miley. Of course I had the kids, and they were a great help; we all supported each other. But Miley gave me something new to think about, something that didn't remind me of Felicity.' He smiles ruefully. 'That little monkey needed a lot of work in those early days – she kept us busy.'

'I can imagine.'

'It gave me a focus, and boy did I need something to focus on. I think I'd have gone off the rails if it wasn't for her.'

'She's one cool customer, that's for sure.'

'She is that.' Jake looks down into the waves and appears to be thinking about something so I don't interrupt. 'Look, Poppy,' he says, suddenly turning to me, 'I'm aware you don't know me that well . . . '

Jake's face is earnest and I wonder what he's about to say.

'I don't expect you to talk about what's happened in your past, that's your business. But if you ever need—'

'What do you know of my past?' I ask sharply. We've been leaning on the harbour railings quite convivially, but now I stand bolt upright, my mind racing. 'Has someone been talking? Has your aunt, that Lou woman, been saying things about me? Has she?'

Jake looks completely bewildered. 'I don't know what you—'

'I bet she has,' I continue, not giving him a chance to finish. 'It's none of her or your or anyone else's business. What happened, happened years ago, and no one was there except me. *No one* knows exactly what happened but me. Understand?'

Jake, still looking confused, nods.

'Right, where does your aunt live?' I demand.

'Bluebell Cottage, up on Jacob Street, but I really don't see—'

But his words come too late; I'm already storming along the harbour towards Jacob Street and Bluebell Cottage.

No one gossips about my family.

No one.

# Eighteen

## Peony – Anger

I bang hard on the blue wooden door and wait.

Jake finally catches up with me. 'What are you doing?' he pants, out of breath from chasing me along the street and up another hill.

'I won't have people tittle-tattling about Will,' I say, banging on the door with my fist.

'Who the hell is Will?' Jake asks.

I turn and look at him, debate for about two seconds whether to answer his question, then turn back to the door. I'm about to bang on it again when it swings open and Lou stands in front of us, looking annoyed and then surprised to see us.

'Poppy, are you feeling better?' she asks. 'Why are you banging on my door? Has something happened?' She looks back at Jake, concerned. 'Is it the children?'

'No, Lou,' he begins from behind me. 'It's—'

'Have you told him?' I demand, interrupting Jake. I know I'm being incredibly rude, but I have to know.

Lou looks puzzled. 'Told him what?'

I give her a meaningful look.

'Poppy, I have no idea what you're talking about. Look, I have to get back inside. Suzy is about to give birth.'

Suzy? Who is Suzy?

'It's happening now?' Jake asks excitedly. 'I thought she wasn't due yet.'

'I didn't think she was,' Lou says, holding open the door for Jake and me to come in. 'But it's happening a few days earlier than I anticipated. Seems Basil got to work quicker than I thought.'

And who is Basil?

As Jake and Lou disappear into the house, I have no choice but to follow. I'm not sure what I'm expecting to find as I enter Lou's pretty cottage and we walk through to her living room, but it's certainly not a brown-and-white spaniel lying in her dog bed in the corner. Blankets and towels surround her, and she's panting and looking very hot and bothered.

'Have you called the vet?' Jake asks, kneeling down next to Suzy and stroking her head.

'Yes, but he's up at Monkswood Farm with a cow that's having birthing difficulties. It seems all the animals in the area want to be born on May Day! I've delivered litters before, though,' Lou says calmly. 'I know what to do. I'm prepared.'

Another dog barks from outside.

'That's Basil,' Lou says, seeing me look towards the back

door. 'He's the puppies' father, and he knows it too! He's been pacing the house for days, waiting – a bit like me.'

'Ah, right.' I look at Suzy again. 'How long before the puppies come?'

'Could be minutes, could be hours,' Lou says. 'They'll come when Suzy's ready. So what was it you both called round for?'

'Oh, it doesn't matter now,' I say. Seeing all this going on has made my temper tantrum seem less important. I'll speak to Lou when she has less on her plate. 'Is there anything I can do to help?' I look down at poor Suzy; she's panting hard, and I'm sure it won't be long before the puppies start coming.

'You could take Basil out for me?' Lou says. 'Like I said, he's completely on edge about the puppies, so a quick walk would do him good. Whether he'll go is a different matter though.'

'Sure, I can try.'

'Is that wise?' Jake asks, 'after . . . I mean, are you sure you feel well enough?'

'Oh, what happened?' Lou asks.

'Nothing, really, I'm fine.'

But Lou turns to Jake for an answer.

'She almost passed out, in the supermarket,' Jake tells her. 'I had to practically carry her out.'

'Oh, you poor thing.'

'I'm absolutely fine now,' I insist, annoyed with Jake for telling on me. 'I feel perfectly well enough to walk Basil for you, Lou, really.'

'Well, you know best, lovey,' Lou says, patting my arm. She heads towards the door. 'Just watch Suzy for me, Jake, will you? I'll be back in a tick. This way, Poppy.'

Lou leads me through to her kitchen, where she collects a red dog lead and some plastic bags, then we hurry out through the back door so Basil can't get in.

Basil is the elderly basset-hound I'd seen Lou with outside the fish and chip shop the first night I arrived in St Felix. He looks up at us with large, doleful, very knowing brown eyes as we enter his garden.

'Hey, Basil, want to go walkies?' Lou asks, brandishing the lead in front of her.

'Woof!' Basil bounds over to us, and Lou attaches his lead to his collar.

'He's no trouble on walks,' she tells me, 'but he's getting on a bit, so he doesn't need to go for miles and miles any more.'

Basil sniffs around my feet. Then he sits down in front of me and looks up in that same knowing way he had when we'd entered the garden.

'You seem to have made quite an impression,' Lou says. 'He doesn't always like strangers. Perhaps he realises.'

'Realises what?' I say, eyeing Basil from above. It's not that I have any issue with dogs, or any animals for that matter. I'm just not used to them these days.

'That you're related to Rose. Oh, don't you know?' she says, clapping her hand to her forehead. 'I assumed someone would have told you. Basil was Rose's dog. When she was taken into hospital, I said I'd look after him. After all, I had Suzy, and they already knew each other, so it seemed the ideal solution. Then of course when Rose didn't return . . . ' As if Basil knows what she's saying, he lets out a low howl. Lou crouches down and strokes his ear. 'I know, fella, I miss her too.'

Basil nuzzles into her hand, and Lou rubs a little harder.

'So he's kind of hung around ever since, haven't you, Basil? Him and Suzy get on fine – a bit too fine, actually, which is why I'm about to deliver goodness knows how many puppies. I thought old Basil was a bit past all that kind of thing and I didn't need to worry, but it seems there's life in the old dog yet – eh, Basil?'

I'm sure I see Basil smile.

'Lou! You'd best get back in here!' Jake calls from the house. 'I think there's one coming.'

Lou thrusts Basil's lead and some bags into my hand.

'He just worries, you know,' she says as she dashes back up the garden towards the house. 'Jake – it's just his way, he doesn't mean anything by it.'

I'm not sure if she's referring to the forthcoming puppies, or to Jake's earlier concerns about me taking Basil out.

'Make sure you clean up his mess,' she instructs as she disappears into the kitchen. 'The Parish Council fine you if you don't!'

I close my eyes for a moment. *Great.*

When I open them, Basil is looking up at me, panting.

'Come on then, you,' I say, leading him out of Lou's back gate. 'Perhaps you'd be good enough to keep it to number ones, if at all possible.'

Lou is right: Basil is easy to handle on the lead. He just pootles along next to me, stopping occasionally to sniff with his big long nose at anything that interests him, and when necessary he marks his territory with a small yellow trail.

I walk him back down into the town, and along Harbour Street, with the intention of us walking along the harbour front and then up on to the cliffs or maybe the beach, depending where the tide is at the moment. It's May so the light is still good at this time, and the earlier threatening clouds I'd thought likely to bring rain when I'd been out with Jake are dispersing.

We've just passed The Blue Canary bakery, all shut up for the night now it's gone six o'clock, and we're just about to walk past Daisy Chain when Basil suddenly pulls up.

I'm not prepared for this, and my arm is nearly yanked out of its socket as the lead tightens behind me.

'What's wrong?' I ask. I look at him sitting firmly on the ground. 'Do you need to go poo-poo?'

I roll my eyes. What has my life become?

Basil just stares up at me, his big dark eyes blinking slowly.

'Come on, Basil.' I tug on his lead. 'Don't be awkward, we were getting on so well there for a while.'

But he won't budge.

Then out of nowhere he starts howling.

Long, loud, pitiful howls that send chills right through me. He sounds a bit like a wolf deep in the middle of some dark dense forest. Except Basil is a slightly overweight elderly basset-hound, sitting on a cobbled street in a quiet Cornish seaside town – a wily old wolf he most certainly is not.

'What's wrong?' I hiss at him, as a few passers-by give us odd looks. 'Why are you doing that?'

Basil stops howling and launches himself at the flower-shop door. Then he begins frantically scratching at it.

'Stop it!' I tell him. 'We've only just painted that! Come on.' I pull on his lead again, but he won't budge. He sits in front of the door, facing it.

'Do you want to go into the shop?' I ask him in a slightly

gentler tone as I realise what might be wrong. 'Is that it?'

Amber has already gone home, so I reach into my bag and pull out my shop key, then while Basil's tail begins to wag very fast, I unlock the door and open it for him. He bursts in, tail still wagging, and sniffs the floor like a bloodhound.

'She's not here, you know,' I tell him. 'If you're looking for Rose, Basil, she's not here.'

Basil ignores my advice and continues to explore the shop. Surprisingly he knocks over very little as he pads about. Rose must have had him in here with her quite a lot; he seems to know his way about. He even goes out to the back and has a look there, so I follow him to the shop counter.

Eventually he returns, tail down, his long ears almost dragging on the floor. He looks at me in disappointment, as though it's my fault he hasn't found his owner hidden in the back room. Then he slowly curls up under the desk in a ball, and I wonder if that's where Rose kept a bed for him when they were here together.

'Oh, Basil, I'm so sorry,' I tell him, kneeling down to stroke him. Then I remember what Lou had done and I rub his ear hard. He lifts his head and pushes his ear into my hand. 'Aw, you like that, don't you?' I say.

I sit down crossed-legged under the desk, and continue to comfort him. It's quite nice being here without all the people, and of course the flowers. The real flowers are all in the newly restored cold store out back, so there's nothing for me to be freaked out by. It's just me, Basil and the shop.

'It stinks when someone dies, Basil,' I tell him as we sit together under the wooden shop counter. 'I know exactly how you feel.'

Basil looks up at me with his mournful eyes.

'It must be harder for you. I guess you don't really know what happened to Rose; one day she's here and the next ... well, you're living with someone else.' I pretend to give him a nudge. 'At least you saw a bit of action living with Lou, eh, fella? That's got to be a bonus at your time of life?'

Basil just yawns.

'But you obviously miss my grandmother, that's why you wanted to come back in here, somewhere you'd feel close to her. Perhaps that's what we all long for, Basil, the chance to feel close to the person we lost. Just that one last time.'

As Basil puts his head on my lap and closes his eyes, I reach out my hand to touch the heart that's engraved under the desk.

*Rebels together forever ...*

# Nineteen

## Pear Blossom – Comfort

Basil and I sit in the shop companionably together for some time, Basil snoring gently as he sleeps contentedly with his head on my lap, and me thinking about St Felix past and present. But eventually I decide we must go back to find Lou and see how Suzy is getting on with her puppies. So I wake Basil and encourage him to join me outside for further walkies.

When we return to Lou's cottage, I let myself in the back gate, take off Basil's lead and refill his water bowl, then I promise him I'll be back when I've found him some food in Lou's kitchen.

'Back in a mo,' I tell him as he curls up on his bed outside. 'You might be a daddy by now, several times over!'

I hunt around Lou's old-fashioned kitchen for some dog food, stupidly looking in cupboards for tins. Then as I stub my toe on a large sack of Bakers dog food standing on the floor, I realise that looking after two dogs as big as Basil and Suzy must require large quantities of food, not silly little tins of Caesar like my neighbour back in London fed her two pugs.

I fill a clean silver dog bowl that I find on the kitchen counter with food, then I take it outside to Basil. He looks up at me as I place the bowl down next to him, sniffs the contents, then allows me to leave it there for his perusal later.

'So much for being desperate to see your offspring, Basil,' I tell him. 'How about I go investigate on your behalf while you take another nap?'

Basil seems to like this idea. So while he settles down with his head on his paws I go inside to see what's happening with Suzy.

I pause as I arrive outside the sitting room door, unsure whether to knock. How much privacy does a dog need when it's giving birth? And it's as I do that I notice something hanging on Lou's wall. That's interesting, I think, looking at an embroidered picture of a sweet pea. It's a bit like the one Amber and I found in the box with the flower journals. I look closer; it has the same initials, VR, sewn into the petals of the flower that ours had.

'Poppy, is that you?' Lou calls from the sitting room, so I leave the picture and head in.

Lou and Jake are sitting on the floor in front of Suzy's basket.

'Come in,' Lou says, beckoning me across. 'It's all over.'

I walk to the basket and find Suzy looking tired but content with five miniature Suzys wriggling underneath her, all vying with each other to get to their mother's teats first and latch on for the longest drink of milk.

'They're so tiny,' I say, unable to take my eyes off them. 'It must have happened very quickly.'

Lou glances at the clock on her mantelpiece. 'You were gone over two hours,' she says. 'That's plenty of time, and Suzy did really well.' She reaches out to stroke her, and Suzy, too exhausted to do anything else, simply closes her eyes to acknowledge Lou's touch. 'Is Basil OK?' Lou asks.

'Yes, he's fine. He was no trouble at all. We went to the shop.'

Both Lou and Jake look at me in surprise.

'He wanted to,' I tell them. 'He was scratching at the door.'

'And what happened?' Jake asks.

'We went in,' I reply cautiously. 'And ... sat for a while. He seemed to like being in there.'

'Poor Basil,' Lou says. 'I think he still misses Rose.'

'I think so too,' I agree.

Lou and Jake exchange a look.

'What?' I ask. 'What's wrong?'

Lou stands up. 'The thing is, Poppy, now that Suzy has had her pups I'm not sure I'll be able to cope with looking after them and two fully grown dogs, and since you got on so well with Basil today ...'

'Oh no,' I say quickly when I see where this is heading. I hold up my hand and back away. 'No way, I have the shop to run, and ...' I search desperately for something else, but realise that I don't have anything else to worry about.

'Me caring for Basil was only supposed to be temporary,' Lou pleads. 'He's an old dog, Poppy, he doesn't take too much looking after – he sleeps most of the time. Besides, he'd so enjoy being back in the shop.'

Jake stands up and gathers up a small bundle of towel.

'While you and Poppy are discussing this, I'll do that thing . . . ' he says, taking a wide berth around me, deliberately keeping the bundle of towel where I can't see it.

'What thing? What's he doing?' I ask as he leaves the room.

'It's nothing, Poppy.' Lou, visibly distressed, glances at Suzy then lowers her voice. 'One of the pups didn't make it,' she says, and her lip begins to tremble. 'Jake and me, we tried so hard to resuscitate him, to give him a chance but . . . ' She shakes her head and begins to sob.

'Oh, Lou.' I look at Suzy and she raises her head for a moment away from her new pups and looks with distress at Lou, her ears down. Then she looks at me as if to say, 'I can't do anything at the moment, you'll have to do my usual job of comforting my owner.'

I take a deep breath and, feeling very much out of my comfort zone, I put my arm around Lou.

'I'm sure you did your best, Lou,' I tell her, sort of half-patting, half-hugging her. 'Suzy knows that. And look –' I gesture towards the basket – 'Suzy has five healthy puppies to thank you for, as does Basil.'

Lou sniffs and reaches into the pocket of her apron for a tissue. 'I know, but he was just so tiny and helpless – the runt of the litter. We tried to save him, but Mother Nature had other ideas.'

'Why don't you sit down,' I say, leading her back over to the sofa, next to Suzy and her pups, so she can see the positive results of her efforts and not dwell on the negative. 'Where's Jake taking him?' I ask delicately, not wanting to upset her. 'The pup?'

'Aw, bless him – he's a good boy. He's having a look in my shed to see if he can find a small wooden box to bury the little fella in.'

I swallow hard. This whole situation is suddenly affecting me in ways I hadn't expected it to.

'I'll go and see if he's OK, and while I'm there I'll put the kettle on. You look like you could do with a nice cup of tea.'

'Oh, that would be lovely, dear.' Lou sits back on the sofa and sighs. She looks almost as tired as Suzy as she sits and gazes contentedly at the puppies. 'Then we can discuss Basil . . . '

I go back through to the kitchen, find the kettle, fill it, then put it on to boil.

Looking out of the kitchen window I see Jake with a spade, digging a hole under a tree in Lou's back garden.

He must have found a box then . . .

I stand at the window for a few seconds, then I take a deep breath and head out into the garden.

'Hi,' I say, as I approach.

Jake jumps, and immediately stands in front of a small wooden box on the grass next to him.

'It's OK, I know about . . . ' I nod at the box.

'Oh . . . ' Jake looks down at it too. 'Yeah, real shame. We tried . . . '

'Yes, Lou said. She's quite upset.'

Jake nods, then he looks up at the tree and I see him take a deep breath. Was he reliving his own pain, as I was mine?

'You can carry on,' I say hurriedly. 'I just wanted to make sure you were . . . well, you know?'

Jake looks at me. 'I was what?'

I kick at a leaf. 'You know, OK . . . after what's happened.' I glance at the box again.

'Yeah, I'm OK. Are you?'

'Yes, *I'm* fine. Why wouldn't I be?'

Jake shrugs. 'Death is never easy to deal with, whatever form it takes.' He looks down at the box. 'Human, animal, it makes little difference if you loved what's now lost to you for ever.'

I remain silent. I desperately want to tell him I know exactly what he means. I know exactly what that pain feels like. But I can't. That ability has been buried too deep inside me to ever resurface.

I'm aware Jake is watching me. Waiting for a response. Still I don't speak.

'So, what about all this responsibility you've been asked to take on lately?' Jake asks lightly, lifting his spade to resume digging. He's obviously decided I'm a cold-hearted bitch with no feelings. 'We all know responsibility isn't your *thing*.'

'What responsibility?' I ask, playing along, hoping he doesn't really think that, but at the same time pleased he's changed the subject.

'First there was the flower shop, and now a dog . . .'

'Basil?' Basil wakes up at his name, and lifts his head. 'Basil?' I whisper this time. 'I haven't said I'll take him yet.'

'But you will.' Jake adds another shovelful of earth to the pile beside the hole.

'How do you know?'

Jake ceases digging, throws the spade into the soil, then wipes a few drops of sweat from his brow with the back of his hand. 'Because,' he says, turning to face me, 'underneath all that hard black armour you wear to protect yourself, there's a heart that beats strong and fast. And it's not just any old heart, Poppy; it's a beautiful, kind and giving heart. Just like Rose's was.'

While I'm still looking at him, surprised once more by his beautiful way with words, he lifts up the wooden box and places it in the hole he's just dug.

'Life stinks, Poppy,' he says, as we both look down into the hole together. 'We both know that. Some of us get a good crack at it, some of us, sadly, don't.'

I'm about to agree, then I stop myself. As comfortable as I feel with Jake, he doesn't know the truth . . .

Oblivious to my hesitation, Jake continues: 'But whatever life throws at you, however bad it is, eventually you realise that *your* life has to go on. Otherwise,' he looks down into the hole again, 'what's the alternative?'

It doesn't always move on, I think. Sometimes it's easier to remain caught in a time you felt happy. A time before the never-ending sadness began.

'Did you ever consider . . . ?' I nod at the hole.

Jake shakes his head. 'No, I had the kids to think about, they needed me more than ever back then. That was enough to stop me going down that route.' He smiles at me. 'People need you too, Poppy. You may not realise it, but they do. You have to move on with your life.'

I'm about to ask Jake which people need me, and might he be one of them, when I feel a wet nose nudge at my hand.

'Basil,' I say, crouching down next to him, putting my arm around his slightly podgy body.

'*He* needs you too,' Jake says quietly from above us.

I stroke Basil's head, but he stands up and leans over the hole.

'Do you think he knows?' I ask Jake.

Jake shrugs. 'Probably, dogs are sensitive like that, aren't they?'

I reach across Basil to pull up a daisy that's growing in the grass.

'Here,' I say, putting it under his nose, 'we'll throw this in for your little boy.' I toss the daisy into the hole on top of the small wooden box, and then Basil and I sit silently for a few minutes together watching Jake fill the hole with the earth he'd dug earlier.

Then before the three of us go back into the house to visit the other puppies, we stand for a few moments with our own thoughts of those we'd lost before.

# Twenty

## Freesia – Lasting Friendship

Jake is right.

I take Basil home with me that same evening – much to Amber's delight. The two of them now get on like best buddies, even rolling around on the floor together in Basil's more energetic moments, which aren't too often these days, poor fella. Basil comes with us to the shop every day, and happily sits under the desk in the new dog basket we bought for him.

Basil and I have a more mature relationship than his and Amber's. We co-habit together quite happily, and make allowances for each other's faults, i.e. Basil puts up with me moaning about him shedding hairs everywhere, and I put up with Basil's snoring.

We also have something in common – a love of cheese. I discover this when I'm happily tucking in to cheese on toast one day, and notice Basil sitting by my side on the balcony – drooling.

Whereas I prefer a good cheddar, Basil has a penchant for blue cheese, particularly Stilton. I know I shouldn't give him too many titbits, but I figure the odd treat now and then won't go amiss.

So even though I don't admit it to anyone, I'm actually really enjoying having him around. He's good company, and our daily walks up on the cliffs and along the beach have become the highlight of my days here in St Felix.

It's just over six weeks since the shop first opened, and we're almost in peak holiday season here in Cornwall. A fact that doesn't seem to have bothered the town too much, which I find both surprising and a little worrying as I sit at the kitchen table in the cottage filling in our accounts books this morning.

Amber and I had come up with a plan for running the shop that seemed to work well for both of us. Amber was quite happy to deal with all the floral stuff – arrangements, bouquets, even the ordering of the flowers was her department. I did all the practical things – the accounts, cashing up at the end of the day, banking and ordering new 'gift' stock – something we hadn't had much cause to do yet, because the shop was doing OK, but not brilliantly.

We still had a lot of support from the residents of St Felix. People would come in to buy bunches of flowers to brighten up their home, or present to someone as a gift, and Amber had had a few orders for birthday and anniversary bouquets – which had been delivered to much happiness and praise from the recipient. That was another of my jobs – delivery. I still had the Range Rover on loan – although I could have done with something a bit smaller to navigate the narrow streets of St Felix – and on the few occasions we had had orders I'd gone out in the 'beast', as I named it, to deliver Amber's beautiful creations.

Even I, someone who pretty much detested flowers in all forms, could see that Amber was extremely talented when it came to things of a floral nature, and I wondered how my mother was managing to cope without her in New York.

She'd rung me several times over the last few weeks to check how I was getting on, and how Amber was doing. I'd only had good things to say about Amber, of course, and, much to my surprise, about being back in St Felix. My mother seemed happy, but much less shocked than I was that St Felix appeared to be doing me good.

'And you're not *seeing* anyone while you're there?' she asks today as I half look at the books, half concentrate on what she's saying over the phone.

In a normal mother-and-daughter conversation this would have meant a man, but in my world it meant a therapist.

'No, Mum, I'm not seeing anyone.' My mother has always found it awkward, talking about my need for counselling. She rarely uses the word therapist.

'And you're sure you're OK like that? We could always find you someone local, if you feel the need? I'll pay.'

'Not necessary. Never felt better,' I assured her, and I meant it. As much as I found it hard to admit, this little seaside town was doing me the power of good. I felt happier than I had in ages, and if it wasn't for the fact the shop wasn't doing too well, everything would be great.

'You're sure you're OK with me keeping Amber here?' I ask her. 'Aren't you missing her?'

'Oh, desperately, but this change will be good for her. I

haven't just sent her there to help you. I'm hoping St Felix will help Amber too.'

'Why does Amber need help?' I ask, wondering what she means.

'Amber will tell you when she's ready, I expect. Look, I have to go, your father is taking me out for lunch – some fancy revolving restaurant, he informs me.'

'OK, Mum, happy anniversary to you both. Give my love to Dad.'

'Of course. Take care, my darling, I'm so happy it's all working out for you there.'

I guess it is, I think as I end the call and stare blankly at my phone for a few seconds. It's a novel experience for me to have things working out. Who would have thought it would happen here?

My grandmother was obviously even wiser than I'd thought.

'Right, Basil,' I say to him as he lies at my feet under the table. 'I think I've had enough numbers for the time being. How about a quick walk before we head back to the shop to see Amber?'

Basil lifts his head, takes a few moments to stretch, then begins to wag his long tail.

There aren't too many people about in St Felix this morning as we begin our walk. It's one of those gloomy, gusty mornings that drive the tourists indoors. The weather here is so changeable; with the turning of the tide a day that starts out like this can change into a beautiful sunny one – and, sadly, vice versa.

But even though the weather is promising bad things, we

take one of our favoured routes: through the town, along the harbour's damp sand while the tide is out, then up the long winding road that leads to Pengarthen Hill. I'm just wondering whether today might be a good time to finally take that trip up to Trecarlan Castle when a vehicle toots its horn. I turn to see Jake's van slowing down and pulling in next to us.

Aside from working at the shop and looking after Basil, I've been seeing a fair bit of Jake over the last few weeks. Sometimes we'll go for a drink together at the Merry Mermaid, or if he's passing by at lunchtime to see Lou at the post office, he'll pop into the shop to say hi. We've even eaten our lunch together a couple of times, leaning up against the harbour wall in the midday sunshine, like we had the day we'd been decorating the shop.

Jake appears to want nothing more from me than to be my friend. Even though the more time we spend together, the more attracted to him I've become, I'm happy for it to be that way if that's what he wants. Jake is great company, relaxed and funny. He makes me laugh a lot, and I like that; there aren't many people who can do that. Between him and Amber, my lips have been finding themselves turning upwards into a smile more lately than they've done in years.

Jake winds his passenger window down as his van pulls to a stop, and two heads poke through the gap.

'Hey, Jake, hey, Miley,' I say, smiling at them both.

'It's a windy day for a walk,' Jake says, shifting across to the passenger seat. 'Poor Basil will blow away.'

Miley leaps from the window down to the pavement to see Basil, who she absolutely adores. Basil, in his usual aloof way, allows Miley to hug him, but doesn't respond.

'Aw, Basil, we know you love her really,' I joke, leaning down and fussing him.

Basil eyes me, then shakes himself, so Miley gets covered with the remnants of sand still left in his coat.

Jake and I both laugh as Miley tries to do the same, and gives herself a full body shake like a dog.

'Are you busy today?' Jake asks. 'Only I was going to ask if you wanted to come up to the nursery later. You said you'd like to visit sometime.'

I don't think I did actually say that. It's more a case of Jake having asked me once and me mumbling something that sounded affirmative to be polite. For weeks he's been offering to show me around his nurseries so I can see where most of the flowers for the shop come from. So of course I've had to keep making excuses not to go. I'm just about coping with a shop full of fresh flowers these days – as long as we keep the door propped open to let in lots of fresh air. But I doubt I could cope with polytunnels and greenhouses stuffed full of the things.

'Yes . . . and I will,' I say, about to make my usual excuse, but I'm saved by my phone suddenly ringing in my back pocket. 'One moment,' I tell him, reaching for the phone. 'It's Amber. Hi, Amber, what's up?' I ask. 'No, I'm not at the house – I've taken Basil for a quick walk . . . Oh, right, have you tried— You have? Right, well, I'd best come back and take a look then . . . No, no plumbers yet, it'll cost too much. Let me have a look first. I'll see you in a few minutes.' I end the call.

'What's wrong?' Jake asks.

'Apparently the sink is blocked at the shop, and Amber doesn't know why. I'll have to go and take a look. So, sorry, it's no-go on the nursery visit today,' I tell him, trying to sound disappointed.

'Aw, shame,' Jake says. 'Look, I'm heading in the direction of town; would you and Basil like a lift?'

'That would be great, thanks.'

Jake slides back over into the driver's seat, and Basil and I climb into the passenger side, Basil sitting in the footwell, Miley sitting on my lap.

Jake grins as he sees us.

'Quite the menagerie you have there, Miss Carmichael.'

'Can you try and get us there as quickly as possible?' I ask. 'Cutting Basil short in the middle of his walk isn't usually a great idea. He likes to pace himself, and . . . ' I hesitate, trying to find the polite way to phrase it: 'his *offerings*.'

'I'm on it!' Jake says as he indicates and pulls out into the road and a not-so-delicate aroma begins to fill the van.

'Perhaps you'd better wind down the window,' I tell him apologetically. 'He is an elderly dog.'

Jake hastily opens his window. 'No worries,' he says kindly. 'Miley often has a similar problem. I'm used to it!'

On my lap Miley hides her face in her hands.

When we arrive at the shop, Jake drops the three of us outside and drives off in search of a parking place.

'Hey, you got here quickly,' Amber says as we pile through the open door. She looks with interest at Miley as she immediately leaps straight for the rolls of ribbons – her favourite items in the shop. 'Were you with Jake? I thought you were walking Basil?'

'We bumped into Jake on our walk and he kindly gave us a lift back,' I tell her while I remove Basil's lead and get him settled with fresh water in his bowl. 'What's up with this sink?'

'It's blocked,' Amber says, as we leave Miley happily playing with the ribbons and head for the back room to examine the sink. 'I tried to empty a vase of water down it but it won't go – look.'

I peer inside the large Belfast sink and see dirty flower water lying stagnant at the bottom of the ceramic white porcelain. I wrinkle up my nose. 'Yuck, it stinks!'

'I know, that's why I was changing the water in the bucket.'

'Do we have a plunger?' I ask.

'A what?'

'A plunger. Oh, what do you call it in America? Like a rubber thing with a wooden handle – you use it to suck stuff out of sinks.'

'Yeah, we call that a plunger too.'

'Do we have one?'

Amber shrugs. 'Haven't seen one about the place.'

The shop bell rings. 'What seems to be the trouble, ladies?' Jake calls, coming round the desk to the back room. 'Do you need a man's help?

'Not unless you have a plunger on you,' I answer, riled as always by Jake's often old-fashioned attitude.

'Well . . . ' Jake grins, and Amber laughs.

'We could maybe borrow one?' Amber suggests.

'Or I could pop back to my house and get one for you?' Jake says. 'Take me a few minutes. But we definitely have one – I used it not so long ago in our bathroom.'

'No, it's quite all right, thank you. I'll take a look underneath. It might be the pipe that's blocked. I've seen my dad do this loads of times.'

'I can do that for you,' Jake offers as I get down on my hands and knees. 'Save you getting dirty.'

'Thanks, Jake, but I don't have my crinolines on today. I'm sure I'll be fine.'

'*OK* ...' Jake says, and I see him and Amber exchange a look as I slide myself under the sink. 'Whatever you say, Mrs Pankhurst.'

'All right, I'm sorry,' I say, squinting up at him from under the sink. 'But a woman can do plumbing, you know.'

'She was like this when I wanted to buy her a drink,' I hear Jake tell Amber while I try to unscrew the pipe that leads up to the sink. I'm quite confident I know what I'm doing, even though these pipes are slightly different and somewhat older than the ones I'd seen my father loosening. 'Quite antsy.'

I know Jake is only trying to wind me up, so I choose to remain silent and deal with my pipe.

'That's our Poppy,' Amber says. 'Soft and sweet on the inside, hard and crisp on her outer layer. Like a lovely M&M candy.'

'Or a really nasty zit,' Jake adds. 'The kind that just explodes everywhere when you squeeze it!'

'Oi!' I snap, trying to sit up but forgetting I'm under the sink. 'Ow!' I cry as my head hits the white porcelain, and rebounds back against the pipe I've just loosened. 'Blah!' I cry, as the pipe falls away from the waste outlet, and filthy, smelly water flows down on to my head.

Jake's face appears under the sink as I'm pushing my dirty, stinky hair away from my face.

'You were right,' he says, obviously trying not to laugh, 'about women plumbers. You've cleared that blockage a treat, the sink is completely empty now!'

# Twenty-one

## Striped Carnation – I Cannot Be with You

I dry myself as best I can with the few small towels we have at the shop, then Jake insists on walking me back to the cottage, leaving Miley happily tying ribbons into Amber's long hair.

'I'll be back in a bit,' he tells Amber, 'once we've got Mario here – or is it Luigi who's the plumber? – into some dry clothes.'

Amber laughs. 'I believe it's both!' she says. 'My brother and I used to play those video games all the time back in the States.'

'When you two have quite finished mocking me!' I protest. 'I'll be perfectly fine walking back to the cottage myself.' I don't want Jake to see, or smell me like this for a moment longer than necessary.

But Jake insists. 'I feel partly responsible,' he says as we walk back to the cottage together. 'Something similar happened to me once when I was unblocking a sink. I probably should have warned you.'

'What happened to you?' I ask, surprised to hear this. Jake has always seemed so capable.

'Bronte helpfully emptied a bucket of floor cleaner down the sink while I was underneath it!'

I grimace. 'I bet you smelled better than I do now though,' I say as we reach the cottage and I open the front door.

'A bit – I had quite the tang of lemon about me, and very clean with all the disinfectant.'

I have to laugh. 'Well, thanks . . . ' I say, dithering about on the doorstep, assuming he will leave.

'I'll make you a nice hot cup of tea, shall I?' Jake offers. 'That wind is mighty cold today – you must be freezing, walking around with wet hair and clothes. You're normally pale, Poppy, but you look almost blue right now!'

'I am a bit chilly – yes,' I have to admit. 'But don't you have to get back to work?'

Jake looks at his watch. 'Call it my lunch hour. Perk of being your own boss. The guys up at the nursery can look after the place for a while.'

'In that case, tea would be great, thank you. Proper tea, mind – none of Amber's herbal nonsense!'

'As if!' Jake grins. 'Tea only comes one way in my book: builder's strength!'

I leave Jake in the kitchen filling the kettle, while I enjoy a lovely hot shower. My grandmother's cottage may be old, but the hot-water system is as good as gold when it comes to running hot baths and showers.

I emerge a few minutes later wearing grey jogging bottoms

and Amber's purple NYU hoody; my towel-dried hair is combed but hangs damply down my back.

'One tea!' Jake announces, setting a steaming hot mug of tea down on the kitchen table. 'Two sugars, isn't it?'

I nod. 'Yes, that's right. Thank you.'

Jake glances at me, then looks away.

'What?' I ask, self-consciously running my hand over my damp hair. 'What's wrong?'

'Nothing. You're wearing colour, that's all.' Jake grins. 'It's like suddenly going from a black-and-white TV to a colour one.'

I look at him, puzzled.

'Oh, sorry, you're probably too young to remember black-and-white TV, eh?'

'No, I do vaguely remember my grandmother having one here, before my parents bought her a colour one to watch gardening programmes on. Anyway, this is Amber's sweatshirt. I borrowed it to get warm.'

'Ah, that figures,' Jake says, nodding. 'Shame, that colour really suits you.'

I feel myself blushing, but luckily my cheeks are already flushed from my super-hot shower. 'Don't start that again,' I bluff, 'about the colour of my clothes – who are you, Cornwall's answer to Gok Wan?'

Jake laughs.

'Anyway,' I continue, always happier when Jake and I are being flippant with each other, 'you're almost as bad as me with your uniform of checked shirts, blue jeans and your staple Timberland boots!'

'Ah, you got me!' Jake says, looking down at his attire. 'Touché, Miss Carmichael.'

My full name is actually Poppy Carmichael-Edwards. My mother and father's names combined. But when Jake calls me Miss Carmichael I get a funny fluttery feeling in my stomach. Like someone has let a kaleidoscope of butterflies loose. So I've never wanted to correct him.

'Shall we take this up to the sitting room?' I ask, lifting my mug of tea. 'It's much nicer on a sunny day than down here in the kitchen.'

'Sure,' Jake agrees.

We head upstairs and settle ourselves comfortably on the sofa, while the sun pours in through the French windows, immediately warming my chilled body.

'Amazing, isn't it,' Jake says looking out of the window, 'how it can look so glorious out there, when in reality it's freezing cold.'

'Joys of living by the sea, I guess. The wind is our constant companion.'

'Isn't it just. I do love it here, though. I always wanted to live by the sea, and now I do, I'm not going to complain.'

'Where did you live before?' I ask as I sip on a very strong, but good cup of tea.

'We lived in East Anglia when the children were very young – Bedfordshire, to be precise, not far from Milton Keynes.'

'What did you do there – grow flowers?'

'No, nothing like that. I worked at the safari park at Woburn.'

I open my eyes wide. This I was not expecting. 'Really? How fabulous. What did you do there – look after the tigers?' I say jokingly, thinking he'll say he worked in admin or something equally boring.

'Not quite – apes, primates and monkeys.'

Of course he did. Now Miley makes more sense.

'Wow, that's a bit different than growing flowers in a Cornish nursery, isn't it – why did you change?'

'My father fell ill,' Jake says sadly. 'He desperately needed someone to take over the family business – only child, see. There was no one else.'

'I know that feeling well,' I tell him. 'The only child and the family business part.'

Jake nods. 'I resisted at first. I liked my job, and I knew it would mean uprooting the family, but the children were still small, and Felicity's family had originally come from St Felix – one of those strange coincidences life often throws at you – so she was very keen to move here.'

Jake falls silent as he's lost in his memories for a few moments.

'Do you ever regret it?' I ask gently. 'The move?'

Jake thinks. 'No. The kids have had a much better life growing up here by the sea, I'm sure of it, and Felicity was always happy here as part of the community.'

'But what about you?' I press. 'Are you happier here growing flowers than you were working with the animals?'

Jake looks at me. 'Poppy, if you're asking me this to try and justify what you've done by moving here, then I can't answer that question for you.'

'Sure, I understand.' I look down into my mug.

'But if you really want to know,' Jake says gently, 'I've always been happy here in St Felix, and that can't be wrong, can it? Being happy.'

I shake my head. 'You're right. The place does seem to have that effect on people.'

'It surely does.' Jake leans forward and picks up a book from the table. 'You seem a lot happier than when you first arrived. Calmer.'

I think about this while Jake flicks through the book.

'Yes, I suppose I am. Do you think we've discovered a sort of Cornish Lourdes?' I ask, thinking about the French town renowned for the healing powers of its waters.

'If we have, it will be great for the town,' Jake says, smiling, 'Imagine all the tourists we'd attract if we could heal everyone that visited of all their woes. What's this?' he asks, holding up the book. 'It's full of names and flowers and problems and stuff.'

I hadn't realised he'd been looking at one of the flower notebooks Amber and I had discovered.

'Oh, it's nothing. We found a bunch of these notebooks in the shop, listing past clients. Amber's been reading up on them.'

Amber was spending every night engrossed in the flower books. She was still adamant we could use them in some way.

'It makes interesting reading,' Jake says, flicking through the pages. 'Did your grandmother really think she was healing people with her flowers?'

'It would seem so,' I say, a tad embarrassed to be admitting this to Jake. I tell him about the other books we'd discovered, and how Amber thought she could turn our fortunes around if we began using them.

Jake nods. 'I guess it wouldn't hurt to try,' he says, much to my surprise.

'Are you winding me up?' I look at him with suspicion. 'You can't be serious?'

'What harm could it do? Look at it this way, Poppy: St Felix needs an injection of something or we're going to lose even more of the businesses on Harbour Street soon. Maybe a magical flower shop could be just the thing we need to bring people in. You said yourself the town is already a healing place – this could fit really well.'

'I don't know . . . ' Much as I adored Amber, her spiritual healing ways didn't sit well with me.

'Your grandmother was a very smart woman, Poppy,' Jake says. 'If she thought this worked, you can bet your life it did.'

'You're right about her being smart. She was definitely that – and loving and kind. I miss her,' I say, surprising myself by this admission.

'You remind me of her – a lot,' Jake says, putting the book back down on the table. 'Not just on the outside, I mean in here, too.' Jake taps his fingers lightly on my chest, and I'm sure he must be able to feel my heart pounding away.

'I hardly think so,' I say quickly. 'My grandmother was a great woman. I'm nothing like she was.'

'Oh, you are, Poppy,' Jake insists, lifting his hand away. 'I can tell.'

Suddenly, without consulting my brain, which would definitely have told me a very emphatic no!, I lean forward on the sofa and kiss Jake. Not on the cheek this time, but right on his lips.

I feel him hesitate for a split second, then he responds. But just as I'm happily sinking into this heavenly feeling of being so close to Jake, I feel him pull away from me.

'I . . . I really have to go!' he says, standing up so suddenly he almost spills his coffee. 'I should be getting back to the shop – Miley . . . you know how she is.'

'Oh ... right, yes, of course,' I reply, my cheeks redder than the scarlet cushion Jake's just vacated on the sofa. As I stare at it, the imprint of his belt still remains in the fabric.

'I'm sorry, Poppy,' Jake says softly, sounding apologetic now rather than panicked. 'I'm not ready for this. It's too soon.'

I look up at him. 'After Felicity, you mean?' I ask, surprising myself again, this time at my bluntness.

He nods.

'But it's been five years, hasn't it?'

'It could be ten for all it matters,' he says, his forehead wrinkling with concern. 'I just can't. Maybe not ever ... Do you understand?'

It's my turn to nod.

'Sure, I understand. Perhaps it's better if you just leave then.'

I turn and look out of the French windows. The sun has disappeared behind a bank of dark clouds. They hover ominously in the sky, predicting unsettled conditions to come.

And as I hear the front door of the cottage open and close, my feelings are a perfect match for the weather.

# Twenty-two

## Trachelium – Neglected Beauty

I sit alone in the cottage for a while, nursing my wounds and trying to get over my embarrassment – what was I thinking of, kissing Jake? He quite obviously isn't ready for a relationship, and now he's told me he probably never will be. I decide I'd better head back to the shop to see Amber and check on Basil.

So I change out of Amber's sweatshirt and into my usual black, trying not to think about the compliments Jake had paid me when I'd been wearing it. Then I gather up the accounts books and mooch back to the shop, wearing the huge mac I'd hidden under the first night I arrived in St Felix. Hiding not only from the rain, which is pelting down on to the cobbles of Harbour Street, but anyone who might want to talk to me too.

Jake's rejection has hit me hard. This is why I never allow myself to get involved with people – they always let you down. I'd stupidly allowed myself to have feelings for Jake, feelings he obviously didn't reciprocate, and as always I was the one who had ended up getting hurt.

Amber and I spend the rest of the afternoon in the shop together. I try not to let my mood dictate our afternoon, but Amber knows me too well, and her constant attempts to find out what is wrong are admirable, but exasperating at the same time.

I wasn't telling anyone what had happened at the cottage with Jake. Living through that rejection once had been bad enough, but twice? It wasn't going to happen.

The awful weather leads to a dearth of customers in the afternoon, and this gives me the ideal opportunity to talk to Amber about the shop and how it's doing. It also diverts attention from my troubles for a while.

'So what are we going to do?' I ask Amber when I've gone over the last six weeks' sales figures with her. 'I know you keep saying it will pick up, but it's not.'

Amber sighs. Always one to look on the bright side, even she looks worried. 'Maybe when the tourists arrive in the school holidays?' she suggests.

'But what if they don't? I was talking to Ant and Dec the other day and they say there's not a huge tourist influx in St Felix in July and August any more – the holidaymakers tend to stick to the bigger resorts up the road. They say if it wasn't for the fact Dec owns their building, they wouldn't be able to survive.'

Amber thinks about this. 'Then we need to attract the tourists *here*, don't we? Away from the big resorts.' She reaches under the counter. 'I know you don't believe in these little books,' she says, holding up the rest of the old notebooks we'd found hidden in the shop. 'And I know you've resisted using them so far. But I think it's worth a shot.'

I look sceptically at the books in her hand and try not to think about what Jake had said.

'Really?'

Amber nods. 'You've seen me reading them – and I've also been doing some of my own research on the net. I believe there's something to this. I think your grandmother must have been using an early form of alternative healing when she had this shop, based around the Victorian meanings of flowers – it's possible it's a gift that's been passed down through the generations since Daisy was first given this book and started her shop here.'

'OK, let's say we – or rather, you – started using these books when you make up bouquets and the like. Do you honestly think it's going to make that much of a difference?'

'Yup, I do,' Amber says enthusiastically. 'There's something special about this shop, Poppy. I felt a magical energy the moment I walked in. I think if we tap into that magic, we might just be able to turn this shop's fortunes around, and possibly the fortunes of St Felix too.'

'OK, tell me,' I sigh, knowing in my heart that both Amber and Jake could be right about this. Daisy Chain has always been a success in the past; there must be something we can do to replicate that.

'Well,' Amber begins, as the shop door, which we've had to close because of the rain, opens, and a lady wearing a red mac and fighting with a purple umbrella backs through the door.

'Gosh, I'm sorry,' she says as she drips water on to the floor, 'but it's awful weather out there.'

'Here, let me help you,' Amber says, hurrying over and taking her umbrella.

While the woman runs a hand over her damp hair, Amber stands the umbrella up in the stand we've installed at the front of the shop to prevent wet umbrellas – a common occurrence in St Felix – dripping all over the floor.

'What can we do for you?' I ask, as the woman removes her mac and water droplets fall to the ground.

'Wait, don't I know you?' Amber asks, looking at the woman with interest.

The woman nods. 'Yes, I came in a couple of weeks ago, and you gave me a special bouquet.'

'That's right, I remember you,' Amber says eagerly. 'So, did it work?'

The woman's face, which until this moment has looked slightly worn and weary from battling the elements, lights up.

'Yes,' she beams. 'It certainly did!'

I look back and forth at their excited faces.

'What?' I ask. 'Did what work?'

'Your magical flower shop!' the woman gushes. 'It's simply amazing!'

Amber makes the woman, who I discover is called Marie, a cup of tea, and while she dries off she tells a delighted Amber, and an astounded me, all about what's happened.

Apparently Marie had come into the shop one day a little upset. She was visiting her family in a nearby town and desperately wanted to make up with her sister, whom she hadn't spoken to in over ten years. She'd come in simply to buy some flowers as a peace offering. But Amber had used the old books of my grandmother's and come up with something a bit different – a bouquet that included purple hyacinth – meaning please forgive me, and hazel, which stood for reconciliation.

'So,' Marie says, after I've caught up on the beginning of the story. 'When I knocked on my sister's door and presented her with the flowers, I thought for one awful moment she was going to slam it in my face. But then the weirdest thing happened. She took the bouquet from me, leaned into it and smelled the flowers. Then she looked at me and said, "Marie, I've missed you. Please forgive me."' Marie reaches for a packet of tissues from her bag, pulls one free and dabs at her eyes with it. 'Sorry,' she apologises, 'it's all so raw still.'

Amber nods sympathetically.

'So then Julie, that's my sister, invites me in, and it's as if we've never been apart. We're like best friends again. We're even going to Alicante together in October with our husbands. And it's all thanks to you girls and your magical flower shop!'

After finishing her tea, Marie leaves the shop promising she will tell all her friends about us and insist that they come here to buy their flowers.

'So,' I ask Amber, after we've sent a dried-out Marie (tear- and rain-wise) on her way, 'you're just *thinking* of using the flower books in the shop, are you?'

Amber grins. 'I told you before, Poppy, the language of flowers is a wonderful, magical thing. You just have to believe . . . '

*

The next day is much brighter, both for St Felix and for me.

Basil and I are taking our usual morning walk. With sunshine beating down on our backs and bright blue skies above our heads, life seems a lot better than it had yesterday. Overnight I've decided that what happened yesterday was nothing for me to be ashamed about, and I mustn't let Jake's rejection ruin my time here.

'You've come so far, Poppy,' I'd told myself as I lay in bed, 'don't let this one incident set you back.' Jake was just one person; I wasn't going to allow him to tarnish my thoughts about everyone here.

'Come on, Bas!' I'd said to Basil as we set off on our walk. 'This is a new day for us, who knows what might happen. It could be great!'

Basil had looked up at me cynically, as if he knew his days were never going to change that much. All Basil was interested in were his walks and a constant supply of food being on hand at all times. Other than that he has nothing to stress about in his life – there are times when I'm quite envious of him.

We're about to continue with our walk along the clifftops, when I turn and look up the path that leads to Trecarlan Castle, just as I had yesterday morning before Jake caught up with us. I shake my head. No, no Jake today.

I'd thought about heading up there to take a look around a number of times since the day I came here with Charlie, but the truth is I'm scared of what I might find. Visits to Trecarlan with Stan had been such an integral part of my childhood in St Felix that the thought of visiting there without him – and, heaven forbid, finding his beloved home derelict – was not something I could face.

But today is a new day, I remind myself. Maybe the time has come to take that first step on a new path. So I take a deep breath, give a gentle tug on Basil's lead, and together we set off up the long road that leads to the castle.

As Basil and I get closer to Trecarlan, and the blurred outline of the grey stone house begins to sharpen, I'm surprised by how little it has changed over the years.

Yes, it's more overgrown than I remember, there's ivy covering the walls and it looks a bit dilapidated with the odd crack in the brickwork, but fundamentally it's much the same as it was when I was a child. As Basil and I stand looking up at the grand entrance, I half expect Stan to come wandering down the steps to greet us.

But I know that isn't going to happen. After Amber and I had spoken about Stan the day we opened the shop, I'd made a few enquiries. According to the handful of people who remembered him, he'd left the castle years ago and Trecarlan has been standing empty ever since.

I unhook Basil from his lead so he can pootle about on his own for a while, then I walk up the stone steps that lead to the entrance of the castle, hoping I might be able to peek through one of the windows. But although the curtains are pulled back, the interior of the house is dark so it's difficult to see anything.

'Basil!' I call to a wandering Basil, currently cocking his leg against one of the gruff-looking gargoyles that guard the stone steps. 'Come along, time we were moving on.'

Basil begrudgingly trots along behind me as we wander through the grounds, and happy memories begin to return as I recognise the places where Will and I played as children.

Stan used to let us come up here as often as we liked. To be honest, I think he quite liked having some company about the place. He had no family, just a few staff that worked for him – his helpers, Stan would call them. There was the lady that came in to clean for him ... I rack my brains, trying to recall her name ... Maggie, that's it! I remember her now. Then there was a husband and wife team that took care of the cooking and gardening full-time ... oh, what were their names? Suddenly these details seem very important and I'm irritated with myself for having forgotten.

Bertie! That was the chap's name, and the woman was Babs.

I remember Babs was always nice to Will and me. She'd provide us with plates of cakes and juice, and sometimes, when she was baking for Stan, she'd let us sit and watch her. If we were good, she'd allow us to lick the bowl and the spoon clean when she'd finished.

Happy memories ...

Sometimes we'd come to Trecarlan alone, and sometimes we'd come here with my grandmother. She was great friends with Stan, and she'd often bring him the leftover flowers from the shop at the end of the week to brighten up his 'dreary old castle' as she'd jokingly call it.

'Something's not right here, Basil,' I tell him as we stop at the back of the castle and I look around. 'If no one lives here any more, then why are the grounds so well kept?'

I'd known something was amiss since we'd started exploring. Even though the castle appears to be shut up, the grass and bushes that surround it have all been pruned and beautifully maintained.

'Hmm,' I say to a disinterested Basil, who's currently engrossed in sniffing the stem of an immaculate topiary bush trimmed into a cone. 'I wonder . . . ?'

The walled area we're standing in front of used to be the kitchen garden. Will and I would sometimes help Bertie plant vegetables here, and when we came back a few months later for another holiday, we'd find our tiny seeds had grown into tasty vegetables that Babs would make into stews and soups for Stan.

I lift the rusty old latch on the wooden gate, praying it isn't locked. To my joy the gate swings open. I call Basil and we enter a derelict kitchen garden that bears little resemblance to Bertie's neat, well-tended vegetable patch of old.

'OK, Basil, if I remember rightly there always used to be a key . . . ' I lean down and lift a loose piece of paving slab, 'right about here!' I say triumphantly, lifting a rusty key in the air. 'And it should fit . . . ' I put the key into the lock in the door in front of me and turn it. '*Here!* I was right!'

I turn the handle of the kitchen door – which used to be blue, but so much paint has peeled away it's hard to tell what colour it had once been – and step inside. 'Come on, Basil!' I call. 'We're going in.'

The interior of Trecarlan Castle is much as I remember.

It's grand – in that the rooms are huge and in some cases ornately decorated, so you can imagine past owners living here with staff tending to their every need. But not so grand that it doesn't seem like a home. That's very much how I remember it – Stan's home. A place we could come to play and feel safe.

The décor may be dated, there's a thick layer of dust covering every surface and large cobwebs in places there shouldn't be, but it still has a certain ambience. A warm, welcoming feel, so that as I wander from room to room with Basil by my side, I don't feel scared or worried what might jump out at me, I simply feel nostalgic for a time when I was young, carefree and happy.

After exploring the house thoroughly, I can't find any signs of life. There's definitely no one living here, the place hasn't been touched for years, that much is clear. But if no one is living in the house, why are the gardens so well cared for?

Eventually we find ourselves at the entrance to the ballroom, which must have played host to many grand events in the castle's history, but which I remember for something much more fun.

While Basil sniffs amiably about the doorway, I walk over to one side of the room and slip my shoes off. I don't know why I check either side of me to see if anyone is coming – old habits die hard, I guess. But with a huge grin on my face I begin to run across the floor. About halfway across, I twist slightly to the side and slide the rest of the way in my socks across the polished wooden floor.

'Ah, that was great!' I tell Basil. 'Will and I used to do the same when we were here.'

'Did you now?'

I swivel rapidly in my sock-clad feet towards the other, smaller door to the ballroom that Stan would tell us was the servants' entrance.

'Who are you?' I ask an amused-looking young man wearing khaki combat trousers and a white T-shirt. I notice he's holding a spade in his right hand.

He doesn't answer but instead says, 'You're Poppy, aren't you?'

'Yes . . . ' I reply hesitantly. 'But . . . '

'I thought so. My sister told me all about you and the flower shop.'

I look blankly at him.

'I'm Willow's brother, Ash,' he says. He walks over to me, brushes down his free hand on his trousers and holds it out. 'Pleased to meet you.'

'Willow, from the Women's Guild – yes, of course. Hello,' I say, still slightly dazed by his sudden appearance. 'Oh, Willow and Ash—'

'I know . . . ' he says, rolling his eyes. 'Trees. My parents were keen gardeners.'

'As are you, by the looks of it.' I indicate the spade in his hand.

'Runs in the family,' he says. 'My grandfather used to be the gardener here many years ago.'

'Oh, you must be Bertie's grandson!' I exclaim, looking up at this broad, tall, blond guy. 'I remember you now, you were just a little fella running around in nappies when I first used to come here as a child.'

'Yeah, that was me,' he says without a hint of embarrassment. 'I wasn't always in nappies though – at least, I hope not, 'cos we lived in St Felix until I was seven!' He winks. 'My parents moved the family back here when my granddad got ill,' he explains. 'We stayed on after he passed away, to be close to Grandma Babs.'

'How old are you?' I ask, trying to work all this out.

'Twenty-two.'

'That would be about right. I stopped coming to St Felix when I was fifteen, although by then I wasn't really running around the castle playing. We'd just pop up to visit Stan when we were here visiting my grandma.'

'Sorry about your grandma,' Ash says sombrely. 'Rose was a lovely lady.'

'Yes, she was, and your granddad too.'

We look at each other, caught in a slightly awkward moment.

'So, you haven't actually told me why you're walking around this dusty old house. Or,' Ash's blue eyes twinkle, 'how you managed to break in.'

'And you haven't told me what you're doing in Stan's old house brandishing a spade.'

# Twenty-three

## Apple – Temptation

Ash and I close up Trecarlan again and walk back through the grounds with Basil, Ash returning his spade to a shed full of gardening equipment.

'So, how come you still do the gardening here?' I ask him after I've explained how I got into the house and why.

'I promised my granddad I would,' Ash says, closing the shed door and locking it. 'When Stan left Trecarlan, my grand-parents did too. Bertie said just 'cos Stan had left didn't mean to say the place had to go to rack and ruin, and he was going to continue looking after the gardens.'

'Aw, that's sweet of him.'

'I know,' Ash says. He gestures towards the path. 'Walking back into town?'

I nod and we set off down the hill together.

'Shortly after Granddad got ill he asked me if I'd look

after the place for him until he got better. But he never did.'

'Again, I'm sorry,' I say, meaning it. 'Your granddad was a lovely man, I remember him well.'

'As was your grandma,' Ash says, and then he smiles. 'So I look after Trecarlan whenever I get the time in between my other gardening jobs, because there's no one else to.'

'Stan never sold up then?' I ask, trying to piece all this together.

'Nope. He still owns the house, as far as I'm aware. He leaves it to the Parish Council to look after the place. And they don't do very much. They don't really have the funds to run a country house.' He thinks for a moment. 'That Caroline can be a bit of a terror though. She went nuts when she found out I was gardening here. Tried to tell me what to do and everything, but I soon put a stop to that.'

'How?'

'I told her if the Parish Council wanted to start paying me to work here then she could tell me what to do. Until then, the gardens were my business.'

'Brilliant!'

'Funnily enough, I never heard another peep out of her. They seem quite happy with me popping in and doing the gardening for nothing.'

'I bet they are.' I think for a moment. 'So what happened to Stan in the end? I've asked around but everyone seems a bit vague about what happened.'

'I don't think anyone knows the details. I reckon he had money troubles – like I said, it takes some wonga to run a place like Trecarlan, and I don't think Stan was all that loaded. Although someone must be paying for his home.'

'His home? Where does he live now then?'

'I'm not sure exactly, but I heard he went to live in an old folks' home somewhere. My granny always says 'Up North' if she ever talks about him – which isn't too often. I think she blames Stan for my granddad's demise.'

'Oh no, that's awful.'

Ash shrugs. 'She's elderly. Bit stuck in her ways. It's easier for her to blame someone else than face up to the fact Granddad smoked twenty a day, and spent five nights a week in the Merry Mermaid!'

We've arrived back in town, and as we stop outside Daisy Chain, I let Basil off his lead so he can go on into the shop to get water. When I stand up again, Ash is looking at me.

'So,' he says, as we linger outside the open door. 'Do you need to go back in and fiddle with your buds right now?' His eyes, set against his tanned skin and scruffy blond hair bleached by the sun, sparkle like naughty sapphires. 'Or can I take you for an early lunch at the Mermaid?'

I feel myself flush, but I manage to reply with a fairly straight face, 'I don't actually fiddle with my buds, I prefer someone else to do that for me.'

Ash grins.

'However,' I continue, 'it's Amber's lunch break very soon, and I have to cover the shop. So I'm afraid it's a no.'

Ash pulls a sad face. 'Ah, I see. Never mind . . . ' Then I see the glint in his eyes. 'In that case, might you be free for a drink tonight instead?'

'Oh . . . '

'We can have a reminisce about Stan, and me in my nappies . . . '

An image of Jake in the cottage yesterday flashes across my mind. So I quickly shake it away.

'Sure, why not?' I agree, without stopping to think about it.

'Great,' Ash says, grinning. 'I'll see you in the Mermaid about . . . eight?'

'Eight's fine.'

Ash gives me a cheery wave as he carries on up the cobbled street, just as Amber appears at the door with an intrigued look on her face.

'Who was that?' she coos, bending to look around me so she can watch Ash walk away.

'Ash – he's a gardener up at Trecarlan Castle.'

'Sexy gardener!' She lets out a low whistle.

'His grandfather used to work at the castle when I played there as a child. I knew Ash when he was little.'

'Bet there's nothing little about him now.' Amber nudges me.

'*Amber* . . . ' I give her a warning look.

'What? You wanna let your hair down, Poppy, have some fun. I thought you were gonna have fun with Jake when I first arrived here, but that doesn't seem to be going anywhere, so why not this Ash?'

She casually turns and walks back into the shop.

'Jake and I are just friends,' I protest, hurrying after her, wondering if we're even that after yesterday.

Amber rearranges some sunflowers in one of the metal buckets. 'Yeah, honey, I know that now, but when I first came here and saw the way you looked at him, I did wonder if there might be something more.'

I can only stare at Amber – she's right, of course, but I'm not about to admit that to her.

'*Poppy*, come on – Jake's fit, not as fit as Lady Chatterley's lover out there, mind, but he's still hot for an older guy.'

'Jake isn't that old,' I reply, trying to sound like I don't care either way.

'He's older than Ash.'

'What's that to do with anything? Jake is thirty-nine; like I said, not old. In fact, I think his birthday is coming up very soon. Bronte mentioned something about a party the last time I saw her.'

Jake's birthday – great. That would be fun now. Oh, why did I have to kiss him and ruin everything?

'How old is Mr Hot?' Amber continues, unusually for her she's not sensing my unease.

'Twenty-two, but I don't see—'

'Ooh, she swings from older man to toy-boy, what a gal!'

'Amber, stop this. Ash has asked me out for a drink tonight, that's all.'

Amber's eyes light up.

'And before you say anything, we're only going to reminisce about old times at Trecarlan.'

Amber raises one eyebrow. 'Is that right?'

'Yes,' I say, heading around the back of the desk, 'it is. Now go and get some lunch – and if you're heading anywhere near the Blue Canary, pick me up a tuna sandwich while you're there, will you?' I wink at her, hoping this will do the trick and she'll move on.

Amber sighs. 'Change the subject all you like, but my sixth sense is tingling about this, missy, and I can't remember the last time that was wrong.'

# Twenty-four

## Nasturtium – Impetuous Love

As I head down to the Merry Mermaid just before eight that same evening I try not to think too much about Ash as I walk. I haven't been on a proper date in ages, and even though I'd insisted to Amber that it wasn't really that, and only a catch-up with Ash, I had a feeling she might be more accurate than me with her predictions for the evening.

So as I head down the road towards the harbour and the pub, I allow the other things on my mind to battle for prominence over my thoughts about Ash.

For a start there's the story Marie told us yesterday about the reconciliation with her sister. Could Amber's choice of flowers really have made such a difference? It must have been a coincidence, surely? Perhaps Julie had been thinking of making up with Marie all along, and seeing her standing on her step had given her just the push she needed.

But what if Amber was right and it had been the flowers. Could it be that there really was something to these books? Amber had admitted to me afterwards she'd used the books to make up bouquets several times already, but Marie had been the first person to come back and tell her they had worked. What if more people started coming back to the shop to tell us it had worked for them too? Ant and Dec remain convinced my grandmother helped bring them together, and the locals are always talking about Daisy Chain being special . . . Even Jake seems to think there's something to it, and despite our falling out, I value his opinion very highly.

My mind wanders to Jake, and a feeling of guilt immediately begins to seep through me.

'Stop it, Poppy,' I tell myself. 'Jake made it quite clear he didn't want a relationship with you, you are doing nothing wrong in going out for a drink with Ash tonight. And that's all it is,' I remind myself. 'Just a drink with an old friend. Nothing more.'

It's Friday night so the pub is already busy when I get there.

I push my way through the locals, and a few tourists, and spot Ash standing up at the bar.

'Hey,' he says, turning around when I tap him on the shoulder. 'You made it. You look great.'

On Amber's advice, and after much coaxing, I've been uncharacteristically adventurous with my outfit tonight. I'm still wearing my customary black in the form of skinny jeans with pixie boots; it's my top that's making me feel uneasy. I've borrowed one of Amber's plainer shirts – still black, but with a host of colourful polka dots scattered haphazardly over the fabric. It's very Amber; I'm just not sure it's very me.

'It's a start,' Amber had said proudly, like a mother helping her daughter dress for her first date. 'Have fun!' she'd encouraged as she'd stood waving at the cottage door, watching me walk down the street.

'Thanks,' I tell Ash now, smiling at him. 'So do you.'

Ash is wearing dark blue jeans and a pale green shirt that makes him look even more tanned and healthy as he leans casually against the bar. 'What can I get you?' he asks. 'The world of the Merry Mermaid is your oyster!'

'I'll have a white wine, please,' I say, just managing to stop myself from asking for 'a pint'. This was definitely an evening for channelling the 'Belle' in me, if there even was such a dainty, elegant thing contained within my four sturdy walls.

'Rita, when you're ready,' Ash calls, opening his wallet and waving a note at Rita.

'You're next, Ash, sweetie,' Rita calls down the bar. 'Oh hello, Poppy, I didn't see you there.' I notice her face registering the fact Ash and I are together as she finishes pulling the pint.

I lift my hand to give her a tiny wave, then sort of drop it in embarrassment. Rita is obviously wondering what's happened to my usual drinking partner, Jake.

'So, how was your afternoon?' Ash asks. 'Were you busy creating lots of beautiful bouquets?'

'No, I'm just a general dogsbody about the shop; it's Amber that does all the hard work. She's the creative one.'

'Really? I'm surprised you kept the shop as a florist's then. Most people would have turned it into a coffee shop or a tearoom, that seems to be all anyone wants these days.'

'Family tradition.'

'Ah, I know all about that. My grandfather was a gardener, my father too, and now little ol' me.'

'Don't you enjoy it then?'

Ash smiles, and I'm treated to the sight of his perfect white teeth. 'Yeah, it's OK. I like being out in the fresh air, and I'm virtually my own boss. It could pay a bit better, but I kinda do what I like when I like, so that's a big bonus.' He pretends to look around him, then winks. 'Just checking none of my clients are within earshot. They might say differently!'

'Ha, well I think you're quite safe tonight,' I reply, pretending to look quickly around the bar.

'Oh?' Ash enquires, flashing another disarming smile at me. 'I'd hoped otherwise ... Ah, Rita, yes, a glass of your finest white wine for the lady, and I'll have a Jack and Coke please.'

I take a deep breath while he's turned away for a moment.

Goodness, Ash is certainly laying on the charm tonight. But not in a fawny, grovelly way, I couldn't bear that. No, Ash's brand of charm is much more dangerous; it's the kind that catches you completely off guard, leaving you tongue-tied, blushing and not knowing what to do. Worst of all, you find yourself liking it.

'There's a table over there, do you want to sit down?' Ash asks when he's got our drinks.

We walk over to a low table against the far wall of the pub, I sit down on the sofa that's at one side of the table, and I expect Ash to take a seat on one of the comfy chairs at the other side. But he doesn't, he comes and sits right next to me.

'Now,' he says, 'let's talk nappies.'

*

For the next half-hour or so we have a fun time reminiscing about old Stan and the castle.

'It must have been such a wrench for Stan, leaving Trecarlan,' I say, thinking fondly of my old friend. 'He loved that place. I'm sure he would never have left unless it was absolutely necessary, and then he'd have clung on until they had to drag him away. Stan may have been a bit eccentric, but he had a good heart. He was always lovely to me and Will.'

'What's your brother doing these days?' Ash asks. 'Didn't he fancy running a flower shop?'

I reach for my glass and am dismayed to find it empty.

'I seem to be empty,' I say, hoping Ash will take the hint.

'Yeah, me too,' he says, holding up his glass. 'I'll go up in a minute, they're a bit busy at the moment.'

'No, my round,' I say, leaping up. 'Same again?'

Ash doesn't really have a chance to answer; I've already left.

I breathe a sigh of relief as I wait at the bar for Rita or Richie to see me. I should have known Ash would ask questions about Will. I should have been prepared.

The pub seems much busier tonight than it has been of late – and I'm surprised and pleased for Rita and Richie. They deserve success, they're a lovely couple. Someone squeezes roughly into the space next to me, and I'm about to tell them to watch it, when I turn around to find it's Jake.

'Hi,' he says looking uncomfortable at seeing me standing next to him. 'I didn't expect to see you in here tonight. Can I get you something?'

'Er . . . no, I'm fine, thank you.'

Oh boy, this is awkward. I glance over at Ash, but he's facing the other way.

'Poppy, let me buy you a drink to make up for yesterday. We're still mates, aren't we?'

Jake seems anxious that I might say no.

'Of course we are,' I reply, relaxing a little. 'Yesterday was just a silly mistake on my part. I'm sorry.'

'Poppy, you've nothing to be sorry for.' Jake places his hand over mine as it rests on the bar. But the contact is too much, and immediately I pull away.

'How about I buy *you* a drink,' I say hurriedly, 'just to show there's no hard feelings. OK?'

Jake nods, but he looks dismayed at my rebuff.

'What would you like?' I ask, hoping Rita or Ritchie will hurry up and see me.

'My *usual*,' Jake says, obviously surprised I have to ask. 'A pint of Tribute.'

'Yes, of course,' I say. 'Richie!' I call, trying to attract his attention.

'Yes, Poppy, what can I get you?' Richie says, arriving at the bar in front of us. He looks startled to see Jake standing next to me. 'Oh, you are with Jake, I knew Rita had got it wrong earlier when she said you were with—'

'A pint of Tribute, a medium white wine, and a JD and Coke please, Rich,' I say, cutting him off.

'Ah, right . . . gotcha.' He winks at me and begins pouring the drinks.

'Three drinks, Poppy?' Jake enquires. 'Are you feeling particularly thirsty this evening?'

'No, the other one is for someone else.'

'But still no pint for you. Plus you're wearing some colour. Golly, you must be out to impress!' I know Jake is joking, and usually I'm much happier when things between us are light-hearted and flippant like this, but Jake is getting a bit too close to the truth.

'No, I just wanted a change, that's all.'

'Nothing wrong in that, change is good.' Jake smiles at me, and I turn away. This is getting more awkward by the second.

Richie finishes pouring my drinks and stands them in front of me. I pass him a twenty-pound note.

'Yours, I believe.' I slide Jake's drink to him along the bar, and our fingertips touch as he goes to take the beer from me. Our eyes meet for a second over the top of the glass.

'Cheers, Poppy,' Jake says, lifting his pint and taking a sip. 'So which is yours?' he asks, looking at the two glasses in my hands.

I lift the wine glass.

'Very nice, and the other is for . . . ?'

I glance over to where Ash is waiting for me.

I think I see Jake flinch slightly as he follows my gaze, but I can't be sure.

'So it's young Ash who is the lucky recipient of the Jack Daniels. Very nice.'

I wait for him to say something else, but he doesn't, he just picks up his pint and takes another sip.

'Right, well, I'd best be getting back over there then. Enjoy your beer.'

For a moment I think Jake is about to say something, but instead he just nods calmly, and I find myself heading back over to Ash, trying not to spill the drinks.

'All right?' Ash asks as I sit down. 'I was wondering, do you remember a time when you and your brother were playing hide and seek, and you let me join in . . . '

While he's talking I drift off with my own thoughts, thoughts about Jake.

Why didn't he say anything while we were at the bar just then? Didn't he care I was in here on a date with Ash? He must have realised that's what it was.

Obviously he had no reason to care what I got up to any more. He'd made that perfectly clear yesterday.

I sulk for a few seconds, before sensible thoughts start filtering into my brain past all the huffy ones.

What was I expecting him to say, even if he did care?

'Ash isn't good enough for you. I was wrong, let me whisk you back to my flower beds and make mad passionate love to you immediately.'

I almost blush at the thought. Anyway, what good would it have done if he had said that? I'd have only been freaked out by all the flowers and run away!

No, I had to get used to the fact that Jake wanted to be my friend, nothing more. If I wanted anything else, I was going to have to look for it elsewhere.

'... and I remember Will getting stuck in the larder, so when my granny Babs came in to start making the lunch that day she got such a shock ... Poppy? Are you listening to me?' Ash asks, tilting his head to one side.

'Of course!' I drop back into the real world with an imaginary thud. 'Will made up a story to cover him being in the pantry, something about him thinking about becoming a chef when he left school. But then he was caught out, because he had to stay and help Babs make sandwiches for Stan's lunch.'

'Yes, that's right.' Ash thinks. 'You were going to tell me about Will earlier: what's he doing now?'

'Will died,' I announce, suddenly wanting to tell someone instead of keeping it hidden all the time. I was tired of secrets. 'He died fifteen years ago.'

'Oh, I'm so sorry,' Ash says, looking quite shaken. 'I had no idea, I wouldn't have kept going on about him if I'd known.'

'It's fine. Sometimes it's nice to talk about him again, and remember.'

'What happened, or would you rather not talk about it?'

I was ready to tell someone Will was no longer with us, but I wasn't ready to go into details.

'No, I'd rather not, if you don't mind.'

Ash takes a long drink from his glass.

'Do you mind if I have a bit of that?' I ask him. 'Suddenly I feel like something stronger than wine.'

'Go for it,' he says, holding out the glass.

I take Ash's glass and swallow a large gulp of the whisky, then another, and a third until the glass is empty.

'Wow,' Ash says, looking impressed. 'You OK?'

'Yeah, I'm fine. Let's get out of here, shall we? It's starting to feel a bit stuffy.'

It's quite hot in the bar, but for once the reason I'm feeling suffocated has nothing to do with the place being crowded or because I've picked up the scent of a bunch of flowers. It's because I'm aware of Jake's eyes glancing across at us every few minutes.

'Sure thing,' Ash says, standing up.

We make our way out of the busy pub into the cool night air, and I stop for a moment to breathe in the fresh saltiness coming off the sea.

'You OK?' Ash asks again. 'Sorry about your brother . . . '

'Ash, I should thank you,' I say, turning towards him. 'It's the first time since I've been back in St Felix that I've been able to tell anyone that. It's as if you've released something in me, something that needed to be set free.'

'Really?' Ash says, moving towards me slightly. He reaches out his hand and gently takes a strand of my hair that's blowing in the breeze and tucks it gently behind my ear. 'Is there anything else you'd like to set free?'

His hand lingers on my jaw, his fingers stroking my skin so delicately I can hardly tell if it's him or the sea breeze caressing my face.

I look up at him and nod.

Ash leans down, his face hovers in front of mine for a second, his bright blue eyes examining my face, until they fall upon my lips, then he leans forward that tiny bit more and I feel his lips on mine . . .

# Twenty-five

## Sweet Pea – Delicate Pleasures

The next morning I wake up in my bed at the cottage and see the wonky ceiling above me.

Nothing odd in that, I do it most mornings as soon as the sun starts creeping through the thin curtains to wake me. What is odd, I realise, suddenly remembering last night, is the extra person lying naked next to me in the bed.

I turn my head carefully so as not to disturb him, and see Ash sleeping peacefully, his face turned towards me on the pillow.

*Oh God . . . I hadn't.*

But I had.

Last night after he'd kissed me outside the pub, Ash and I had gone a bit mad. We'd run along the harbour, then up over the other side of the hill that St Felix is perched on, to the beach, where we'd taken off our shoes and run laughing and kissing along the length of the sand, until Ash had taken me in his arms and kissed me so hard and fast that we almost did it right there on the sand.

But I still had a little bit of sense about me, and managed to peel him off my body long enough to suggest we might have a more comfortable time if we headed back to the cottage.

When we'd got back we'd crept in quietly in case Amber was still awake. She'd told me before I went out that she was going to take a bath, do some meditation, and have an early night.

So Ash and I had sneaked straight into my room, trying to be as quiet as we could. It did cross my mind I was being a bit reckless – after all, I hardly knew Ash, and he was a fair bit younger than me. I may have done many things in my life that were irresponsible, but sex wasn't usually something I messed about with.

But this felt right. I needed to let off some steam, and Ash, apart from being very attractive, had been the catalyst to make me want to do so.

And best of all, I didn't think about Jake once.

It had been quite some time since I'd woken up with someone in my bed next to me, and it felt as awkward today as it had always done.

I wonder how sound a sleeper Ash is. I move, and he doesn't stir. So I pull back the sheets and sit up. He shuffles a bit, but his eyes don't open. So I lift myself slowly off the bed and grab my PJs from the chair. I wish I had a dressing gown I could sexily slip into, but I hadn't expected to be staying this long in St Felix when I'd originally packed, so it isn't something I have the luxury of this morning. I take one last look at him still sleeping, and then I slip out of the door.

'Well, well, well!' Amber says, eyeing me from her place at the sink as I enter the kitchen. 'Look who snuck out of the love nest early!'

'What do you mean?' I ask, wandering over to the fridge to get juice.

'Come on, Poppy, I may be a bit ditsy sometimes, but I'm not deaf. I heard you sneaking lover boy into the cottage last night.'

'Ah . . . that.'

'Yes that,' she says, as she dries her hands on a towel. 'Well?' she whispers. 'What's he like?'

I'm surprised Amber isn't more shocked that I slept with Ash on what I wasn't even admitting to her was a first date.

'He's very nice,' I reply coyly.

'Nice as a person, or *nice*,' she grimaces, 'in bed. Because the two are very different things . . . '

'*Amber* . . . ' I flash my eyes at her. 'He's a nice person to be with, and . . . ' I flush. 'Pretty good in the other department too.'

'Ooh, jackpot!' she says, pulling an imaginary handle.

'Somebody won something?'

We both turn and see Ash walking through the kitchen door. His hair is dishevelled and he's pulled on his jeans, but his feet and his very well developed chest are bare.

'I think Poppy has,' Amber says, raising her eyebrows at me.

'Tea, Ash? Or coffee?' I offer.

'Coffee would be great,' he says. 'Do you mind if I jump in the shower?'

I see Amber swallow hard.

'No, go right ahead,' I tell him. 'You'll find fresh towels on the side.'

'Thanks. See you in a bit.'

'Wow,' Amber says as soon as he's gone. 'You are one lucky lady, Miss Poppy.'

'He is pretty fit, isn't he?' I can't help but smile.

'Er . . . ya!'

'I'm surprised you aren't more shocked that I brought him back here last night.'

'Nah.' Amber waves her hand. 'I knew you would.'

'How? When I was insisting to you it wasn't even a date.'

Amber taps the side of her head. 'Never doubt the powers of Amber,' she says. 'I know many, many things before they happen.'

'OK . . . ' I wave my hand, not wanting to know more. I had no need to know if she'd read her cards, or her crystals or whatever else she could find. 'But I bet you can't predict what I'm going to do next?'

'Make Ash breakfast?'

'Haha! See, that's where you're wrong.' I walk back towards the door Ash has just gone through. 'Even you couldn't predict this one, Amber. I am going to join him in the shower . . . '

'Poppy, you minx!' I hear Amber call after me as I reach for the bathroom door.

Later that day Amber and I are back in the shop waiting for a young couple, Katie and Jonathan, to arrive for their appointment with us. In a few weeks' time Daisy Chain will be providing the flowers for their wedding in a large country hotel about half an hour away from St Felix.

It's the first wedding we've been asked to do, and Amber is understandably nervous at the prospect.

'But I've never done a wedding on my own,' she said when we'd first been approached. 'Your mom always did all the organising, I just helped out.'

'You'll be fine, Amber,' I'd assured her. 'You're a brilliant florist. The bride wouldn't have specially asked for you if you weren't.'

'The bride asked for Daisy Chain to do the flowers, not me,' she'd said, still looking worried. 'It was your grandmother's reputation that sealed the deal.'

Eventually I'd managed to persuade her this was something she could do – and do well – and we'd had a preliminary meeting with the bride to discuss her requirements.

This afternoon Katie's back with her groom, Jonathan, to discuss the designs Amber has come up with for the wedding, and to confirm how many flowers will be required – plus the all-important cost.

'So,' Amber says as we wait for them to arrive, and she puts the finishing touches to a birthday arrangement for a grandmother of pale pink roses, meaning grace, and white lilies, meaning majesty. 'What's happening with you and lover boy?'

I roll my eyes as I watch her. Since Marie's visit, Amber has been quite open about her use of the flower books for guidance in her arrangements, and she will happily inform me which flowers she's using and why. The science of it – I preferred to call it that rather than magic – was fascinating, but I still preferred to let Amber deal with the actual arranging of the flowers. I wasn't ready to be that hands-on just yet, even though I had to admit I was finding being in the shop much easier these days.

'I assume you mean Ash?' I reply, pretending to be aghast. 'We've only been on one date!'

'But what a *long*, and if I might say, very *noisy* date that was.' Amber winks as she places her final stem into the green oasis holding her arrangement in place.

I blush. 'He says he'll call me, if you must know.'

'Ooh, like "I can't *wait* to see you again" call you? Or "I'll see ya around" call you?'

'I guess the first. But—' I cut Amber off before she can say anything. 'It's not anything serious. Ash isn't that kind of guy, and I'm not interested in anything too heavy right now.'

Amber shrugs. 'OK, if you say so.' But as she swivels the arrangement round on the desk to check it, she murmurs, 'Not with Ash, anyway.'

'What did you say?'

'Nothing!' she sings. 'Oh look, here's our bride and groom, I'll just take this out back.'

Katie and Jonathan appear in the doorway of the shop, and I go over to greet them.

'Hello,' I say, shaking Katie's hand. 'And you must be the happy groom,' I say to a not-too-happy-looking Jonathan, who shakes my hand dismally. 'Is everything all right?' I ask as they sit down on the chairs we've placed in a corner of the shop for our meeting. 'You seem worried.'

Katie looks at Jonathan as if she's going to burst into tears.

'The wedding is going to have to be cancelled!' she says, fighting back tears as Amber appears from the back room and hurries to join us. 'Our perfect day is off.'

'No, it's not, darling.' Jonathan puts his arm around Katie and tries to console her. 'Not yet anyway,' he says to us.

'But why?' I ask. 'What's happened?'

'The hotel has had a mix-up with our booking,' Jonathan explains, while Katie sniffs on his shoulder. 'They say they can't hold our wedding on that day because they already have another wedding booked. The other couple take priority because they paid their deposit first.'

'They can't just cancel you altogether,' I insist. 'Surely they can offer you another date instead?'

Katie shakes her head sadly. 'Not anything that works for us. It's either midweek or much later in the year – they're fully booked. That's why we wanted to hold our perfect day there, because they have such a great reputation. Plus their grounds are absolutely stunning, it would have been perfect for our photos.'

'It happens,' Amber says. 'When I was at the florist's in New York, we had a couple who got double-booked at the Plaza! Can you imagine a hotel like that double-booking you? It worked out well for them in the end though – they got married in Central Park, it was very romantic, so I hear. Much nicer than the Plaza would have been.'

'Maybe you could find somewhere else?' I suggest. We can't afford to lose this booking, it's too important, both financially and for Amber's confidence.

Jonathan shakes his head. 'Nope, everywhere local is fully booked throughout the summer. We may have to put it off until next year . . . '

Katie lets out another huge sob, and scrabbles in her bag for a tissue.

Amber produces a beautiful white lace handkerchief and passes it to her instead.

'Thank you,' Katie sniffs. 'You're both so lovely, that's why we wanted you to do our wedding. It would have been so special to have had Daisy Chain providing the flowers. My mother was a huge fan of your grandmother's way with flowers; she never stopped raving about her before she died. Your grandmother did the flowers for her funeral.'

I nod. I'm thinking. Something Amber said has given me an idea.

'How would you feel about having a different sort of wedding?' I ask tentatively, my brain still trying to keep up with all the ideas that are suddenly flooding in. 'Like Amber's New York couple?'

'How do you mean?' Jonathan asks, looking dubious.

'I have an idea... I can't promise anything, but if it works out it would guarantee you something much more memorable than a dull old country hotel. And,' I add when I see I've got them interested, 'your photos would be absolutely stunning.'

# Twenty-six

## Chamomile – Energy in Adversity

It's all very well coming up with an idea, but how on earth am I going to bring it to fruition, I wonder as I tap on the cover of my notebook with the end of my pen, and take another sip of my orange juice.

I'm sitting in the Merry Mermaid waiting for Amber. This will be our first proper meeting to discuss the wedding since I put my idea to Katie and Jonathan earlier today. The shop had been unusually busy after they'd left us – looking an awful lot happier than they'd been when they arrived – and we'd not had a chance to discuss my plan any further.

My idea was for Katie and Jonathan to hold their wedding at Trecarlan Castle. I was sure I could persuade the Parish Council to agree. Why not? The place wasn't being used for anything, and it would be a fantastic setting for a wedding.

I smile to myself as I think what Stan would make of the idea. I know he would love it. He liked nothing better than to see Trecarlan filled with people; he always said the house was miserable on its own. I knew he would agree to my idea if I could only ask him. But I didn't know where Stan was, and no one else seemed to know either. So I was just going to have to try to persuade Caroline and the rest the Parish Council to give it the green light in his absence.

'Evening, Poppy. On your own tonight?' Woody asks, standing hesitantly by my table in his civilian clothes: a navy blue sweater, dark blue jeans, and a blue-and-white check shirt.

'Yes – I mean no. I'm expecting Amber in a bit.'

Woody's eyes light up at the mention of her name.

'Why don't you sit down with me, Woody?' I say, grinning at him. 'She'll be here soon.'

Woody tries unsuccessfully to look cool about my invite. 'That's nice,' he says, hovering by the seat next to me. 'But it really doesn't bother me either way, you know?' He rubs the palm of his hand over his hair to smooth it down, and glances towards the door.

'Yeah, right, whatever you say, Woody.' I wink.

He pretends to be shocked, then drops the fake expression. 'OK, you've found me out,' he says, sliding into the seat next to me. 'I do find your American friend a very attractive lady.'

I just adore Woody's style, he's very ... *proper.* Yes, that's exactly what it is. Polite and proper should be Woody's middle names.

'I'm sorry, how impolite of me, can I get you a drink?' he asks, looking at my glass.

‘No, I’m fine just now, thank you,’ I say, lifting my half-drunk orange juice.

‘So what are you up to?’ He nods at my notebook.

‘Ah, it’s a long story.’

‘I like stories, why don’t you tell me?’ says Woody, glancing towards the door in case Amber has arrived.

I need as many people onside as possible if I’m going to persuade the council to let me do this. And it wouldn’t do any harm to have our local police constable as one of them. So I tell Woody about the couple and their setback, and my idea for the wedding.

‘What a lovely idea,’ he says when I’ve finished. ‘You have my blessing. I love a good wedding, me. I always end up crying though. Ruins my hard man reputation.’

I smile at him. ‘Yes, I bet it does.’

‘So how far have you got with your plans?’ he asks, sliding my notebook across the table. ‘Oh,’ he says, when he sees the blank page. ‘It’s still in the early stages then?’

I grimace. ‘The thing is, I’ve never done anything like this before. I really don’t know where to start.’

‘Teamwork,’ Woody says knowingly. ‘That’s what they taught us in the army. In a team: Together Everyone Achieves More.’

‘Cool, I like it. So you were in the army too?’ I ask, surprised by this. Gentle Woody as an officer of the law I can about believe. But a soldier?

‘I was before I joined the force. Not for too long, mind,’ he adds. ‘We weren’t really suited, the army and I.’

‘Yes, I can imagine that ... I mean, I think you’re much better in charge of a small seaside community like St Felix. It suits you.’

'Do you think?' Woody looks surprised.

'Yes. A place like this, you have to know how to treat people to get the best out of them. You need a *delicate* touch.'

Woody nods thoughtfully. 'Yes, I like that. I do have a delicate touch. My sarge at police training college always said I was a soft touch. I guess that's why they sent me here.'

I smile at him again. 'You bet it is.'

Lovely Woody was definitely one of my favourite people here in St Felix. Aside from being very proper, he was also kind, and very gentle and understanding with everyone who needed his help. Even though Woody didn't have a hope of ever preventing any crime here in the town, or achieving the air of authority he longed for, everyone knew Woody, and more importantly everyone loved him.

'You were saying something about team work,' I remind him.

'Ah yes. I may not have been here in the town that long, Poppy, but during that time I have learnt that places like St Felix run on committees, organisations, societies and the like. You won't get far without them onside.'

'You mean like the Women's Guild?'

'Yes, and the Parish Council.' He screws up his face. 'They're a tough nut to crack. Even I've had problems with them. Me, in my position!'

'I'm not looking forward to dealing with them – especially Caroline. I don't think she likes me very much.'

'I don't think Caroline likes many people,' says Woody. 'But you can deal with her, Poppy, I know you can. And do you know how I know?'

I shake my head.

He leans in towards me. 'Because you already have someone very important on your side.'

'I do?'

'Yes.' Woody nods keenly. 'Who in a small town such as this commands the most admiration and respect from people?'

'Erm . . . '

'Who do people look up to and listen to when they talk?'

'Clarence?' I try, hoping I've got it right with our local priest.

Woody looks dismayed, but carries on regardless: 'Yes . . . Father Claybourne is definitely *one* of your allies, *and* . . .'

There's more than one?

'Jake?' I ask, shrugging my shoulders.

Woody tries not to let his irritation show as he leans back in his chair.

'Yes, I'm sure Jake has your back too. But I feel the description applied more to myself than the local flower grower.'

'Oh! Well, it goes without saying, Woody, surely?' I reach forward and grab his hand. 'Of course I know you're on my side.'

Woody blushes and looks down at my hand holding his. 'Whatever I can do to help – you know that?'

'Ooh, what are you two up to!' Amber calls as she appears behind us, peeping over our shoulders.

Woody immediately snatches his hand away and leaps up, knocking over his chair in the process. 'Nothing! Nothing at all, Amber!'

Amber grins. 'As if, Woody. Poppy only has eyes for Jake anyway!'

Amber picks up Woody's chair for him and heads around to the other side of the table. 'Thank you, Woody,' she says, as he dives in front of her and whisks her chair back from the table. 'Very kind.'

I stare at her across the table while Woody enquires if Amber would like a drink.

'Guinness, please, Woody,' she replies, and he heads off to the bar. What?' she asks innocently, seeing my glare.

'What you said about Jake,' I hiss. 'Didn't you mean Ash?'

'Oops, sorry, slip of the tongue!' Amber grins, not looking at all embarrassed she's said the wrong name.

'Will you stop trying to get me and Jake together! We're just friends and you know it. There's nothing more going on between us and there never will be.'

'Sure, I understand,' Amber says, not looking as though she believes me.

'It's the truth!'

'And you know 100 per cent that Jake feels that way?'

'Feels that way about what?'

We both turn in the direction of the deep, gentle voice joining our conversation.

'Hey, Jake,' Amber manages first. As she turns back she pulls a face at me that Jake over her shoulder can't see.

'Feels that way about ... women buying men drinks!' I recover, breathing an internal sigh of relief. 'Amber said you were still against it, and I said you were fine about it after I bought you one last night.'

Jake looks at us, puzzled, as Woody arrives with Amber's Guinness.

'Oh, Jake, you're here.' Woody glances with dismay at the pint he's just bought for Amber. 'Can I get you anything?'

'A pint of my usual would be great, thanks, mate.' Jake pats Woody on the shoulder and sits down in his seat.

Woody sighs and heads back to the bar.

'So, no Ash tonight?' Jake asks, casually picking up a bar menu from the middle of the table.

'No, he's at a stag party in Newquay,' I tell him, feeling most awkward discussing Ash with him. 'He'll be back tomorrow.'

'Nice. Can't remember the last time I went to a stag do,' Jake says, browsing the menu. 'I'm sure he'll have fun.'

I glance at Amber. She grimaces.

'Yes, I'm sure he will,' I say tersely. Obviously Jake isn't at all bothered about Ash. My assumptions last night had been spot on.

'So, are you getting food tonight?' Jake asks, looking up from his menu.

'Erm . . . ' I turn to Amber.

She nods enthusiastically.

'Yes, why not?' I say, determined not to feel so awkward around Jake. 'We only had time for a quick snack at lunch, the shop was really busy today. I notice Richie has an ale pie on his specials board tonight, that's always good.'

'Sounds good to me!' Jake says, putting down the menu. 'What about you, Amber?'

'I'm vegetarian,' Amber says. 'I'll have whatever the veggie option is.'

'Don't you find that limiting when you go out to eat?' Jake asks with interest. 'I admire what you're doing and everything – and I love animals, don't get me wrong – but I'd miss my meat if I had to give it up.'

'It depends where you go. Most restaurants have at least one non-meat option on the menu these days, if not more.'

Jake nods. 'Well, good on you. It's a great thing you do for our animal friends.'

'Talking of which, where's Miley tonight?' I ask, suddenly missing her. Basil is back at the cottage, snuggled up in his bed. But Miley's unlikely to be doing the same.

'Bronte is making some sort of collage tonight for her art project at school, and Miley loves sticking stuff with glue. We figure it's best to give her something we don't mind being stuck down to play with, rather than finding our socks stuck to the walls when she's a bit bored one day.'

Amber and I are both laughing as Woody returns with Jake's drink.

'Cheers, Woody,' Jake says, holding up his pint of beer. 'My round next.'

We all decide on, then order, some food from Rita at the bar, then we begin chatting amiably around the pub table while we wait. The earlier awkwardness I thought might be there between me and Jake seems to melt away, and Woody and Amber are getting on very well too.

'Poppy is going to try and hold a wedding at Trecarlan,' Woody tells Jake. 'And lovely Amber is going to do all their beautiful flowers.' He smiles dreamily at Amber.

'Really?' Jake asks, looking at me in astonishment. 'How on earth are you going to do that – it's derelict, isn't it?'

'No. It's just not lived in. Mad Stan, the previous owner, had to go into a home when he couldn't live there any more.'

'*Mad* Stan?' Jake enquires. 'I've never heard him called that before.'

'That's what the locals used to call him. Stan was a bit . . . eccentric, I guess you'd call it. How long have you lived in St Felix if you don't remember Stan?'

Jake thinks. 'Erm, we moved here about seven years ago when I got the flower business, and we were here two years before . . . well, you know.'

I nod hurriedly. 'Perhaps that's why you don't remember Stan then. He must have left before you arrived.'

'Stan sounds fabulous,' Amber says. 'I love elderly people – they have so many interesting stories to tell.'

'You'd love Stan then, he was always telling stories. Not all of which I think were true.'

'You still haven't explained why you're going to hold a wedding at the castle though,' Jake persists.

I quickly fill him in on what happened in the shop earlier.

'Well, good luck with that,' he says, looking doubtful. 'I can't see Caroline letting you hold a wedding there.'

'Why not? She doesn't own Trecarlan.'

'You'd think she did the way she carries on. She's very protective of it. But then Caroline seems to have taken it upon herself to be in charge of all of St Felix.'

'Well, not this time,' I say. 'Trecarlan was Stan's house, not hers, and I intend to breathe some life back into the old place with or without Caroline Harrington-Smythe's permission!'

We talk about the wedding and Trecarlan some more, deciding that if I am going to try and hold a wedding at the castle next month, not only will I need the blessing of the Parish Council, but the help of some of the townsfolk of St Felix too.

'You need to hold a meeting,' Woody suggests. 'The people here are very helpful, and I know they'll chip in, like they did with your shop.'

Jake nods. 'He's right, whatever you might dislike about living in a tight-knit community, the people here always try to help each other when someone's in need.'

'That's what I love about this place,' Amber says affectionately, 'the closeness. Coming from New York, it's like a different world.'

'Do you miss it?' Jake asks. 'Being here in little old St Felix can hardly compare to the Big Apple.'

'I miss the energy,' Amber says. 'Nothing can compare to the buzz of Manhattan. And of course I miss my friends and family over there, big time. And I'll definitely miss New York in the fall this year.'

'Is it pretty?' Woody asks. 'I've never been to America.'

'Oh yes, very. If you go upstate, the colours are even more intense and beautiful than in the city.'

'It sounds amazing, Amber,' Woody says, hanging off her every word like a puppy waiting for a treat from its master. 'I'd love to go there one day. I'm sure it's wonderful.'

'It is, Woody, you'd love it. But St Felix is a wonderful place too, don't ever doubt that. I miss things about the States, sure, but here –' she gestures around the room – 'in this friendly pub, on the beautiful sandy beaches, walking the quaint little streets, and visiting your olde worlde harbour with its colourful boats bobbing around – it's . . . ' She searches for the right word. 'It's safe. Here in St Felix I feel safe, like nothing or no one is going to get to me.'

I notice that Amber's bottom lip is quivering as she finishes her impromptu speech. She hurriedly picks up her almost empty pint glass and drains the last of her second Guinness of the night.

'If Richie doesn't hurry up with those meals, I'll be quite tipsy soon,' she says, and her eyes are a bit misty. 'That's what you Brits say, isn't it – tipsy?'

We all nod, touched at Amber's emotional speech, but at the same time mystified.

'Right then, my round!' she announces in a tight voice. 'Same again, everyone?'

Without waiting for an answer, Amber leaps up and heads off to the bar.

'Is she OK?' Woody asks, looking worriedly after her. 'She seems a bit upset.'

I watch Amber at the bar as she waits to order from Rita.

'Yes, I think so,' I say, remembering what my mother said on the phone yesterday. 'But I have a feeling there might be a bit more to our Amber than a few crystal beads and some incense. I think she's hiding something.'

'What sort of something?' Jake asks, looking up at Amber waiting at the bar.

'I'm not sure. But knowing St Felix, whatever it is, I bet being here is already making it better.'

# Twenty-seven

## Lobelia – Malevolence

Amber and I stand together in the ballroom of Trecarlan, the evening sun filtering through the windows and highlighting the dust covering every surface, and the cobwebs hanging from each corner of the room.

'I didn't know it was this bad,' Amber says, looking around her. 'How are we going to transform this into a wedding venue?'

'We will. I've already had numerous offers of help from people in St Felix.'

The offers had started coming in that night at the pub. As soon as we'd told Rita and Richie what we were hoping to do for Katie and Jonathan, they'd immediately begun putting the word out with their customers. News spreads fast around St Felix, and I'd been inundated with people volunteering to help with the cleaning-up process, or offering to lend a hand with the décor, music and catering.

So all I had to do now was turn the offers into something

concrete and we'd be away. I'd called an emergency meeting of the Parish Council to discuss what I wanted to do, and we were meeting with them on Thursday to get the go-ahead.

'We're only here today,' I tell Amber, 'to work out exactly how we're going to run this. I've never done anything like it before, have you?'

Amber shakes her head. 'And to think a couple of days ago I was worrying about a few flowers! Now you've got us organising the whole wedding. How did that happen?'

'I don't know.' I shrug. 'This really isn't my sort of thing at all. I just wanted to help them, you know. They seem such a lovely couple.'

'Ahh . . . ' Amber points to my chest. 'I told you there was a heart in there somewhere, and I think we've finally found it!'

'You're hilarious,' I tell her, rolling my eyes. 'How about you get that pad out of your handbag while I stop laughing, then we can start making some notes.'

'Don't bother, Amber!' A shrill voice which sounds worryingly like Caroline's calls across the ballroom. 'Because no wedding is going to be held here.'

We both turn to see Caroline striding across the ballroom floor wearing a navy Barbour jacket and green Hunter wellington boots.

'What makes you think you can tell us what to do?' I snap, annoyed that she's already trying to ruin things. Caroline and I haven't had much to do with each other since my first night here in St Felix, but I've bumped into her enough around the town, and heard so many negative things about her from people that I know her reputation is well deserved. She could make real trouble for us if she put her mind to it.

'Because the Parish Council simply won't allow it,' Caroline says, untying a paisley scarf from her head. 'You don't have a licence, for one thing.'

'A licence?' Amber asks, bewildered.

'Yes, my American friend,' Caroline gloats, patting her hair into place. 'A building here in England needs to be approved by the local council to make it legal to hold a civil wedding ceremony on the premises. If you try to hold your wedding here it will be illegal and I shall have you arrested.'

'Oh really?' I ask, trying not to look smug.

'Yes, I think you'll find that's the law,' Caroline smirks, folding her arms in front of her tiny chest.

I smile back at her with equal warmth. 'Except, Caroline, we don't want to hold the ceremony here, only the reception. And *that*, as far as I'm aware, does not require express permission from the council, and is most certainly *not* illegal, now is it?'

Caroline's body stiffens slightly but she continues unabated.

'It makes no difference,' she says, with a toss of her head. 'You will still need a licence for entertainment and presumably you will want to serve alcohol too. I shall oppose you at every turn.'

'I think you'll find those are matters for the district council, not the parish council,' I counter, glad I've done my research. 'And as far as I'm aware, Caroline, even you don't have any control over them?'

Caroline eyes me coldly, knowing she's beaten.

'What have you got against us anyway?' I continue in a gentler tone. I honestly didn't understand why Caroline was being like this about the wedding. 'This is nothing to do with you, why be so mean about it?'

But Caroline doesn't follow my lead; instead she sighs

dramatically and rolls her eyes. 'One,' she begins, 'Trecarlan is part of St Felix's history, and I see no good reason a historic building such as this should be desecrated by using it as nothing more than a party venue. And two,' she continues before I can respond, 'two is more personal.' She gives me an icy stare. 'The Carmichael family have never got on with the Harringtons, so annoying you, Poppy, is my way of avenging past betrayals.'

She looks at us both for a moment before nodding smartly, her job done. 'Good day to you both,' she says swivelling around as best she can in her Wellington boots and striding off across the ballroom.

'W-what?' I stutter in disbelief as I watch her leave. 'What on earth are you talking about – betrayals?'

'Ask your friend Stan!' she calls, not looking back. 'A little bird tells me you two were quite pally in the past.' Then before she disappears out of the door she turns to face us one last time. 'Oh, wait a minute,' she says, a triumphant glint in her eyes, 'you don't even know where he is, do you? Well, goodbye, girls. And good luck!'

'What on earth is she talking about?' Amber asks, looking at me aghast. 'Past betrayals? I feel like I'm in one of your English costume dramas and we should be wearing corsets and long dresses ... Come to think of it, that might be fun!'

'I have absolutely no idea, Amber,' I sigh, still staring after Caroline. 'But I'm not about to let her stop us. I have an idea how we can get the approval we need to hold a wedding reception at Trecarlan – and at the same time hopefully discover just what on earth she's going on about.'

'How are we going to do that?'

'By finding a very dear friend of mine.'

# Twenty-eight

## Verbascum – Take Courage

After our encounter with Caroline, I speak to Ash about the possibility of visiting Babs at her cottage, and he arranges for me to visit his granny the next day.

Ash and I are getting on just fine. He's lovely to spend time with – always super chilled and relaxed. Sometimes I take Basil to the beach to watch Ash and his mates surf the waves that wash up on to St Felix's long stretch of sand, and afterwards, if the weather's good, Ash and I picnic on the beach together, snuggled up on, or under, a blanket with Basil contentedly nibbling on a cheese sandwich at our side.

Ash tries on more than one occasion to get me to mount a board with him. But I insist my surfing days are over, and I'm happy to watch him ride the waves while I enjoy being out in the fresh air.

I surfed with Will. I don't surf any more.

I hadn't realised how much I missed the taste, smell and feel of sea air until I returned to St Felix. Living in London and the various other cities I've inhabited over the years, I'd got used to the tight, smoggy air. I'd forgotten how clean, fresh and invigorating sea air was, and now I couldn't get enough of it.

'I'm just going to see Babs!' I call to Amber as Basil and I get ready to leave the shop. 'Are you sure you'll be OK on your own?'

'Yes, I'll be fine. Good luck, Poppy,' she replies, reappearing from the back room where she's currently creating a bouquet for a young man to give to his girlfriend when he proposes. Word of Amber's magical bouquets has begun to spread, and we've been getting requests from all over Cornwall from people wanting our help. 'I really hope Babs can tell you something about this Stan,' Amber says. 'And not just for the sake of the wedding. It sounds to me like you really need to see him again.'

Before I can answer, the shop door opens and our fifth customer of the day walks in. And it's only 10 a.m.! We'll have to take on someone else to help us if this continues; Amber can't possibly look after the shop and arrange all the flowers, and it's inevitable there are going to be times when it's impossible for us both to be there.

'I've heard you do *special* bouquets?' the woman says to Amber as Basil and I head out the door. 'My mother has been ill recently, and . . . '

Basil and I leave Amber to it – this is most definitely her department.

We've got to the point we can always tell when a customer's

going to ask for one of Amber's special bouquets. Often they'll hover outside the shop window for a while, looking shifty, then they'll come in and pretend to browse for a bit. Once they finally get up the courage to ask if we could make them up a 'special' bouquet, I hand them over to Amber, who very discreetly asks what their issue is, then disappears out back to consult her books before creating the perfect bouquet for them, always tied with a white ribbon.

As Basil and I walk down the street, waving to Ant and Dec as we pass – the bakery also seems exceptionally busy today – I think about Stan.

Amber's right, of course. I should have tried to locate Stan as soon as I arrived in St Felix, but what with the shop and then Basil to look after ...

No, I couldn't kid myself; these were simply excuses. I hadn't gone in search of Stan because I knew that seeing him again would remind me of past times here in St Felix with Will. Even though I'd managed to talk to Ash about Will, I knew Stan would want to reminisce even more, and I wasn't sure I was ready for that yet.

But I had to do this. It was important, not only for Katie and Jonathan, but for me too.

So as we walk towards Babs's cottage, pausing occasionally so Basil can do his thing, my mind is very definitely on the past.

'Oi! Your dog!'

Shaking myself from my memories, I see Basil about to cock his leg against the side of a mobility scooter. 'Gosh, I'm so sorry,' I tell an elderly lady carrying a string bag full of shopping. 'Basil!' I pull him away from the wheels. 'No!'

'Oh, it's Basil,' the lady says, easing herself on to the seat of the scooter. 'I haven't got my glasses on, I didn't recognise you, lad.' She reaches in her handbag and pulls out a pair of spectacles. 'There, that's better,' she says, putting them on. 'Now,' she bends down to stroke him, and Basil, as always, laps up the fuss. 'I haven't seen you in ages, boy. How are you?'

She looks up at me. 'Poppy?' she says. 'Is that you? You were just a young girl the last time I saw you.'

I look more closely at her.

'Babs!' I exclaim. 'I'm just on my way to your cottage.'

Babs nods. 'That's right, young Ash said you were coming over. I was just getting some cakes in.' She rolls her eyes, 'Can't even make me own these days.'

'Oh dear, how are you? Ash said you hadn't been too well lately.'

'I have to admit, I've seen better days,' she says, gesturing to her buggy. 'But you have to get on with it, don't you? I heard you were back in town and looking after Rose's shop. I'd have popped in, but I haven't been out much lately; touch of bronchitis hit me real bad, it did. But I've escaped today and been allowed out on me own for a while.'

'Well done.' I haven't seen Babs for so long I barely recognise her. She's lost a lot of weight, and has got a lot greyer in the hair department. 'I heard about Stan,' I say, wondering if it's too soon to mention this. 'How he decided to sell the castle and move away. It's a shame it had to come to that. He loved that place.'

'Hmmph,' Bab says. 'Or so he let everyone believe.'

'How do you mean?'

Babs looks furtively up and down the street, then she beckons for me to lean in so she can lower her voice.

'Stan changed in the years after you stopped coming to Trecarlan, Poppy – and not for the better, either. He was getting on a bit, and I don't think he was playing with a full deck a lot of the time.'

'Oh, poor Stan. What happened?'

'Well, I'm not one to gossip, as you know . . . ' She looks shiftily about her. 'But Stan got in with a bad crowd. There was a lot of drinking went on up at the castle, and –' she looks up and down the street, but the weather has done one of its U-turns and there are ominous rainclouds gathering overhead, so anyone who'd been out enjoying the sunshine first thing this morning has already taken shelter. 'Gambling,' she whispers, so quietly I can barely hear her.

'Really?' I can't imagine Stan running the sort of debauched gambling ring Babs seemed to be implying.

Babs nods. 'Regularly held parties up there, he did. He'd let all 'n' sundry into the castle. He asked me to cater for his parties, but I said no. My job was to look after him, not a load of hoolie-billies with more money than sense. So,' Babs puts her hand to her chest, 'he got in outside caterers!'

Stan might as well have let in serial killers. This would have been the ultimate insult to Babs.

'That's awful, Babs. I can't imagine Stan doing that – not to you. He loved you and Bertie.'

'Hmmph.' Babs folds her arms across her chest. 'You'd think so, after all we did for him. But the way he treated us, we were obviously just servants to him – nothing more.'

'What are you talking about – what did he do?'

This was all very odd. It didn't sound like the Stan I remembered at all.

'Well, one night Stan had another of his parties. Me and Bertie weren't involved, of course. But we heard he had another load of these hoolies staying with him – from *London*.'

Babs spits the word out as if it's toxic. 'They came up in their fancy cars, lording it up all over St Felix before they even went to the party. I reckon they pissed off half the town that day with their airy-fairy ways. Sorry for me language, dear.'

'Don't worry about it. What happened next?'

'I don't know exactly what happened when they went up to the castle that night, I can only surmise.'

'Surmise away.'

'Well, there was the usual carryings on: too much drink and goodness knows what else. But the outcome was, Stan lost all his money – in a card game.'

'No!'

'Sadly 'tis true. It wasn't long after that Stan moved out, and we lost our jobs.' She purses her lips. 'Me and Bertie had given that man our lives, and then he turns around and does that to us.'

'B-but it doesn't make sense,' I say, trying to piece all this together. 'Stan would never have risked his home and your livelihood on a card game.'

Stan may not have had any family, and few friends, but I know he cared about his 'helpers'. This just doesn't fit with the man I remember.

'Them's the facts, Poppy. I've told you all I know, and some what I heard on the quiet.' She sighs. 'My Bertie took ill shortly after all this went on, so maybe we were best out of there as it turns out. When he died, they said it was a stroke caused by heart irregularities. I still say he died of a *broken* heart from being evicted from the place he loved. He'd worked at Trecarlan since he was a nipper. But you know Bertie: he vowed he was going to carry on looking after the gardens, even though we wasn't being paid no more. Bless his soul.'

'I was so sorry when I heard about Bertie,' I say. 'Ash told me.'

She smiles a toothy grin. 'I hear you and my grandson have been seen stepping out together. I may have been banished to my cottage for the past few weeks, but I still keep my ear to the ground.'

I feel my cheeks turning red.

'He's a good lad, is my Ash,' Babs says. 'He's a looker for sure, a bit like his granddad was when he was younger. But his heart is in the right place. He'll watch out for you.'

'Thank you,' I tell her, but I want to ask more about Stan. Something doesn't sound right about all this. 'So did you ever see Stan again after that?'

Babs shakes her head. 'No, he went to a home Up North somewhere. What with that and Bertie, I just never got around to visiting him.' She leans in towards me. 'Tell the truth, there was bad feeling, you know, after we lost our jobs, and then I lost Bertie. So I didn't really want to go. Then after a while it seemed too late to try and make amends.'

'Of course, I quite understand in the circumstances. I don't suppose you know which home it was, do you?' I ask hopefully. Maybe I could phone them.

'No, dear, sorry. Lou might know though. I think she visits him occasionally.'

That's good of Lou to travel so far to visit Stan, I think; they must have been close.

'Thanks, I'll ask the next time I see her.'

'You were always a good girl, Poppy,' Babs says, looking up at me from her scooter. 'Mischievous, but good at heart. I was sorry to hear about your brother – terrible business.'

'Yes ... well ... you know.' I look down at Basil, who's having a rest on the floor beside us. 'Looks like Basil wants to get going,' I say, tugging on his lead to wake him up.

Basil yawns and grudgingly looks up at me.

'It's nice seeing you again, Babs. Now you're up and about, you'll have to call in and see us at the shop sometime.'

'Oh yes, I'd like that. You must pop in and have a cup of tea with me, too.' She nudges me. 'And you look after that grandson of mine, you hear? He's a good boy, that one. Don't worry too much about that Stan, he was always a bit of a rascal, even when he was young. It was going to catch up with him one day.'

I wave to Babs as she heads off on her scooter, bobbing along the cobbled street.

'Right, Basil,' I say, making a U-turn in the street. 'Looks like we're off to see your old mate, Lou.'

'Hi, Poppy, Hi, Basil,' Lou says, opening the door to greet us. Lou is wearing painting overalls, has her hair tied up in a scarf and is holding a paintbrush.

'Oh, have I caught you at a bad time?' I ask as she stands back to let me in.

Lou's hall, which was full of trinkets and pictures the last time I was here, is stripped bare, and half the walls are painted blue.

'No, I could do with a break, and it's always a joy to see Basil.' She rests the brush on an open tin of emulsion and bends down to fuss him. 'The puppies are in the kitchen, if you want to go and see them? Basil will be fine with them now.'

We head into Lou's kitchen to find a riot of activity, as five puppies bound around, chewing on brushes, rolling in blankets, and generally getting up to mischief.

I let Basil off his lead, and he goes over to investigate.

'Tea?' Lou asks, filling the kettle.

'No, I can't stay long. I have to get back to the shop. Amber's got a lot on at the moment.'

'It's all going well then?' Lou asks.

'Yes, it's definitely picking up.'

'Good, I'm glad to hear it,' Lou says, putting the kettle on to boil and turning to face me. 'I had a feeling things would improve. Now, what can I do for you? I'm sensing this isn't simply a social call.'

'Do you know where Stan is?' I ask without any preamble.

'Yes, of course I do. Why, would you like to visit him?'

I nod.

Lou goes to a drawer and pulls out a white business card. 'Here,' she says, handing it to me. 'Camberley House, it's a lovely residential home up in Bude.'

'Bude! But I thought Stan was a long way away – Babs said "Up North".'

Lou smiles. 'Well, it is North Cornwall.'

'If I'd known he was so close, I'd have gone before,' I say, staring at the card.

'Would you, though?' Lou asks gently. 'Maybe you've waited until it's the *right* time to go, for you and for him?'

'How do you mean?'

'Poppy, you've had a lot to deal with since you arrived here in St Felix, and I'm not just talking about the shop and dear old Basil. Perhaps you weren't ready to see Stan before.'

I look across the kitchen at her.

'But now, Poppy,' she says deliberately. 'Now I know you are.'

# Twenty-nine

## Chrysanthemum – Truth

I'm back in the Range Rover again, heading out of St Felix for the first time in ages.

I drive along the narrow twisty roads, thinking all the time about Stan, Will, and what I'm going to do today.

When I arrive in Bude, the satnav helpfully directs me through the busy streets teeming with holidaymakers, until on the other side of the town we drive down a quiet residential road, and I'm instructed I've 'reached my destination'.

Camberley House is a large modern bungalow situated on an extensive plot amongst immaculately mown lawns and perfect flower beds. I park my car on the gravel drive and climb out. As I do an elderly man smiles at me as he hobbles past with the assistance of a wooden stick.

'Reception is that way,' he calls, pointing in the direction of the front door with his stick. 'You look a bit lost, dearie.'

'Ah, thank you,' I say, looking towards a frosted glass door. 'Yes, it's my first time here.'

'Well, I'm sure whoever you've come to visit will be glad to see you,' he says, nodding. 'We usually are.'

He gives me a quick salute and hobbles on his way, so I head towards reception.

Just inside the door I find a cosy hallway with a polished wooden table acting as a reception desk.

'Good afternoon,' says a smartly dressed lady sitting behind the table. 'Welcome to Camberley House. How can I help you?'

'I'd like to see Stan, please, if I may?'

'Stan?' she questions. 'Do you have a surname?'

'Er ... ' I hadn't thought about this. I only knew him as Mad Stan the Pasty Man. 'I don't actually know his surname.'

'Hmm ... ' The woman looks quizzically at me. 'We can't let just anyone in here, you know, there are rules, and our residents' care and safety is foremost here at Camberley.'

'Oh yes, I completely understand. It's just I used to know Stan a long time ago, when he lived down in St Felix. Do you know Trecarlan Castle at all?' I ask hopefully.

The woman looks blankly at me.

'A woman called Lou comes to visit him quite a lot?'

She carries on looking stonily back at me from her desk.

'Do you have a Stan here that likes to eat pasties?' I try as a last resort.

The woman's face lights up. 'Oh, you mean Stanley,' she says, smiling now. 'Of course, Stanley can never get enough pasties, even though his teeth don't really like them these days. Who should I say is calling for him?'

'Poppy,' I tell her quickly before she changes her mind. 'But he might not remember me. Like I said, I haven't seen him since I was fifteen.'

She rings a bell, and another, younger woman, this time in a green uniform, appears.

'Melanie, can you please tell Stanley that Poppy is here to see him.'

Melanie nods. 'Certainly.' And she disappears back where she came from.

'She won't be a moment, please take a seat.' The receptionist gestures to a brocade chaise longue behind me.

I sit down awkwardly on the seat, and look around while the receptionist returns to her computer screen.

This is all very efficient, and not at all what I was expecting. After what Babs had told me about Stan losing all his money, I'd wondered if I might find him living in some ramshackle old folks' home, with paint peeling off the walls and incompetent staff.

Camberley House, from what I've seen so far, seems very well run, although I knew from reading and hearing stories about residential homes that what you saw on the surface wasn't always the real story.

'Stanley will see you,' Melanie says, reappearing. 'Please come this way.'

I follow Melanie through a long corridor full of closed doors, and I can't help wondering what's behind them.

'Just offices,' she says, guessing what I'm thinking. 'Nothing sinister, I can assure you.'

'Sorry,' I apologise. 'You hear so many awful stories about places like this.'

'Yes, I know. It's despicable what goes on in some care homes. The trouble is, we all get tarred with the same brush when those stories come out, when the truth is there are so many homes out there giving wonderful care to the elderly and infirm. You just don't hear about the good ones.' She pauses at a glass door and pushes it open. 'Here we are: our day room.'

I follow Melanie into the room, and instead of a room full of elderly folk sitting around in high-backed chairs with blankets over their legs, I am surprised to find a hub of activity.

There are a number of white- and grey-haired octogenarians playing pool and table tennis, a group of residents playing Scrabble, and a couple of folk on computers at the side of the room surfing the Internet.

'Now,' she says looking around, 'where's Stanley got to? He was by the pool table a few minutes ago. Ah, I spy him, he's over by the window, waiting for you.'

We walk through the sea of movement to two armchairs by a window, and then I see him.

'Poppy, my girl!' Stan struggles to stand up from the chair, so Melanie helps him. 'I can't believe it's you after all this time.' He hugs me and I feel the fragility of his body against mine.

'Stan, it's good to see you,' I say as I stand back to get a better look at him.

The Stan I remember was tall and broad with a loud voice and bellowing laugh. This Stan seems to have shrunk in stature; I'm taller than he is, and his voice these days is croaky and weak.

'I'll leave you two to it,' Melanie says. 'Just call me when you've had enough of this one's tall tales.'

'Melly, my girl,' Stan says, easing himself down into the chair, 'you know every word that leaves my lips is the truth.'

'Aye, and I'm Kate Middleton,' she says, smiling. 'I'll just go and polish my crown.'

Stan smiles after her as she weaves her way back through the room, speaking to the residents as she goes. 'She's a good lass is that one. Sit down, child, and let's catch up.'

Stan tells me all about his life at the home. All the activities they get up to, outings they have, and friends he has made over his years at Camberley. He has to pause to remember sometimes, his mind not recalling as fast as he'd like it to. But I listen patiently, giving him time to reminisce.

'So now I've told you all about me, what about you?' Stan asks. 'What have you been doing all this time – and more importantly, how are you getting on in that flower shop? I half thought you might bring me a posy, like the old days.'

'No, no flowers, but I did bring you this,' I say, reaching down into my handbag. I produce a paper bag and pass it to Stan.

'Ah, this is just like the old days,' he says, sniffing inside the bag. 'Fresh this morning?'

I nod. 'From the Blue Canary bakery.'

Stan looks puzzled.

'Oh, it used to be Mr Bumbles, but it has new owners now. They're very good though,' I assure him.

'I'll save it for my tea then.' He smiles, putting the bag down on the table next to him. 'The pasties they give you here aren't much cop – supermarket rubbish. That will go down a treat, thank you. So tell me all about Daisy Chain. Lou said you were back in St Felix. Such a shame about your grand-mother though – fine, fine woman she was.'

'Yes, she was,' I agree, thinking about her.

'But now the shop has fresh blood – a new chance to shine, and it will shine brightly with you at the helm, I'm sure.'

I shrug. 'Perhaps. We're doing all right.'

'Only all right? Are you using the *books*?'

'You know about those?'

'Of course I do. That shop has been special since the original Daisy took it on in Victorian times. She used the Victorian language of flowers to produce her own form of the magic, but the whole shop is charmed. Shall I tell you a story?' he asks, his eyes lighting up.

'Sure,' I say, remembering how Stan used to love telling us tales as children. Much as I want to get on to how he ended up moving away from Trecarlan, I guess it can wait for a few minutes.

'Well, the old story goes that the ground the shop was built on was once blessed by the Cornish sorceress, Zethar. Zethar was being tried for witchcraft, but she escaped her persecutors, fled, and found herself in St Felix. The townsfolk took pity on her plight, and hid and looked after her until her persecutors had ridden through the town. In return for their kindness, Zethar cast a spell over the building she had been hidden in and the ground beneath it, saying that whoever inhabited any building built on the land in the future would be protected from harm. Then she cast a final spell over the whole town, saying that anyone who came here would always be safe, and find happiness and contentment within its boundaries whatever their plight might be, and that's how St Felix got its name. Because Felix means—'

'Happy!' I finish for him. 'Yes, I'd forgotten, but I did know that. But really, Stan,' I say gently, 'I'm not eight years old now. Do you expect me to believe that fairy tale you just told me?'

'Whether you choose to believe it is up to you, but it's the truth,' Stan says, leaning back in his chair.

I know I should leave it. Stan is an elderly man, what harm would it do for him to believe his stories were true? But I just can't, fairy tales, myths and legends didn't sit any easier with me than Amber's holistic and spiritual ways, or the notion that certain types of flowers could heal people – even though I'd heard first-hand accounts of it happening.

'How do you know it's the truth?' I ask. 'That story is centuries old; someone could have made it up when they were a bit bored one day.'

Stan regards me through a pair of sharp sea-green eyes. 'You don't change,' he says eventually. 'Even as a young girl you were always questioning my tales.'

'Was I?'

Stan nods. 'Your brother would just sit and listen politely, but you,' he smiles, 'you would always want proof, and the reasons why.'

I open my mouth to reply, but Stan continues:

'And that's good, Poppy. You *should* question things; you should want to know why. *Why* is a very difficult thing to answer sometimes, though . . . ' He watches me for a few seconds. 'Is the magic working?' he asks. 'In the shop, first of all?'

'Well . . . ' I choose my words carefully, 'Amber's special bouquets are proving very popular.'

'Does she tie them with a white ribbon?'

'Yes.'

Stan smiles approvingly. 'And secondly, is the magic of St Felix working for you?'

'How do you mean?'

'Are you feeling better since you returned? After what happened, it was understandable that you'd stay away. But I didn't think it would be for so long. I don't think any of us did.'

'Yes ... well ... ' I mumble, 'it was difficult to come back ... after Will.'

'Fine young man, he was. Honourable, trustworthy, fine-looking fella, too. The good always die young.'

I swallow hard.

'I heard about Bertie,' I say, deliberately changing the subject. 'Such a shame. But Babs is doing well. I saw her the other day.'

Stan's cheery demeanour immediately changes and his face fills with sorrow as he remembers. 'They were good helpers to me. I never meant for them to lose their jobs when I left the estate. The woman she said she'd keep them on. She gave me her word.'

I knew Stan wouldn't have left Babs and Bertie in the lurch.

'Which woman, Stan?' I ask. 'Who said she'd keep Babs and Bertie on?'

Stan furrows his brow. 'I'm trying to recall her name. Bossy woman, loud voice – shrill, you know?'

Oh, I knew all right.

'Was her name Caroline, by any chance, Stan? Caroline Harrington-Smythe?'

'Yes, that's her. She said she'd guarantee them their jobs if I left the Parish Council in charge of Trecarlan.'

Caroline strikes again.

'But why *did* you leave the castle, Stan?' I hesitate before continuing: 'Did you lose all your money in a card game?'

Stan's head drops, and he looks down into his lap.

'The truth please, Stan,' I ask him gently. 'I need to know.'

'The truth is I was broke, Poppy,' Stan says, lifting his head, sadness etched all over his face. 'I no longer had the funds to run Trecarlan. It costs a lot of money to run an estate like that.'

'I'm not surprised you were broke if you were gambling all your money away. Babs told me about your parties.'

'Ah, dear old Babs, she always did like to gossip. Yes there were parties, parties that I hosted at Trecarlan. There was a lot of money won and lost in that house during that time. But I wasn't the one gambling, I was merely allowing others to do so on my premises. It wasn't legal, I know, but it was lucrative for me and for Trecarlan. It allowed me to keep hold of my beloved home for a while longer.'

Stan looks wistful as he thinks about his former home.

'The castle was badly in need of repair; there were cracks in places there shouldn't be. Big cracks that, left untreated, were making the whole building unstable. I had two choices: sit by and watch the place fall down around me, or take a chance on something illegal and allow those parties to go ahead.'

'So what happened?' I prompt, feeling sorry for him but at the same time wanting to know the truth.

'There was a police raid one night – tip-off, apparently. Luckily I got off with a fine; the judge was lenient with me because of my age and my reputation as . . . how can I put it?

A tad mad!' he winks. 'But the fine was bad enough. It meant I had no money left for the estate, no way of making any more money, so I had no choice but to leave and come here to Camberley to live. Luckily, I had a few things from the castle I could sell to fund my fees for a few years, but it won't last for ever.'

Stan looks at me with a mixture of fear and dread in his eyes. 'When that money runs out, Poppy, I'll have to leave my friends here, and . . . ' Stan swallows hard. 'To tell you the truth, I'm not sure what will become of me,' he says, his voice trailing away. He pats his weak legs. 'These things don't work properly any more. I'm hardly in a position to look after myself.'

'Oh, Stan,' I say, leaning forward to take his hand. 'It won't come to that. I won't let it.'

Stan grips my hand. 'Poppy, it's lovely to see you again. Really, I can't tell you what it means to me. But I'm not your concern. You have a life of your own. Responsibilities.'

'That's where you're wrong, Stan,' I tell him, looking straight into his kind old eyes. 'You looked after Will and me when we were young, and it's time for me to return the favour. You, Stan, are now my responsibility, and I won't hear otherwise!'

# Thirty

## Orange – Generosity

'We have to get ready to leave,' I tell Ash as he tries to prevent me climbing out of bed. It's 6.30 p.m. on a Wednesday evening, and Ash was only supposed to be 'popping round for a bite to eat', before we headed out to the Merry Mermaid for a meeting about the Trecarlan wedding. But as so often happens when he 'pops round', we'd ended up in bed, and now I'm running extremely late.

'Let's stay and snuggle a bit longer?' Ash pleads. 'It's comfortable here, and the weather outside is shit. Why do you want to leave?'

'I don't *want* to leave,' I tell him, stroking his hair as he holds me in his muscular arms. 'I *have* to. I can't miss this meeting tonight, it's our final one before the wedding on Saturday.'

Stan had given his permission for us to hold a wedding at

Trecarlan, silencing Caroline and the Parish Council for the time being. Several members of the council had come to offer their help with the wedding, so I knew my problem was definitely with Caroline. But I still hadn't a clue why.

In an effort to coordinate all the helpers, I'd taken Woody's advice about teamwork and had attempted to form a wedding committee – not very successfully to begin with.

As Jake had predicted, everyone had been keen to volunteer their services to help the young couple out, and the tiny village hall had been packed when we held our first meeting. But trying to channel all their ideas and enthusiasm into action had proved tricky. In the end I'd asked if people could separate themselves into those that only wanted to help out on the day, and those who'd like to form a committee with me to organise the wedding in advance, and asked them to put their names down on two pieces of paper accordingly.

The subsequent meetings of the newly formed committee had been much more successful, and I was happy with the way things were coming along. But even though by this stage they could easily have coped without me, I didn't want to abandon them tonight. To my surprise, I was actually enjoying organising the wedding.

'Please?' Ash asks, his head tipped to one side as he looks at me.

'No . . . you're not going to persuade me this time. I have to go.'

'Not even if I do this?' Ash asks, manoeuvring himself in the bed so he can begin gently kissing my neck.

'No . . . ' I protest, even though I can feel myself succumbing to his charms.

'Or this?' Ash asks, kissing along my neck and down on to my chest, so I shudder with anticipation.

My defences destroyed, I feel myself surrender . . .

'I'm so sorry I'm late!' I apologise, as I arrive at the reserved table in the Merry Mermaid. I notice an official-looking sign in the middle that says *Wedding Committee Only* as I hurriedly sit down on the one remaining chair.

'Are you OK, Poppy?' Lou asks. 'You look a little flushed.'

I glance at Amber, who grins at me, knowing full well where I've been. Then I can't help looking across the table at Jake.

He sees Amber grinning, then he looks at me with disappointment.

I immediately drop my eyes, and examine the neatly typed minutes in front of me. Much to my annoyance I feel my cheeks flush even redder.

'Yes, yes, I'm fine, thanks. So, where shall we begin?'

'At the beginning?' Jake says tersely, gesturing to the piece of paper in his hand. 'Willow has done a sterling job of typing up an agenda and the minutes of the last meeting.'

I look around the table for Willow. 'Thanks, Willow,' I say, smiling at her. 'That's very efficient of you.'

Willow blushes slightly. 'Well, I was voted secretary,' she says proudly.

'And you, as chair, Poppy, need to get a move on with this meeting,' Jake reminds me. 'Some of us haven't got all night.'

I glance at Jake. Gee, why is he so tetchy this evening? It couldn't just be the fact I was late, surely?

*

We work through Willow's agenda, and everything seems to be set for the big day on Saturday. Ladies from the Women's Guild, led by Harriet and Willow, are going to decorate the tables and the ballroom for the wedding reception. Rita and Richie will be catering the first two courses of the dinner and laying on a bar for the evening. Ant and Dec will be doing the desserts and of course the wedding cake. Local bands and musicians will provide the entertainment – Charlie's been busy finding suitable acts for us. So that left just one thing, which everyone strangely seemed the most excited about: the flowers.

'The flowers will make the whole event,' Belle had enthused at one of our earlier meetings, 'especially the way Amber makes them up.'

'How are your *special* arrangements going?' Lou had asked quietly, and the others had all pricked up their ears.

'They've been going very well,' said Amber. 'I'm getting more and more people asking after them all the time.'

It was true; Daisy Chain was getting busier by the day. And it wasn't only the special bouquets that were bringing people in; the more traditional floral items for weddings, christenings, birthdays and anniversaries were also in demand.

Our meeting eventually comes to a close and everyone begins clearing their stuff away. I wave across to Ash, who'd appeared during our meeting and found himself a quiet spot at the bar while we finished off. He lifts his pint and wanders over.

'How'd it go?' he asks, kissing me on the cheek, while slipping his arm around my waist.

'Good, thanks. Katie and Jonathan seem happy, anyway.' I give them a wave across the table.

Katie blows me a kiss in return.

'So, Jake, what are you doing for the wedding?' Ash asks, as Jake attempts to summon Miley so he can slip away from the meeting.

When Jake turns to face us, his eyes fall on Ash's arm placement.

'I'm providing the flowers,' he says quickly, about to turn away.

'Is that it?' Ash asks lightly. 'I'd have thought as a member of Poppy's committee you'd have been doing more than that?'

Jake eyes me briefly, before returning his gaze to Ash.

'And I'd have thought as Poppy's boyfriend you'd have been doing a bit more to help than propping up the bar.'

'Good point, mate,' Ash agrees, lifting his pint. 'Poppy, your wish is my command. I'll do *anything* you say.' He winks at me, and I know he's not talking about the wedding.

Unfortunately, so does Jake. He deliberately turns away and engages Belle in conversation. Belle seems more than happy to oblige.

'Charming,' Ash says. 'Seriously, though, Pops, what *can* I do? I feel I'm letting you down.'

'Of course you're not,' I reply, my mind still on Jake. Is Ash's presence bothering him that much? Or is this just my heart overriding my brain when it comes to Jake? I haven't seen much of him lately. Other than helping out with the wedding, and delivering flowers to the shop, Jake appears to have been giving me a wide berth. 'There'll be something for you to do on Saturday for sure.'

'Right, until then my job will have to be keeping the boss happy, won't it?' he says, kissing my neck.

'You're doing a very good job of that already,' I tell him, and as I reach up to kiss him, I try to erase all thoughts of Jake permanently from my mind.

# Thirty-one

## Stephanotis – Happiness in Marriage

The wedding, to my absolute delight – is a huge success.

In the days beforehand we'd cleaned, scrubbed, and polished the areas of the castle that would be on show to the guests, with help from the local Brownies, Guides, Cubs and Scouts. Then teams of ladies from the Women's Guild had decorated the entrance hall with homemade bunting and ribbons, and the ballroom with white tablecloths, shiny cutlery and pristine white crockery, to brighten up the mahogany tables we'd found hidden in cupboards at the side of the ballroom.

Caroline has tried to be involved, as I'd thought she might, making sure people did not stray away from the areas of the castle I'd agreed with the Parish Council would be used for the wedding. When she's tried to take over anything else, I've been quick to step in and put her in her place. Something she has not taken kindly.

Amber and a small team of helpers have decorated both the ballroom and the castle entrances with a mixture of flowers that are perfect for a wedding: pinks – pure love; stephanotis – happiness in marriage; pink roses – grace; purple roses – enchantment; calla lilies – modesty; and stocks – you will always be beautiful to me. The flowers look fabulous, and everyone has been commenting on them. Even I can see what positivity and joy they've brought to the wedding, and to the guests who are taking such delight in them.

The mother of the groom informs me ecstatically that the Merry Mermaid's catering is absolutely delicious. And Ant and Dec's profiterole tower and extravagant wedding cake go down a storm with the wedding party and guests alike.

So the wedding is a triumph. Not only for Amber and me, but for the whole of St Felix.

It's evening now and the mahogany tables have been pushed back by a team of helpers from Bronte's school (who've also doubled as waiting staff), to allow room for dancing. The band is currently playing rock 'n' roll tunes from the fifties and sixties while people jive and twist on the dance floor.

'We did it,' Amber says, as we watch the happy couple dancing. Katie has her long white skirt pulled up above her knees so she can move with ease, and Jonathan, who's very red in the cheeks, has lost his jacket and tie and rolled his sleeves up. The crowd applaud as he scoops up his new bride and twirls with her in his arms. 'We somehow pulled off a wedding, Poppy!'

'I know, it feels great, doesn't it? Mind you, it wasn't only us – it was the whole of St Felix that pulled together to create this.'

'Just like they did with our shop. Oh, what a wonderful place this is!' Amber sighs euphorically. 'I can't imagine this happening in the States.'

'I can't imagine this happening anywhere I've ever lived either. Apart from Bronte's mates, who deserve a bit of cash for the work they've put in, everyone that came forward and offered their help did it for free. All Katie and Jonathan had to do was cover our expenses and the cost of the food. This entire wedding happened purely out of the goodness of peoples' hearts – it really is amazing.'

'You see there are some good people out there,' Amber says pointedly. 'You shouldn't judge everyone by past experiences. I know I don't.'

I turn towards her.

'No offence, Amber, but you haven't had the same background as me. Life's been pretty shitty in the past.'

'No offence, Poppy,' Amber says, sounding unusually irritated, 'but you have no idea of the shit I've had to deal with in the past either!'

Before I have a chance to apologise or ask her what she means, Amber storms off.

'Amber, wait!' I call after her, but she's already striding down the castle corridor in the direction of the kitchen. I'm about to follow her when Charlie and Bronte arrive by my side.

'Hey, how are you doing?' I ask them, glancing back to the corridor. But Amber has disappeared from sight. 'You both did a great job tonight. Well done.'

'Thanks, Poppy,' Charlie says. 'It's been a great success,

hasn't it? Do you think you might do more events like this here? It's a fab venue.'

'Oh, I don't know about that – this was only supposed to be a one-off to help Katie and Jonathan.'

'Only we'd like to hold dad's birthday party here,' Bronte blurts out.

'Bronte!' Charlie glares at her. 'Not so loud. It's supposed to be a surprise!' He leans in to me and continues in a low voice: 'It's Dad's fortieth birthday in a couple of weeks and we're organising a surprise birthday party for him. It was going to be at the Merry Mermaid, but the guest list is getting so long, I think we're going to need a bigger venue.'

'It would be sooo cool if we could hold it here,' Bronte pleads. 'Do you think the mad guy would let us?'

'Stan isn't really mad,' I tell her. 'He used to be a bit eccentric, that's all. Er . . . ' I look around the ballroom at everyone enjoying themselves. Having this many happy people in the castle today has breathed life back into Trecarlan; I could almost feel the place smiling.

'We'd do all the work,' Charlie insists. 'You wouldn't have to do anything, I promise.'

I think about Jake, and holding a birthday party here at Trecarlan for him.

'No,' I say, watching as the eagerness in their faces turns to disappointment. 'If you're going to hold a party for Jake, then I definitely want to be involved. Count me in!'

'Yay!' Bronte calls as Charlie shushes her again.

'I'll speak to you about it another time, OK?' I tell them. 'I . . . I just need to go and deal with something else right now.'

*

I'm prevented from heading straight to the kitchen by people coming over to thank me for such a great evening, and then by Katie, who pulls me on to the dance floor, grabs a microphone, and makes everyone drink a toast to me.

When I finally get to the kitchen, I find not only Amber sitting at the big heavy wooden table in the centre of the room, but Woody and Jake too.

Woody has been acting as master of ceremonies all evening, a job he's thoroughly enjoyed. Jake, as far as I was aware, hasn't been involved today other than supplying us with flowers. So I'm surprised to see him.

Amber is drinking wine straight from one of the many bottles supplied for tonight's celebrations. She lifts it up as I come into the room.

'Ah, here she is, little Miss Gloomy,' Amber says, taking another slug of the wine. 'Did you know, boys,' she addresses Woody and Jake, 'that no one's problems are ever as bad as Poppy's.'

'She's had a bit to drink,' Woody says apologetically. 'Jake and I found her like this a few minutes ago.'

'That's right, they did!' Amber says, grinning at them both. 'My knights in shining armour, aren't you?'

'Amber, I'm sorry,' I say, hurrying to her side. 'I didn't mean to say what I did. It came out wrong.'

Amber wobbles to her feet, and throws her arm around my shoulder.

'I know you didn't, my friend.' She rests her head gently on my other shoulder, but then it shoots right back up again. 'Poppy, you know you've really got to get over it . . . whatever *it* is . . . You know, the thing, the thing that makes you wear this,' she gestures to my customary, though slightly smarter than usual, black attire. 'Honey, you've got to let it go.'

I just nod. This isn't the time or place to begin justifying myself to Amber. She's obviously put a fair amount of wine away in the time it took me to get here.

'What are you doing here tonight?' I ask Jake, as Amber slides back into her seat. 'I thought you only had time to supply us with flowers today?'

'I've been helping in here,' Jake waves a hand at the large pile of washed and dried plates neatly stacked on the worktop. 'Castles tend not to have dishwashers, so I've heard.'

'Sorry,' I say, feeling guilty. 'I didn't know you wanted to be involved in the actual wedding day.'

'You never asked me, did you?'

We stare at each other for a few seconds, the silence broken only by the sound of Amber glugging from the bottle.

'Great wedding!' Woody says brightly, trying to lighten the mood. 'I'd love to get married one day.'

When no one speaks, he carries on: 'I think marriage is a wonderful institution. Solid, you know.' He brings his fist down on the table to emphasise his point, but a bit too hard. 'Ow,' he says, shaking his hand.

'It's not always that way,' Amber says, as if thinking aloud. 'Sometimes it can go very, very wrong.'

'Yes, that's also very true,' Woody says as he rubs his sore fist with his other hand. 'My parents got divorced when I was young. I was mainly brought up by my mother and my aunt.'

'No –' Amber waves her bottle over the table – 'I don't mean divorced, I mean *really* go wrong, like when violence enters the marriage.'

'That's a nasty business,' Woody says, while Jake and I just listen. 'When I was training we had to attend a domestic violence incident.'

'What did the man do?' I ask. I absolutely loathe that kind of behaviour: men thinking they can use their fists on a woman because she doesn't conform to their way of thinking. It's barbaric, no better than cavemen.

'Oh, it wasn't a man doing the beating, it was a woman,' Woody says, remembering. 'She – apologies for my language, ladies – but she beat the shit out of him. The ambulance took him to hospital and everything.'

'Did he press charges?' Jake asks.

Woody shakes his head. 'Nope. He was too embarrassed that his wife had done that to him to take it further.'

'That's terrible,' I say, shaking my head. 'If anyone tried anything like that with me, I wouldn't hesitate to ring the police.'

'You don't know that, Poppy,' Amber says quietly. 'You don't know until you're in that position.'

'Oh, I know all right, I—'

'No, you *don't!*' I'm surprised by Amber's tone. '*You* don't know, Poppy, but I do.' She looks around the table and lowers her voice. 'I know exactly how it feels because I've been there. I've been beaten. And by my own husband too.'

We all sit around the table shocked into silence by Amber's admission.

'When, Amber? When did this happen?' I'm the first to ask. I just can't believe this. I'm shocked not only by Amber's story, but by the fact I didn't even know she was married.

Amber looks up from where she's been staring at the table, and instead of the usually bright, bubbly, confident Amber, I see a vulnerable, scared young woman.

'It's been happening on and off since we got married about two years ago. Not many people know. Ray, my husband, is highly regarded in the business world in New York. But behind the scenes he's into all sorts of shady dealings. He knows how to hide anything he doesn't want the world to know about – including a beaten wife.'

I see Woody bristle.

'Did my mother know?' I ask, piecing everything together.

'Yes,' says Amber. 'I started to miss days off work, and then when I did come in I couldn't hide my bruises well enough to fool her. She was great with me though, let me stay at her place until I got back on my feet. And she helped me find a new apartment too.'

I feel a rush of love for my mother well up inside me.

'That's how I got into this new spiritual way of life. I met some people in my apartment block and they started telling me their beliefs and it all made sense to me. I was happy for the first time in ages. Everything was going great until Ray found out where I was. He tried to get me to move back home, but I refused. Like I said before, Ray has some shady connections, so I was scared of what he might do. When I told your mom, she suggested I come here to get away from everything for a while.'

I'm aware we're all staring at Amber in a mixture of amazement and horror.

Of all the things I thought Amber might have kept hidden, a violent marriage wasn't one of them. Amber was so confident, how could this have happened to her? And how had she managed to get over it and rediscover the ability to be so happy and positive about life?

'Are you safe here?' Jake asks with concern. 'Can your husband find you?'

'On his way to being an ex-husband, thank goodness.' Amber shakes her head. 'No, Poppy's mom said she'd tell them I'd run away, and she had no idea where I was. And that's what I have done in a way: run away from my problems instead of confronting them.'

'No, you haven't done that,' I insist, sitting down next to her and putting my hand over hers on the table. I knew better than anyone what it was to run away from what was bothering you. 'You've done the brave thing. You've stood up to him by making your own way in the world, and I for one am glad you did. I'd be lost without you in our little shop. I'm so pleased you came here.'

'Me too!' Woody insists, making a very un-Woody move by taking Amber's other hand in his.

'Amber, we all love having you here in St Felix,' Jake adds. 'And Poppy's mother is right: you're safe here with us. St Felix is very good at healing old wounds. I can vouch for that.'

Amber squeezes both our hands, then pulls them away to grab her bottle.

'Then let's raise a toast to St Felix,' she says. 'I don't want to remember this evening in a negative way – the wedding has been too beautiful and too romantic to finish it on a sour note. Come on, let's raise our glasses!'

As Amber quickly opens another bottle, we each grab a mug or glass and hold it out to be filled.

'To St Felix,' Amber says, as we all lift our glasses. 'To its wonderful healing ways, its gorgeous views, and its lovely, lovely people! I wouldn't want to be anywhere else in the world right now. And,' she continues, just as we're about to take a sip of our wine, 'to love. Let love always find a way of finding us!'

'To love!' we all agree, and I can't help taking a quick glance at Jake.

And I'm surprised to see he's doing the same to me.

# Thirty-two

## Goldenrod – Careful Encouragement

As summer reached its height we were seeing a lot more holidaymakers in St Felix. Daisy Chain, along with many of the other shops on Harbour Street, was starting to turn a healthy profit. And it wasn't only our regular flowers and Amber's special bouquets that were making money; we'd begun to sell a lot more of our flower trinkets too.

So much so that many of the original bits and pieces that Belle had supplied me with for the shop had already sold out. So I'd approached the makers of these items, personally this time, to ask if they'd like to supply the shop on a regular basis. Thrilled, they had agreed. As a result, Daisy Chain featured the work of many local artists displayed amongst the flowers.

This afternoon I'm off to see Bronte at her house, to talk to her about whether she'd like to sell some of her creations in the shop.

Aside from the ceramic work Jake had shown me on the night we'd gone to her school, I'd noticed that Bronte made a lot of her own jewellery – some from papier mâché, some from beads, and some from items she found on the beach like shells, pebbles, sea glass and tiny bits of driftwood. It was all really pretty and very different, and observing the type of people we were attracting to the shop, I knew it was something Daisy Chain's customers would like.

The rest of the shops in Harbour Street didn't sell the sort of items we did; they were either practical, everyday shops that sold food, newspapers or stationery, or they went for the traditional seaside wares: buckets and spades, ice creams, sun cream and beach towels. Apart from Belle with her studio, no one else dared to do anything differently. It was a shame because Harbour Street and St Felix had so much potential. The few empty shops at the higher end of the street could be filled with so many things other than another charity shop, which I had been afraid we'd get if things didn't pick up. But with the town a lot busier now, I had high hopes that new businesses might eventually be attracted back into St Felix.

So this morning as Basil and I walk up Primrose Hill to our meeting with Bronte, I'm in a buoyant mood even though I'm slightly concerned about visiting Jake's house. I've come during working hours in the hope he'll be busy in the nursery, but he lives on the same land he grows his flowers on, so I'm crossing my fingers I won't have to see him, or too many of his flowers. I've been a lot better around flowers lately, but even so I don't want to chance being exposed to so many of them – that might be taking things too far.

Basil and I arrive at the nursery and walk through a gate and up a long path leading to a pleasant-looking farmhouse, and as I ring the bell and stand back to wait, Basil immediately lies down to rest while I take a quick look around me.

I can see a few polytunnels, lots of greenhouses and some fields spread out at the back and sides of the house, and I can't help but shudder at the thought of all the flowers that might be lurking in there – hundreds of the things, all condensed into one place . . .

I'm hoping that Jake isn't home. Not because Bronte and I need to discuss his birthday party; I've already had several secret meetings with Bronte and Charlie in the back room of Daisy Chain, and our plans for a party at Trecarlan are coming along a treat. No, the reason I don't want to see Jake today is because I'm afraid he'll suggest a trip to see his flower empire. Although, the way Jake has been with me lately, it seems highly unlikely.

Jake's changed since Ash and I got together. He no longer pops into the shop at lunchtime, and he never asks me to join him for a quick drink at the Mermaid after work. As much as I like Ash, this distance Jake has put between us saddens me greatly. I don't want to gain a boyfriend and lose a good friend, but that's what seems to have happened.

'Hey, Poppy. Hey, Basil,' Bronte says, opening the door. 'Come in.'

We follow Bronte into a tidy hall with pictures hung neatly on the walls, and then through to a spotless kitchen where she has laid her jewellery out on a large scrubbed wooden table for me to see.

'Can I get you a drink?' she asks. 'Coffee or tea?'

I get the feeling that the usually confident Bronte is nervous.

'What are you drinking?' I ask, looking at a can on the side.

'Diet Pepsi,' she says. 'Would you like that?'

'Yeah, that would be great.'

Bronte gets me a can, and Basil a bowl of water, then we sit and examine her jewellery, talking about how she makes it, where she gets her inspiration from, and what sort of things she could make for the shop.

'Are you sure people will want to buy my jewellery?' she asks. 'It's just a hobby.'

'Do you ever make jewellery for your friends?'

'Sure, that's all they ever want for birthday and Christmas gifts.'

'And do they wear it?'

'Yes, all the time.'

'There you go then. That's all I need.'

'This is amazing!' she says. 'I can't believe my jewellery is going to be in a real shop.'

'Is your dad OK with all this?' I ask, wondering if Jake is here.

'Dad, yeah, he's cool. He was the one who encouraged me to keep making my stuff when I thought about giving up.' She pauses, then confides: 'Mum and me used to do all these kinds of things together before she died. She was very arty – Dad says that's where I get it from.'

I nod.

'I mean, we didn't make jewellery like this – I was only ten when it happened. I think we used to make bead necklaces though, and I remember us painting and drawing together.'

She screws up her face. 'It's hard sometimes to remember. Does that sound awful, Poppy?'

I shake my head. 'No, I know what you mean; as time goes by our memories become slightly hazy. Doesn't mean you love your mum any less though. It just means new experiences are taking up the space that's allotted in your head for memories.'

'I like that,' Bronte says, nodding slowly. 'It makes sense. Like a flash drive that's full and there's only so much space on it. My memory flash stick is so full I need to remove some data from it to allow new stuff to be uploaded.'

'Yes.' I smile at her. 'Something like that.'

'Hey, Dad,' Bronte says, looking towards the kitchen door. 'You're back already! Poppy is here checking out my jewellery for her shop.'

Jake pauses in the doorway and smiles at us, then walks into the kitchen. Miley jumps from his shoulder, and immediately goes to the fruit bowl on the kitchen counter.

I wonder how much of what I was just saying Jake heard.

'Just one, Miley,' Jake instructs the monkey, who is already unpeeling a banana with great dexterity. 'I hope she's offering you a good price for it, Bronte,' Jake comments as he heads towards the kettle.

'I certainly am,' I reply. 'I think Bronte's jewellery will go down a storm.'

'She's a very talented lady is my Bronte,' Jake says, winking at her. 'Tea?' he offers, looking at me.

'I'm fine, thanks.' I lift my can.

'Do you want to take the bits you like right away, Poppy?' Bronte asks. 'I've a box upstairs I can put them in for you.'

'That would be great, thank you.'

Bronte heads for the stairs. 'Back in a mo.'

Jake turns and leans against the kitchen counter while he waits for the kettle to boil. It feels a bit awkward for us to be on our own like this; it hasn't happened for what seems like ages.

'She's over the moon you've shown an interest,' Jake says, and noticing a snoozing Basil he comes over and crouches down to fuss him. 'She keeps talking about going to art college when she's old enough.'

'She'd do very well at it,' I tell him. 'She has talent.'

'Just need to sort out what Charlie is going to do now. He has one more year of A-levels then it's uni time for him, but he still doesn't know what he wants to do.'

'Charlie is very different to Bronte, but I'm sure he'll find his way. I bet you'll miss them when they go to college.'

Jake stands up from where he's been fussing Basil and heads towards the boiling kettle.

'Truth is, Poppy,' he says with his back to me as he puts a tea bag in his mug and pours boiling water over it, 'I don't know what I'll do here without them. The place will seem deserted.'

I wait for Jake to continue but he doesn't, he just stands very still gazing out of the kitchen window. Miley, sitting next to me on the table, looks up at Jake, then she leaps across the kitchen units and offers him the rest of her banana.

'Of course I'll still have you, you little monster,' he says stroking Miley's head. 'No, you keep the banana, thank you.'

Miley turns from Jake and looks at me, and I'm sure I see her shrug.

I get up and go over to the counter where Jake is making

the tea. This seems to jolt him into action; he grabs the milk and sloshes far too much into his mug.

'Damn,' he says under his breath.

'Don't you like it milky then?' I ask, smiling.

He turns to me and I see his eyes are misty.

'Oh, Jake,' I say, putting my hand over his as it rests on the kitchen worktop. 'When it happens – and like you said, there's another year to go before Charlie leaves for uni, if that's what he decides to do – it will be OK, I'm sure it will.'

Jake looks down at my hand, but he doesn't attempt to move his own.

'How do you know it will?' he asks. 'It was bad enough when I lost Felicity – at least I had the children for company. This time it will be just me when they're gone.'

'But you have your friends in St Felix, and you have Lou.' I know this sounds weak.

'Yes, I know, and I'm grateful for them, of course, but sometimes . . . ' He struggles for the right words. 'When it's just you, on your own, and you close the door on the world outside, it can be very lonely to have only your memories for company. I felt like that every night when I lost Felicity.'

I know exactly what he means, and I want to tell him I know, but I can't, it just won't come out, so I squeeze his hand instead.

Jake looks up at me. 'Poppy, I—'

'Couldn't find the box!' Bronte announces from the door, marching back into the kitchen. She stops and stares at Jake and me, apparently holding hands by the sink. We immediately pull away from each other, and Bronte, her head down, carries on as if she's not seen anything. 'It was under my bed of all places,' she says, rapidly placing the items of jewellery into a decorated shoebox.

'This is fab,' I tell her, hurrying over to the table. 'If I pay you for these now,' I reach for my bag, and pull out my purse, 'then you can make some more, like we discussed – yes?'

'Sure,' Bronte says quickly. She glances at Jake then at me. 'That would be great.'

I pay Bronte and gather up the box of jewellery, still annoyed with myself that Bronte had seen the two of us like that. 'I was wondering, Bronte,' I ask, as a thought suddenly comes to me, 'if you'd be interested in a part-time job at the shop?'

Bronte stares at me. 'Really? You want me to work at Daisy Chain?'

'If you'd like to. We're a lot busier these days, and I'm sure Amber would be happier spending less time in the shop and more in the back room creating her bouquets and arrangements. What do you think?'

'Definitely!' Bronte says, her eyes shining. 'I'd love to. Is that OK, Dad?' she asks, looking at Jake.

'Of course.' Jake looks at me. 'Thank you, Poppy,' he says, and our eyes meet again.

I quickly look away. 'Well, I'd better be getting off. Pop in and see me at the shop soon, Bronte, and we'll discuss it further. Right, where's that dog of mine?'

We all look around for Basil, who up until a few moments ago had been snoozing peacefully under the table.

'And where's Miley?' Jake asks.

We all rush out into the hall to find Basil wandering around in a slow circle with Miley riding on his back holding on to his collar.

'Oh, Basil,' I say, grinning at him. 'What is she doing to you?'

'Training him to ride in the Grand National by the looks of it,' Bronte says, and we all laugh.

'Would you like to see where all your flowers come from while you're here?' Jake asks hopefully. 'You did say you'd like a tour sometime.'

Oh lord, I couldn't say no after the way Jake was a few minutes ago. Plus it was lovely to have Jake talking to me again; I'd missed him. 'Sure,' I reply, my words catching in my throat. 'Why not?'

Bronte remains at the house while Jake walks Basil, Miley and a very hesitant me up to his nursery. It's much larger than I'd thought it would be: there are about a dozen greenhouses lined up along one side of the land, some fields of rich dark soil with a few polytunnels, and two of Jake's four staff. He introduces me to Gemma and Christian, who are busy trundling wheelbarrows full of compost over to one of the greenhouses so they can begin filling pots with new seedlings. Then we walk over to another greenhouse and Jake holds the door open.

'B-but what about Basil and Miley,' I say, looking over my shoulder. Basil is walking along sniffing the ground like a bloodhound, and Miley is trying to imitate her idol.

'They'll be fine,' Jake says, gesturing for me to go inside. 'We'll only be a minute.'

I take a deep breath and step inside a greenhouse full of brightly coloured flowers.

'This is the batch that will go out tomorrow,' Jake says proudly. 'To your shop, and the many more I supply around the area. Some will go up to Covent Garden tonight, for the market tomorrow.'

'Really?' I ask, trying to breathe without taking in too much of the smell, which is extremely hard to do. The scent of the flowers in here is overpoweringly sweet.

'Yes, these are my flowers at their very best.' He steps away from the door, further into the greenhouse. 'These beauties are in peak condition – come see.'

I have no choice but to step further into the greenhouse. Either side of me on great long tables are more flowers than our little shop could hold ten times over. I can see carnations, chrysanthemums, lilies – I try not to look any further down the greenhouse for fear of spotting a rose.

'How do you get them just right?' I ask, avoiding looking at the flowers too much, by concentrating hard on Jake. 'Don't some go to waste if they're past their best?'

'No, we keep the glasshouses at different temperatures – colder to hold them back from blossoming too early, and warmer if we need to bring them on a bit faster.'

'What temperature is this one?' I ask, as Jake moves closer to me. Today he's wearing blue jeans, tan Timberland boots, and my favourite of his many checked shirts. It opens just far enough to allow me a glimpse of the beginnings of his sandy-coloured chest hair. Swiftly I look up at his face as I realise where I'm gazing.

'This one is just perfect,' he says in a low voice, looking at me.

I open my mouth to speak, but nothing comes out. Jake moves closer to me, so I can feel his warm breath on my face, he leans down towards me and . . .

'Do you have roses in here?' I suddenly demand as a familiar scent begins to engulf me.

'What?' Jake asks, looking confused.

'Roses – I think I can smell them.'

'Yes, about two hundred. They're down at the bottom of the glasshouse, did you want to see them?'

'Two . . . two hundred roses . . . in here?'

'Yes, but—'

'Sorry, Jake, I really gotta go.' I run for the door of the greenhouse and as I fumble with the handle, I begin to panic even more, terrified I can't get out.

A large hand reaches over me and opens it with ease.

I stumble out and begin taking large gulps of fresh air as quickly as I can.

'What on earth is wrong, Poppy?' Jake asks, following me. He shuts the door of the greenhouse behind him, and it's as if he's just wiped out all the roses on the planet by doing so. My breathing begins to recover, and I become a sane (well, fairly sane) person once more.

'Nothing, I just remembered I have to be somewhere. Now.' I begin to walk back towards Jake's farmhouse. 'Come on, Basil!' I call, and to my relief for once he obeys and follows me.

'Ah, right, I see what you're doing,' Jake calls after me, not moving. 'I get it – this is payback time.'

I turn to look at him, and for a split second wonder whether to tell him everything.

'No, you don't get it,' I mumble to myself as I turn and carry on down the hill with Basil next to me. 'That's the thing. No one does.'

# Thirty-three

## Pink Carnation – I Will Never Forget You

The next day I'm sitting in the gardens of Camberley House with Stan. It's a hot sunny afternoon, so we sit in two deckchairs, partially shaded by the branches of a huge oak tree.

'Are you OK, Poppy?' Stan asks, looking at me with concern. 'You seem a bit subdued today. Is everything going well with the plans for the birthday party?'

I'd asked Stan if we could use Trecarlan for Jake's birthday party, and of course he'd agreed.

'It's good to know the old gal is being put to use,' he'd said with pleasure in his eyes. 'I don't like to think of her standing empty.'

'Everything is going fine,' I tell him now. 'With the party at any rate.'

'And with everything else?' Stan asks.

I glance at him. 'Not so well.'

'Is it the shop?'

I shake my head. 'No. We're doing better than ever.'

'Friends?'

'Kind of.'

'Kind of . . . Hmm, let's see, then it must be your love life?'

I'm silent.

'Is young Ash giving you grief?'

'Oh, no, Ash is lovely. We get on great.'

'Do you?' Stan asks, his eyes narrowing.

'Yes. Ash is lovely to be with. Chilled, relaxed. Just what I need right now.'

Stan studies my face before speaking. 'Those are telling words – "right now". If Ash is perfect for you "right now", then who is it that might be perfect for you in the future?'

'I don't know what you mean,' I lie.

I know exactly what Stan means because Amber said pretty much the same thing when I got back from Jake's yesterday . . .

'How did you get on?' Amber asks, looking up from some sweet peas she's arranging in a vase.

'With . . . ?' I ask, letting Basil off his lead.

'Bronte?'

*Bronte.* With everything that had happened with Jake, I'd almost forgotten that's why I'd gone over there in the first place.

'She's definitely going to supply us with some of her jewellery. It's very good.' Damn, I'd been in such a hurry to get away, I didn't go back to Jake's house to collect Bronte's box. I'll have to text her and ask her to bring it down to the shop when she comes in to talk about the job. There was no way I could go back to Jake's, not after what had happened. 'And I've asked her to work part-time in the shop – weekends, that kind of thing. When you're busy with arrangements.'

'That's a wonderful idea! I like Bronte.' Amber smells the flowers, then places them down on one of the tables. 'Did you see Jake while you were up there? He came into the shop earlier. When I said where you were, he dashed off pretty quickly.' She gives me a meaningful look from under her big lashes.

'Yes, I did, briefly. He arrived home just as I was finishing up with Bronte. Then he showed me around his nursery. Why?' I can't bring myself to tell her about the greenhouse, that would only complicate things. And things were already complicated enough.

'No reason. I thought he'd probably head home when he knew you were there.'

I watch Basil noisily lapping water from his bowl until it's nearly empty. 'Hey, fella, let me fill that for you again,' I say, picking up the bowl and heading out the back to the sink.

'So what if he did?' I call to Amber. 'It's his house.'

'It is indeed. Made even more inviting knowing you're there, no doubt.'

I carry Basil's water bowl through to the shop and set it down next to where he's crashed out on the floor after his excursion.

'Explain yourself, Amber,' I say sternly, folding my arms and turning to face her.

'I only say what I see,' Amber says, unfazed. 'And I see not one, but two hunky men interested in our Poppy.'

'Don't be ridiculous!' I leap in, a bit too quickly. 'We've been through all this before. Jake is not interested in me, I can tell you that for a fact. And you know full well I'm with Ash now.'

Amber merely nods. 'Yep, so you are. But for how long?'

'What?'

'For how long? Ash is only a temporary solution to your troubles. He's like a pretty Band-Aid covering up a wound. What you really need, Poppy, is a surgeon to stitch that wound up for you permanently.'

I knew what Amber was getting at with her analogy, but I chose to play dumb, and luckily we were interrupted by customers wandering in.

Now, sitting in the garden with Stan, I think again about what she said.

'Is there someone else, Poppy?' Stan asks. 'You don't have to tell me, of course. But I was a bit of a looker in my time, you know. I had my fair share of female attention. I do know something about complications of the heart.'

I smile at Stan. 'I bet you were!' I say, then I sigh. 'Yes, there's someone else. But not in that way. It's someone I've liked for some time – since the first day I came to St Felix, as it happens. But the trouble is he's never shown any interest in me.'

Until yesterday. But was that just a spur of the moment thing? Had Jake meant to try and kiss me, or was it just wishful thinking on my part?

Not that I was ever likely to find out now. Jake obviously thought my running away was an attempt to get back at him for the time at the cottage when I'd tried to kiss him and he scarpered.

'I find that very hard to believe,' Stan says, his eyes wide. 'A pretty girl like you?'

'It's kind of you to say, but I hardly think so, Stan.'

'Now you listen to me, my girl. I may be an octogenarian, but I can still spot a beautiful young lady when I see one, and you are it. You wear a bit too much black for my liking, and you could smile more often, but underneath all that there's a radiant beauty waiting to emerge.'

'Oh, Stan!' I get up and hug him. 'You say the nicest things.'

'I only speak the truth, my dear. And if an old man like me can see it, and Ash, then why can't this other fella too?'

'Jake's complicated,' I say without thinking as I sit back down on my chair.

'Oh, it's Jake is it? Lou's nephew.'

I blush. Damn, I hadn't wanted to reveal his name.

'But isn't that the fella you're arranging the birthday party for?' Stan's brow crinkles.

'It is.'

'Ah . . . the plot thickens.'

'I'm just doing that as a favour to Jake's children – Bronte and Charlie. They're good kids, and they want to give their dad a special birthday.'

'As do you,' Stan says, nodding slowly. 'Right?'

My turn to nod.

'Ah, Poppy, the human heart is a complicated thing. It rarely ever works in the way we want it to, without heartache and pain.'

'Tell me about it.'

'But what I do know is life often has a way of pushing us down paths we don't want to go, but find ourselves glad we did.'

'Perhaps.'

'How about I tell you a story?' Stan asks. 'It's a long tale, but bear with me, it'll be worth it.'

'Sure. Why not?' I say, indulging him as usual in his favourite pastime.

I settle back in my deckchair to listen while Stan takes a deep breath and begins:

'Many years ago in 1846 Queen Victoria visited Cornwall – did you know that? It was her only official visit here.'

I shake my head.

'So, to celebrate her visit, a local craftswoman embroidered a set of four pictures for her as a gift. On the day the Queen visited her town the woman managed to hand the pictures to the Queen's lady-in-waiting, who showed them to the Queen there and then. The craftswoman was thrilled, as you can imagine.'

'Yes, I'm with you so far,' I say, wondering where all this is going.

'Good. Well, the Queen's lady-in-waiting had her eye on the then owner of Trecarlan, Lord Harrington. He was the MP for the area, and used to visit London frequently to attend Parliament. He and the lady-in-waiting moved in the same circles, and they'd had a bit of a fling when he was in London. So when she got the chance to visit his home ... well, I don't need to go into details. Let's just say they made the most of the opportunity!'

'Goodness, and there was me thinking the Victorians were all uptight and polite!'

Stan grins. 'That is just a fallacy; it was all going on behind the scenes. Anyway, the lady-in-waiting had to make a quick escape from the castle one day when she was summoned back to the Queen's side earlier than expected. In her rush, she left behind her bag containing the pictures, and a handwritten note she was supposed to be delivering from the Queen to the craftswoman to thank her for the lovely flower embroidery.'

'So the pictures remained at Trecarlan?' I ask.

Stan nods. 'Not long after that, ownership of the castle changed hands. Sordid business, if local gossip is to be believed. Apparently Lord Harrington was up to his old tricks again, this time with the daughter of a local landowner.' Stan tuts and shakes his head. 'When they were found out, the father threatened Harrington with a very nasty fate if he didn't stay well away from his daughter. But it was too late, the girl was already pregnant. So, to avoid a fate worse than death, Harrington fled the castle, taking most of his possessions with him. But he left behind the pictures, not thinking them to be worth anything. You'd be surprised at how many owners that house has had over the years, Poppy. Why, I could tell you some stories—'

'This one is fine for now, Stan,' I say, trying to keep him on track.

'That was when my family, the Marracks, took over Trecarlan,' Stan says, his eyes gleaming with pride. 'That young girl was my great-great-grandmother, and the Marracks have lived in the castle ever since.'

'Wow, that's an amazing story,' I say. But there's one detail in his story that's bothering me. 'Stan, you said that the previous owner of Trecarlan was called Harrington, is that right?'

Stan nods.

'Could he possibly be any relation to Caroline Harrington-Smythe?'

'Yes, I believe he might be,' Stan says, as if it has only just occurred to him. 'I remember when she told me the Parish Council would look after Trecarlan, she mentioned that she had some sort of heritage there. But I never made the connection.'

'Hmm . . . ' I say, mulling it over. 'If that's true, it might explain why Caroline is always so difficult when it comes to Trecarlan. Some bit of ancient history meant her family didn't inherit the castle and yours did. But what it doesn't explain is . . . why she has a problem with *me*.'

'Ah, that's easy,' Stan says, leaning back in his deckchair. 'I remember that one.'

'You do?'

'Yes. Do you know why Daisy and William came to St Felix to open the original Daisy Chain shop?'

'Er . . . no. I assumed they liked the seaside and wanted to live there.'

Stan shakes his head. 'It was because Daisy's grandmother lived in St Felix. She was a maid at the castle in her younger days.'

'So?' I ask, not following this.

'Daisy's grandmother, so the story goes, was the person that dropped Lord Harrington in it. She'd seen everything that had gone on at the castle while she was working there.'

'Ah . . . it all makes sense now. That's why Caroline has a problem with me – my ancestor was responsible for her not inheriting Trecarlan!'

'It would seem so,' Stan says. 'History is a strange thing.'

'Well, good on my family for stopping the Harringtons from having the castle, that's what I say. Caroline certainly wouldn't have made a very good lady of the manor.'

Stan nods in agreement. 'If it hadn't been for Daisy's grandmother, we might not be sitting here in this lovely sunshine together.'

'Exactly! So what happened to those embroidered pictures? Are they still in the castle?'

Stan shakes his head. 'No, and this is the second part of the story. Stick with me, Poppy, I said it was long. As I mentioned earlier, in my day I had my fair share of female attention from the ladies of the town – your grandmother included.'

I open my eyes wide. I hadn't expected to hear that, but then my grandmother always did seem to have a soft spot for Stan.

'After your grandfather passed, Rose and I spent a great deal of time together, and during our time, as a sign of my affection, I gave her one of the embroidered pictures – the one of a purple rose.'

'Oh yes!' I exclaim, remembering. 'We found it in one of the old boxes that were stored away in the shop. That would explain why it had the initials VR stitched into it – Victoria Regina! Once you know about the Queen Victoria connection, it all makes sense.'

'Rose kept her picture then?' Stan asks, looking pleased. 'I hoped she might. Do you know what purple roses mean, Poppy?'

'I do, as a matter of fact; Amber used them as one of the wedding flowers. They mean enchantment.'

'Exactly. Your grandmother was always utterly enchanting, which is why I gave her that particular picture.'

'How lovely, but I don't see . . .'

'Patience, Poppy, I'm getting there, give me time. You'll remember there were four pictures in this set. The second, I gave to another lady friend of mine, who I think you also know – Lou.'

'Stan, you old devil! Lou, too?'

Stan smiles sheepishly. 'What can I say? There were a lot of lovely ladies in St Felix back then, it was the seventies, it was all about free love. Lou's picture was of a sweet pea – it means delicate pleasures, and Lou was—'

'No, Stan! Enough information, thank you,' I tell him, but I'm smiling when I say it. Who would have thought old Stan was such a ladies' man! 'Lou still has hers too,' I tell him. 'It's hung up in her hall. I noticed it in a cluster of pictures the day Basil's puppies were born.'

'Good old Lou,' Stan says. 'It was such a joy when I heard she'd returned to St Felix. I'd missed seeing her.'

'So you had Rose, Lou, and who else on the go?'

'Oh no, only one lady at a time, Poppy, give me some credit.' He raises his white brows at me. 'There were only ever three ladies in my life I cared about, that's why I gave them each a picture. The last was Isabelle. She wasn't in St Felix long though, her family took her away shortly after we got to know each other. Her gift was the embroidered picture of a pink carnation, it means I will never forget you – and I didn't, Poppy, I still remember her as if it was yesterday.' He looks wistfully across the Camberley gardens as he remembers, and I let him sit with his memories for a few moments.

'I wasn't promiscuous, Poppy,' Stan insists, coming back to the present day once more. 'I don't want you to think that. I held these ladies in great esteem, that's why I gave them each a gift as a sign of my deep affection. Valuable gifts.'

'It really is a lovely story, Stan, but why are you telling me all this?'

'Love comes wrapped in many different packages, Poppy. Sometimes it's fleeting – like Lord Harrington's affairs – sometimes much of it comes around at once – like my ladies of St Felix. And sometimes,' he swallows, 'sometimes, you fall in love with someone who can't be yours, but you never forget them – like Isabelle.'

'Oh, Stan.'

'No, no, I'm not telling you this so you can feel sorry for me, Poppy. I'm telling you so you understand that, whatever sort of love it is, it's always for a reason. Love is too powerful an emotion for us to feel it otherwise. You mark my words; your feelings for Jake will be for a reason. Just you wait and see.'

# Thirty-four

## Heliotrope – Devoted Affection

It's the evening of Jake's fortieth birthday party, and Amber, Ash and I walk up the hill to Trecarlan Castle.

Amber is wearing a beautiful, long, rainbow-coloured dress with gladiator sandals. Having been through my entire wardrobe and not found a single thing suitable to wear, I've borrowed another of Amber's dresses: a gorgeous gown in duck-egg blue – a colour I don't think I've ever worn in my life, and would certainly never have chosen for myself if Amber hadn't encouraged me into it. The dress has embroidery all over the fitted bust and thin straps, with a loose, flowing, gossamer-soft skirt below.

It's a good job Amber and I are a similar size or I don't know what I'd have done. Amber seems able to create endless different outfits, some of which she brought with her from New York, and some she's made up from items she picks up in the charity shops of St Felix and the surrounding area.

Bronte, Charlie and myself have instructed all the guests to get to the castle fifteen minutes before the birthday boy is due to arrive at 7.30 p.m., and Woody has been put in charge of getting Jake to the party. None of us have a clue how Woody's going to get him there, but Bronte and Charlie have told me not to worry, it's all in hand.

When we arrive at the castle we are ushered inside by Charlie and told where to go and hide. Ash and Amber seem quite excited by all the subversive behaviour, but I can't help wondering just how much Jake will enjoy being surprised like this. Jake has always struck me as being very down-to-earth and practical, I'm not sure surprise parties are really his idea of fun. On the other hand, Jake's kids mean the world to him, and knowing they were the ones who'd organised this bash, he would make damn sure he enjoyed it.

As we arrive in the ballroom, I realise just how popular Jake is in St Felix. The place is already packed out with people holding glasses of fizz, eagerly waiting to congratulate him. There is a huge birthday banner hanging over one wall, leaving no one in any doubt as to what age Jake is turning today, and the white tablecloths that had looked so serene and elegant at the wedding are decorated with colourful helium-filled balloons and confetti 40s.

At the appointed time we all squeeze into a tiny room behind the main ballroom. Stan had once told me it was for ladies to powder their faces during the huge balls that were held at the castle in the last century. But as we all squeeze together in the dark like sardines, it's hard to imagine an elegant powder room with ladies gossiping about their beaux.

'Ssh,' someone hisses, 'he's here.'

We all stand as quietly as we can, waiting for our signal, and then we hear Jake's voice.

'What the hell is going on, Woody? Why have you brought me here?'

'Go!' someone shouts, and we all jump out of the powder room calling 'Surprise!'

But it's not just Jake who gets a shock. So do we when we see him standing in the middle of the ballroom with his arms handcuffed behind his back.

'What the hell?' he cries, seeing us all.

'Happy birthday, Dad!' yell Bronte and Charlie, rushing forward to hug him with Miley in their arms.

Jake tries to hug them back, but finds he's still incapacitated.

'So this is why you arrested me in my own home!' Jake exclaims, turning to Woody, as Miley climbs on to his shoulder. 'I thought you'd lost it!'

'Sorry, Jake,' Woody says, pulling a key from his pocket and unlocking the handcuffs. 'It was my job to get you here without you guessing what was going on, and that was the only thing I could think of that was guaranteed to work.'

'Arresting me?' Jake says, rubbing at his wrists.

'I did check with Bronte and Charlie first,' Woody says, looking embarrassed. 'They said you wouldn't mind.'

'I bet they did,' Jake says gruffly, turning to his children. 'However ... ' He stops pretending to be cross and grins. 'I think I can forgive you. This all looks amazing!'

'Have a drink, Jake,' Lou says, thrusting a glass of bubbly into his hand. 'Happy birthday!' she says, lifting her own glass.

'Thank you, Lou.' Jake turns around to face his guests.

'Cheers, everyone!' He lifts his glass in a toast. 'And thank you all for coming!'

The party is a great success; one of the local bands we had at the wedding is playing, and people soon begin flooding on to the dance floor to boogie the night away. There is plenty of booze (another pop-up bar provided by the Merry Mermaid) and refreshments (provided by St Felix's new catering team of Richie, Ant and Dec).

'How fabulous is this?' I ask Charlie a bit later when I bump into him at the buffet table. 'You and Bronte have done brilliantly.'

'We couldn't have done it without you, Poppy, and the rest of the town chipping in to help,' he says. 'Everyone wanted to be involved again, that's how we ended with so much stuff.' He gestures to the long table. 'Even after Ant and Dec offered to cater for us, we still had loads of offers of sandwiches and desserts. We didn't know what to do with it all.'

'That's because your dad is so popular.' I look at the plates of food set out on the table. 'It seems to be disappearing rapidly. I don't think you'll have a lot left.'

'I know, the people of St Felix sure are hungry!'

'My son!' Jake comes over and wraps his arm around Charlie. It looks as though he's had quite a few drinks already. 'Aren't I the luckiest dad in the world to have two fantastic children?'

'Yes, without a doubt.' I smile at Jake. It's good to see him again. We haven't seen each other properly since the strange events at his nursery, and I'd wondered if tonight might be a bit awkward. But judging by the look on Jake's face it's anything but.

'And can you believe how old I am today, Poppy?'

I open my mouth to reply, but he continues: 'Forty! Forty years old – when did that happen?'

I shake my head.

'I just wish Felicity was here to see all this.' He throws his arm out to the ballroom. 'She always loved a party, especially birthdays.' The happiness in his face changes to sadness.

Charlie puts a hand on his father's shoulder. 'I'm sure Mum is here in spirit, Dad.'

Jake nods. 'Yes, you're right. Did I ever tell you, Charlie, what a good kid you are?'

Charlie grins. 'Just a few times tonight.'

'Good, good,' Jake says, patting him on the back. 'Now then, Poppy,' Jake says, swaying a little as he lets go of Charlie. 'Do you dance?'

'Er . . . '

'Because *I* feel like dancing, and you are by far the most attractive dance partner I can see in the room. Plus,' he leans in towards me and whispers, 'I don't see Ash anywhere, so we'll be OK.'

Jake's words make my cheeks flush bright red. Is he coming on to me? Was I right about what almost happened in the greenhouse?

'Oh Ja-ake!' Belle comes wafting over; she's wearing a long red halter-neck maxi dress, which is cut very low on her slim back, and gold sandals. 'I haven't had a chance to wish you a happy birthday yet!' She kisses him on the cheek.

'Thank you, Belle,' Jake says politely. 'I do hope you're enjoying yourself tonight.'

'Well, I would be,' Belle replies, pouting, 'if only I could find a dance partner . . . '

'I was just saying I felt like a dance!' Jake responds, grinning. 'What are we waiting for!'

He grabs Belle's hand and pulls her on to the dance floor, where he proceeds to wrap his arms around her waist, and swing her around, while Belle laughs hysterically.

'Sorry,' Charlie says, seeing me forlornly watching them. 'Dad's a bit drunk. I'm sure he would rather have danced with you.'

'Oh no, it doesn't matter,' I tell him quickly, turning away from the dance floor. 'I'm not one for dancing much anyway.' I give a fake smile, which I'm sure Charlie knows isn't genuine.

'Hey,' Ash says, arriving at our side. 'What's going down?'

'Nothing,' I reply brightly, kissing him. 'How are you enjoying the party?'

'Yeah, it's good.'

I get the feeling Ash is only saying this for Charlie's benefit.

'You've done well,' he tells Charlie. 'Organising this. When I was your age I was only interested in surfing and girls.'

'And what's changed?' I tease.

'Ha, funny.' Ash puts his arm around my waist and kisses the side of my neck. 'You know you're the only woman for me.'

For some reason I feel uncomfortable when he says this. 'Charlie likes to surf, don't you, Charlie?' I say, changing the subject fast.

'I would, given the chance,' Charlie says wryly.

'Then what's stopping you?' Ash asks.

'You have to be in the right crowd, don't you, to be in the surfing gang.' He eyes Ash knowingly.

Ash thinks about this. 'I guess we are a tight-knit group, but we're always open to newcomers.'

Charlie looks like he doesn't believe him.

'What are you doing tomorrow?' Ash asks.

'Not much,' Charlie replies. 'Probably clearing up here.'

'Well forget that!' Ash declares. 'Life's too short to tidy!'

I nudge him hard.

'OK . . . ' he says looking at me. 'Don't forget that. But when you've finished clearing up, why not come down to the beach? The surf should be well up, according to the forecast.'

Charlie shrugs. 'I don't know . . . '

'Come on, man up! Do you wanna ride those waves or not? The rush is mad!'

'OK then, I will!' Charlie says, grinning.

'Do you have a board?' Ash asks. ''Cos you can borrow one of mine if not?'

'I have a board, just don't use it very often.'

'Then we'll have to get her waxed up!'

Ash and Charlie begin to talk enthusiastically to each other about surfing, and after a few minutes I decide this might be a good time to slip away. I have something important to do.

After Stan had told me the story of the Victorian pictures, we'd talked some more about his collection:

'Stan, would these pictures be worth anything, do you think?' I ask, an idea springing into my mind. Ever since he'd confided in me about his financial situation, I'd been trying desperately to think how I might help him remain at Camberley.

'Oh yes, without a doubt. Especially if they could be sold as a set with the letter from Queen Victoria. If we knew where they all were, it would be a very valuable collection indeed.'

I nod, still thinking. 'Well, we know where the purple rose is – I have that back at the cottage. The sweet pea is definitely at Lou's – I've seen it myself.' Although the last time I'd been in Lou's cottage, the hall walls were bare because she was decorating. But I was pretty sure she wouldn't get rid of the picture if Stan had given it to her. 'But what about the other two?'

'I left one at the castle,' Stan says, looking shame-faced. 'A forget-me-not.'

'Why did you leave it there? You must have known it was worth something.'

'I was in a bad way when I had to leave Trecarlan, Poppy. I barely remembered to pack my toothbrush, let alone a picture of a flower I'd long forgotten the importance of. And the picture is worthless on its own, the value comes from it being part of a set.'

'Of course.' Not wanting to dwell on the subject of him losing his home, I ask, 'But what about the picture of a pink carnation, the one you gave to this Isabelle? That can't be in St Felix. How on earth are we going to find that one?'

'Oh, what does it matter, Poppy?' Stan sighs. 'That was all a long time ago. You need to concentrate on the present, on your flower shop and your beaux.'

'No, Stan, I won't rest until I know you're secure here at Camberley. I owe it to you.'

'Poppy, love, you don't owe me anything.'

'I do, Stan. I abandoned you for over fifteen years while I wallowed in my own misery. Now I'm going to make it right.'

I take a quick look around the ballroom; everyone seems to be busy dancing, drinking or chatting.

'I'll be back in a bit,' I murmur to Ash.

'Yeah, babe,' he says, immediately turning back to Charlie. Finding a fellow surfer seems to have cheered Ash up no end.

I take another quick look around the room. Jake is still dancing with Belle, the tempo has slowed, and they are swaying to the music together. Belle's arms are draped provocatively over Jake's shoulders, but Jake's hands, I'm relieved to see, are resting formally on Belle's waist. As I watch them I notice he's looking around as if he's wondering how to get away. Amber has asked Woody to dance – it must have been that way around; I'm sure Woody wouldn't have had the nerve to ask Amber. Lou, surprisingly, is dancing with Ant, and Rita and Richie are busy serving drinks to Dec at the bar. Great, everyone that might notice is otherwise occupied, there's no one else that will miss me if I slip away for a while.

Unnoticed by Charlie and Ash, I make my way towards the door. Then, taking one quick look to check I haven't been seen, I slip out into the hall.

Stan had told me that he'd hidden the last picture, along with the original letter from Queen Victoria, in the cellar of Trecarlan.

So that is where I'm heading.

This was my first opportunity since Stan had told me the

story to be at Trecarlan without someone else present. On my previous visits I'd either been with Bronte and Charlie, overseeing the arrangements for tonight, or Amber, setting out the beautiful pedestal arrangements full of flowers from Jake's nursery. Even when I had tried to come up here with Basil on the pretence of a walk, Ash had intercepted us along the way, saying he was heading up to the castle to trim the lawns.

Tonight, even though the castle is full of people, everyone's busy having fun in the ballroom. There's not a soul in sight as I head through the main hall, then down some stone steps into the original servants' quarters, flicking on lights as I go. Although we'd used this area of the castle during the wedding, it was freaking me out a bit, being down here on my own. The castle was hundreds of years old, what if it had ghosts?

'Stop it, Poppy,' I tell myself. 'There's no such thing. You've been spending too much time with Amber.'

The cellar entrance, as I recall, is not far away from the kitchen. I'd noticed it the other day when I'd been down here. But as I rattle on the handle of the wooden door, I realise it's locked.

Damn!

Where would the key have been kept?

The kitchen, perhaps? I remember Babs keeping a collection of keys pegged up on some black iron hooks inside her pantry. Could they possibly still be there?

To my delight and amazement not only the black hooks but the keys are still there – and they're all labelled too! I grab the one that says 'Cellar' and head back out into the corridor.

For a moment I think I hear footsteps, but when I stop and listen all I can hear is the distant sound of music from the ballroom. 'Stop imagining things!' I tell myself. 'Otherwise you'll never do this for Stan.'

And that really is my driving force in all this – Stan. I genuinely feel I let him down by not being around when he had to leave Trecarlan. Maybe, if I'd known, I could have helped him, possibly even prevented it from happening. But I was too caught up in my own trauma back then to even think about St Felix, let alone return here.

I approach the wooden door, slip the key into the lock, and as if by magic it creaks open to reveal stone steps leading down into the darkness of the cellar.

Luckily in this modern age I don't need to carry a lantern. I'm able to flick a light switch to illuminate my way.

When I get to the bottom of the steps I find myself in a large cellar lined with wine racks, each holding vast quantities of bottles; there's wine, champagne, whisky . . . It's like being in the cellar of a pub, except the bottles are all dusty and forlorn, like they've been waiting a long time for someone to return to select them to help celebrate a birthday or complement a dinner party.

Stan had instructed me to head to the far right of the cellar and find a narrow passageway. Unlike the rest of the cellar, the passageway isn't lit so I flick on the torch on the back of my iPhone and feel my way along even more racks till I come to the very end. I notice that in this part of the cellar most of the racks are empty. I count three shelves up, five spaces across, and reach my hand up to feel in that space where a wine bottle should be.

But there's nothing there. It's empty. I shine my phone up on to the shelf, in case I've made a mistake with the counting, but there's nothing, just empty spaces where bottles once lay waiting to be drunk.

How odd. Stan had been adamant that's where he'd hidden the picture and the letter, inside a tin box to protect it.

I'll have to speak to him again. There's obviously nothing here, so maybe Stan had made a mistake, or remembered it wrongly. I sigh and turn to make my way back. I've only taken a few steps towards the light of the main cellar when suddenly everything goes black. Thank God I have my iPhone, I think, lifting it up higher to guide me out of the cellar.

It's then I hear a sound that strikes fear into my heart.

The sound of the cellar door being shut above me, and then locked.

# Thirty-five

## Sweet William – Gallantry

I'm frozen to the spot for about ten seconds, then, realising that's not going to help matters, I use the tiny beam of my phone to run towards the stairs and cautiously make my way back up them.

When I get to the top I push gently on the doors just in case I'd heard wrongly and they weren't locked after all. But they don't budge an inch.

I'm about to call out for help, when I remember I'm not supposed to be down here, and if someone did hear me I'd have to explain why I was here instead of at the party. Stan had told me to say nothing about the pictures to anyone unless we found them all. He didn't want everyone – especially, Lou – knowing about his other ladies if it could possibly be avoided.

Damn! What was I going to do?

I sit down on one of the steps to think.

After a few seconds I light up the screen on my phone hoping to find a signal, but there's none. So my plan to call Amber and get her to come and unlock the door for me is immediately down the pan.

*OK* . . . I think again.

Stan used to say that Trecarlan was filled with secret passages constructed back in the days it had stood as a fortress overlooking the sea, protecting St Felix. But Stan told us so many tales about Trecarlan when we were children that we gave up believing him in the end. If Stan was to be believed it had been used as a refuge by King Arthur when he was resting from battle, by Cavaliers hiding from the Roundheads, and by British spies during the Second World War.

But what if Stan was right about the secret passages? And what if one of them led out from here?

It's a long shot. But what choice do I have?

I climb down the steps again, and use my phone to guide me for a few minutes while I look for alternative exits. Then the thin beam of light falls on some packing crates stacked in a corner.

*I wonder . . .*

I manage to prop up my phone on one of the wine racks, giving me just enough light to see what I'm doing. I grab hold of one of the crates, expecting it's going to be heavy, but surprisingly I find it's quite light.

I lift that crate down, and then another, until I've moved about six crates, and it's then in the dim light that I see it: another door . . .

I pull the rest of the crates aside, and pray as I grab the rusty wrought-iron handle that it won't be locked.

Hallelujah, I silently cry as it turns easily in my hand.

I go back to the shelves and grab my phone. Then I take a deep breath and step into the tunnel, closing the wooden door behind me.

The tunnel is actually more like a corridor; the floor feels smooth and dry under my feet, as though it's been well worn by people passing through over the years. Luckily I hadn't worn the high heels that Amber had tried to make me order off the Internet when we were choosing our outfits; I'd opted instead for a pair of sparkly silver pumps that we'd spotted in the charity shop in St Felix. But flimsy pumps to me were still silly shoes, I'd have been much more confident walking along in my sturdy old Doc Martens on this floor, especially when I can't see where I'm putting my feet half the time. I can only hope this tunnel isn't adjacent to any sewers; I love animals, but rats I could really do without.

The floor might feel dry, but the walls are damp beneath my hand as I feel my way along the corridor, worrying as I go just where this tunnel is going to come out.

Finally, when I feel like I've been walking for ages, I see tiny specks of light up ahead – hurrah!

I pick up speed, hurrying towards the light, and as I get closer I realise the reason I'm seeing tiny specks of light is because I'm looking at the stars.

The tunnel must lead outside!

As I arrive at the tunnel's mouth there's a very fine opening for me to squeeze through, before I find myself in a small cave. As I step towards the opening of the cave, a great waft of salty sea air hits my lungs, a welcome relief from the musty air I've been breathing for the last few minutes. Another step and I realise the stone floor has given way to wet sand: I'm on a beach.

But which beach?

St Felix is situated on a curved peninsula jutting out into the sea, so when you look out to sea from various points on its coastline you can often see parts of the town from where you stand.

But tonight I can't see any lights in front of me, just an endless sea, lit only by an almost full moon.

There's only one place on the St Felix coastline that has a beach where that happens, I realise. The steep cliffs where I often walk Basil, and where Charlie had showed me the lookout point where he liked to sit when he wanted some peace.

I look up above me, and thanks to the moon I can just make out the ledge where Charlie and I had sat that day, looking down on the jagged rocks.

So that's where this tunnel comes out, just below Trecarlan Castle. I go out on to the tiny beach as far as I can without the waves reaching my feet, and I can just make out the windows of the house dimly lit from inside.

Hearing movement above me, I instinctively duck back into the cave.

'Poppy?' I hear my name being called. 'Is that you down there?'

Cautiously I make my way back on to the sand.

'It is you!' the voice says.

I look up and see Jake leaning over the ledge.

'What on earth are you doing down there?'

'I could say the same to you!' I call back. 'Shouldn't you be at your birthday party?'

'There must be easier ways of having this conversation,' Jake shouts. 'I'll come down, shall I?'

'No!' I cry out, having visions of Jake scaling the sharp rocks in the dim light. 'It's dangerous. You might hurt yourself!'

'Not if I follow the path down. I'll be fine.'

'There's a path?'

'Yeah, look to your left.'

I do as he says and in the moonlight I can just make out a set of rough steps leading up from the beach, a bit like the ones that had led down to the viewing ledge.

'No, I'll come to you,' I say. If Jake comes down here we might both get stuck, and there's no way out through the locked cellar.

'OK, but be careful,' Jake calls with concern. 'It's quite steep.'

Slowly I make my way up the rocky steps as best I can in the silver pumps.

Jake reaches out a hand for me to take as I get close to him, and as his fingers close around mine I finally feel safe.

'OK?' he asks, as I climb the last few steps to stand facing him, still holding his hand.

'Yes,' I say. 'I feel very secure now.'

Jake looks down at our hands, still entwined, but he doesn't let go.

'How did you know this place was here?' I ask, content for us to stay in this position.

'Charlie told me about it. I often come here to sit when I need to think. I don't know how he found it though, it's quite tucked away.'

'He told me about it too.' I decide it's best if Jake doesn't know the real reason Charlie discovered the ledge. 'It's beautiful here, isn't it? Very peaceful. You feel as though nothing else matters in the world when you sit here looking out at the never-ending sea.'

Jake looks at me. 'That's very poetic of you, Miss Carmichael.'

'Well, I try,' I say, winking at him.

'So how did you get down on that beach if you didn't know about the path, but you knew about the ledge?' Jake asks. 'That doesn't add up.'

'I think we'd better sit down, Jake, it's a long story . . .'

While we sit on the little ledge together looking out at a perfect view of moonlit sea and twinkling stars, I tell Jake the whole story. Why I was on the beach, why I'd been in the cellar, and what I'd been looking for.

'But who would lock you in?' Jake asks, mystified.

'I have no idea. Perhaps someone saw the door unlocked and thought they'd better secure it?'

'Maybe,' Jake says, still thinking. 'So if the picture and letter *aren't* in the cellar, then where are they?'

'I don't know. Perhaps Stan got it wrong. He's getting old, his memory isn't what it used to be.'

'But from what you've told me, he seems pretty compos mentis. I doubt he'd have got something like that wrong – the pictures seem to mean a lot to him.'

'Yes, you're probably right. I'll ask him next time I see him. Now,' I say tapping my hand on his thigh. 'It's *your* turn to tell me why you're AWOL from your party! A party which,' I glance at my watch, 'we had better return to. People will be wondering where the birthday boy is!'

'Yes, I know.' Jake turns his gaze to my hand, which is still resting on his thigh, so I hurriedly retrieve it. 'We'd best be getting back.' He starts to stand up, but I prevent him by grabbing his hand. 'Ah-ah, you're not getting away with it that easily, mister! I told you my story, what about yours?'

Jake sits down again.

'I just needed some air, that's all,' he says, not sounding very convincing. 'I'd had quite a bit to drink, I needed to sober up.'

'You came all the way down here to do that? Why not just take a stroll in the castle grounds?'

'OK, OK,' he sighs. 'If you want the truth, I needed breathing space. Some time to think.'

'At your own birthday party?'

He nods. 'It's special times like this that make me think of Felicity even more. Whether it's my birthday, the children's birthdays, anniversaries – you know the kind of thing.'

I nod.

'But tonight seemed different somehow. It struck me the most when I was dancing with Belle.'

Oh great. I could tell where this was going . . .

'What did?' I hardly dare ask. Please don't tell me you felt guilty because you want a relationship with her.

'I felt guilty.'

Here we go . . . I brace myself for the inevitable.

'Guilty, that I'd behaved badly towards you, Poppy.'

*Oh!* I prick up my ears.

'You see, the thing is, I like you – I like you a lot.'

*But* . . . There will be a but, I know it!

'But, it's been so difficult for me, having these sorts of

feeling for someone after all this time. I haven't felt like this since Felicity. She was the only one I ever felt this way about. I never thought it would happen again. In fact I told myself it wouldn't.'

I squeeze Jake's hand.

'And then you were so lovely the day you kissed me. So understanding when I said I couldn't. I wondered if it might ruin our friendship, but it hasn't, has it?'

I shake my head.

'And then I nearly kissed you that day in my greenhouse, but sensibly you made a hasty exit. I was being stupid; I'd left it too late. You'd already found someone else.'

I had?

'Ash is a good guy, Poppy. Much younger than me, of course, much more suitable for you. I'm pleased you've found someone. Really I am.'

*But . . .*

But this time there is no but.

'We'll still continue being friends though, won't we?'

I find myself nodding.

'Good. As long as I have that then, I'm happy. Right,' Jake says standing up, pulling me with him. 'I feel much better now. Time to return to the fold, my public awaits!'

As I climb the narrow steps from the ledge, then walk back up the short path to the castle making polite chitchat with Jake, my mind is buzzing with recrimination.

Did I let that just happen? Did Jake tell me he had feelings for me, and I didn't respond . . . I didn't tell him I felt exactly the same way?

Had Jake gallantly stood back to allow Ash to continue being my suitor, in the type of chivalrous gesture you might have expected to see at Trecarlan hundreds of years ago?

As I walk back inside the castle with Jake, part of me wishes he hadn't been so gallant, that instead he'd challenged Ash to a duel at dawn for the hand of the fair Lady Poppy.

It had never been like this when I was a child. When I played at being a princess at Trecarlan, I always rode off with my handsome prince at the end of the day.

# Thirty-six

## Potentilla – Beloved Daughter

The next day is a Sunday, but the shop still opens for business at midday.

It's my turn to be on duty with Bronte, which is usually a lot of fun. I've been getting on really well with her since she started working at the shop, and I enjoy hearing all about her latest teenage exploits.

I'm out back making a cup of coffee when I hear the shop door open. 'Hi, Bronte!' I call.

Disappearing from the party for a long time last night meant I hadn't had time to drink too much alcohol, so I'd been spared the hangover that many St Felix residents would have woken up with this morning.

But after a particularly rough night's sleep – where I dreamt I'd been locked in a high tower like Rapunzel, and Jake and Ash, wearing huge silver suits of armour, had jousted on horseback, and the results hadn't been too pretty – a shot or two of caffeine is going to be needed if I'm to get through the next few hours.

'Howdy,' Bronte calls, coming into the back room. 'How are you today?'

'Good, thanks. You?'

'Yeah, I'm OK.' Bronte hangs her bag on the peg behind the door. 'Did you enjoy the party?'

Jake and I had returned to the party after our talk and attempted to sneak in quietly in the hope no one had noticed we'd been gone.

Except people had.

Jake had immediately been interrogated by his children. And I'd been questioned by Amber, and then Ash.

Amber hadn't been too bad; I'd explained as quickly as I could what had happened and where I'd been, and as usual she'd taken it all on board with no drama. Ash, however, had not.

'You've been where?' he'd asked, astonished. 'And with who?'

I try to explain again, except I was leaving out the part about the cellar. Ash was too close to Babs and Trecarlan to tell him the truth about the pictures yet.

'And you expect me to believe that? You spend getting on for two hours away from this party, and part of that time you just *happened* to bump into Jake who just *happened* to be outside too? What do you take me for, Poppy, a fool?'

'No, of course not,' I'd protested.

'What were you really up to, hmm? I know you and Jake are friends – but is that friends with benefits now?'

'Stop it, Ash,' I'd pleaded. 'It wasn't like that.' I'd tried to placate him, suggesting that we go back to the cottage, sleep it off and then talk about it in the morning.

'Na-ah!' he said, pulling away as I gently tried to take hold of his arm. 'I gotta get outta here and think for a bit. On my own.'

'Ash!' I called to his disappearing figure, as he strode towards the door of Trecarlan.

'Later, Poppy!' he called with a dismissive wave of his hand. 'Much later.'

'Yes, it was good,' I lie now. 'Coffee?' I offer.

'Nah, I had a Red Bull on the way up here, thanks. What ya looking at?' Bronte asks, seeing me staring at the embroidered picture of the purple rose I'd propped up on the side this morning.

'Oh, it's nothing really. Just something that was found here under the floorboards of the shop. It belonged to my grandmother.'

Bronte comes over. 'May I?' she asks, lifting the picture. 'Hmm . . . that's cool.'

'Is it?' I say, surprised she likes it. 'I didn't think it would be your sort of thing.'

I wander back into the shop, and Bronte follows me.

'It isn't. But I think we have something very similar hanging up on our landing at home.'

'You do?'

'Yeah, it's not the same flower, ours is pink – a carnation, I reckon. But it looks just like this one, same embroidery, same initials stitched into the petals of the flower.'

'Are you sure?'

'Yes, definitely. It was Mum's, I think. We had to pack a load of stuff up recently, 'cos Dad is going to decorate. I packed it into a box with the other pictures that were hanging on that wall.'

'So where is it now?' I ask, wondering how on earth the picture had ended up on Jake's wall. Had Felicity bought it somewhere?

'I guess it's in one of the boxes of stuff stacked in the shed. I'll ring Dad and see if he can take a look. He should be up by this time, but I think he'll be nursing a pretty bad hangover. The party went on pretty late after you left with Ash. Did you know Ash took Charlie surfing this morning?' Bronte asks as she hangs on her phone waiting for Jake to answer. 'Charlie was well up for it when Ash called to tell him the surf was up.'

I'm pleased Ash had still taken Charlie out. After he'd stormed off, I was quite worried about him.

'He's not answering,' Bronte says, pulling the phone away from her ear. 'It's going to voicemail. Told ya he was in a bad way last night! I'll try again.' But this time when she dials we hear the sound of a phone ringing outside the shop doorway.

'Dad?' Bronte jumps as Jake appears at the door. 'I was just ringing you.'

'I saw,' Jake says, holding up his phone. 'But I was close by, so I thought it would be easier to speak to you in person.'

Jake glances in my direction as he enters the shop properly. 'Morning, Poppy, are you well?'

I nod hurriedly, still feeling a little awkward after Jake's confession last night.

'Dad!' Bronte calls, trying to regain his attention.

'Yes, my darling daughter,' Jake says, rolling his eyes. 'What can I do for you?'

'You know those pictures that were at the top of the stairs? The ones I took down so you could decorate – they were Mum's, right?'

Jake flinches slightly at the mention of Felicity. 'Yes, some were. Why?'

''Cos Poppy has a picture just like one of them – look.'

Bronte hands Jake the embroidered picture.

'If Bronte is right,' I tell him, 'it sounds as though you might have one of the missing pictures I was telling you about last night.'

'You mean Stan's pictures . . . which one?'

'The pink carnation?'

Jake's brow furrows. 'Oh yes, I know the one you mean. I never thought anything of it when you were telling me last night. But seeing this –' he holds up the picture of the purple rose – 'I can see the resemblance. I think that picture belonged to Felicity's mother. Felicity kept a number of her possessions when she died and we had to clear out her house. But why would Isabelle have had one of Stan's pictures?'

'Maybe she bought it somewhere?'

'I don't think so. For as long as I knew Felicity, her mum kept that picture in pride of place on her mantelpiece.'

A customer comes into the shop, so Bronte hurries over to serve them. I can see her still trying to listen to our conversation as she does.

'Wait a minute, what did you say Felicity's mother's name was?' I whisper, as something clicks in my mind.

'Isabelle, why?'

'Because that was the name of the girl Stan fell in love with, the person he gave his third picture to – it *must* be the same woman.'

'It's a mighty coincidence,' Jake says, frowning.

Bronte is still trying to hear what we're saying, so I guide Jake out into the back room.

'Perhaps, but what was Felicity's family background? If you don't mind me asking, of course,' I add, realising I could be treading on delicate ground here.

'No, it's fine, I don't mind telling you. She grew up with her mother near Oxford, then—'

'Mother?' I interrupt. 'What about a father?'

'Isabelle brought Felicity up on her own as a single mother. Felicity never knew who her father was.' Jake smiles. 'I think I told you before how keen Felicity was for us to move back here because her mother had grown up in St Felix. Isabelle had to leave suddenly though; I think when she fell pregnant with Felicity. Having babies out of wedlock was frowned upon in small towns like this, even in the seventies.'

I stare at Jake.

'What?' he asks.

'It all fits, doesn't it? What you just said, with Stan's story. He told me Isabelle had to leave St Felix suddenly and he never knew why.'

'Oh ...' Jake says suddenly realising. 'But if this Stan is Felicity's father, that would mean ...'

'That Bronte and Charlie have a grandfather they've never met and –' I swallow as a lump forms in my throat – 'that Stan has the family he's always longed for.'

# Thirty-seven

## Dianthus – Make Haste

Jake and I dash to Jake's house, having called Amber and told her what's happening so that she could go to the shop to be with Bronte.

It took her a while to get there because she'd been up at Trecarlan helping with the clean-up operation, which hadn't been due to start until this afternoon.

'What's going on?' Bronte had asked. 'Why all the secrecy?'

'No secret, Bron,' Jake had said. 'We just want to make sure the picture stays safe if it's as old as Poppy thinks it is.'

But Bronte had not looked convinced.

'Are you going to take Basil with you?' Amber had swiftly changed the subject for us, and we'd all looked at Basil curled up in his basket.

I'd gone over to him and rubbed his ear. 'What do you think, Bas? Do you want another walk?'

Basil had looked up into my eyes, then he'd licked my hand before settling back down and closing his eyes.

'We had a long walk this morning,' I'd told the others. 'He seems quite tired, perhaps it's best just to leave him to rest.'

So we'd set off for Jake's house just the two of us.

When we arrive we immediately go around the back of the house to one of the sheds that stands there.

'Right,' Jake says, opening the door. 'The boxes are in here, I believe. Let's see if this picture really is the right one.'

He pulls out a couple of cardboard boxes packed with pictures and ornaments, and we look through the contents.

'That's weird,' Jake says after we've been through both boxes. 'It should be in here.'

'Could it have fallen out?' I ask, looking around the inside of the shed. But all I can see are a couple of bikes and a lawnmower.

Jake shakes his head. 'No, I distinctly remember Bronte packing all the stuff carefully into boxes.'

'Would Charlie know anything?' I ask, desperate to find the picture. If this was the right one, we only had to find the missing Trecarlan picture and we had a full set.

'He might,' Jake says. 'Let's go see.'

We head into the house.

'Charlie!' Jake calls. 'Are you here?'

Charlie appears at the top of the stairs with Miley. He has a towel wrapped around his middle and has obviously just come out of the shower. Miley looks like she might have joined him – her fur is all damp and fluffy.

'Yeah, Dad, what's up? Oh hi, Poppy, didn't see you there.' He gives me a wave. 'Thanks for arranging that surfing session with Ash this morning. It was the best fun I've had in ages.'

'Not a problem,' I say, not looking at Jake.

But Jake has his arms full – literally. Miley has slid down the banisters to greet him.

'Hey, Miley,' Jake says, catching her and deftly hoisting her on to his shoulder. 'Ooh, you're all wet. Have you been letting her go under the shower again, Charlie?'

Charlie, grinning, just shrugs.

'Do you remember those boxes of pictures and stuff from the landing that Bronte packed up?' Jake asks him.

'Yeah.'

'What happened to them?'

'They went into the shed, didn't they?'

'What, all of them?'

'The stuff we wanted to keep, the other lot went to the jumble.'

Jake looks at me.

'What jumble, Charlie?' he asks quietly.

'For the church. You said yesterday to put a box of stuff out for the Women's Guild who'd be by to collect some for their sale.'

'And did they?' Jake asks, screwing his face up.

'Sure, Willow came by yesterday morning. Why?' Charlie asks. 'What's wrong?'

'It must be in there,' Jake says, looking at me. 'The stuff must have got mixed up. It's the only explanation.'

'And you say Willow Wilson has it?' he calls back up the stairs.

'She was the one who collected it,' Charlie says. 'Why, what's wrong?'

'I'll explain later,' Jake calls. 'Right now we have to go to Willow's.'

Willow's cottage is over on the other side of town.

'What if she's not home?' I ask worriedly as I march along next to Jake. He takes such big purposeful strides that I'm jealous of little Miley riding along on his broad shoulders.

'Then we come back another time,' Jake says firmly. 'We have to find this picture, Poppy. If what you say is true and Stan is indeed Bronte and Charlie's grandfather, then I want to help him.'

'But it's Felicity's picture,' I continue. 'Don't you want to hold on to something that was hers?'

Jake stops walking. 'Poppy,' he says, turning towards me, 'I have many things that were Felicity's, and even if I didn't, I would always have my memories. The picture is the past, and we should always concentrate on the present. If this picture can help Stan, then I'm all for doing what we can with it.'

'Thank you,' I tell him as we begin to walk again. 'Do you think Lou will feel the same when we tell *her* about the pictures?'

'I know she will,' Jake says. 'She's always had a soft spot for Stan. She often talks about him. But until today I didn't know why.'

By the time we arrive at Willow's, the sun is starting to sink behind her roof as the afternoon turns into evening.

Willow answers the door just before Jake can knock a second time.

'Oh, Jake . . . ' she says looking surprised to see him. 'Er . . . lovely party last night.' Then she sees me. 'And Poppy too?' she says, sounding rather less friendly. She glances behind her. 'What can I do for you both?'

'Did you pick some jumble up from my house yesterday?' Jake asks, quickly getting to the point. Miley climbs down from his shoulder and sits quietly in his arms as though she senses something serious is happening.

'I did, yes, it was most generous of you, Jake, thank you.'

'Can I have it back?'

'What?'

'I'd like the box back, please, it contains something it shouldn't.'

'Oh I'm not sure—'

'Please, Willow, it's important,' I beg.

Willow gives me a cold look. 'Sorry, can't,' she says flatly.

'Why not?' Jake asks, while I'm wondering why Willow is behaving so oddly.

'Because she doesn't have it any more,' a voice says from behind Willow, and we see Ash appear, looking tired and dishevelled.

It's the first time I've seen him since last night. I'd had every intention this morning of finding him and apologising, but things had got out of hand with the pictures, and the day had slipped by before I knew it. I wonder how much of what happened last night Ash had told his sister? Quite a lot, if her behaviour towards me is anything to go by.

Ash glares at me behind Willow's shoulder. Then he sees

Jake and his expression darkens further, so Miley covers her eyes.

Jake, sensing all is not well, looks from one of us to the other.

'Right, well, if you don't have it, Willow,' he continues, obviously deciding now is not the time to prompt for further information, 'then might I ask exactly where my box of jumble is?'

Willow looks at me with disdain before turning to Jake. 'I'm only telling you this, Jake, because I don't blame you in any way.'

'Right . . . ' Jake nods. 'That's good you feel that way about my jumble.'

Willow is the one to look confused now. 'All the jumble for the sale is being held in one place,' she says eventually.

'And that is . . . ?' Jake prompts.

'At Caroline Harrington-Smythe's house.'

'Caroline!' I say, as the door closes on Willow's cottage and Jake and I are left outside. 'Of all the people. If I ask Caroline for anything she'll say no – she hates me.'

'Then let me do the talking,' Jake says. 'She won't say no to me.'

We begin to walk to Caroline's house on the outskirts of St Felix.

'So what's up with you and Ash?' Jake asks casually as we march along.

'Oh, that. I think I upset him at your party.'

'Why?'

'He knows it was you I was with last night when I

disappeared, and he thinks . . . ' I pause. 'He thinks something went on between us.'

'Oh.' Jake pulls a face. 'That's not good. Perhaps if I spoke to him. Told him there's nothing going on. That we're just friends . . . '

I look at Jake and desperately want to scream, 'But we're more than that, aren't we?' Luckily for me, at that moment we bump into Lou out walking Suzy.

'Where are you two off to in such a rush?' she asks. 'And without Basil.'

'He was a bit tired,' I explain. 'I left him at the shop with Amber, but –' I look at my watch – 'I expect they've shut up and gone home by now.'

Lou looks at Jake expectantly.

'Oh, just tell her, Jake,' I say, 'she'll need to know soon anyway.'

Lou looks at us, puzzled. 'Tell me what?'

Jake and I explain everything to do with the flower pictures as quickly as we can – including Stan's story of how they came to be in the hands of the owners they're with now.

'Well,' Lou says when we've finished, 'it doesn't surprise me one bit. That Stan was always a bit of a devil when he was younger.'

'You're not upset?' I ask. I had been worried what Lou might think about Stan and his 'other women'.

'No, of course not. It was all a long time ago, and if these pictures can help old Stan in his twilight years, then good luck to you.'

'You'll give us your picture then?' I ask, surprised she's agreed so easily.

'Well, I would if I had it,' Lou says sadly.

'What do you mean? I saw it hanging on your wall not that long ago.'

'Yes, indeed it was. It's been there for many a year. But I took it down when I decorated, and when I went to hang it up again it was gone. I've looked everywhere around my house, but nothing.'

'That's very odd,' Jake says. 'Lou, are you missing anything else?'

She shakes her head. 'Nope, just that.'

'Has anyone unusual been at your house?' I ask, my senses beginning to tingle. 'Anyone who wouldn't usually be there?'

'No, not that I can think of. I don't have many visitors. I always go out to meet people. St Felix is a lovely place for meet-ups, you know.'

I sigh, it seems we've no sooner found one picture than we've lost another.

'Wait a minute,' Lou says, 'the Women's Guild held their committee meeting at my cottage a few weeks ago. You might say that was unusual – we normally go to Caroline's or someone with a bigger house than mine. It was a bit of a squeeze.'

Jake and I turn to each other with the same look on our faces.

'Caroline!' we say in unison.

# Thirty-eight

## *Marsh Marigold – Desire for Riches*

We arrive at Caroline's house. It's completely enclosed in its own grounds, surrounded by a high red-brick wall, and as we walk cautiously up the drive, it's all I can do to remain calm.

'It's her, isn't it?' I seethe, as our shoes crunch along the gravel. 'She's the one behind all this!'

'We don't know that, Poppy,' Jake says. 'It might just be a coincidence.'

'Yeah, right, and I'm Claudia Schiffer.'

Jake grins at me. 'You may have changed since you've been in St Felix, Poppy, but not *that* much!'

'You know what I mean. I'll tell you what, Jake, if it's not Caroline behind these missing pictures then I'll . . . I'll . . . I'll promise you never to wear black again, and you'll see me forevermore in all the colours of the rainbow!'

'Blimey, you are confident,' Jake says as we approach the

house. 'I have to say, I like the thought of seeing you forevermore. I'd half thought you might disappear at the end of the summer and head back to London.'

Jake's words throw me completely off kilter. 'I can't say the thought never crossed my mind, at least not when I first came here,' I tell him honestly. 'But now ... things are different. There are things ... *people* here I care about.'

'Good,' Jake says as we arrive at the front door. 'I'm very pleased to hear it.'

We've agreed that while Jake goes to the front door, I'll nip out of sight with Miley so neither of us will antagonise Caroline any more than necessary. So while he does just that, I hurry around the side of the house carrying Miley in my arms, so whoever answers the door can't see us.

I hear Jake ring a doorbell, and then Johnny, Caroline's rather wet husband, answers.

'Evening, Johnny,' Jake says companionably, 'is Caroline in?'

'You've just missed her, Jake. She popped into the town for a few provisions for dinner. But she'll be back shortly. Why don't you come in?'

Jake glances towards where I'm lurking.

I give him a quick nod.

'Sure, thanks very much, Johnny,' he says, and disappears into the house.

Right, now what? I wonder, feeling a little lost without Jake by my side. The sun has completely dipped in the sky, and it's looking like we'll have a beautiful sunset later.

Deciding I need to find somewhere to hide with Miley until Jake comes back, I take a look around me, but all I can see are immaculately kept lawns, trees and flower beds. I can hardly keep Miley amused behind a bush, she's already wriggling in my arms, so I let her climb up on my shoulder, and she settles for the moment.

'Right, you,' I whisper to her, 'let's see if we can find somewhere to go.'

We creep carefully along the perimeter of the garden, avoiding any open spaces, so if necessary we can hide behind something if anyone should appear. We've nearly run out of places to go when I spot a pretty flower-covered arbour with a bench beneath, tucked away at the end of the garden.

'That will do,' I tell Miley, heading over there. 'Now,' I say, sitting down on the bench. 'You behave while Jake is away, you hear?'

Miley jumps up on to the trelliswork that surrounds the seat, and immediately climbs all along the clematis that covers it. Then she picks one of the many purple flowers and jumps down to hand it to me.

'Thank you,' I tell her, taking the flower. 'That's very sweet of you.' Suddenly I realise what I'm doing: I'm completely surrounded by flowers, and the sight and smell of them isn't making me feel nauseous. I look at the flower in my hand, then I lift it to my nose. Even this close, the scent isn't bothering me.

I think about how I've been with flowers recently. Apart from the isolated incident at Jake's nursery, the ones in the shop really haven't been bothering me for quite some time. I've been so focused on Amber and her special bouquets, events at Trecarlan, the Victorian pictures, and helping Stan, I haven't noticed how at ease I've become with them. I recall what I said to Bronte, about our brains only being able to hold on to so much information before they had to let some go. Had the part of my brain that detested flowers been squeezed out by more important concerns? It had taken this simple gesture of Miley's to put it all into perspective for—

Miley!

I look up at the trellis, but I can't see her. So I stand up and look on top of the arbour, but she's not there either.

I search the area we've been sitting in, calling her name as quietly as I can.

Damn. Damn. Damn. Where has she gone?

The light is fading fast, and there's a very definite pink tinge to the sky as I desperately search the garden, no longer worrying whether I'm seen. I have to find Miley; Jake will never speak to me again if I've lost her. I think about Basil and how I'd feel if someone lost him while they'd been taking care of him, and my heart tugs at the thought of losing my special friend.

But then I spot her, sitting like an unusual weather vane on top of a modern-looking red-brick outbuilding. I hurry over before she can disappear again.

'Miley!' I hiss. 'Come down here this minute!'

But she just sits on top of the building preening herself.

I try to think what Jake does when he wants her to come to him. So I hold out my arm, like a keeper summoning a great bird of prey.

'Please, Miley!' I call. 'Come down now.'

Miley looks at me inquisitively.

'We can go and see Basil later if you come down?' I offer, hoping the mention of her hero might help.

To my surprise it does! She swings herself gracefully down from the roof, and into my arms.

'You terror,' I tell her, giving her a tickle. 'I thought I'd lost you.'

I'm about to move away from the building and head back towards the house, hoping that Jake might be finished with Caroline by now, when I spot something through one of the windows.

Attached to the walls of the outbuilding are a number of long shelves, a bit like the ones in the cellar at Trecarlan, and stacked neatly on top of each one are rows and rows of green and brown wine bottles.

'Gee, that place is stocked pretty tightly,' I tell Miley, 'it's like their own private off-licence. They must like a drink!'

*Like a drink* . . . I'm about to turn away, when I remember all the bottles missing from the cellar at Trecarlan, when Stan had clearly told me there would be wine stored in the racks, so I take a closer look.

'Come on, Miley,' I tell her, as we turn away and head purposefully for the house. 'We are going to pay Mrs Harrington-Smythe a quick visit.'

# Thirty-nine

## Orchid – Refined Beauty

Miley and I stand calmly on Caroline's doorstep and ring the bell.

Johnny answers again. He's holding a large glass of red wine.

'Good evening, Johnny,' I say in my best polite voice, trying not to look at the wine. 'I'd like to speak with Caroline if I may?'

'Er . . . she's with someone right now,' Johnny says, looking hastily behind him.

'That's OK,' I say, walking straight past him into the hall. 'I can wait.'

'Johnny, what *is* going on out there?' Caroline calls, appearing from a room to the left of their large hallway. 'Do we have another guest? Oh, it's you, Poppy,' she says, and her smiling face immediately tightens into a scowl.

Jake follows her into the hall.

'Poppy,' he says, acknowledging me as Miley scampers across the floor from my arms to his. 'What are you doing here?' He gives me a meaningful look.

'Has she given you your picture back yet?' I ask calmly.

'Actually I was just about to go and get it for Jake.' Caroline looks between the two of us suspiciously. 'But now I'm not so sure . . . '

Jake pulls a face that suggests by charging in unnecessarily, I've messed everything up.

'Oh, you'll get it for him all right,' I say, my voice much calmer than I feel. 'And you'll fetch Lou's picture of the sweet pea, and Stan's picture of the forget-me-not while you're at it. And,' I say before Caroline can interrupt, 'the letter from Queen Victoria too.'

Caroline's face gives nothing away.

'I have no idea what you're talking about,' she says, glancing quickly at Johnny.

'Oh, I think you do. You see I found your homemade cellar in your garden just now, with a little help from Miley.' I wink at her, sitting happily on Jake's shoulder again.

'So? We're allowed the odd glass of wine, aren't we?' Caroline lets out a nervous laugh. 'What's wrong with that?'

'Nothing, nothing at all, if the wine you're drinking hasn't been stolen from someone else's cellar!'

'Johnny, remove this . . . *person* from my house!' Caroline waves her hand limply in my direction. 'I don't need to stand here listening to these ludicrous accusations. I have more important things to do with my time.'

'Like steal pictures? Yes, we know,' I say as Johnny looks at me but doesn't make a move. 'I've seen the wine in your pretend cellar, Caroline. It's Trecarlan's wine. And we both know how I know that, don't we?'

'Johnny!' Caroline shrieks suddenly, making Miley jump with fright and hide in Jake's arms. 'I told you to change the labels, but oh no, you said no one would ever see them!'

'Would someone please tell me exactly what is going on here?' Jake asks.

Caroline turns away with her arms folded while a shame-faced Johnny stands looking like he always does – good for nothing.

'Seems it's down to me to explain then,' I say, eyeing them with contempt. 'Now, where to begin ... How about we start with the fact you stole bottles of vintage wine from the cellar at Trecarlan Castle, bottles that had their own unique Trecarlan labels attached to them, and you began doing this when you found yourself, as chair of the Parish Council, left in charge of the house?'

Caroline doesn't flinch, but Johnny drops his eyes and stares intently at a threadbare patch on the carpet.

'Or how about when you were down in the cellar, stealing the wine, you just happened to find a package containing an embroidered picture of a forget-me-not, together with a letter from Queen Victoria, which you realised on further investigation might be worth rather a lot of money, if you could only find the other three pictures in the set?'

I wait for a response from Caroline this time. She scowls, but says nothing.

'OK ... how about when you spoke to a few of the more – how can I put this kindly – *gossipy* older members of the

Women's Guild, you found out what might have happened to the other pictures, and that they might still be in the vicinity. But when you started your search you couldn't even find the one you knew was most likely to still be in St Felix . . . the one that belonged to my grandmother.'

Caroline twitches slightly, but still doesn't speak.

'You looked, Caroline, didn't you? You looked hard to begin with. That's why you lost interest in the shop after a while and let the other ladies of the Guild take over and run it, because you couldn't find what you wanted in there. In fact, I think you gave up looking for the pictures altogether for a while, until you happened to be in Lou's house one day and saw her picture, isn't that right?'

Caroline turns and glowers at me, but she still won't say anything to incriminate herself, so I continue:

'But you couldn't take Lou's picture of a sweet pea off the wall there and then, could you? No, Lou would have immediately noticed it was gone and been suspicious. So you waited, and your chance finally came when Lou was decorating and removed the picture herself. Then you suggested that the Women's Guild hold their next committee meeting at her house, and hey presto! the picture of a sweet pea is suddenly yours.'

'Caroline, is this true?' Johnny asks, shocked.

*Ah, he must have known about the wine, but not the pictures.*

Caroline looks guiltily up at him and nods.

'Shall I continue?' I enquire.

'There's more?' Johnny asks in astonishment.

'Only a few more loose ends to tie up,' I tell him. 'The jumble was the next thing, wasn't it, Caroline? You must have gone out and bought several lottery tickets the day the picture of a pink carnation, the third in the set, found its way into your house accidentally in a box of jumble!'

'And then *you*,' Caroline hisses, spinning on her heel to face me properly, 'you, Poppy Carmichael, had to come along and ruin it for me. I should have known it would be a Carmichael that would spoil everything. You always do! Tattletales, aren't you? It's in the blood.'

Jake and Johnny both look mystified now as they listen to us.

'Trecarlan Castle and those embroideries would have been mine anyway if it wasn't for the Carmichaels sticking their noses in where they're not wanted. I wouldn't ever have needed to go looking for four stupid pictures if I'd inherited what was rightfully mine in the first place.'

'What is she talking about?' Jake asks me.

'Tell you later,' I whisper. I don't want to stop Caroline when she's in full recriminatory flow.

'*Stanley Marrack*,' Caroline says scornfully, 'didn't deserve to be living in a wonderful house like Trecarlan. He was using it to host a debauched gambling ring – did you know that about your precious Stan, hmm?' she asks me. 'It was about time the Marracks got their comeuppance. So when the authorities happened to find out what was going on, he had to leave the castle in disgrace, just like my ancestors did. And the sweetest part about that was, he had to come to me, a Harrington, and ask if the Parish Council would look after the castle. It was the ultimate revenge.'

'It was you!' I exclaim. I hadn't worked that part out. Actually, a lot of what I'd said over the last few minutes had been complete guesswork, but it appeared I had got it spot on if Caroline's reaction was anything to go by. 'You were behind the anonymous tip-off! And,' I cry as something else occurs to me, 'you were the person that locked me in the cellar, weren't you?' I shake my head. 'I can't believe you did all this because of some piece of ancient history, some feud between our families that's centuries old.'

'Some people never forget, Poppy,' Caroline says, quite slowly and deliberately this time. '*Some* people take their families very seriously. Unlike you, it would seem, neglecting yours for years on end.'

'You see, that's where you're wrong, Caroline,' I respond in an equally determined voice. 'I take my family very seriously. What you've forgotten is that Stan is my family, every bit as much as Rose was. And no one messes with my family. No one, do you hear. Especially not a Harrington!'

'I can't believe you did that,' Jake says as we walk back into St Felix under a gorgeous salmon pink sky. He's holding Miley and I'm clutching my bag, which has three small embroidered pictures of a pink carnation, a sweet pea and a forget-me-not, along with a faded letter from Queen Victoria zipped safely inside. 'You were amazing back there.'

'Perhaps,' I say, trying to sound calm, even though I can still feel myself shaking.

'I thought you went incredibly easy on the Harringtons, considering it was Stan's home they were plundering. You're usually so protective of him. I think I would have just called the police.'

'If they don't come through on their promises, I definitely

will. I bet Woody would be in his element getting to the bottom of all this.'

'Ha, he would that,' Jake says.

'But what's the point in causing more problems? I don't want this ridiculous feud carrying on down the generations. Especially now we know Stan does have a family to pass things on to – he has grandchildren!'

Jake nods. 'Yes, it would seem so. We'll have to go and see him though, and talk to him about all this before I tell the children.'

'Of course, I'll need to go and tell him about the pictures too. He's going to be overjoyed to see them. Best of all, if our plan comes together, he won't have to sell them!'

Jake grins. 'That was crafty, Poppy. When will you tell him about that?'

'When the time is right.' I wink. 'I'm just so happy for him. A family is all Stan's ever wanted, and now he has one.' I sigh. 'Life is good, Jake. Very good.'

'You know I don't think I've ever seen you this happy?' Jake says, stopping and turning to face me as we reach the harbour. Miley jumps from his arms and scampers over to investigate an empty coffee cup blowing along the path. 'When I first met you, you were so down about life, so sad. You tried to cover it up, but I could see past all that. You see, I've been there and worn the *I'm fine* T-shirt too.'

I smile at Jake. How did he know me so well?

'You were one feisty lady, Poppy, and you'd bite at the tiniest of things. But you've changed since you've been here, changed for the good. I really think St Felix has healed you, just like we said it could.'

'Do you really think I've changed that much?'

'Definitely. Last night at my party you looked beautiful in your pale blue dress. But it wasn't the dress that was making you look like that, it was you, Poppy. This will sound very corny, but you've blossomed since you've been here. Blossomed into a beautiful, intelligent and caring young woman.'

'You've told me enough times I should wear more colour,' I reply lightly, attempting as always to deflect a compliment. 'Maybe I actually listened for once!' But I'm very aware of Jake moving closer to me. It's like the moment in his greenhouse all over again. I can feel his breath on my face, and see his laughter lines at the corner of his eyes, mixed with more prominent lines caused by worry and heartbreak. 'Your analogy before, very clever, considering my name.'

Jake screws up his face so even more lines appear. 'Oh, I've just realised what I said – about a blossoming Poppy! That makes me sound even more old-fashioned and corny than you probably already think I am.' His head drops, but I put my hand under his stubble-covered chin to tilt it up again.

'Don't be silly,' I tell him. 'I don't think you're old-fashioned – or old, for that matter. I like it that you think about me in the way you do – I always have. I like the fact you've noticed I've changed, because that's true too.' I pause for a moment. 'I also like *you* very much, Jake—'

But I'm prevented from saying more because suddenly my lips are otherwise engaged, as Jake presses his soft, warm mouth to mine.

I'm beginning to relax and enjoy this feeling of being so close to Jake once more, when he pulls away.

*No! Not again . . .*

'I'm sorry, Poppy, I shouldn't have done that,' Jake says, looking shocked.

'No, it's good,' I tell him, moving towards him. What could be wrong this time? I wanted Jake and Jake wanted me – it was perfect.

'No, it's not good . . . you've got a boyfriend.'

Oh. I realise I've kind of forgotten about Ash in the heat of the moment, and it's *very* hot indeed where I'm standing right now. Even the breeze coming off the sea as the waves splash up against the harbour wall next to us isn't cooling my ardour.

'Ash and I aren't really serious,' I tell him. 'We're just friends . . . with benefits, if you know what I mean?' I cringe; that was the term Ash had used about Jake.

'But still, you shouldn't be kissing other men.'

I have to admit I quite like this 'proper' side of Jake.

'Even if I enjoyed it?' I say seductively as I lean forward to kiss him again, but our lips don't quite meet before I hear someone calling my name.

I turn and look into the hazy light of the evening, and it's then I see Amber hurrying towards us along the harbour front. Immediately I know there's something wrong.

'What is it?' I ask, breaking free from Jake and rushing towards her.

Amber's face looks terrible, and she's very pale.

'Amber, what's happened? I thought you were going on a date with Woody tonight?'

Amber puts her hand on my arm.

'Poppy, it's Basil . . . '

# Forty

## Michaelmas Daisy – Farewell

Through a blood-red sky, as the sun finally sets on St Felix, Amber, Jake, Miley and I rush back to the cottage and into the sitting room, where we find curled up in his basket what appears to be a sleeping Basil, with Woody kneeling down next to him. Woody immediately stands when I come into the room.

'I'm so sorry, Poppy,' he tries to say as I barge past him to get to Basil.

'Basil?' I say softly, kneeling down next to his basket. 'Wake up, Basil.'

I reach out to stroke him but he doesn't flinch, his always warm body, which I'd cuddled into many a time since we'd known each other, is already beginning to feel cold.

'He was quiet in the shop all afternoon,' Amber says with tears in her eyes. 'After I'd taken him back to the cottage,

Woody and I decided not to go out because we were worried about him. But then Basil seemed to rouse a little, and he even managed some of his dinner. He seemed quite happy before he curled up in his bed to go to sleep, didn't he, Woody?'

Woody nods furiously.

'We decided to stay in and watch a DVD anyway,' Amber says, 'so we didn't leave him. But when I got up to check on him halfway through the movie, I realised something was wrong. I tried to wake him, but he didn't respond. I tried calling you, Poppy, several times.'

'My phone was on silent,' I tell her weakly. I'd switched it off while I was in Caroline's garden.

'So when we couldn't get hold of you, Woody went out to look for you, didn't you?' Amber turns to Woody, and he puts his arm gently around her shoulders.

'We think he must have passed away in his sleep,' Woody says, visibly upset.

'He looks very peaceful,' Jake says, passing Miley to Amber. He kneels down next to me, and pats Basil on his side. 'The old fella had a good life. And a happy one too.' He puts his hand on my shoulder. 'We'll need to call the vet, Poppy. It's too late for them to do anything, but they need to know.'

'No!' I cry, flipping his hand away. 'No, he can't be dead, he's Basil, he's always with me. He's my friend.'

I try again to wake him, but his eyes remain closed, his expression peaceful, like he's having one of his long naps after he's had his dinner.

'Oh, Basil,' I sob, cuddling one last time into his fur. 'You were the only one that really understood. The only one that I could tell *everything* to. What will I do without you?'

My tears fall on to Basil's body, and are immediately absorbed into his brown and white fur.

Jake stands up and fetches a blanket from the chair.

'He's at peace now, Poppy,' he says gently.

'Yes,' Amber says, crouching down next to me with Miley. 'He's gone to be with your grandmother. He'll be happy again. You know how much he missed her.'

'I know he did,' I sob. 'But I'll miss him too, he was my best friend.'

Little Miley wriggles out of Amber's arms, and stands in front of Basil.

We all watch her, wondering what she's going to do. But she reaches out her paws and wraps her arms as far around Basil's neck as she can, to give her hero one last hug. Then she climbs back into Amber's arms, and buries her face into Amber's chest like she's sobbing.

Moved by Miley's emotional reaction, I reach out and stroke one of Basil's long soft ears for the last time. Then I look up at Jake and nod.

Jake gently lays the crochet blanket over Basil's body, covering his head last.

'Goodbye, my wonderful, grumpy friend.' I smile as tears stream down my face so hard I can barely see any more. 'I hope they have lots of cheese up there. Then I know you'll be happy.'

I take one last look at the blanket, then I stand up and turn to Jake. He wraps his arms tightly around me, while I bury my face into his chest like Miley had done to Amber, and then I sob long and hard into his warm checked shirt.

*

For the rest of the evening, Jake and I cuddle together with Miley on the sofa, not too far away from Basil.

All four of us had tried to drink the customary healing cup of tea together, then Amber had made us all some food, which none of us had wanted, before Woody had returned home and Amber headed off to bed to get some sleep, after Jake had assured her he'd look after me.

Jake and I then dozed together on and off through the rest of the night – me, dreaming horrible nightmares about Basil being arrested and banged up in jail for being drunk and disorderly, then me returning to the cottage to find Caroline curled up in Basil's basket with a glass of red wine by her side.

I awake with a start after that particular dream, and hope for one moment that it *has* all been a dream, and Basil will be sitting at my feet demanding a walk or his breakfast.

But no, as I see the basket with the blanket covering it, the same feeling of emptiness and sorrow engulfs me once more.

I gently wriggle away from Jake's embrace, and leave him sleeping soundly on the sofa, with Miley not too far away covered with a blanket on the rocking chair, and walk over to the French windows, opening them as gently as I can, before stepping out on to the balcony.

It's daylight already, and last night's sunset seems to have been correct in predicting a beautiful morning in St Felix. I stand very still watching the sun's rays dancing off the top of the waves as they race along into the harbour, eventually becoming hypnotised by a never-ending stream of rhythmical sounds and rolling movement. Over and over the waves keep coming, until, with no one to tell them how or when, they simply turn and work in reverse, pulling the sea and all its inhabitants back out towards the horizon.

After I've stood on the balcony for a few minutes, I hear a voice.

'Are you OK?' Jake asks from the doorway. I turn to see him looking dishevelled and bleary-eyed, he can't have had much more sleep than me, and the stubble that had just begun to show on his face last night is even more apparent. 'You've been standing there ages, looking at the sea.'

'You've been watching me?'

'You looked so peaceful. I didn't want to disturb you.' Jake, still wearing his clothes from last night – a pair of blue jeans and a crumpled checked shirt with the odd mascara stain on it – steps out on to the balcony with me.

'The sea is an amazing thing,' I say, turning back to watch. 'It's a never-ending circle. No one is its master, it does its own thing.'

'But it does it very well,' Jake says, and I feel his arm around my shoulders. 'Life is a circle, Poppy, a never-ending round of birth and death. Sometimes people and animals we care about leave us to make room for something else to live or be born into this world.'

'How do you mean?'

'Basil may have left us so that another dog can take its place in someone's heart, and look out for them like Basil did for you, and you did for Basil when Rose was no longer able to. You both needed each other and were there for each other.'

I feel the tears welling up in my eyes. 'Oh, Jake, that's a beautiful way to put it,' I tell him, and I can do nothing but hug him once more, while he wraps his arms around my body and holds me.

'Someone told me something similar when Felicity died. I can't say it took the pain away, because nothing ever does that, only time. But it helped a little.'

I lean back in his arms.

'I don't want to take her place, you know?' I suddenly tell him. 'No one could ever do that. Felicity was your wife, the mother of your children. I just . . . well, I just like being with you, a lot.'

Jake nods. 'I know, I feel the same. The reason it took me so long to do anything about it is I thought I was being disloyal to Felicity's memory, and I was scared. Scared of appearing unfaithful to her, and scared of how I felt about you. I know I've told you before, but this is the first time I've cared like this about anybody since Felicity. It scares me, Poppy, I never thought it would happen again.'

'Oh, Jake,' I say, stroking his face. 'I'm scared too.'

'Why are you scared? Because I'm older, because I have a family?'

'No, of course not. I told you last night your age doesn't bother me, and I think the world of Bronte and Charlie, you know that.'

Jake's face is quizzical as he looks down at me. 'What is it then?'

I take a deep breath. 'I'm scared of loving someone and then them leaving me. It hurts. It hurts a lot.'

'I know it does.' He brushes my hair away from my face as the wind tries its best to cover it back up again. 'Are you talking about a particular person that left you?' Jake asks. 'We've all had losses in our lives that have affected us – family, friends, animals too,' he gestures back towards the sitting room and Basil. 'But nothing ever hurt like losing Felicity. I thought my life was over. It was only the kids and then Miley that got me through. Without them, I'd have lost the plot.'

'I did,' I tell him, still looking up into his kind, deep brown eyes. 'I lost the plot for a while. I went way off the rails too, if we're looking for euphemisms for a mental breakdown. Actually it wasn't a while, it was more like fifteen years.'

Jake opens his eyes wide. 'So when did you regain *the plot*?'

'Not long after I came back to St Felix.' I look at the town down below us, then I shake my head. 'I can't believe I'm saying this, but this town, an enchanted little flower shop, and a group of lovely people, you included, have done more for me than fifteen years of therapists ever did.'

Jake doesn't look in the least shocked by my revelations.

'You know I'm going to ask this, Poppy,' he says gently, 'but what on earth happened to you, for you to need *fifteen years* of therapy?'

# Forty-one

## Rosemary – Remembrance

Jake makes us all a cup of tea and some toast.

Amber has woken up too and has joined us in the kitchen.

I think she realised something was up. The moment she appeared from her room, she asked if we wanted to be left alone.

'No, Amber, it's about time I told you this story too,' I'd said, gesturing for her to join me at the table. 'You deserve to know the truth as well.'

Amber had looked at Jake, who just shrugged, then she'd sat down at the kitchen table opposite me while Jake had made us breakfast.

Now we're all sitting around Rose's scrubbed wooden table, waiting. Waiting for me to begin my sorry tale.

'OK, I'm ready,' I tell them eventually, putting down my cup of tea.

As they both sit watching me, I take a deep breath and begin.

'You both know that I used to come to St Felix on holiday when I was young?'

They nod.

'I used to come with my older brother, Will. We didn't visit every school holiday; Mum and Dad would sometimes take us other places. But for a few weeks each summer Will and I would take the train down from London as far as we could into Cornwall, then Rose would pick us up at the station in her little banger of a car and drive us the last few miles to St Felix.'

I smile as I remember my grandmother's red Mini.

'Will and I loved St Felix. We were never happier than when we were playing on the beach, or in Rose's shop, or up at Trecarlan Castle with Stan telling us tales of the castle's past. We didn't really believe his stories, especially as we grew older . . . ' I pause for a moment to reflect. 'It's so bizarre to think that some of those stories might actually have been true.' I shake my head, 'Sorry, I'm getting off track. So, like I said, we were never happier than when we were staying with Rose. Will and I got on really well, far better than brothers and sisters should. Naturally, we'd argue occasionally; I was a lot livelier, I guess you'd call it, than Will. He was quiet and studious, but the best brother I could have wished for. I was always getting him into scrapes, but he never once told on me – he was loyal like that.' I stop again, memories of Will flooding back into my mind and heart.

I look at Jake. 'Your two remind me a lot of Will and me when we were that age. Charlie is very like Will was, and Bronte, well she has that wild streak in her that I had in me.'

'Don't I know it!' Jake agrees, and we all smile for a moment.

'So, anyway,' I was getting to the difficult bit of the story, the part I never talked about with anyone. Not even any of the therapists I'd had had been able to coax this particular story out of me. 'One time when we were staying here with my grandmother I wanted to go to this concert up at Padstow, but Will didn't want to go – bands and concerts weren't really his thing. But I kept badgering him to take me. I was only fifteen and I knew that Rose wouldn't let me go on my own, but if Will went, at seventeen, Rose would think I was safe.'

I swallow hard. If only I hadn't done that . . . if only I could turn back time and change that decision.

But I'd learned over the years that, however hard I wished, whatever bargain I made with God, it never happened, and my life carried on the same miserable way.

Amber puts her hand over mine. 'Take your time, Poppy. We're in no hurry.'

I nod, but like pulling off a plaster, I knew the quicker I did this the less painful it might be.

'So in the end Will relented and we went to the concert together. It was his worst nightmare: a huge field packed full of party-goers out to have a good time. I thought it was marvellous, and the most exciting thing I'd ever been to, and I dragged Will as far into the centre of all the mayhem as I could. We were squashed together like sardines in that field; I think the farmer had allowed too many people in that night. But I felt exhilarated and was loving every minute of it.'

I can feel myself getting clammy as I remember exactly what it felt like that night: hot, sweaty and loud. Very loud. I pull my hoody, that I'd put on to get me warm after standing out on the balcony with Jake for too long, back over my head. I lay it down on the chair next to me, then I flatten down my hair. 'Sorry, getting a bit hot.'

Jake and Amber nod sympathetically, but I know they just want to hear what happened next.

'So we were enjoying ourselves, jumping away to the music with the rest of the crowd – well, I was, I'd never felt so alive.' I wince at my choice of words, but the other two don't know why and wait patiently for me to continue. 'Then, in between songs, I turn around to see how Will is doing.' I stop and try to breathe evenly; retelling this is beginning to feel like I'm reliving it. 'But he looks ill, very ill – even in the dark I can see that. Then I notice he's clutching at his neck and he can't breathe properly. Suddenly he drops to the ground, and people around him move aside to give him some air . . . ' I'm aware I'm talking as though it's happening right now in front of me, and it really feels as if it is, the pain and panic is just as real and intense. 'So I kneel on the grass next to him, but now he's closing his eyes. I scream then, scream really loud, and even more people turn to see what's happening. But no one does anything to help, and I don't know what to do to help him. So I begin shouting, asking people to get an ambulance and fast. But no one seems to be doing anything, and no one comes to help us. And all the while the band keeps playing – they don't know any of this is happening, we're right in the middle of a huge dark field, they can't see us.'

I take deep breaths and exhale to try and calm myself.

'It's OK, Poppy,' Amber soothes. 'Take your time.'

I nod at her. 'It's then that Will reaches out for me, and I take his hand. He squeezes my hand so weakly that it scares me, but I continue to hold on tightly, all the time praying someone will come, praying that my brother will be all right.'

I glance at Jake, but I barely see him, because I'm right back in that field, living every horrific moment of it over again.

'And it's then that I know he won't be OK. It's as if someone is trying to tell me something, because the band have started singing their biggest hit, "Flowers on a Breeze", and above us thousands of rose petals are being blown across the field from one of those great wind machines. The rose petals float down, landing on Will's body, they cover his face, and I try to push them away to keep his airways clear, but they just keep coming, more and more petals, cascading down on us, and it's then that I feel Will's grip begin to loosen on my hand.'

I close my eyes as I sit at the kitchen table, the memories too real and too painful to bear.

'I'm aware I'm screaming,' I continue. 'I'm aware that the crowd is parting and someone's coming through. And it's then they arrive, the paramedics in their green uniforms. I get pushed aside so they can do their job, and I lose my grip on Will's hand. But I know it's too late. I know as his hand slips out of mine, I've lost him for ever.'

I open my eyes to look at Jake and Amber. Amber has tears streaming down her face, like she had last night with Basil, and Jake looks drawn and pale as if he's living through his own personal anguish again as well as mine. Even Miley sits quietly in the corner, playing with some plastic bottles Amber had given her.

'They told me afterwards they just couldn't get through the crowds of revellers, that's why they didn't come sooner,' I explain. 'They tried to help him, tried to revive him there and then using those big electric pads you see on *Casualty*. But they couldn't bring him back. He died before they got there.'

I lift my trembling chin and look them both in the eyes. 'My lovely brother died in a muddy field covered in stupid rose petals.' I bang my fist on the table in frustration. 'And if that wasn't bad enough, it was all my fault.'

# Forty-two

## Weeping Willow – Melancholy

'No, Poppy!' Amber cries out across the table. 'Don't be silly, of course it wasn't your fault!'

'It was! If I hadn't persuaded him to go to the concert, it wouldn't have happened.'

'Did he have a heart defect, like Felicity?' Jake asks sombrely.

I nod. 'Yes. That's what the post-mortem found.'

'Then you know it wasn't your fault. It could have happened at any time.'

'But if I hadn't dragged him there, if we hadn't been in the middle of a field, then the paramedics would have got to him quicker. They might have saved him.'

'That's an awful lot of mights and ifs,' Jake says. 'You don't know that, Poppy, and beating yourself up over it isn't going to bring him back. Believe me, I know: I tried long enough.'

'So is that why you don't like crowds and flowers?' Amber asks. 'It makes sense you wouldn't, after what happened.'

'You noticed?' I ask. 'I thought I'd hidden the flower thing quite well since I've been here.'

'Of course I've noticed,' Amber says supportively. 'I was just waiting for you to tell me why.'

'When I first returned to St Felix I hated flowers with a vengeance, and not just because of the rose petals at the gig, but because of all the flowers that were sent to our house afterwards in condolence, and then all the flowers that were at Will's funeral. That used to be what I associated flowers with – death. It's roses I have the most issues with, obviously; the rest I could just about hack, but roses . . . ' I shudder. 'Just the sight or smell of a rose can make me feel nauseous; make me feel like I'm back in that field. All my therapists have tried to cure me of it, and all of them have failed.'

'Is that why you ran away that day at my nursery?' Jake asks. 'Because you could smell the flowers?'

I nod. 'I'm so sorry; I know you thought it was to do with you, but really it wasn't. It was all those roses you said you had stored in there.'

Jake smiles a little. 'That's a relief. I was convinced it was me.'

'For some reason I've been a lot better recently. It's as if Daisy Chain and St Felix have helped to cure me. I can see now how happy they make people. In fact, how happy they'd started to make me feel – until last night.'

Amber nods. 'Yes, it's always amazed me that flowers can mean so many different things to so many people. One moment they're in sympathy, the next celebration. What other living thing can represent so many different emotions?'

We all think about this for a moment.

'So, tell us some more about Will,' Jake says quietly, breaking into our thoughts. 'You've mentioned therapy before. Did you go off the rails a bit after his death?'

'Not a bit, a hell of a lot,' I tell him. 'I went from being an A-grade student who promised much, to . . . ' I smile. 'I suppose you'd call me a juvenile delinquent. I was in trouble with the law, was sectioned for my own good, then when I'd got through that and they thought I was safe enough to be let out, there was a string of jobs, none of which I could hold down for long. I was the black sheep of the family. Whereas everyone else followed into the family business, I refused to follow tradition.'

'That's not always a bad thing,' Jake says. 'Sometimes I wish I'd done the same.'

I put my hand over Jake's. I know he's talking about his job with the animals.

Suddenly there's a knock at the door, and we all look at each other in surprise.

'It'll probably be Woody, wondering how we all are this morning,' Amber says as she jumps up to answer it.

'Hi, Amber.' I hear Ash's voice at the open door, and I immediately pull my hand away from Jake's. 'Is Poppy in?'

Amber steps aside and Ash comes through the door looking fresh-faced, unlike the rest of us. He's wearing a white T-shirt and blue jeans, and his eyes immediately fall on me sitting at the table, and then they move very quickly to Jake.

'Jake?' He looks at him questioningly. 'I didn't think you'd be here at this time of the morning, and –' he casts his eyes suspiciously over Jake's attire – 'still wearing the same clothes you had on yesterday.'

'I think I'd better go, Poppy,' Jake says, standing up. 'I'll go back to my house first, get freshened up, then I'll contact the vet for you.'

'Thanks, Jake,' I say, looking up at him. 'For everything.'

'Any time.' Jake leans down and kisses the top of my head. 'I'll be in touch later.' He summons Miley, and heads for the door.

'Ash,' he says, acknowledging a bewildered-looking Ash as he passes. 'Go easy, she's had a tough night.'

Then he leaves, and my heart drops to my toes. Jake has been such a wonderful support over the last few hours that I don't know how I'm going to face up to everything without him. I still couldn't bear to look in the direction of Basil's basket, and I had no idea how I was going to go about telling Ash I had to break up with him . . .

Ash waits for me in the kitchen while I get changed, and I hear Amber telling him about Basil.

When I return, Ash comes over and puts his arms around me. 'Pops, I'm so sorry about Basil,' he says. 'I'll miss the old fella, really I will. I'm also sorry for being so off with you at Jake's party. I've been talking to Willow and she's made me see what an idiot I was. Can you forgive me?'

I'm glad when Ash suggests we take a walk together; it's a beautiful morning and we decide to walk through the town and across to the beach. We've spent so many happy hours together here with Basil that I feel even worse about what I'm about to do.

The beach is packed this morning with holidaymakers enjoying picnics and building sandcastles. I don't know what has happened to St Felix this summer, but every day the town seems to be getting busier and busier with visitors.

The sight of so many people enjoying the town lifts my spirits a little, but my joy is short-lived. A Labrador runs past us after a ball, and I'm reminded that Basil is no longer here with us.

'It's OK to be sad,' Ash says as we pause for a moment to watch the waves.

'I know,' I tell him. 'I'll miss Basil so much though. He was more than just a dog, he was my friend too.'

Ash puts his arm around my shoulders, and immediately I'm reminded of Jake doing the same this morning.

'I'm sorry again about what happened,' Ash says softly. 'I shouldn't have gone off in a strop at Jake's party. I should have trusted you. I know you wouldn't cheat on me with Jake.'

His last sentence hangs in the sea air, like a seagull riding on a gust of wind.

'It's fine, really,' I assure him. 'I shouldn't have left you for so long alone at the party. It wasn't fair.'

'Ah well, I had Charlie to chat to. Nice lad. He's going to come out with us again. He really seemed to enjoy riding the waves. He's a natural.'

'That's great. Thank you so much for doing that for me.' I turn and look at Ash properly for the first time since we've been here on the beach. 'Please don't ever think I don't appreciate it.'

Ash looks at me with a puzzled expression.

'I would never think that, Poppy. I'm always glad to help

you.' He pauses for a moment as if he's considering something, and his arm drops away from my shoulder. 'So what *was* Jake doing banging on Willow's door yesterday, demanding his jumble back? You haven't told me yet. Seems a bit odd.'

We find a space to sit on the sand, and then I tell Ash all about Stan's flower pictures, and what had happened at Caroline's house.

'Go, you!' Ash says punching his fist triumphantly in the air. 'Stan will be over the moon. I'll have to pop over and see the old fella sometime, now we know where he is. Maybe we can go together?'

I close my eyes. I have to do this sometime.

'Do you think it's karma?' I ask, then open my eyes. 'Finding all the pictures to help Stan, then Basil dying? Something good happens, so then something bad has to happen to balance out the universe.'

'You're sounding more like Amber every day,' Ash says, grinning at me. 'No, don't be silly; it's just a coincidence. You did a good thing for Stan, Poppy. Don't lose sight of that.'

'Perhaps . . . ' But what about what had happened between me and Jake last night – that was good. But the bad thing was I now had to break up with Ash as a result. Maybe Amber spoke more sense than I gave her credit for. But I knew it was Jake I really wanted, and it wasn't fair to string Ash along.

'Ash,' I say, at the same time as he asks, 'What was Jake still doing at your house this morning, Poppy? Did he spend the night?'

I knew Ash didn't really believe me about Jake. The things he'd said this morning had been Willow's thoughts and words.

'No – I mean yes. Yes, he spent the night at the cottage, but it wasn't anything like that. Honestly, Ash, I'm telling you the truth. He was just there comforting me about Basil.'

'You like him though, don't you?' Ash asks, not looking at me, concentrating instead on a small boy building sandcastles with a shiny red plastic bucket.

'Yes, of course I do, but—'

'And he likes you enough to kiss you this morning.'

'That was on my head,' I protest. 'It didn't mean—'

'Oh, I think it did,' Ash says, in a heavier tone than I was used to hearing from him. He still isn't looking at me. 'I'm not stupid, Poppy; I see the way the two of you look at each other, and not just this morning but when I've seen you together before. It's written all over your faces. Are you in love with him?'

'I . . . ' I have to think about Ash's question a tad too long. 'Yes, I think I might be,' I tell him honestly. 'I'm so sorry, Ash, it was nothing you did. I really like you, honestly I do.'

'But not *love*,' Ash says in a tight voice. He looks at me. 'Right?'

I shake my head.

Ash pulls himself to his feet and brushes the sand off his legs. 'Not that it makes any difference now, Poppy,' he says, looking down at me, 'but it might interest you to know that while you only *liked* me, I was very much in love with you.' As he gazes down at me still sitting on the sand, I'm sure I can see tears in his eyes.

'Oh, Ash,' I say, scrambling to my feet, 'I'm sorry, I didn't know. If I had I—'

'You'd what?' Ash looks at me with anguish in his eyes. 'You wouldn't have fallen in love with Jake? I don't think so.'

I don't know what to say; I try to put my hand on his arm, but he turns away from me.

'See ya around, Poppy,' he says, and he begins to walk off across the sand, his voice quivering as he speaks. 'It was fun while it lasted.'

'Ash!' I call out to him, but either he doesn't hear me or he chooses not to.

I look around the busy sand, and for a moment I long for the deserted beaches that I'd known when I first came back to St Felix, or a sudden shower of rain, so everyone would disappear indoors and I'd be left on my own for a while.

But I know that isn't going to happen. St Felix is jam-packed with people on this sunny morning, and I can't begrudge the town that joy. I need to think of somewhere else to go; somewhere I can be alone with my thoughts for a while …

And then I remember.

Keeping my head down and without speaking to anyone on the way, I head away from the beach, back across the town, and up to the cliffs. Then just like Charlie had shown me the day we'd opened Daisy Chain, I carefully climb down the grassy side of the cliff, find the stone steps, and descend to the little viewing area.

I sit and watch the gulls circling over the sea like we had that day; their graceful artistry as they swoop and dive for their food mesmerises me, yet at the same time allows me to put my thoughts into some sort of order as I sit there.

I'd never been able to come here with Basil when we'd been on our walks; it would have been too dangerous trying to get him down the narrow steps, poor old thing.

I manage a smile as I think about Basil. I'd tried to give him a happy last few months here on earth. We'd taken lots of walks together, which I was pretty sure Basil appreciated more than anything else, even his cheese. And he'd been great company for me, as I hope I'd been for him. I'd told Basil things I'd never told anyone before, and he'd just sat and listened to me without passing any more judgement than a twitch of his ear, or a lick of his tongue.

I'll miss him more than anyone could know.

I'll also miss Ash.

I never wanted to hurt Ash, I liked him a lot. He was great fun, and we'd had some good times over the summer, but I just didn't feel the same way about him as I felt about Jake.

The last time I'd sat here on this ledge it had been with Jake. We'd sat here in the moonlight together during his birthday party. That was the first time I'd heard him say he had feelings for me.

But having feelings for someone didn't mean you necessarily wanted to be in a relationship with them. I'd told him this morning I didn't want to take Felicity's place, but was Jake really ready to take the next step?

I think about all these things as I sit peacefully on the ledge, allowing the rhythmical sounds of the sea to wash over me as they had so many times since I'd returned to St Felix, calming my mind and soothing my soul.

# Forty-three

## *Lily of the Valley – Return to Happiness*

As I stand looking out over St Felix harbour, I feel something cold and wet nudging at my ankle, so I bend down to stroke it.

'Hey, Bill,' I say to the puppy at the end of a thin red lead. 'Are you ready to go walkies again?'

A week or so after Basil's death, Jake, Amber, Woody, Lou, Bronte, Charlie and I had walked up to the top of Pengarthen Hill where Basil and I used to take our daily walks together, to scatter his ashes over the cliffs into the bay.

We'd watched sadly as Basil was swept up by the strong wind that always blew on the cliffs, and was carried out to sea. Even little Miley was sombre and quiet as she watched, from the safety of Jake's arms, her friend disappearing into the sunset.

It was a poignant day for many of us. Saying goodbye to

Basil brought back all the pain of his death, and memories of goodbyes we'd said to loved ones before.

But after our impromptu ceremony, Lou had a surprise for me. We all walked back together to Lou's house, where she told us she'd laid on a light supper.

Basil had been the last link between Lou and my grandmother, and his death had hit her hard. To comfort us both, we'd taken to walking the remaining two puppies from the litter – the others had all found new homes – up and over the cliffs every evening. They'd had all their inoculations and were excited to be allowed out; they didn't have the stamina to go on the kind of long walks Basil and I used to do together, but they were a great comfort in my grieving process.

Yes, I'd been grieving for a dog. I would never have allowed myself to admit to that before, but Basil had been part of my St Felix family, and he was much missed.

'I have an announcement to make,' Lou called, as we stood in her kitchen enjoying soup and homemade bread. 'I've finally found a home for the last puppy.'

Everyone turned to hear Lou's announcement.

'As you know, I always said I would keep one of Suzy and Basil's pups, but I've struggled to find a home for the last one. Actually, I tell a lie,' Lou had told us, her blue eyes glinting. 'I never even looked for a home for this little fella.' Lou bent down to stroke one of the puppies. The one with the look of a miniature Basil: the same multi-coloured markings, the same way of sitting with his long ears cocked to one side, trying to con you into giving him food. 'Because I knew all along where he was going to go. Poppy,' she looked up at me. 'This one is all yours.'

I protested, of course, saying no one could ever take Basil's place, but secretly I was thrilled to bits. This little fella had been my favourite from the start, back in the days when I would occasionally bring Basil to visit the puppies. He was a quiet, reflective pup and he reminded me a lot of the regal and dignified Basil.

So I'd named my new puppy Bill, after my brother William.

'Right then,' I say to Bill now, 'if you want to go walkies, then that's what we shall do!'

We walk back into the town and up along Harbour Street, squeezing through the crowds of people who've packed into St Felix today.

News of Amber's special bouquets has spread beyond the Cornish borders. In part through word-of-mouth from delighted customers who've had amazing things happen to them after receiving one of her white-ribbon bouquets, and in part because Amber had unwittingly made up one of her 'special' bouquets for a journalist.

The cynical reporter had come into Daisy Chain one day asking for a white-ribbon bouquet, as they'd become known, and had taken Amber's selection of flowers away thinking she'd be able to write a scathing report about a charlatan flower shop in Cornwall claiming their bouquets could work miracles. But to her amazement, after years of trying and failing to conceive a baby with her husband, within days of returning from St Felix she found out she was pregnant. They are expecting twins next spring.

Her miraculous story was first published in a local newspaper, and then picked up by a national broadsheet. Then we were asked to do an interview on *This Morning* – my mother nearly exploded with joy when I told her we'd met Philip Schofield. So now we had people arriving in St Felix by the busload to buy one of Amber's bouquets, and to take photos of the 'Enchanted Cornish Flower shop' as the tabloids were calling us.

Daisy Chain's new-found fame has changed St Felix from a sleepy Cornish town into a bustling tourist attraction, and it's busier and happier than I've ever seen it before.

Prospective traders have flocked to the town to look at the empty shops on Harbour Street with a view to opening new establishments come spring next year, and the current owners of shops are rushed off their feet, and having to take on extra staff to cope with the sudden influx of tourists. But most importantly, everywhere I look, people are constantly smiling, whether they're new to the joys of St Felix or they've lived here all their lives.

Today, as the sun shines joyfully down on a town packed with happy holidaymakers, I'm reminded of my time here as a child, and how Will and I would run through the busy streets with a pasty in a paper bag for Stan . . .

Pasties! That reminds me, I'm supposed to pick one up for Stan.

On the way back to the shop I stick my head around the door of The Blue Canary bakery so I don't have to leave Bill outside. Ant, on seeing me, promptly fills one bag with a giant Cornish pasty, and a second with three custard tarts.

'Wish Stan well for me,' he says, as he hurries back into his shop, which has a rather long queue of hungry customers waiting. 'Fantastic fella, he is, with some great tales of St Felix. I could listen to him all day!'

'I'll tell him that,' I say, smiling. It's great to know Stan's stories are entertaining people again.

Back at Daisy Chain I'm happy to see we have a few customers, but not too many. So I take Bill in past the desk and give him a drink of water out back.

'Where's Stan?' I ask Bronte, when she's finished serving her customer.

'I just sold three pairs of my earrings to that lady,' Bronte says happily, putting some notes into the till. 'Granddad? Charlie came and took him out for a stroll.'

Once we'd found out that Bronte and Charlie were more than likely Stan's grandchildren, Jake and I had taken them to Camberley House a number of times to visit him. The day Stan first met his grandchildren is one I will remember for ever.

Over lunch Stan had entertained Bronte and Charlie with his tales of Trecarlan, and they in turn had told him stories about their own lives. They all got on so well, it was as if they'd always known each other. And seeing them with Stan brought back many happy memories of the time Will and I had spent with him. Except this was Stan's real family, a family he never thought he'd have.

To give him a treat, and a break from Camberley, this week Stan has been staying with Jake at his house. I'd wanted him to come and stay with me at the cottage, but it just wasn't big enough to accommodate the wheelchair Stan needed to get around. So he'd happily gone to stay with his 'new family', as he liked to call them, and I'd been spending as much time as I could with him while he was here.

Yesterday we'd visited Trecarlan Castle together for the first time in over fifteen years. It had been a very special moment for both of us. Then today we'd brought him along to the shop, so he could see how we were doing things at Daisy Chain these days.

I check on Bill, who's already sparked out in his bed in the back of the shop.

'I'm leaving Bill here, Bronte,' I tell her, as I grab Stan's pasty. 'He'll be asleep for a while. I'm off to find your granddad.'

'Sure thing, boss!' Bronte calls, as she makes another appointment for someone to see Amber. 'See you at four o'clock then, Mrs Hurley.'

'Wait a moment, Poppy!' Amber calls as she finishes with her current customer, or client as we were now calling all our special appointments. 'I have something for you.'

'What?' I ask, as Amber disappears out to the back room.

'This,' she says, producing a small bunch of blue, white and pink flowers tied with a white ribbon. 'It was left on the doorstep this morning.'

I look at Amber suspiciously. 'Did you do this?' I ask her. 'It looks like one of yours.'

She shakes her head. 'No, nothing to do with me. Look –' she points at the flowers, 'there's a card.'

I turn the posy around and pull out a small white envelope, the type we send out with our bouquets. The card inside is handwritten.

*Want to know if this is good or bad? Then go and find the one we once thought mad . . .*

I look at Amber. 'What is all this about?' I ask her suspiciously. 'Are you sure this is nothing to do with you?'

Amber shakes her head again. 'Definitely not. But it's a lovely choice of flowers – there's iris in there to denote a message; white stocks – you will always be beautiful to me, and delicate pink phlox – our souls are united.'

'Hmm . . . ' I look at her suspiciously. 'But what does the card mean? Go and find the one we once thought mad?'

'It's Granddad!' Bronte shouts excitedly. 'Everyone used to think he was mad, didn't they?'

I sigh. 'Well, I suppose I was going to find Stan anyway, so what difference is it going to make if I do as the card says?'

'Oh, Poppy, do play along,' Amber says disapprovingly. 'Have some fun for once!'

'OK, OK,' I say, putting the flowers down on the table.

'No, take them with you!' Bronte insists.

I narrow my eyes at them both. 'Don't for one minute think I don't know this is something to do with you two,' I tell them. 'OK, I'll take the flowers. See you both later.'

As I leave the shop with Stan's pasty and my flowers, I turn back to look at them, and I see them quickly high five each other.

'Nothing to do with you,' I mutter, weaving my way through the crowds. 'Yeah right.'

I find Stan down by the harbour, sitting in his wheelchair surrounded by children. He appears to be enthralling them with an impromptu storytelling session. So I wander over and sit down on a bench next to Charlie, who seems to be enjoying the story as much as the children.

'. . . and then when the pirates returned to Trecarlan they

found their treasure was gone!' he tells the children, who are sitting quietly in front of him, their eyes wide with anticipation.

The parents are hanging on his every word too. 'Did you know all that went on up at Trecarlan Castle?' one of the parents says to another.

'Nah, he's making it up, isn't he. Word is, the fella's a bit doolally.'

'Yes, I heard that too, but he sounds coherent enough, and that castle does have some history, even if it's not quite as exciting as he's making out.'

'I wonder what will happen to the place. It seems a shame for it to be left empty, doesn't it?'

'Yeah. My mother told me it was a lovely place years ago. Focal point of the town.'

'And that,' Stan says to the children, 'is the story of how Trecarlan saved an Indian princess's jewels.'

The children applaud enthusiastically, and call for more. But Stan holds up his hand. 'Later perhaps, Stan needs his rest now, children.' He waves at Charlie and me, and we go over to him.

'Ah, more satisfied customers,' Stan says, looking happier and more alive than I've seen him in ages.

'They love you, Stan,' I tell him. 'And so do their parents, for keeping the little ones entertained.'

'Never mind them, I was entertained too,' Charlie says, grinning. 'I love Granddad's stories.'

Stan's face lights up when Charlie calls him that.

'Right, Charlie,' he says, 'how about you go get your granddad a little . . . no, make that a large pasty from the bakery?'

Charlie glances at me.

'I'll be fine, Charlie,' I reassure him. 'You go.'

Charlie winks at Stan then heads off in the direction of The Blue Canary.

'You can never have too many, can you, Stan?' I say, lifting my pasty up from behind my flowers.

'That's my girl!' Stan says, taking the bag from me. He looks at the flowers. 'Very nice, who gave you those?'

'No idea.' I shrug. 'It's some sort of mystery; I'm playing along though.'

'Good, good,' Stan says. He seems not overly surprised by this. 'Now then, how are things?'

'Just look at all the people.' I wave a hand, indicating the crowds swarming all over the harbour with their chips, pasties and ice creams.

'Yes, it's like old times here today,' Stan says, looking around him. 'The magic is definitely working again.'

'What?'

Stan grins up at me. 'The flower magic. I assume you and Amber are still using your grandmother's old books to make up the bouquets? I've seen Amber tying them with a white ribbon just like Rose used to.'

'Yes, we are but—'

'You must see it, Poppy, the connection?'

I look blankly at him.

'St Felix was always a busy little town while the flower books were being used through the generations. It was only when your grandmother became ill and there was no one to create the magic that problems arose. As soon as you and Amber picked up the reins, St Felix started to recover.'

Now I think about it, the town did start to get busier about the same time as Amber began creating her white-ribbon bouquets, and the more she did, the busier it got. But surely that was coincidental. Wasn't it?

'Anyway, I wasn't asking how the town's doing,' Stan continues. 'Or even the shop, before you try that one. I meant with *you*? How are things with Poppy?'

'Good,' I say hesitantly, still thinking about the flower books.

'*Good*,' Stan repeats. 'Is that it? Come on, Poppy, I'm an old man – give me something to live for.'

I smile at him, and decide to let it go. What did it matter whether the upturn in St Felix's fortunes was down to magic or not, it was happening, that was the main thing.

'You'll live for ever, Stan!' I tell him, laughing. 'Things are going great.'

'Really, in which department?'

I blush. 'You know full well, you tease: with me and Jake.'

'Ah, you and Jake . . . I'm pleased to hear it. You make a fine couple.'

Jake and I had been getting on extremely well since the night of Basil's death. We'd spent lots of time together, just as we had when I'd first come to St Felix, and it had been lovely. But it never seemed to go any further, and I was beginning to wonder, even after Jake's declarations a few weeks ago, if it ever would.

'Jake's a good man,' I tell Stan. 'He's a great friend to me.'

'So you're happy?' Stan asks hopefully.

'Yes, of course I am.'

'Then I'm pleased for you, my dear. It's about time – you can't hold on to the past for ever. Which is why I've come to a decision.' Stan takes hold of my hand. 'Poppy, I don't think you and Will ever truly realised how much joy you brought me coming to Trecarlan to spend time with me when you were small. It made my long lonely days in that castle bearable, and gave me something to look forward to.'

I'm about to speak, but Stan stops me by holding up his other hand.

'No, let me finish. It was always my intention that one day you and Will would run Trecarlan. It was,' he insists, 'and actually it still is, in my will that you should both inherit it. Sadly, Will is not with us any more, so it falls to you, Poppy. I would like you to have Trecarlan to run as you see fit.'

'What? No, Stan, you can't do that. Trecarlan is your home.'

'It's not my home any more,' Stan says. 'It was many years ago, but Trecarlan needs new blood now, someone who will look after and nurture it, and put it to good use. And that person, Poppy, is you. I want you to go on with the good work you've already been doing over the past few months.'

'But . . . what about your real family? What about Bronte and Charlie? Shouldn't they inherit it?'

'You are as much a part of my family as they are,' Stan says, 'if not more so. I'm sure we can sort something out with Jake so the children will be a part of Trecarlan if they wish to be. But I've always wanted you to have my home, Poppy, and I'd be very grateful if you'd do me the great honour of accepting my offer.'

I look at Stan, and then I look up at Trecarlan sitting high on the hill over St Felix Bay. I'd spent some of the happiest times of my life up at that castle, and now I didn't see why I couldn't spend many more there.

'Yes,' I say, kneeling down next to Stan. 'If you really want me to look after Trecarlan for you, then I shall.'

'Poppy, I knew you'd say yes,' he says, his thin hand cupping my face. 'You've made an old man very happy.'

'Are you absolutely sure about this, Stan? What about the Parish Council – they might kick up a fuss?'

Stan shakes his head. 'Now that Harrington woman has resigned they'll be *sweet*. That's what you youngsters say, isn't it?'

I nod. After I'd given Caroline and Johnny my conditions for me not going to the police, they'd acted almost immediately. Caroline had resigned as chair of the Parish Council and president of the Women's Guild, and Johnny had made sure the second part of my request was dealt with promptly too.

'Poppy, I've never been surer of anything in my whole life. I want you to fill Trecarlan with joy and laughter. Make it come alive once more, like it was in the old days, before it became a lonely old man's house.'

'I will, Stan,' I promise, leaning over his chair to give him a hug. 'You have my word.'

'I know you'll do a good job with Trecarlan, Poppy,' Stan assures me. 'And if you make a profit, maybe you can help me fund my stay at Camberley. But I won't have you selling the flower pictures for me. I gave them away as gifts. They're not mine to sell any more.'

'Of course, Stan. I wouldn't dream of selling the pictures if you don't want them sold. Maybe we can display them at the castle for future visitors to see and enjoy?'

'That's a wonderful idea!' Stan says, his face lighting up. 'I'd like that very much.'

I have a quick internal debate as to whether this would be a good time to tell Stan the other condition I'd negotiated with Caroline and Johnny for my silence. But I decide perhaps this isn't the moment to let Stan know he'll be able to stay at Camberley House if he wants to – because Caroline and Johnny

Harrington-Smythe will be paying his fees there indefinitely . . .

'I have something else for you, Poppy,' Stan says, interrupting my thoughts. 'I think you'll find a rather delicate posy of flowers hanging off the back of my chair that have your name on them.'

'What?' I ask, looking around the back of his wheelchair. I unhook the bunch of colourful flowers that's hanging there by a white ribbon, and look with suspicion at Stan.

'Are you in on this too?' I ask.

Stan just winks. 'You now have two rather lovely posies. This one contains pansies, meaning think of me; alstroemeria, meaning devotion; and it's entwined with ivy, meaning fidelity. So go on, open the card, lovely.'

I open the envelope, and there's a card inside in the same handwriting. This time it says:

> *So you found the mad one, now you need to find me.*
> *Come to the place where it's like nothing else matters in the world, and together we can look out at the never-ending sea.*

'It's the ledge,' I tell Stan. 'The secret ledge on Pengarthen cliffs.'

'Well, what are you waiting for?' Stan says, encouraging me. 'Go, go!'

'But I can't just leave you.'

'Ah, here comes Charlie with my pasty,' Stan says as Charlie wanders over almost on cue. 'He'll take it from here. Now go to the cliffs. I think you'll find something there that will make you happy for a very long time to come.'

# Forty-four

## Baby's Breath – Everlasting Love

As I hurry along to the cliffs, my mind is buzzing with everything that's just happened.

Stan was giving me Trecarlan! It was amazing, and wonderful, and scary all at the same time.

I was honoured of course, and incredibly happy, but I was also in shock. What was I going to do with a castle? How could I make it into the joyful place that Stan wanted it to be?

'Ah, you'll figure it out, Poppy,' I tell myself as I arrive at the cliffs and begin to make my way tentatively down the stone steps. 'Trecarlan will help you to, it's good like that.' As I reach the slightly firmer ground of the ledge, I'm content knowing that whatever happens now, or in the future, my life is going to be spent here in St Felix, where I've always been most happy.

As I half expected there might be, there's another posy

waiting for me on the ledge, bound by another white ribbon. This time it's made up entirely of colourful tulips.

I lay my first two posies down, so I can pick up this one, and I find another envelope tucked inside the flowers. So I read the handwritten message aloud:

> *'Tulips – A declaration of Love.*
> *Want to know who wants to tell you this?*
> *Then look carefully over the edge of the cliffs.'*

I do as the card says and go to the edge of the cliff, then I peep over the top, down on to the beach below.

In the sand someone has carved a huge heart, and inside the heart are the words:

*P & J was 'ere.*
*Friends and Lovers*
*Together forever . . .*

It was just like the words in the heart that Will and I had carved underneath the desk in the little flower shop so many years ago.

As I'm staring down at the sand I see a person emerge on to the beach below.

Jake.

'You made it then?' he asks as he climbs up on to the ledge next to me. He takes my hand as I move away from the edge of the cliff.

'You did that?' I ask, pointing down towards the tiny beach

in astonishment. 'The heart – it's just like the one under the desk in Daisy Chain.'

'I know. I knew how much that meant to you, and I wanted to do something equally special to show how much you mean to me.'

Jake removes the posy I still have clutched in my hands, and lays it down on the stone ledge with the others, then he takes hold of both my hands, and turns me to face him.

'If you didn't know it before, I'm in love with you, Poppy Carmichael,' he says, his dark eyes gazing down into mine. 'Every feisty, argumentative, brave, loving, wonderful part of you.'

'Really?'

'Of course,' Jake says, smiling. 'I've loved you since the day you pushed yourself into my van looking like a drowned rat.'

'I hardly think—' I begin, but he renders me speechless by putting his finger gently to my mouth, which he then quickly replaces with his lips.

'I'm not very good with words, Poppy,' Jake says when he finally removes his lips from mine. 'I've been wanting to tell you properly for so long how I felt, but it never seemed the right time. There was always something in our way.'

'I disagree,' I tell him, and I see his face fall. 'I think you can be pretty amazing with words. You've said some lovely things to me since I've known you.'

Jake smiles with relief.

'And I knew all this was you,' I tell him, gesturing to the posies on the ledge. 'Well, I desperately hoped it was. But why all the flowers?'

'You were OK with them then?' he asks. 'I wondered if I

was doing the right thing, sending you flowers – given your past issues. But they all had such wonderful meanings, and could say everything I was finding it difficult to.'

'The language of flowers,' I say, thinking about Amber and the books. 'Who would ever have thought when I came here to St Felix, that flowers, the one thing that gave me the most grief, would be the thing that would remedy all my troubles?'

'You're right,' Jake agrees. 'It does seem pretty odd.'

'There were no roses in my special bouquets though?'

Jake shakes his head. 'No, I thought that might be pushing things a bit too far. I know you're fine with them now, but they will never be your favourites. Shame though, Amber said they had some of the loveliest meanings.' He slaps his hand over his mouth.

'Amber was in on this too? I knew it!'

'Along with Bronte, and Charlie, and Stan,' Jake admits. 'And Lou gave me the idea in the first place. I'll take credit for the heart though, that was all mine.' He wraps his arms around my waist and pulls me closer to him. 'I'm sorry, Poppy, I'm not very romantic, am I?'

'Jake,' I say gently, stroking his face. 'I wouldn't want you any other way. I love you exactly as you are. Hearts and flowers have never really been *my thing*, have they?'

Jake grins as I wrap my arms around his neck.

'You're *my thing*, Jake. You, St Felix, and a little flower shop by the sea. You're all the things I need.'